DESIRING THE HIGHLANDER

Cole swallowed and the aching hunger that had been driving his emotions and actions swelled to new levels. "God, Elle," he groaned, his voice thick and husky, "you are so incredibly beautiful."

Ellenor arched her back, twisting, her body begging to be touched. Cole complied. He bent down and closed his mouth over hers for a long, searing moment.

Ellenor gripped his shoulders. Her body was screaming for more of his touch. His fingers were tormenting her with their light, stimulating caresses. She needed his mouth on her, tasting her as he did before. "Please, Cole, touch me."

"I am, love," he whispered and brushed his mouth against hers.

"No," she moaned. "Touch me," she begged, only half aware she was voicing her uninhibited request, "like you did before."

Cole knew exactly what she wanted, what her body longed for, and reveled in the thought he could make such a beautiful, strong woman weak with need for him. "Tell me. Tell me exactly what you want, Elle, and I will give it to you . . ."

Books by Michele Sinclair

THE HIGHLANDER'S BRIDE

TO WED A HIGHLANDER

DESIRING THE HIGHLANDER

Published by Zebra Books

Desiring
The
Highlander

MICHELE SINCLAIR

ZEBRA BOOKS
KENSINGTON PUBLISHING CORP.
http://www.kensingtonbooks.com

ZEBRA BOOKS are published by

Kensington Publishing Corp.
119 West 40th Street
New York, NY 10018

All Kensington titles, imprints, and distributed lines are available at special quantity discounts for bulk purchases for sales promotion, premiums, fund-raising, educational, or institutional use.

Special book excerpts or customized printings can also be created to fit specific needs. For details, write or phone the office of the Kensington Special Sales Manager: Attn. Special Sales Department. Kensington Publishing Corp., 119 West 40th Street, New York, NY 10018. Phone: 1-800-221-2647.

Zebra and the Z logo Reg. U.S. Pat. & TM Off.

ISBN-13: 978-1-4201-0854-5
ISBN-10: 1-4201-0854-9

First Printing: December 2009
10 9 8 7 6 5 4 3 2 1

Printed in the United States of America

Prologue

Creag Mhor Summit, above Glen Lyon, 1301

Crouched low, Cole crawled his way up to the edge of the cliff. His elbows and knees were caked with mud from the morning's rain, but he didn't care. Just as he didn't care what his older brother had to say about what he could and couldn't do. Arriving unseen, where so many were gathered who knew him and his family, proved he was more capable than his brother believed. And in just a few hours, every Scottish soul within ten miles would be too busy battling the English to worry about whether a young Highlander should be fighting alongside them.

Inching forward, he felt his arm sink almost wrist deep into the wet earth and he bit back an expletive. His dark brown hair was crusted with the muck. But crawling through mud, while irritating, was better than on the jagged rocks that covered most of the broad ridge. And walking to the peak was out of the question. The trees that did pop up along this section of the flat-topped hills were so scarce the only way to avoid detection was by staying low. Hence the scrapes, the bruises, and the mud. But he would suffer them all again to be right where he was—here at Glen Lyon, where the next big battle against the English would be fought.

The frigid spring wind caused his shirt to billow. He shivered, but not from the cold. From anticipation. As if nature knew what was about to happen and changed the weather, eager to help the Scottish achieve another victory.

He breathed deep the heather-perfumed air and smiled. The thin-skinned English with all their armor hated the damp, cool temperatures that accompanied these hills. And soon, they would have even more reason to hate the Highlands.

He edged up the last few feet, feeling quite brilliant and enormously brave about tricking his eldest brother and making his escape. His best friend Rob had been right. This *was* a lot better than training and a hell of a lot more fun than working for the stable master, taking care of the horses.

On the battlefield below, Highland boys would become men, and when all was over, he would be one of them.

No longer would his brother refuse to allow him to train with the soldiers despite the fact that he was sixteen and just as tall as half of them. But most of all, he would no longer be known as the third son, or one of Conor's younger brothers, or worst of all, the boy McTiernay. People would know him by his name. Cole. And they would be scared.

A sandy-haired figure crouched low at the cliff's edge bent his head back and issued Cole an exasperated look. "What took you so long?"

"*Mo Chreach!* I had to hide the horses way down there!" Cole hissed back as he edged his way up to his friend's side. Cole's bright blue eyes peered over the ridge and took in the grassy slopes that led to a wide col. Tomorrow—possibly even this afternoon if the English arrived fast enough—there would be a battle on those grounds that would rival Stirling Bridge.

"Are they hid good?"

Cole nodded, knowing that Rob was just as sensitive—maybe even more so—about being discovered by their comrades. "What's happening?"

Rob shrugged. "Not much. Most of the men have been getting the spearheads ready. The English are coming from over there. You can see something shining through the trees every once in a while if you look long enough."

Cole turned to stare, hoping to get a glance at the sun-stricken armor. He had no idea how long he had been studying the trees for armored movements when Rob gave a halfhearted yelp and pointed.

Immediately, Cole shifted his gaze and followed Rob's finger pointing down toward two figures standing no more than fifty yards below them. Cole's heart lodged in his throat. He was unable to speak.

"Cole, isn't that . . ."

"Your laird," Cole finally managed to get out. "And my brother. The *blaigeard* must have followed us."

"*Mo Chreach!* Do you think he told my father?" Rob choked.

Cole scoffed. "Of *course* he told your father. His being laird requires him to do what is right, not what you or I want," Cole answered, mimicking one of Conor's favorite lectures. Cole couldn't remember his father ever once saying something so trite, and *he* had been a great laird.

Three months ago, his father had turned fifty-eight years old. A week later, he was dead, leaving seven sons to mourn him. He had seemed incredibly healthy, and maybe in the body he had been. But his heart had left seven months prior with his wife. Cole had never seen his father so lost as in those months after his mother died. Her death had been unexpected and unfair.

Some of the McTiernay families living close to the clan border had taken ill, and she had insisted on going out to help. Soon after her arrival, she had fallen prey to the mysterious disease herself, dying only a few days later. Cole's father had never recovered from the loss. Some say he had welcomed his own sickness, letting it invade and take over so that he could once again see his one and only love.

Be that true or not, within a week of falling ill, he had slipped away and Cole's eldest brother, Conor, had suddenly become laird of one of the largest Highland clans in the Grey Corries.

Cole had lost not only a father that day, but also his freedom. The morning after the burial, he had gone to the fields determined to begin his training with the soldiers. His best friend Rob had been practicing for nearly a year and a half, and Cole's father had promised he would soon be joining his friend in the daily drills. But when Conor had turned him away and sent him to work in the stables, an icy resentment had begun to grow. Over the weeks, then months, as Conor's pledges of personally overseeing Cole's training were preempted repeatedly by more pressing clan needs, the resentment changed to anger and now defiance.

"Your brother's going to kill you," Rob quipped, stating the obvious.

"And your father isn't?" Cole retorted.

"*My* father is a farmer. And while he resents my desire to train and fight, he certainly wouldn't leave his crops and follow me."

Cole cocked his head and reconsidered his brother's stance. "I don't think Conor did follow us."

"What do you mean? If he isn't here because of us, then why? To fight? I thought you said he didn't think MacDonnill should have picked the Strath Tay for a battleground."

"I did," Cole murmured, remembering every word spoken that afternoon. He glanced around, hoping to find familiar faces, someone to indicate another reason for his brother's untimely arrival. His peripheral vision told him that Rob was doing the same . . . and was just as unsuccessful as he was. "We're in serious trouble," Cole sighed.

"Yeah," Rob agreed. "But why is the laird here if not to fight and not because of you?"

Cole folded his arms and laid his forehead down on them. "Oh, he's here because of me. I just don't think he followed us. If he had, he would have stopped us long before we got here. *Na*, he just knew where we were going."

"How?"

Cole glanced at his friend's face. The youthful features were filled with incredulity. Though nearly two years older than Cole, Rob would be forever plagued with people assuming he was younger than he actually was. He had a slight build, dark sandy blond hair, and dimples that were more like craters in his cheeks than simple indentions. Often ridiculed by the warriors as being too young to play soldier, Rob had been near desperate to find a way to prove he was not a boy, but a man. When Cole reported what he had overheard about a battle at Glen Lyon, Rob had instantly decided that he was going and that Cole was coming with him. It was time they both proved something to their elders.

And there was no better way to silence tongues than to fight in a victorious battle.

Cole watched as Conor spoke animatedly with another much older man. He couldn't hear them, but knew his brother was not pleased with the man's answer. Even at a distance, the black scowl of Conor's displeasure was easily seen. His brother could go from calm to angry in the blink of an eye, but usually only with his men or those he considered family. Rarely did Conor allow anyone else to see his displeasure.

Cole nudged his friend with his elbow. "Hey, Rob, who is that with my brother?"

"Um, I think that's Olave. He's some Highlander who used to fight with Wallace before he left for France. Olave came to camp one time and all the older soldiers could talk about was his skill with every weapon known to man. He doesn't look like much to me," Rob added with a snort.

Cole watched the argument change tone. Olave shook his head. Conor then picked up a stick and knelt on the ground, sketching something in the loose soil. He looked worried . . . hell, his brother looked *scared*. Cole glanced at his surroundings and reexamined them with new eyes. He studied where the English were positioned and where his comrades were preparing to meet them. A sinking feeling overcame him, and Cole began to suspect his brother had been right.

Almost two weeks ago, a handful of eastern Highland lairds had arrived with ideas about luring the English into a battle that would weaken their forces, leaving Stirling Castle vulnerable for recapture. Conor had welcomed them and listened to their plans patiently. And then he had refused to join their campaign.

Most of the lairds—especially MacDonnill—had made clear their disappointment, saying how Conor's father would never have forsaken an opportunity to free Scotland. The barely veiled implication that Conor was a coward and lacked his father's leadership skills had not been lost on anyone.

Sitting hidden behind the wooden planks separating the Great Hall from the servants' preparation area, Cole had listened intently, waiting for his brother to roar and drive a fist into the man's skull. But nothing had happened. Conor only reasserted that it was foolhardy to believe that sheer Scottish bravery could defeat English archers, and that the Strath Tay was perfect ground for the English longbow to find its target.

The lairds had ignored him, and they had been wrong.

McTiernays were known for several things. Their large, well-trained army, their aptitude for leadership, their ability to command both loyalty and dedication of their clansmen, even their own skill with a sword. But those who truly knew them would say their ability to outstrategize even the most cunning of enemies was their greatest strength. Some believed that it was this reason above all others that kept Edward I from trying to invade the McTiernay stronghold. Only a fool marched knowingly to his death. And Edward I and his commanders were a lot of things, but they were not fools.

Cole had never seen a battle, being only sixteen, nor had he ever fought for his life, but McTiernay intuition was flickering through his mind, revealing what was about to unfold. "Rob, come on, we're getting out of here."

"Why? Isn't it too early to join MacDonnill? The battle is hours away from starting . . ."

Cole's eyes darted over the strath. The valley was a death trap. Those few Highlanders who did survive the archers' arrows would be heavily outmatched. It was not the English numbers which were about to be weakened; it was theirs.

"We aren't joining the battle," Cole said and began to retreat.

Rob reached out and grabbed Cole's arm. "If your brother being here bothers you so much, then leave, but I'm staying."

Cole stared into his friend's eyes. "It's suicide, Rob. The English have us flanked on two sides, and judging by the amount of armor starting to shine through those trees, we have less than a tenth of the men. It's going to be a slaughter."

"You're wrong. Look, MacDonnill is moving men even now to attack."

Cole watched in horror as MacDonnill split his forces. Sounds erupting from the field below suddenly filled his ears as the Highlanders began to yell and clank their swords, forecasting victory. But Cole knew miserably that it was not to be theirs.

The cliff provided an excellent vantage point of the staging area. From here, almost anyone could see what was about to happen. Anyone but Rob. His friend had never understood the art of strategy. Having trouble thinking ahead, Rob always addressed the problem facing him, not the one coming. Even now, he couldn't see how the battle would unfold, but Cole could. Mac-Donnill had just sent over a hundred men to their deaths, and he doubted the English would be stupid enough not to take advantage of the mistake.

"What do we have here?"

The snarl came from behind them, accompanied with the clatter of metal made only by men wearing bulky armor. With all the noise below, Cole had not heard them approach until it was too late. His heart began to pound even faster realizing the mistake.

"Looks like two Scottish whoresons dressed like women."

Rob shifted to look at them, but Cole refused to turn around. One of them kicked his shin. "'Ere now, don't you know enough to look at your betters when they are speaking to you?"

Out of the corner of his eye, Cole could see Rob stare with open mouth at the man. His friend spoke only Gaelic and had no clue what filth the English soldiers were spouting. Cole wished he were so blessed with ignorance. His father's closest friend, a Highlander who lived near the English border, had made sure all the McTiernays were well versed in the English tongue. He believed, as did his father, that one had to understand the enemy before he could defeat him. Cole had always refused to speak the words, but he understood them.

Just as he understood he was about to die.

He could feel his broadsword burning next to his thigh, but having it did little good. One movement toward it would bring instant death, and reason prompted him to do whatever he had to do to stay alive.

He flipped over as they ordered and surveyed the depressing reality of his situation.

Three men of varying height towered over them. It was impossible to tell how broad they were with all the metal they wore, but from their eyes, Cole could see who was in charge. The man was standing a little over ten feet away, leaning on the hilt of his sword, which he had stabbed into the ground, and from the glint in his black eyes, Cole knew the man was a heartless bastard fully intent on killing them.

The one closest to Rob kicked him in the ribs. When Rob instinctively reached for his sword, the man stomped on his friend's hand. Cole could hear the bones snap under the weight. To Rob's credit, he didn't scream, but just stared back. He was just as aware as Cole that they were about to die.

"Hey now, I don't think you will be needing that today," the English soldier sneered, kicking the broadsword away. "And I would apologize for the hand, but I don't think you will be needing that either."

"What do you think they're doing up here?" another asked. "Scouting? You don't think they were planning on fighting, do you?" Cole suspected he had been brought along for his brawn, not his intelligence.

"Even the Scots aren't dumb enough to let their boys fight a man's battle."

One soldier poked Cole in the side. "Hey, how old are you?"

Rob immediately cried out, *"Sguir!"* yelling for them to stop. "My brother's only a boy! He knows nothing but farming. I am the one you want."

The instant Rob shouted his lies, the soldiers responded. A foot weighted by iron links crashed down upon Cole's chest. Hearing the choking sounds Rob was making, Cole guessed the same had happened to him. The English wanted them to feel helpless and weak, and damn their souls, it was working.

"What did he say?" one of the men asked. "The dregs can't even talk right. I don't think they understand a damn word we're saying."

The leader's eyes flicked from Cole to Rob and back to Cole again. Finally, he spoke. "The gaping one doesn't," the leader finally decided. "But the dark-haired boy does. You understand every word we are saying, don't you? Just who are you? A farmer boy wanting to play soldier?"

His voice was deep and had a sick tone to it. The man had more than just a willingness to kill; he enjoyed the act itself. His question also proved he understood enough Gaelic to interpret some of Rob's lies.

Cole leveled his hard gaze and let all emotion drain out of him. He was not afraid of dying and it must have shown because the leader chuckled and approached, his cruel smile growing larger as if he just thought of a delightful game involving pain and death. The soldier pinning Cole down adjusted his stance, but did not free him.

The leader swung his polished blade around and pointed it at Cole's neck. Cole could feel Rob squirming and heard him choking. That's when Cole grasped it was not Rob's chest they were using to pin him down, but his windpipe.

Cole felt as if the hand of God had swooped down and torn him in half. The part with any emotion, any feeling, was screaming to save his best friend, to do something, say anything that would get the bastard to lift his foot and let Rob breathe. But the other part— the part that controlled his actions—refused to move. Every emotion, every foolish hope and childish dream he had ever had, was shriveling, leaving only a cold, empty shell in its place.

Cole stared in silent defiance as the leader slowly pressed the tip of his sword into his throat. Warm blood began to trickle down the side of Cole's neck and then past the back of his ear. When Cole remained unresponsive to the pain, the metallic edge began to move upward, unhurried, to slice the skin. Bit by bit the blade carved its way up the neckline, stopping at the curve of Cole's chin. The man was waiting for him to fight back, put up some type of resistance. His enjoyment rested upon reactions—a cry, a flinch, a whimper . . . anything to let him know that Cole was afraid.

But Cole wasn't afraid of dying. What he was most afraid of was living.

The leader must have seen it. Somehow, he had recognized that one weakness. The man smiled cruelly, lifted his blade, and then nodded at the soldier to his right. A second later, Rob's raspy gasps filled the air. No longer was his friend pinned, dying for lack of breath. The leader then pointed at Cole and said, "Tie up the bastard. We wouldn't want him to suddenly feel heroic and get in the way of our fun."

Cole heard one of his ribs crack as a foot collided with his side, forcing him to roll over. His arms were yanked back as a coarse rope was slipped around his wrists, binding them tightly together. But not once did his bright blue eyes lose their lock on the maniacal leader as he walked over to his friend's side.

He leered at Rob and then returned his attention back to Cole. "I'll admit that I had thought to kill you first, but I have come to realize your death means little to you. So I have changed my mind. You will watch me kill your pathetic farmer-boy brother and the slaughter of your countrymen. And *then* it will be your turn. Maybe by the time your legs and arms are tied to horses, you will feel more inclined to fight back."

Then, without any more preamble, the evil man brought his sword high up in the air and then straight down, goring Rob right through his stomach and into the ground. A scream filled the air. The strike was meant to kill slowly, painfully. Then the madman struck again, his crazed smile growing each time Rob shrieked in agony.

Cole knew he was only getting started. The man would continue his merciless attack finding more and more ways to exact pain before Rob finally succumbed to his death. And there was nothing Cole could do but watch. He knew if he closed his eyes for even one second, the English lunatic would think he had won.

Suddenly, a trumpet blasted over the strath and a man riding an armor-covered horse broke over the ridge. Pausing only briefly to assess Cole and then Rob, who was now writhing on the ground, he rode straight to the leader. "Lincoln wants you and your men on the west bank now."

The confidence the leader had worn just moments ago dissolved upon hearing the order. "The west b . . ." He moved to look over the ridge at the troops below. For the first time since locking his eyes on the murderer, Cole broke his gaze and looked out.

The English archers who had lined the western flank, ensuring the doom of the Scottish cause, were gone. Somehow, MacDonnill had maneuvered a handful of men behind them and they now lay dead. The battle would now be fought between the English cavalry and Scottish spearmen, a much more equitable turn of events. Cole knew who was behind the miracle. His brother. Conor must have somehow talked some sense into MacDonnill, and the pompous laird, recognizing his perilous situation, had listened. The English numbers were still significantly greater, but there was now a chance.

The English soldiers must have seen the same thing. The leader pivoted, ordered his men to get their horses, and grabbed his sword still protruding from Rob's abdomen. But just as he jumped on his mount, he turned to face Cole. "This changes nothing. Watch your people pray to God as they meet with their end, and when I return, it will be my turn to listen to you beg for mercy."

And then he was gone.

Cole collapsed and closed his eyes, listening to his heartbeat. He tried to feel something . . . anything.

Fear, anger, remorse. There was nothing. Then he heard Rob.

"Cole . . ." Rob's voice was weak and close to death.

Cole scooted awkwardly over to his friend. "I'm here." He wanted to say hold on, I'm going for help, you are going to be all right, but each time he tried, the words got caught in his throat. All he could mutter was "I'm here" again and again, hoping to reassure his friend that he would not die alone.

"Do something for me."

Cole swallowed. "What?"

"Live. I have a dagger in my belt. Use it to get free and then I want you to make every English *blaigeard* pay for what they do today."

"I will." Cole choked on the two words. Hearing his dying friend speak in such pain was making everything seem more real, more awful. The detached part of himself was slamming back inside and his heart was wrenching.

"Don't forget me and what they did. Promise me, Cole. Promise me you won't forget."

"I promise."

"And Cole . . ." Gurgles of blood started sputtering from Rob's mouth. "Tell my father . . ."

But before he could finish the request, his eyes glazed over and Cole knew that his best friend since he had been four years old was dead. A deep hatred began to slide over his skin, slipping into his pores. The urge to join the ensuing battle below was paramount. He would find the English leader with cold black eyes and drive a blade straight through his heart.

Twisting around, Cole fumbled with the back of Rob's belt for what seemed an eternity. Then he felt the small cool blade on his fingers and slid the tiny weapon out of its casing. A minute later, he was free.

Picking up his broadsword, he swung it high in the air and then began yelling as he descended the steep slope to join the battle.

Crazed, detached, almost unaware of his actions or what he was doing, Cole began swinging his weapon haphazardly at anything covered in armor that was moving. He plunged and sliced and created a bloody swath through every English soldier he encountered, searching for the one man who had dared to mutilate Rob.

Then he found him. He was sitting atop his horse, behind the fighting, among several other English leaders, confident that he was safe. Cole was charging the small group when a lone arrow appeared and found its target. The man came down off his horse with a crashing thud. The others immediately rode off hoping to avoid being next.

Cole screamed in fury and ran up to the Englishman hoping to find him alive. But revenge was not to be his. The arrow had pierced his jugular and the man was dead. Cole cried out and was about to behead him when suddenly his weapon was stripped from his hands. Turning to attack, Cole encountered Conor, who threw his sword down and gathered him in his arms.

"It's over now, Cole. It's over. He's dead."

Cole shook his head. "It will never be over," he whispered. "And I won't forget."

Chapter 1

Fàire Creachann Keep, off Loch Shieldaig, 1311

Cole McTiernay leaned back in the worn chair and outstretched his long legs, crossing them at the ankles. He stared out one of the few windows in the keep that had not been broken by years of wear and neglect. Clouds had begun to thicken around the Highland mountains of Torridon, and with each minute that passed, their humid masses sank just a little lower down the rugged primeval slopes. It had yet to start raining, but drops would begin to fall any moment. The unusually cold and damp spring weather had done little to help the moods of those in the room—including his own.

As choices go, it should have been a simple one and Cole was baffled why it wasn't. Newly formed clans needed chieftains and chieftains needed an army, financial means, and the ability to make difficult decisions. All of which he possessed and Lonnagan did not. Those differences alone should have dictated who would be laird.

But not for these stubborn people.

When he had been approached to lead the nomadic clans of the northern Highlands, he had halfheartedly agreed. His men and their families desired a home and he, too, was restless and needed a change. Then word had come that another was being considered. And after ten days of endless discussions, Cole was no longer confident he was going to be the one selected. Even more surprising, he wasn't sure whether he would be disappointed or relieved.

Heavy footsteps came up from behind. Controlled and methodical, they could only belong to one man—his older brother. Cole craned his head, gave a slight nod in acknowledgment, and then returned his gaze out the window to the lapping waters of the sea. "Made a decision?"

"No," Conor grunted, not even trying to hide his frustration, "and you know why."

Cole sighed and bobbed his head slightly. "I'm leaving in the morning."

"None too soon. You and Dugan haven't been making things easier."

"He's easily provoked," Cole replied with a slight shrug.

Conor wanted to throttle his younger brother. The man had perfected the persona of one who was detached and unconcerned about the plights of others, but it wasn't true. One only had to look into his eyes to see the sorrow Cole carried. An ache brought about from profound sadness. But Cole never would allow anyone to look long enough, deep enough, to see anything but indifference. Until he learned how to drop his guard, share his thoughts, and allow someone to grow close to him, his pain would never heal.

Cole McTiernay was the third of seven brothers, and all could be exasperatingly stubborn when they wanted to be, but Cole was famous for his obstinacy, especially when it came to his hatred of all things English. Over the years, Conor and his brothers had tried to get him to open up. But each time they pushed, Cole would emotionally retract, burying himself behind some distant, impenetrable wall. Eventually, he and his brothers had stopped trying.

Conor often wondered if that had been a mistake. Did they give up too soon? Or had they been wise to back off in fear of pushing their brother away altogether? Cole was an incredible soldier, a superb strategist, and a worthy leader, but as a man, he was hollow inside. He lacked something . . . something that made one want to face a new day. Conor had hoped this opportunity would give Cole the drive missing from his life, but after the heated discussions that had taken place the past couple of days, his brother acted as if he cared even less about the possibility of becoming laird than he had before.

"It's been a lousy week," Conor mumbled, looking for another chair.

"It's been a lousy *two* weeks," Cole corrected. "You were lucky and missed the first half."

"So mocking Dugan, trying to make him look like a fool, was your way to perk things up?"

"Dugan is a fool. I just exposed it for all to see."

All seven McTiernays had a dry sense of humor, but Cole was a master at sarcasm. He could deliver clever yet slicing remarks with such a straight face, it was hard to tell if he was serious or just amusing himself. In today's case, it mattered little, for the damage had been done. "Dugan's not the fool you make him out to be."

Cole shrugged. "If he wasn't, then it shouldn't have been so easy to make him sound like one."

"He's a good man. And while I agree he might not be the most tactical of soldiers . . ."

Cole stiffened. "Try heedless, foolhardy . . ."

"But he could make a good leader," Conor tried again. "He understands and relates to people. An ability *you* have yet to attempt, let alone master. Why is that, I wonder?"

Cole's jaw clenched. For nearly a week, he had been tolerating Dugan's propensity to discuss ad nauseam the most nonsensical topics. And though Cole refused to admit it out loud, he didn't believe Dugan to be unintelligent. The man had proven himself a talented soldier—even capable of being heroic. And his friendly overtures to the clan would have been exceptionally brilliant, if they had been intentional. Dugan, however, didn't have a strategic bone in his body. His friendliness, easiness with others, and almost effortless ability to gain a person's trust had been natural and unplanned.

What truly bothered Cole was the man's incredible shortsightedness. Dugan just reacted to whatever was happening directly in front of him, never considering the consequences of his statements and ideas. And for the past couple of days, Cole had been exposing that weakness time and time again. So no, he wasn't threatened by Dugan; he was just confounded at everyone's inability to recognize the depth of the man's shortcomings. Who cared if he was nice? These people needed a leader . . . not a friend.

Cole twiddled his thumbs. "Dugan staying?"

Conor shook his head. "Left already. Your last barbs about his ideas of where and what should serve as the residence for these clansmen left him with little choice."

"His *ideas,* as you put it, were ill-conceived just as most of his other plans, and everyone who heard them, with the exception of Dugan, knows it. You say he's a good man, and he may be, but if he becomes laird of this motley group, don't be surprised if you're back here in a year trying to figure out how to clean up his mess. And when that happens, don't bother asking me to pick up the pieces, for the answer will be no."

Cole stood up and glanced at the small group of lairds sitting around a broken-down table on the far side of the room. They had assembled here almost two weeks ago to determine what to do about the northern nomadic tribes. Leaderless from either disease or war, the various clansmen had banded together informally over the years just to stay alive. Their continual raids upon neighboring clans and stock had gone from annoying to invasive and then intolerable. This gathering was a last effort to achieve peace. Many Highlanders had died in recent years securing Scotland's freedom, and while no one relished more killing, if a new laird was not agreed upon soon, more deaths were inevitable.

"After this week, I doubt anyone would be clamoring your name if that happened. And while a few of us have similar doubts about Dugan's ability to run a clan, we have none whatsoever about his *desire* to be here and lead these people."

Cole grunted. Was that the crux of the difficulty in deciding who should be laird? Who *wanted* it more? And if that was it, Cole wasn't sure how to respond. He knew he *should* be concerned about the outcome of the discussions, but with each passing day, he had found himself caring a little less.

He never asked for the opportunity—what some called honor—to lead the lawless, prideful bunch, nor did he ever aspire to it. But Dugan had.

Just a year younger than Cole's twenty-seven years, Dugan Lonnagan had seen a fair number of battles and had won more than his share of fights. Unlike Cole, however, Dugan had no army, no means to support one, and no money to maintain one even if he did have it. Those reasons alone had led Cole to believe the question of who should be the next laird to be simple. Yet, the past two weeks had proved it was a much more complicated selection than Cole had anticipated it would be.

It was coming down to ability versus personality.

Dugan was tall—though Cole still dwarfed him— good looking with dark sandy brown hair, and possessed an easy nature that drew people to him as if he were honey and they were flies. Conversely, Cole lacked the patience and talent for simple conversation— especially with women and children. His reticent nature prompted him to communicate in a direct style that tended to keep people away, not beckon them to his side. In short, Dugan Lonnagan was everything that Cole was not.

So whom should they choose?

Dugan was beloved by many of the clansmen, but Cole would bring with him key alliances with neighboring clans. Then again, Cole's name and battle success could also bring enemies—namely the English, while Dugan was relatively unknown to the southern enemy. And yet, nearby adversaries would discount Dugan, but fear Cole and his army.

Complicating the decision further was the concept of influence. Several Highland lairds believed Dugan could be easily manipulated to do what they wanted. Unfortunately, clans led by weak men often became unwanted burdens to their neighbors. Conversely, Cole would listen to suggestions and ideas, but he would heed only his own counsel when making decisions and compromises. And anyone who'd had doubts as to just how hardheaded and stubborn Cole could be, had learned otherwise two weeks ago when he convinced everyone to convene at Fàire Creachann. Cole had announced then that if he were to be chosen as laird, the abandoned, crumbling fortress would serve as the new clan's home. A decision incredible to many—including Dugan.

An unintelligible grumble erupted from the far side of the room. Tempers were flaring again. Conor shifted his stance and was about to return to the group when he paused. Hesitating, his silver eyes met Cole's blue ones. At thirty-seven, Conor was just ten years senior to his younger brother, but in the past few years, Cole had grown to match him in height and breadth. That and his steady gaze reminded Conor that Cole was no longer a young man in need of counseling. He was an adult and had proved it many times. If Cole wanted to walk away from the opportunity in front of him, he could do just that. Conor only wanted him to do it for the right reasons.

"You have always been your own man, Cole. That's probably one of the reasons I think you would be so good for these people. You would not let them and their volatile opinions get in the way of a good decision. Dugan also has much to offer, but until either of you learn to accept and grow beyond your shortcomings, these people are doomed—regardless of who is selected."

Conor laid a hand on Cole's shoulder briefly and squeezed. "One last thing, I know you plan to go directly back to your men, but would you swing by and stay with Laurel at least for a few days and make sure she is all right? Schellden has just sent word that he wants to join the discussions and the others have agreed, so it will be at least another week maybe even two, before anything is settled. And I . . . I need to know she's all right."

Cole nodded. "I'll let her know what's going on," he agreed, understanding his brother's concern. His wife was nearing the end of her second pregnancy, and while this one was advancing normally, unlike her previous route to motherhood, Conor was still worried.

"Thanks. I know word would be sent if I needed to return, but I would still feel better if you were there. Laurel has a way of fooling those around her, but she's never been quite as good at conning you into doing her bidding."

Cole fought from rolling his eyes. His brother's half-English, half-Scottish wife could sweet-talk the devil into a confession. And though Cole tried to remain immune to her wiles, he had found himself on more than one occasion realizing he had been duped into some activity he had had no intention of doing. And while he didn't exactly mind, it was somehow unnerving to know a woman was able to get the best of him.

Cole nudged his mount forward to the edge of the outcropping and looked across the rambling hills to the valley below. The morning sun was still low in the sky and the cool nip in the air felt almost warm compared to the frosty mornings of the Highlands. The valley below was still shaded by the hills surrounding it. Nestled in its center was a rather large tower. Wooden cottages encircled the stone structure and dotted the landscape until their numbers thickened again at the valley's edge. There, peeking out from the surrounding woods, was a small, active abbey that appeared to be the heart of the village.

Donald observed the straight back of his commander and then followed Cole's gaze. The scene looked very ordinary, and very English. "That's supposed to be Durchent Hall?"

Cole nodded once. "Aye."

"Doesn't seem like they're expecting you."

"Don't know and don't care," came Cole's short reply, knowing Donald would not take offense. He had served under him for almost four years and was as close to a friend as Cole had.

Cole still had no idea how Laurel had tricked him into making this journey. He certainly hadn't willingly agreed. In fact, he definitely remembered saying no. Several times. And yet, here he was. And all to acquire something his sister-in-law treasured very much. Cole had told her to wait for Conor, but she threw a whole bunch of nonsense at him about how it couldn't wait and how she could trust no one else. That only someone who abhorred the English could be entrusted with what he was to bring back. That alone should have warned him to refuse and mean it, but fact was he needed something to do as he waited for a decision that would dictate the course of his future. Unfortunately, procuring the mysterious treasure required a short excursion into the one place he had always refused to tread. England.

He heard Jaime catch up to them. He had asked only two of his men to ride with him, knowing that both were good in battle, levelheaded, and most of all, understood him. And what they didn't understand, they didn't try to change.

Jaime halted his mount next to Donald's. "Commander," Jaime prompted, unable to see Cole's current grimace, "do you want to stop and rest the mounts before continuing?"

"No." Like most of Cole's answers, this one was short and left no room for discussion. Before sundown, he fully intended to be back on Scottish soil. He might be forced to ride on English lands, but he refused to walk on them, eat on them, or even donate his piss to the flora. "We ride on."

The sun was high by the time the group had made its way down the series of smaller hills and into the woodland surrounding Durchent Hall. They rode until they broke free of the trees to where a massive square tower stood visually overpowering the rest of the buildings surrounding it. Cole was unimpressed.

A young boy was busy removing stone and wood from a cart, when Cole called out to him. "Find your baron and tell him that we come for what belongs to his sister."

After overcoming his shock, the boy dashed into the tower with the message. Minutes later, a different, much chubbier, and somewhat better dressed adolescent came running out, breathing heavily, stating the baron would receive them in his presence room.

Cole arched a single brow and stared at the lad. "And just who are you to speak for the baron?"

"I'm . . . I'm . . . the herald," the boy rasped out.

Jaime twisted the reins he was holding and leaned forward. "Tell your baron that we will be *received* by no Englishman. If he wishes to speak to us, we will hear his words here."

The young herald stood in stunned silence for several seconds, opening and then closing his mouth. Cole pointed to the keep's partially opened gates. "Go now, herald. Speak our words to your baron and be sure to tell him that we will be leaving before the sun reaches your trees."

The boy looked at the landscape and realized the sun would be setting below the tallest trees any minute now. He glanced back at Cole and gulped before scurrying back inside.

Fifteen minutes later, the herald returned huffing. He was red and obviously uncomfortable with his message. "My lord says that he meets with his guests only on his terms, not theirs. He bids you to join him in some drink and food."

Cole smiled and the young lad blanched. He always thought it amusing that his smile was considered more frightening than his scowl. "That is good news then, herald. For it means I no longer have any reason to stay." Then with a flick of his reins, Cole turned his mount around and headed home.

Ellenor Howell stood staring out the small slotted window in her room in disbelief. The three men sitting on their enormous mounts were not like any of the Scotsmen she had ever seen. Most were big, but these three were huge. Not just in size, but also in sheer strength. The muscles in their arms and legs peeking out from their strange garments bulged with latent strength. And while the sight of all three of them together was alarming, it was the dark-haired man in the middle who caused the hairs on the back of her neck to twitch.

He was the one in charge.

Maybe it was how he sat, or maybe it was how he stared disdainfully down at her brother-in-law despite being surrounded by English soldiers, but the large Scot was not just in command of his small group, but all those present. Ellenor had no doubt the arrogance spewing from the giant was something he could support easily with deeds.

The Scot's shoulder-length hair was tied back, causing his face to appear severe and emotionless, almost as if it were cut from stone. The effect mirrored the rest of him. Hard and well defined. Never had Ellenor dreamed men could come in such sizes or with such strength.

The knowledge chilled her core.

The Scot adjusted a long bow that was hooked over his shoulder, and then casually tapped the handle of his sheathed broadsword. Only a fool would believe he was anything other than highly skilled with both weapons. This man was not afraid of anything. She had been wrong to assume the baron's men had forced him to return. Something else compelled him to come back, for he certainly didn't *want* to be here.

Ellenor turned her eyes toward her brother-in-law, who was glowering in the center of the courtyard. A slight man of medium height, Ainsley Cordell's auburn hair only accentuated his ruddy cheeks. His matching brown eyes were usually haughty, filled with disdain for anyone whom he did not consider a peer. But today, they lacked their normal unwarranted pride. It was as if Ainsley knew he was outmatched by the strangers, both in strength and mental agility. Still, that did not keep the fool from trying.

"You are an arrogant man," Ainsley barked without effect. "You refuse my hospitality and then have the gall to summon me outside my own home."

Ellenor watched as the Scot eased his grip on the reins. His mount, tired of standing for so long, began to dance from side to side. "And you are a desperate one, baron," came the bored reply.

The Scot's unspoken refusal to get off his monster horse and address Ainsley eye to eye was a blatant attempt at intimidation. And it was working. Despite herself, Ellenor smiled at the idea. Ainsley was just like her elder sister, a greedy soul, believing his status and wealth gave him power over others. *What desperation haunts you so much, baron, that you would have your men chase after these giants and endure such humiliation?* Ellenor asked herself.

A minute later, she had her answer.

"I understand you have something for me." The Scot's words were unconcerned, as if he were talking about some trivial item. Ellenor wondered just what it was Ainsley wanted to give him.

"I see my message was received. I was beginning to have doubts. But in answer to your question, I have what you want," her brother-in-law responded with a mixture of renewed confidence and relief. "But I want your word that you will take whatever I give you and never return."

Ellenor felt her body go cold.

After her father died, Ainsley had pretended to be the dutiful brother-in-law and eagerly assumed the role as her guardian, believing it could gain him even more of what he already had by marrying her off to a wealthy nobleman. Soon afterward, Ainsley had realized his mistake and wanted Ellenor gone by any legitimate, legal means. That had been six months ago. And after months of searching, Ainsley had finally found someone willing to relieve him of his familial burden.

Scorn entered the Scot's stare. "Englishmen have no concept of honor so why would I give my word to one?" Ellenor held her breath. "Rest easy, baron, what you have will leave with me. That I have vowed to another. It belongs to you no more."

"That's where you're wrong, Scot. No one owns what I give you, and God help the poor soul who thinks he does," Ainsley replied, finally sounding like a baron in control of the conversation.

Ellenor exhaled slowly. All her prayers, all the months of planning and preparation, were now worthless. If that giant of a man intended to take her with him, he would succeed.

She had only one remaining option. She had to make him change his mind.

* * *

Cole felt the looming tentacles of a trap. He had suspected one the moment Laurel had managed to finagle his promise without disclosing exactly what he had been sent to retrieve. He had sensed it again when the baron had his men ride after him, beckoning his return. Never, however, did Cole dream the nature of the trap to be the kicking disaster being coerced toward him.

It was a woman, or what looked like it had been a woman at one time. Her long chestnut-colored hair had been unwashed and unattended for days, if not weeks, and was a nightmarish concoction of tangles. The once deep emerald green gown she wore was covered in dirt smudges and frayed along the hems.

The sound of a new rip along one arm echoed across the small courtyard as she fought her captors. The woman was struggling for her freedom with all her might. Even now, Cole could see blood dripping from her nails as she clawed the cheek of one of the men dragging her.

As she neared, her eyes darted everywhere looking for any possibility of escape. The woman hated her captors, but clearly did not want new ones.

Cole watched expressionless as the frustrated guards tugged her to his mount's side. He gazed down as the woman shook loose the soldiers' hold. Her defiant posture, her dress, the condition of her arms and hands . . . she appeared to be quite mad. Then, she looked up, and as if caught in some spell, her dark green and gold eyes held his blue ones.

Her face was filthy, but it did not conceal the collection of well-defined features. A soft lower lip slightly fuller than the upper was stretched into a scowl that held both fear and audacity. Framed in deep brown lashes, eyes too large for her face were tight with strain and lack of sleep. A sudden gust of wind whipped at her clothing and hair. The few brown tendrils not tied in unwashed knots danced across her face, but she refused to brush them away.

Whatever game she was playing, she had been playing it for a long time. The woman was many things, but she was not crazy. She was as sane as he and every other person present.

Cole glanced at Donald, who was staring wide-eyed at the woman's back. The look in her eyes when she had been dragged between them had been borderline maniacal.

Believing her act to be true, Donald shifted his gaze to the baron. "What have you done to this woman?"

The moment Donald spoke, the female hissed and leaped to attack, but before she could inflict injury, Cole reached down and grabbed her hands firmly but not painfully in his grasp. She thrashed only for a moment and then stopped. With his long arm outstretched, she could not reach him or his horse with her kicks. Her jaw tightened, and she flicked him an icy look that he suspected could chill many a man. But her quick acceptance of the situation reinforced Cole's suspicions.

"No one did anything to her," Ainsley answered and threw a bag to Donald, who easily caught the bulky item. "She is my wife's younger sister. After her father's death, she became deranged. No one knows why. Those are her things, at least the ones my wife tells me were important to her at one time." Swallowing, Ainsley wiped his hands on his tunic and said, "Good-bye, Ellenor. Gilda would be here to wish you well, but I thought it would be too hard on her. She does love you."

Cole watched the woman's eyes narrow with fury

before she spat on the ground. No, madness did not swirl in those large hazel depths—hatred did.

For several seconds, Cole observed in hidden amusement as she threw rapier glances at the baron, causing him to shrink under her stare. Then, she turned her eyes toward him, assessing him as if he were a new challenge. "Leave, Scot, while you can. For you don't want me. No man does."

Without breaking his gaze, Cole reached behind him and yanked free the leather strip that had been holding back his hair. He wrapped it around her wrists. "Aye, in that you are right."

The woman's expression turned to one of outrage as he cinched the knot. In one smooth upward movement, she attempted to crack her fists against his jaw, but Cole was far more agile than she had anticipated.

"Damn you," she hissed.

Cole captured her chin between his thumb and forefinger, raising it. "Can't condemn a man who has already been damned. And know this now, *babag*, I hit back."

Her defiant eyes glittered with anger, and for an instant, Cole felt his pulse race. She wasn't afraid of him. It was rare to look a woman in the eye and not see the urge to flee reflected back at him. There was a significant amount of fear churning in the dark green depths, but he was not its cause.

He abruptly released his hold and she lost her footing. With her hands bound, she could not reach out and soften her landing. Donald instinctively grabbed her shoulders and tried to help her stand upright again. The second he touched her, she started screaming and jerking wildly. The more she thrashed, the tighter Donald's grip became.

Cole nodded to Donald, who hesitated for a moment and then let go. The instant she was free, she turned and nailed Donald in the groin, and then flew to Cole's side like a wild creature seeking refuge.

Donald grabbed his horse's mane to keep from keeling over in agony. "Insane bitch," he grunted, "you will pay for that mistake."

Stupefied that any woman would attack a man twice her size, Jaime nodded in agreement and then added, "Starting with being tied to the back of my horse."

Cole signaled Jaime to remain seated. Couldn't either of them see she was terrified? And now Cole knew why. The woman hadn't been feigning madness to annoy the baron, she did it to keep him and his men away.

He looked down at her huddled form hovering near his leg. She was scared of everyone. Everyone except him.

Without taking the time to explore why she had selected him for protection, Cole reached down and hauled her thin frame onto the section of saddle between his groin and the pommel. He could feel her back stiffen as he squeezed her tightly so that she couldn't speak. He yanked out his broadsword and pointed it at the baron. "Do not look to Scotland again to solve your problems. If you do, you shall be doing it at the end of a sword."

Grabbing his horse's reins, Cole swung his mount around and entered the forest enveloping the Cheviot Hills and the keep. The woman grabbed the mane of his horse to steady herself and looked back at him. He thought for a moment she was going to beg to be returned, but instead she pointed her finger at the nervous baron behind him and shouted, "May you and my sister get all that you deserve!"

"Be silent," Cole ordered as he began to weave in and out the trees.

Ellenor straightened her shoulders. "Or what? You'll make me walk?"

"Considering how bad you smell, that suggestion has its advantages, but I would rather endure your stench than stay any longer on English soil. So that leaves—"

"Do not pass me off to one of your men," Ellenor spat. Her eyes sought his, seeking reassurance but also warning him of the hell she would bring if he tried to make her ride with anyone else.

"Gagging," Cole clarified. "I will gag you, *babag*, until we reach our destination. Be silent and don't tempt me further."

He glanced down at her to make sure she understood. Hot, furious tears brimmed in her eyes. "My *name* is Ellenor. Ellenor Howell," she said through clenched teeth, ignoring his warning.

For a brief moment, Cole thought she might have understood his Gaelic insult for her hazel eyes had flashed bright green with recognition and pain. But then her expression turned cold as she issued him a challenging smile. Gesturing to the horizon just becoming visible between the tree limbs, she snickered, "Your precious homeland is beyond those large hills, and the sun will soon set. So I hope you can ride as well as I reek, Scot."

Then with the skill of someone who had ridden horses all her life, she swung a leg over the horse's neck and sat on the saddle astride, reducing their physical contact.

Her regal defiance surprised him, and Cole found himself intrigued. She was unpredictable, spirited, and most of all . . . a survivor. He had seen it in her eyes. This woman had endured pain and persevered.

He met her smile with one of his own. "Are you challenging me, lass?" He laughed and flicked the reins. "Because I do love a challenge."

Chapter 2

Ellenor was furious. And mostly at herself.

Halfway up the slope of Windy Gyle, she made a silent vow never to assume anything again about the dark-haired Scot holding her hostage. The knoll was nothing special in of itself. Grass-covered and rounded, it was one of the bigger hills of Cheviot, but definitely not the largest. In less than a half an hour, they would be passing its summit. And by doing so, the small group would no longer be in England, but in Scotland . . . just as the arrogant hulk had promised.

Practically the moment Durchent Hall and her weasel of a brother-in-law had disappeared from sight, the gait of the group changed to an aggressive lope that made her pulse skitter. For a short while, Ellenor feared she would fall to her death. The mount the Scot rode was enormous, just like he was, and it didn't seem possible the large animal could be agile enough to safely traverse the deceptive hills. But as one possible travesty after another was averted, Ellenor could no longer delude herself into believing the Scot's accurate riding was from luck. The man was highly skilled. Moreover, at the speeds they were moving, his expertise was far greater than hers. It rankled. She was good at very few things, but until today, she had met no one better on a horse.

All of her life she had been riding up and down these hills and rarely could a man keep up with her in fear of their horse losing its footing. There were holes and hidden patches of thick muck that could instantly stop a horse traveling too fast. And yet, the huge giant and his friends seemed to be gifted with foresight. They mysteriously found the few passes that remained traversable during the wet spring weather and knew how to avoid the enticing traps of grass-covered sludge.

The idea the dictatorial Scot and his companions could navigate terrain she knew far more intimately galled her enormously.

Ellenor glanced at the western sky. The sun was partially hidden behind some thin clouds and maybe one or two hours from setting—more than enough time to cross the peak and enter the Lowlands of Scotland. *Damn him*, she cursed silently. They would be sleeping on Scottish soil, and Ellenor had no doubt the *uamhlach* would gloat.

Even now, the silent triumph sparkling in the cave dweller's eyes was maddening. *Smile all you want, blue eyes, but tonight, all the laughter will be mine*, Ellenor promised herself. The man may have interrupted her plans but that didn't mean she couldn't resurrect them.

Two weeks ago, she had finally snuck away enough coin to buy her way into an Irish nunnery, far away from the baron, her sister, and anyone else who had ever known her. She had just been waiting for news of an arriving ship. Unfortunately, everything she needed was still at Durchent Hall. It would be a long trek back, but she could do it. Then she would disappear and, hopefully, start to forget.

The horse weaved unexpectedly and Ellenor felt herself slipping. Suddenly, a big arm pulled her close and cradled her to keep her from falling. An overwhelming sense of security came over her. She was bound and furious about being taken somewhere without her consent, but in that instant, she also felt protected. Something she had not felt since her father had died.

Ellenor glanced back at the large Scot and blatantly assessed him. Two thin plaits of his dark brown hair were braided along his scalp just above his ears. Both hung loose among the rich shoulder-length mass left free after he used the leather strip that had been holding it back to bind her wrists. A long white scar starting at his chin looked old and deep and terrible. His mouth was hard, set in a permanent scowl, and Ellenor tried to envision him smiling. She couldn't do it. With high cheekbones, an arrogant nose, and an inflexible jaw covered with the growth of a day-old beard, his face matched the rest of him, cold and unforgiving. There was no softness about him anywhere. Just raw, controlled power.

He should have terrified her. So why did he, of all people, make her feel safe? Even as she asked herself the question, she knew the answer.

He hated her.

His eyes were the brightest blue Ellenor had ever seen, but their brilliance held no warmth. Only pain reflected back, hurt and a type hollowness one had to recognize in one's self to see in others. Something had happened to this man. Something unmentionable. Something that had changed the very core of who he was. As a result, he despised her and all that she represented.

That was the reason she felt safe in his arms. Her tenuous trust in the Scottish warrior, however, did not extend to his comrades.

His brown-haired companion had been silently

boring holes in her head their whole ride north. Ellenor
didn't care and held no sympathy for him or his sore
groin. He should never have grabbed her. The one with
wild red hair had also been stealing glances, although
his looks were not one of lust, but of pity. She stank and
looked unmanageable. Both states of repulsiveness had
been by design, and both served a purpose. They kept
men like them away.

At least until today, when she had suddenly lost control of her fate.

Renewed anger heated Ellenor's blood and her pulse
began to pound violently. She had long ago vowed never
to allow any man to control her life again, and she
wasn't about to let the overgrown Scot command her
destiny. Ellenor narrowed her eyes and faced forward.
She needed to think.

She needed to regain her freedom.

Over an hour later, Ellenor was desperate. Her attempts at convincing her Scottish captor to cut her
bonds had all failed. Her seemingly brilliant plan hadn't
worked even once.

The concept had seemed sound. Relax her grip, and
then while pretending to fall, cry out for help. After a
few times of catching her, she would blame her bonds
and to avoid the process repeating itself, he would
remove them.

Unfortunately, each time she began to slide off the
monstrous animal, the oaf had let her, forcing her to
save herself barely in time. Only once had she waited
too long and had been unable to break her fall.

Fear had ripped through her as the horse's legs
pounded the earth, never easing from their deadly pace.
Her hip had passed the animal's massive fore flanks,

evoking a real and terrified scream. Only then did a large hand come down, grab her in a bruising grip, and dump her in a mortifying manner back atop the horse.

Humiliated, she decided her next solution would be something far less dangerous. Regrettably, it was also exceedingly more painful.

Brilliant plan number two consisted of good behavior and silence. Why she had thought *that* would work would forever be a mystery even to her.

For almost an hour, she had sat straight backed in mute defiance. Periodically, she would hint her desires by demonstratively twisting her bound wrists. As a result, her lower back was on fire and her rear end was sore from improperly sitting in the saddle.

From him . . . nothing.

Well, Scot, if you won't free my bonds for my sake, then maybe you will for your own. She was down to her final idea. Talking. Slowly, though. Simple stuff, like who he was and where they were going. Trust was the key.

Ellenor twisted around and stared at him, waiting to be acknowledged, even if just by a passing glance. The infuriating man ignored her. She took a deep breath, told herself to remain calm, and asked, "Do you remember my name?"

Cole smiled to himself. She had lasted much longer than he had anticipated, but he *had* been right. Once silence had not worked, he had been sure she would try its opposite. He wondered which vocal tactic she would employ. Pleading? Crying? He hoped not. Both were annoying, and for a strange reason, he felt beneath her. Cole hoped the English lass would be more honest. "Aye."

"And?" Ellenor pushed.

"There's English and then there is abhorrently English. Your name falls in the latter category."

Ellenor blinked. She should have been insulted, but she was too shocked to muster the anger. The uncommunicative Scot had just answered her with more than a single word. In fact, his English had been eloquent.

The damn man had surprised her *again*.

"Well . . . good," she stammered. "And how about you? Do you have a name? Are you by chance from a local clan?"

Silence.

Ellenor pursed her lips. "Perhaps a . . . MacInnes?"

Her captor's rigid face suddenly came to life and Ellenor felt a ray of hope shoot through her. It was unlikely Ainsley had reached out to his dead sister's clan for assistance, but if he had, it was probably the one place in Scotland she would be willing to go. However, before true excitement could build, the contrary giant cocked a single brow and said, "Nay."

Ellenor waited for him to follow his answer with some clarification but none came. Pasting on a fake smile, she returned to face the front. "I didn't think so," she sighed. "Most of them are rather good looking . . . and long winded," she added at the last moment, hoping to compel him into conversing with her.

In truth, she had no idea what the MacInneses were like, with the exception of Laurel. Ainsley's sister had left nearly four years ago to live with her Scottish grandfather, Laird MacInnes. On the way, her small guard had been ambushed and almost all had been killed. Those that had survived had returned reporting of her death. "Is it by chance . . . Douglass?"

The unmistakable revulsion in her voice startled Cole. First MacInnes and now Douglass, both clans from Laurel's past. The Englishwoman must suspect who had ordered him to find her and was fishing for a confirmation. That, he was absolutely not going to provide.

While the woman had been assessing him, he had been considering her as well. Aside from her more appalling characteristics of stinking and speaking with a repugnant English accent, he had to admit she was resourceful, persistent, and surprisingly intelligent. All three spelled trouble. If Laurel knew her, then she knew Laurel as well, and no doubt would try to use their relationship as leverage to get what she wanted, starting with removal of the leather strap securing her wrists.

Cole felt a sharp thump on his rib cage as one of her elbows "accidentally" collided with his chest. She glanced back for a second and that's when he noticed her eyes. Their hazel color had turned into a deep green that was so dark they were almost black. Hatred boiled within her and it was aimed at him. For a moment, he was clueless as to why. What had he done? Then he realized by *not* answering her question, she had jumped to the wrong conclusion of just who he was. "I am no Douglass," he said with conviction. "They fear me. I don't fear them."

And they did.

Three years ago, the Douglasses learned a deadly lesson. Attack a McTiernay and die. Attack a McTiernay's woman and die screaming. Now, when members of the Douglass clan saw the dark McTiernay tartan of greens and blues, they hid rather than faced him.

Soft, slim fingers reached out and grabbed his forearm. Cole looked down and watched in both horror and fascination as the Englishwoman twisted almost all the way around in the seat. By the time she let go, she was precariously perched on the back of his horse's neck between the withers and the crest. When after several seconds she didn't falter, he knew his suspicions about her riding abilities were correct. At the pace they were riding, he should have been forced to hold on to her nearly the whole time to keep her upright. Instead, the only time his assistance had been truly needed was when she had pretended to fall off his horse and nearly succeeded.

He had to admit she was far from dull. Even now, she was trying to give him the same withering stare she had issued the baron upon their departure, but it lacked the venom the other had possessed. It amused him, and without thinking, the corners of his mouth lifted into a half smile. He was about to return his attention to the terrain when he felt something push firmly into his chest. Looking down, he saw one outstretched finger poking out from her bound hands. His half smile seemed to add intensity to her stare.

Frustrated, she gnashed her teeth and asked outright, "If I am to be dragged away from my home and family, may I at least know the name of my captor?" She pulled her hand away from his chest and wagged it in front of his face. "And think twice about ignoring me, Scot."

"Or what?" he asked, grabbing her wiggling finger. "Just what do you think you are in a position to do about anything, *babag*?"

A sinister smile invaded Ellenor's eyes. "Or I'll sing. I happen to know a lovely *English* bard song about Richard the Lionheart that I especially enjoy when I am riding. It has many verses to keep me entertained while I wait for your answer."

Cole almost choked with unexpected mirth. It had been a long time since someone surprised him. It had been even longer since he had engaged in a battle of wills with a clever opponent. He could threaten to gag her, but deep down he knew he wouldn't.

"McTiernay. My name is McTiernay," he said with resignation. A look of satisfaction crept into her green and gold eyes and he almost choked again. She actually believed she had won this battle.

Ellenor licked her lips. *McTiernay.*

She rolled the name around in her head, but did not recognize it. She had heard of most of the clans on the border from either her father or Ainsley, and that name had never been among them. He could be from a smaller clan she had never heard of, but instinct told her otherwise. This man came from much farther north. He was one of the Scots who had driven Edward I crazy with their fight for independence. A fight she secretly endorsed.

"And so are you the only McTiernay or are there others in your clan?"

Cole shot her a strange look. "There are others."

"And . . ." she prompted.

"And what?" Cole asked, confused as to what she was asking.

"Your name!" Ellenor huffed. "What is *your* name? Not your clan's. You know . . . like Elmer Harold Ludlow of the clan McTiernay," she offered, intentionally using the most English-sounding names she could think of.

He immediately stiffened and Ellenor thought for a second her ploy might work. Then he glanced down at her with eyes so blue they compelled one to stare into them. They held not annoyance. Instead, amusement glittered back. The beast actually thought her attempt at provoking him into an answer was funny.

Well, prepare yourself, McTiernay, for if you won't tell me your name, I think I just gave you one. Her inner dialogue did nothing to remove the look of triumph in his eyes, but it did make her feel better.

Wrenching her gaze free from his, Ellenor stared at the opening of his leine. The breeze caught his shirt and she could see the spattering of dark hair across his chest. It looked silky to the touch. She tried to look elsewhere, but his shirt continued to billow and her eyes were drawn to the inviting V the hairs created down the length of his torso. His stomach was rippled like the rest of him. Muscles on top of muscles. As male physiques went, McTiernay had one of the best she had ever seen.

"See something you like?"

Ellenor's head snapped up, realizing she had been caught. Refusing to admit defeat, she coyly replied, "If you mean something I would like to pummel, then yes. I see something I like." Then she squeezed her eyes shut and tried once again to figure him out.

The one question that kept cycling through her mind was *why*. Why would a man—especially this one—travel all the way from northern Scotland to haul a crazed woman back with him? But then again, she wasn't crazy, and he had known that from the beginning.

Ellenor opened her eyes and caught him looking at her. She cocked her head to the side, moved to cross her arms, and grimaced as she was reminded of her bound wrists. She took two deep breaths and said, "You know I am not mad."

"Aye."

"If you knew I was not mad, why did you not say so to the baron?"

Cole shrugged. "Because it would have changed nothing."

He had looked at her when he answered, not just passively, but deeply, as if he wanted her to understand that she *was* coming with him. She could fight it, but she would lose. A sharp retort came to her tongue, and yet, she couldn't utter it. Something in those sapphire depths held her captive, a suppressed warmth she had not expected to see.

This man felt deeply; he just didn't want to. He had learned how to cut off his emotions and she imagined very few had ever gotten close enough to see something other than a remote coldness reflecting back at them. Ellenor wondered if her own eyes mirrored the same kind of pain.

"I think you find me handsome."

If it were possible, Ellenor would have throttled her own throat. That was twice in less than a handful of minutes he had caught her staring at him. "Not at all," she lied. "I was simply curious about the scar on your chin. I was wondering how a man could get that close to the end of a sword and live?"

Ellenor had never seen a face deaden quite as quickly or as thoroughly. Her comment had inadvertently triggered a horrific memory. She knew. She recognized the icy hollowness evading every part of him. It happened to her each time someone said or did anything that yanked her back to the night her life changed. Her body went numb, her emotions dissolved until there was nothing left.

If she didn't do something quick, the Scot would shut down and resurrect impenetrable walls made of nightmares. Then, she would have no chance of convincing him to cut her bonds. She needed to snap him back to the present, now.

"So, McTiernay, you've made it quite clear you did not wish me to come with you. You had the chance to leave me behind and yet you didn't. You could even now drop me off and be on your way. I assure you I won't return to my sister's home. The baron would never know."

"If I were going to 'leave you behind' as you put it, I would have done so."

Ellenor chewed on his answer and realized his reason

for getting her was not complicated, but simple. He had been sent to get her, and that was what he had done. Why she had been pretending to be mad or why Ainsley had desired her immediate departure mattered nothing to the overgrown beast. She would be sitting exactly where she was even if she *had* been mentally unbalanced.

"What about . . ." Ellenor choked out, grabbing Cole's leine as his horse suddenly slowed its gait. "Hey, Scot! Make up your mind! Either keep me alive or take me back, but don't kill me on this monster of yours!"

She let go of his shirt and Cole flicked his tongue out across his lips, smothering an instinctive smile. Any other woman would have undoubtedly required saving. Then again, they wouldn't have been sitting backward perched on his mount's neck. But not this Englishwoman. Her reflexes were immediate and accurate. Her snipe didn't come from fear; it came from lack of control.

Ellenor Howell was just as disturbed by him as he was by her.

The woman had practically probed him with her eyes a few minutes ago, and he sensed she glimpsed something . . . something he didn't want her or anyone else to see. So, he had teased her, and her comeback, while innocent, had revived emotions he had long ago suppressed.

Indifference, Cole whispered to himself. That was the only way he was going to survive the next few days. "Steud is not a monster. He's a horse. And you would not have been in danger if you had been sitting properly and not jumping around all the time."

Ignoring his comment, Ellenor asked, "Did you say Steud?"

"Aye."

Ellenor muffled a laugh but could not keep from rolling her eyes. What kind of man named his horse . . . *horse*? "Why did you slow down? I thought you were in a rush to get back to your precious Scotland."

"I was."

"But then . . ." Ellenor halted in midsentence as she answered her own question. They had just crested Windy Gyle. England was now behind them. "Well," she began with a huff, "I suppose you are pleased with yourself, Scot, but I could care less where we are just as long as it's not Durchent Hall."

"Then we are finally of accord, *babag*."

"We are most certainly *not* in accord, *Elmer*. My hands are tied. I am incredibly uncomfortable and I am finding it harder and harder to remain atop your *monstrous* horse."

"I suggest you try harder," Cole returned, refusing to react to her latest nickname for him.

Ellenor's jaw dropped open. The man was actually smiling. Not a large one that spanned from cheek to cheek, but the sides of his face were definitely crinkling and Ellenor was positive it qualified as a grin for the hulking brute. Probably a large one.

Laugh while you can, Scot, for it will be I who will be laughing last, Ellenor vowed. "I have tried," she replied with mocking innocence. "But I can no longer sit as I am, and sitting facing the front without support is also painful. That leaves only one choice. You."

"What do you mean me?" Cole shouted, unaware his voice had risen several levels.

"Simply that I shall have to rest against you," Ellenor replied calmly, knowing how bad she stank. And then taking a deep breath, Ellenor gripped his tunic, turned back around to face the front, and commenced to wiggle even farther back into the seat. When she was done snuggling against him, her whole backside was touching him from his shoulders down to his groin. Then, she sucked in her breath and waited.

For well over a year, she had successfully avoided being in the presence of a man, let alone touching one. Now, suddenly, she was practically lying in the arms of one that radiated more primitive masculinity than any man she had ever met. And instead of screaming and clawing her way to safety, her instinct was to get even closer.

She felt no abhorrence, no repulsion. The taste of bile and the uncontrollable need to flee did not invade her every sense. There was only an unfamiliar desire to touch him and discover if the rest of his body was just as hard and solid.

Licking her lips, Ellenor tried to ignore the confusing messages her own body was sending her, but it was impossible. A hypnotizing warmth seeped through his tunic and her gown and into her skin. His powerful chest was huge, and with each step his horse took, she could feel his muscles move to keep both him and her atop the animal's back. The Scot could overpower her anytime he wanted to, but instead of feeling caged in by his strength, she felt protected by it.

Cole was anything but unmoved by her new attempt at freedom. He knew she was not trying to use her femininity to induce him to loosen her bonds, more likely the opposite. The woman had been hoping her odor would make her nearness unbearable. And while she didn't smell good, it was far from repulsive. His men had stunk worse than she ever could, even if she continued to abstain from bathing for another month. Moreover, he was not about to concede to her latest challenge.

Pushing her back upright, he grunted, "I suggest you try harder to find another position."

"And if I cannot?"

"Then I will find one for you . . . starting with across the back end of my horse."

A sudden shower of angry sparks flashed from Ellenor's eyes. She whirled around to face him and almost fell. He caught her, but she shrugged him off. "You wouldn't dare, Scot."

"Oh, I certainly would."

There it was again! That damn grin. Except it was a little larger this time. The intolerable beast was laughing at her. Maybe not out loud, but the man probably didn't know how to. His awkward grin was practically guffawing at her and all from the possibility of her lying prone across the ass of his mount.

"Don't you have any compassion?" she wailed.

Blue eyes dropped to hers and any warmth shining in them just a moment ago had been sniffed out by that single question. They darkened considerably until only cold navy stones remained. His face was once again void of emotion. "No."

Ellenor swallowed. His voice had been low, even, and full of disdain. His antipathy toward her had all of the sudden become personal, but she had no idea why. She had done nothing to him. "You . . . really hate me, don't you?"

Cole broke free from their locked gaze and concentrated again on the jagged trail. "I despise all who are English," he said simply.

"I didn't say the English. I said *me*."

She waited for him to say something, to explain, to tell her she was wrong, but his mouth was set in a grim line, indicating he had said enough. "That's it? That is all you have to say?"

More silence.

"You insufferable oaf. You don't even know me! At

least *my* reasons for detesting you are based on personal interaction," Ellenor hissed, waving her bound wrists in the air so that he could not mistake her meaning.

Cole bristled. He didn't want to admit she intrigued him and that in some odd way he respected her determination to control her fate, despite the way she went about it. He hated the English, and every word she spoke aloud proved her ancestry. Honor demanded that he despise her and so he did. Everyone had accepted his position long ago, and until today, no one had questioned the intelligence of his stance. If he hadn't explained his reasoning for his blanket hatred of the English to his own family and clan, he certainly wouldn't explain himself to her. Besides, she was wrong. His grounds for disliking her *were* personal.

"Do your reasons for disliking me include reeking?" Cole shot back. "Trust me, mine do."

Clenching and unclenching her bound hands, Ellenor fought the rising need to strike him and said through gritted teeth, "I stink because I have not been able to bathe."

"Nay. You stink because you *chose* not to bathe."

Denial was pointless. The man was infuriatingly right. People had begged her to wash herself, but she had adamantly refused. Precious isolation had been hard to attain and being offensive had allowed her to keep it. Acting out of control was difficult to do for prolonged periods, but smelling foul, while uncomfortable, was easy to accomplish and even easier to maintain. Not to mention that the more she stank, the more everyone left her alone.

Unfortunately, that was no longer the case.

It appeared she had company, whether she liked it or not. Better yet, it was not her stench that would keep his hands off her, it was who she was—an Englishwoman. If she had to be in a man's arms, there were no safer ones than this Highlander's.

"And I suppose you are going to make me take one," Ellenor remarked, waiting for his order to bathe the second they made camp. And she would. One of her most favorite things in the world was a bath. It mattered not where—a tub, a river, a lake—she just loved the feel of water against her skin. Nothing was better.

Cole chuckled against her shoulder blades and Ellenor felt something inside her deflate. A bath was not in her near future.

"You obviously enjoy your stench, *mùrla*. Why should I stop any English from being what they are?"

Ellenor had had enough of his name-calling. First, it was a filthy female and now he was referencing her horribly matted head of hair. Despite the oaf's belief otherwise, she did not like to reek. Her odor even offended herself, and since it was no longer necessary, she had no intentions of staying that way. Squaring her jaw, she announced, "I shall bathe when we stop."

"Not tonight."

Ellenor stiffened at the casually issued challenge. "And why not tonight? I have decided to bathe, and I will, Scot. You have no idea how stubborn I can be when I have decided upon something."

"Aye, I have an idea." Cole couldn't help admiring her spirit. He had no idea what hell she had endured to cause her to walk the path of feigned madness and stench, but the woman was a survivor and she had not become one by succumbing to anyone's decrees.

"Then you concede?" she said with a hint of smile.

"That depends."

"On . . ." she pressed. The man's short answers were infuriating. If only her sister and Ainsley had spoken so little, isolation would not have been so appealing.

"On how you enjoy your baths."

Ellenor realized the man would continue with his vague comments until she really did go mad. He expected her to press for explanations, and maybe most women would have, but she was not most women. It was time he learned that fact.

Throwing back her head, Ellenor let out a peal of laughter. "You make no sense, Scot. Maybe it is you who is mad, not I."

"I make sense, and stop calling me a Scot."

"Why? That's what you are."

"My home is the Highlands."

"So, you are still a Scot."

"I am a *Highlander*," Cole replied evenly. If the woman was intentionally trying to provoke him, she was surprisingly effective. She was not only impossible to ignore, she seemed to read him and his reactions in a way very few could.

Ellenor clucked her tongue. "Last I heard, the Highlands were a part of Scotland. Therefore, you *are* a Scot."

Cole's jaw clenched. He forced it to relax. "You and your sister share the same father and therefore the same blood. I am as close to a Scot as you are to your sister."

Ellenor sat mum. This Highlander had never even met her sister, but he had made his point. She and Gilda were far different people, and always had been.

"I need to know, are you or are you not going to unbind me when we camp?"

"I am not."

The answer was so short and final it almost made her give up trying. Almost. "And just why not? What is it that you hope to achieve by perpetuating my irritability?"

"You are not mad, woman, but you are obviously not above acting like you are," Cole began, surprised by his willingness to explain himself. "I am not in the mood to be scratched, or bitten, or kicked in an attempt at freedom."

Ellenor couldn't deny having the impulse to do just what he feared, but she doubted she would have acted on it. She was desperate, but not stupid. She didn't want to assault him. She just wanted to leave. "What if I promise to behave?"

"You will be freed only when I am assured that you will not flee."

"*Damn,*" she muttered, uncaring if he heard her or not. "Just who *are* you? Why do you care if I run off? I am nothing but a burden to you, I stink, and most of all, you hate me."

Her comment rattled Cole. He didn't hate *her.* Fact was he admired her. And surprisingly, she had not felt like a burden. It wasn't often someone held his interest, but this lass did. He found himself anxiously awaiting her next ploy. And her eyes . . . gold flecks swam in the deepest green he had ever seen. Each time he peered into them, he got lost. But if she ever knew any of that, he would lose all control, over her and himself. "I am the man who has been charged to escort you north. That is all you need to know."

"No, it is not! I need to know where I am going, who you are, and where you are taking me."

"These questions will be answered in time."

"Maybe in your time, *Scot,* not mine."

"Aye, I'm glad we understand each other, *babag.*"

Furious at lacking the power to retake control of her life, Ellenor sat in silence as Cole weaved in and out of the forest. The hills had grown steep again, and the sight of fresh water was disappearing along with the sun. The ground was slippery with mud, and Ellenor suspected they would be stopping at the next decent spot to camp. And when they did, bound or not, she intended to escape.

Thinking about how she would traverse these hills on foot, Ellenor was unprepared when the horse stumbled slightly on the slick ground. She almost fell when firm hands instantly grabbed her arms, dragging her back to safety. She had been deep in thought unaware of what had happened or who was holding her. A cold sweat enveloped her as memories of a man's hands holding her down filled her mind.

"Are you all right, lass?" Cole asked, concern lacing his question. He had never seen a human being turn so pale so fast. It was as if all the blood had drained out of her.

Ellenor blinked. "What . . . ? What did you say?"

Cole shook his hands. Ellenor looked down and realized she had a white-knuckled grip upon them. "I won't let you fall," Cole said softly, hoping to allay her fears.

Ellenor stared at his fingers. They were long and large and rough with calluses. The power and strength of his hands were unmistakable, and at any time, he could have wrenched them from her grasp. Instead, he was waiting patiently for her to let them go.

She eased her grip, but didn't fully release it. She looked up and found his eyes searching hers. They were the deepest, most intense hue she had ever seen. Darker than the sky. Clearer than the sea. A woman could get lost in eyes like his if she let her guard down. They seemed to reflect understanding. He didn't know why she needed to be the one to let go, but he recognized her pain. It was the kindest thing anyone had done for her in a long time.

And for a moment, Ellenor almost reconsidered running away.

* * *

Cole threw the leg bone of the rabbit he had been chewing on into the fire. He offered to do the same for Ellenor, but she opted to glare at him and toss the bone in herself. Shrugging, he stood and announced, "I'm going to scout the area and will return shortly." Then he paused and added in Gaelic, "And if our *aoigh* decides she no longer wants our company . . ." He paused, looked back and gave her his half grin. "Then let her go."

A minute later, he was gone. Ellenor sat in shocked silence, wondering if she could have misunderstood . . . but she doubted it. After her father died, she had stopped venturing into town alone, ending her secret lessons in the Gaelic language. However, before that, the old Scottish smithy had told her that, with the exception of Laurel Cordell, she was the finest student he ever had. She had similar compliments from the abbess who had taught her how to read and speak French and Italian. She had a mind for languages and found them easy to digest and learn, but never did she dream she would actually have a need for one of them in her lifetime. Tonight, the once-useless talent had both calmed and inflamed her fears.

Since they stopped to make camp, the three Highlanders had chatted intermittently in their language about various topics. Most of them uninteresting— horses, the flat terrain, and the painfully slow pace they had been forced to endure. Ellenor had almost given away the fact that she could understand their speech by making a sarcastic comment, but held her tongue just in time. And the price for her silence had paid off.

She had learned the name of her captor—Cole. He was the third of seven siblings and they were headed to the home of his eldest brother and laird of their Highland clan. The brother was married, and by the sporadic comments—quite happily. However, nothing in the conversation explained why his brother had ordered Cole to go south and bring her safely back to him.

Ellenor could only surmise two reasons. She was to be married, which was unlikely, but possible. The thought of building alliances with an English baron might appeal to some. The other reason was labor, but even that was a stretch. Why go to so much effort to punish a single Englishwoman whom you don't even know?

"Do you think she will try and run?" The question came from one called Jaime Ruadh—or Jaime the Red, which was appropriate for his wild hair was an incredible shade of bright crimson.

His friend, Donald, shrugged and stoked the fire. "Hope so."

"You're just sore about earlier," Jaime chided. He was still gnawing on the rest of the rabbit so his words were slurred and half-articulated.

"More like pissed. All I did was try and keep the wench from falling."

"She was just scared of you."

"I don't care if she thought I was the devil," Donald retorted, adjusting himself once again. "You don't kick a man that hard . . . there . . . especially when he has to sit in the saddle all day."

"True," Jaime agreed. "And I've seen no remorse from the lass."

Ellenor's eyes widened and quickly looked away. All afternoon she had been returning Donald's evil glares, believing her violent reaction had been justified. He had grabbed her from behind and she had wanted him to let go and never think about touching her again.

"The damn *mùrla* is no more capable of remorse than she is of shame. No woman should allow herself to smell the way she does."

Jaime took a last bite, licked his lips, and threw the

bone in the fire. "Come on now. I've smelt worse. Hell, *you've* smelled of worse."

"I'm not a woman."

"And you're not sick in the mind, either."

Donald stood up and pointed in her direction. "If that woman is mad, I'm a married monk."

Jaime glanced in her direction and caught Ellenor staring at them. "Aye, I wondered myself. She avoids our company, but not the commander's. Doesn't make sense."

"It's because she's the last person in the world he wants with him and she knows it. Wench actually takes comfort in the knowledge."

"Wonder why," Jaime murmured, ignoring his friend stalk around the campsite to where he'd placed his things earlier.

"Don't know and don't care," Donald mumbled as he grabbed his rolled plaid. "I just want to get back to my woman, a woman of quality, who happens to know how to take care of herself."

Jaime adjusted his own saddle and leaned back, chuckling. "Better prepare yourself, friend. Your Brighid seems to get along with the English. They just might become fast friends."

As Donald sharply denounced any possibility of Jaime's prediction coming true, Ellenor slipped off the large log and headed toward the thickest part of the brush surrounding the campsite. Relief went through her when she made it to the other side without any sounds of her breaking brittle branches, notifying them of her exit. She doubted they would have stopped her, but she didn't want to take any chances. Not even to get the bag, which held her few remaining possessions.

As she moved deeper inside the dark brush, very little light from the partially veiled moon was getting through the thick branches. Ellenor waited for her eyes to adjust and then began to look for something that could free her from the leather straps binding her wrists. Spying a fallen tree with a broken narrow branch protruding from it, Ellenor straddled the log and pulled both wrists as far apart as she could. Then she carefully began to saw the exposed leather back and forth against the sharp edge of the break. What felt like an eternity later, the leather snapped, and for the first time in months, she felt truly and completely free.

There was no Ainsley, no threat of marriage, no pretense of madness . . . nothing. And based on what that Highlander had said to his men, she was also free from him.

Cole watched in fascination as the woman trudged on through the ever-darkening woodland. She had been fighting her way through some difficult foliage for over an hour and had fallen several times. Still, she had forged ahead. He had no idea where she was going based on the wild path she was taking, but the woman was heading toward the deepest part of the forest. The region was full of prey, but with all the noise she was making, he had seen more than one animal scamper away in fear.

It was a calculated risk to let her try and run, just as it had been a tactical decision where to camp. Normally, he would have ventured closer to the River Teviot for the night and let her bathe, but then he would have been forced to keep her bound another day. Access to the shoreline would have only fueled the dogged determination to get away he had seen in her eyes. This forest was difficult to navigate in daylight. At night, it was near impossible, and Cole needed her to succumb to the idea that she was safer with him than on her own.

The constant cracking sound of twigs and branches suddenly ceased. Apprehension flooded him. The noise the woman had been making could have led the dead to her location, and consequently, he had felt comfortable keeping his distance to prevent her from accidentally seeing him.

Cole started moving quickly to the last place he heard her, praying he had been the only one stalking her movements. His fears dissipated as he soon as he saw her huddled form. She was sitting on the forest floor with her arms locked around her knees rocking back and forth . . . crying.

He stepped into the small area and the crack of twigs breaking immediately caught her attention. Instinct caused her to grab the closest thing to her and leap to her feet.

Waving the half-rotted stick around, Ellenor demanded, "Who goes there? Tell me now or I will scream. I have three enormous Highlanders traveling with me, so I suggest you think your plans over again before you take another step."

Cole grabbed the waving stick and, with a single twist, plucked it from her grasp. "So it is now we three who are traveling with *you*, is it?"

He had been prepared for a spicy retort or to chase her if she chose to run away, but he had not expected the woman to throw herself—weeping hysterically—into his arms.

"Cole, thank God, it's you."

An unexpected shudder went through him. His name echoed in the black stillness as she mumbled it again and again. The sound of it seemed to ease her fears. He tried to remain indifferent, telling himself that she didn't know what she was doing or saying, but found it impossible as her slim body melded to his.

"Aye, lass, it's me," he whispered, threading his fingers through her thick, tangled mane. Had he really forgotten how wonderful a woman's body could feel, or was Ellenor's embrace so very different from every other he had known?

"I . . . was so scared. I was lost and . . ." Ellenor's voice caught in her throat as she became aware of their tight embrace. She was clinging to him and he was comforting her. His hands were in her hair and his huge frame practically engulfed her own, holding her gently to him.

And the last thing she wanted was to pull away.

"You were running away," Cole finished for her.

"No," Ellenor mumbled into his tunic, followed by a sniffle. "I was at first, but I haven't been for some time. I was trying to get back to you."

Cole could not recall a single time a woman had ever come to him, let alone embraced him, for comfort. He had been told he was cold, menacing. Yet, this woman— someone who feared men—was crushing herself to him, burying her head into his shoulder.

The fiery, hot-blooded creature from this afternoon had a vulnerable side Cole was sure she let very few see. He had no idea why Ellenor trusted him, but for some reason she did. The resulting abrupt need to protect her was so strong, so unexpected, his mind floundered and his body took over.

His arms stole around her and gently held her to him, rocking her, soothing her. In return, her soft feminine curves arched into him, seeking his touch. The rapid rise and fall of her chest pressed her breasts against him, and he could feel the pulse in her neck pounding against his skin.

And then the warmth of her body was gone.

Ellenor pulled away, startled by her reaction . . . and his. The man hated her, didn't he? She hated him, didn't she? Unconsciously she smoothed back her unruly tawny curls as if her hair were brushed and styled and frantically sought for something to say. "I . . . could use some water."

Cole told himself the feeling that had swept over him when she broke off their embrace was relief. Comforting women was not something he had practice with, and if asked, he would say proudly he hoped never to be as well versed in the activity as his two older brothers. And yet . . . it was she, not he, who ended their contact and that needled him. He was tempted to pull her back into his arms just so he could prove to her and himself he was just as impervious to their touch.

Instead, Cole reached out and took her hand in his. "Come with me. There's a small stream by the campsite." She didn't resist and he pretended not to notice how delicate her wrist was.

A half hour later, Ellenor cursed as she stared into the moonlit water trickling through her fingers. The stream was barely deep enough for her to cup her hands. Just as she had been warned, bathing was out of the question. This pitiful brook was probably the very reason the infuriating man had chosen where to camp. Thick woods and a stream that was no more than ankle deep. He wanted her dependent upon him and too afraid to run away.

And damn, if she wasn't just that.

She had actually jumped into his arms, whispering words of gratitude, uncaring that he was a man, that she was demonstrably afraid, that she wanted . . . no, needed to be comforted. She had allowed herself to become the worst thing ever to be . . . vulnerable. *Well, never again, Scot,* Ellenor vowed. *Never will I need you or anyone else ever again.*

"Did you say something?" Cole called out.

Ellenor's head snapped up, realizing he might have heard her. "Yes, I did," she barked and pulled off her slippers. "I said damn. Damn this so-called stream, damn these impenetrable woods, and damn you, Scot, for ruining any chances I had at a life."

The chuckle rising in Cole's throat was suddenly stifled as he quickly moved to dodge two slippers being hurled surprisingly close to his head. "You have a strange way of thanking someone."

She didn't answer him directly back, but the words "colossal-sized lout" and "cave dweller" were hanging in the air.

In less than a day, she had given him more nicknames than had been bestowed upon him in a lifetime. She used his proper name when frightened, called him a hulking giant or lout when exasperated, Highlander when she was being sarcastic, and Scot when her frustration was morphing into anger. And if he wasn't mistaken, he was fairly certain she had called him an ass at least twice while setting up camp, each time after she realized he had tricked her.

Any one of these less than flattering labels should have given him reason to take offense and possibly retaliate on some level. Nevertheless, Cole felt no compunction to do either. Just the opposite. Her outbursts made him feel something that he had no longer thought possible. Simple happiness. Not pleasure from accomplishment. Not satisfaction as a result from some deed. Just a strange kind of contentment.

Ellenor picked up a nearby rock and threw it at him. A second later, she heard it bounce off a tree. She had missed. "*Thanking you?* Why, you . . . you . . . big, hulking, inconsiderate . . . giant. For months, I have gone without regular baths and behaved irrationally to the point I offend even myself, forgoing all that I enjoy. And for what? To be picked up and dragged away by a towering Scot and his two faithful companions days away from escape." Ellenor picked up another rock. This time she threw it into the stream, watching the water splash and settle back down as the pebble sank the short way to the bottom.

She reached down for a third pebble and glanced behind her shoulder to see if he was watching her. The moonlight revealed that he was. More than that, he was grinning. This time it was a full-fledged grin. This afternoon she hadn't thought his cheeks were capable of a real smile. And now, Ellenor wished fervently they weren't.

The man had dimples. Deep ones.

If she had been told about them, rather than having witnessed them, she would have thought the idea ridiculous. Warriors as large he was, who had the ability to make a man quake with a single look, didn't have dimples. And this Highlander was definitely a warrior. His strong and rigid face was not made to be soft and welcoming, but that was exactly what it became when he smiled. Warm and unguarded, and disturbingly disarming.

His broad and firm mouth suddenly became generous and his compelling blue eyes sparkled with life in the moonlight. Tousled dark brown hair, overly long and slightly curly, recaptured into a ponytail only added to the transformation. The man oozed masculine charm, but at the same time, maintained whatever it was that spoke of his subtle, but substantial power.

In total, Cole McTiernay was exactly what Ellenor had dreamed all her life a man should be. He was tall, strong, and surprisingly gentle. And when smiling . . . almost too handsome.

She was in the presence of one of the most masculine, physically intimidating men she was ever likely to meet. Incredibly, he was also the most honorable. With him, she was safe. And with this man, that knowledge was dangerous.

Since the moment her eyes had met his and felt a jolt of connection, a sense of awareness she could not put into words, had come over her. With every word, every touch, it had only grown.

The night her father died, she lost a piece of herself. Since then, Ellenor had not thought it possible to feel connected to anyone or anything again. But here she was, bending over a small brook, stealing glimpses at a Highlander who supposedly hated her, feeling not dead inside, but very much alive.

Drying her hands off on her bliaut, Ellenor rose and was about to return to his side when her right foot slipped off the smooth rock upon which she was standing. Instinctively, she tried to correct her stance and regain her balance but the uneven ground seemed to reach up and grab her other foot, dragging her down.

With a gurgled exclamation, she fell in the brook with her hands and rear taking most of the painful landing. Cold water lapped around and over her legs sending shivers down her spine. Her cheeks were already flaming from embarrassment when she heard it.

Laughter.

Not small giggles that could easily be stifled, but the kind of laughter that incapacitated one, nearly choking them because of a lack of breath. Cole McTiernay's head was completely thrown back and he was roaring with laughter. At her.

Ellenor suddenly felt a desire to end his smug expression

with one of her own. *Smile, Cole McTiernay. Laugh. But you are about to learn a lesson you will never forget. Never challenge an Englishwoman. Especially this one.*

Waiting until his eyes locked with hers, Ellenor favored him with a blindingly bright smile and stood up. Ignoring the steady drips from her drenched state, she reached down, flicked the emerald folds of her bliaut aside, and grabbed the bottom of her chemise. The sopping, tattered material easily tore as she ripped a sizable chunk from the hem.

The laughter stopped.

"Just what the hell do you think you are doing?" Cole demanded.

Ellenor blinked and pasted on what she hoped to be an innocent expression. "I believe I am about to take a *bath*, Highlander. Was it not you who said I could take one this evening?"

"You can't bathe there. It's barely ankle deep!"

Ellenor looked down. "Yes, that does make it more difficult." She paused and took an exaggerated breath. "And I agree this is far from ideal, but I refuse to sleep with grime all over my skin for another evening. So just stand over there and face the other way. I will try to be quick."

Cole opened his mouth to say something but nothing came out. She was already beginning to work the knots of her bliaut loose and any moment would be standing only in her shift.

Ellenor eased the last loop free from its bonds, shimmied out of the bliaut, and threw it on the bank. With the torn piece of linen still clutched in her hand, she leaned down, dipped it into the cool water, and began to rub her face and neck, washing away the filth and grime. It was as if every smudge represented her life these past few months and she not only had the chance to start anew . . . she wanted to.

Cole stood with open mouth, frozen, unable to stop himself from staring. With a large chunk of her chemise missing, her shapely legs were now exposed and the moonlight ensured he saw every inch of them. Cole swallowed, feeling more unsure of himself than he ever could remember. She had a slim, wild beauty about her that pulled at him in a way he could not explain.

"You're staring, McTiernay. That tells me either you have never been acquainted with a woman or that I have just managed to put you into a state of shock. Either answer works for me," she said with a shrug. Unconcealed amusement laced every word.

Realizing she was right, Cole pivoted and marched over to a fallen log, mumbling curses—all aimed at himself. The damn woman's soul was not a persevering one—it was unrelenting. She survived on pure stubbornness, enforcing her agenda however and whenever she could. Before it was by *not* bathing, and tonight it was *by* bathing.

Thump. Splash. Thud. Thud. Splash. Cole resisted the urge to turn around. "Just what are you doing? How long does it take an Englishwoman to simply wipe herself off?"

"Maybe if a certain Highlander had not made it so very clear how bad I smelled, not very long. But as I am going to wash my hair . . . or at least rinse it, I shall be a bit longer."

Without thinking, Cole spun around. "How the hell are you . . . ?" His voice caught in his throat as he answered his own question. Thud. Splash. Thud. Two more rocks added to the formation of a crescent-shaped wall cupping the current of the stream. It resulted in about a foot or more of water.

Ellenor pointed at her accomplishment and smiled. "Well, what do you think? Pretty smart, even for an Englishwoman."

Cole just nodded and turned back around. Seeing the genuine pleasure in her face made his stomach do flips. It had reached her eyes, her voice, her whole body radiated with delight over such a simple thing. He guessed it had been a long time since she had felt true accomplishment, almost as long since he had felt the urge to laugh.

Something white flashed in his peripheral vision, landing on the thicket beside him. It was her chemise. He didn't know why, but he had assumed she would bathe in the thing. "Are you crazy?"

"You know I am not," Ellenor replied and lay down in the cool water, letting the current play with her hair. She had no soap, but this was still next to heaven. It had been almost two weeks since she had last washed herself and the experience had been hell, itching constantly, dreaming of warm water laced with rose petals.

"What kind of woman strips down to her skin when a man is just a few feet away?"

Ellenor stared up at the star-filled sky. She had not considered if she should undress or not. It had been instinct. For years, she had slipped out of the house and gone skinny-dipping in the small pond near her home. No one had ever known. Consequently, she had never wondered what a temptation it would be to a man.

But this one is untemptable, Ellenor whispered to the large crescent-shaped moon. Untemptable *and* honorable. Cole would keep his back turned, and it was not because she was English. A man intent on rape had no need to like his victim. No, Cole wouldn't turn around because he had one thing most men of her acquaintance didn't—integrity. Keeping his self-respect meant more to him than any quick romp ever would.

"Are all Englishwomen so bold?"

Ellenor mulled over his question, wondering if he had known other women from her homeland. "Only those who have no other choice," she finally answered. "Or would you have me return to camp and fall asleep soaking wet? Not the most intelligent idea, even for a Scot."

"Well, this *Highlander* is leaving and I am not leaving alone."

Ellenor gulped and sat up. She had pushed Cole enough. He might not rape her, but he definitely wasn't above walking over and pulling her out of the water— nude or not. "Wait. I'm getting out. If you could, just reach over and throw my shift back to me."

He did as she asked and she mumbled thanks. A minute later, she was back on the bank donning her chemise. Her bliaut, still damp from her earlier fall, was not so easy to put on and she mumbled her aggravation.

Cole turned around to see what was causing her so much frustration and felt the wind rush out of him.

The semibath had worked a miracle. Along her arms and the small of her back, the thin worn fabric hugged her damp skin, hinting at the shapely figure hidden beneath. And though both her garments were still soiled with multiple days of dirt and sweat, she now looked fresh and unspoiled.

"Can you get them?"

Cole blinked. "Get what?" he asked, realizing she had just asked him a question.

Ellenor pointed on the ground beside him. "My slippers. Could you give them to me?"

Cole bent down to retrieve the two items that had been used as projectiles less than a half hour ago. He tossed them to her and watched her easily snatch them out of the air with an appreciative smile.

The woman was making him crazy. Earlier, she could not hurl enough objects at him, but now, her rich honey-and-cream sort of voice was letting him know just how completely at ease she was with him. Ellenor Howell was becoming a serious complication. One he didn't want. One he immediately intended to rectify with a little distance.

Ellenor quickly slipped on her shoes and dashed into the woods after Cole. He was moving so fast through the thick limbs Ellenor wondered if it was a deliberate attempt to lose her. Just as she was afraid that it would work, she saw firelight. They were back at camp. Jaime and Donald were asleep on one side and Cole was already across the clearing. He was holding a clean plaid and picking up another that had been used as a buffer between his saddle and the horse.

He laid them both on the ground and pointed to one that came from his mount. "That should keep you warm enough."

Ellenor glanced at the dark blue plaid. She felt clean for the first time in weeks, and in moments, she was going to smell like horse. Worse, she had no choice but to accept what he was offering and the hulking giant knew it. The air was already quite cool and would be thoroughly cold by morning.

Mustering an evil stare, she said with a thin-lipped smile, "Thank you, although I wonder if it isn't your horse I should be sending my appreciation."

Cole lay down and tucked an arm underneath his head. His mouth curved into an unconscious smile. "Go ahead, but I doubt *Steud* will understand a word you're saying." He chuckled softly and closed his eyes.

Ellenor fought the urge to throw her slippers at him

again. Instead, she tiptoed over to where Donald was sleeping and pulled free the bag Ainsley had tossed at him earlier. With her back to Cole, she sat down on a log close to the fire and rummaged inside the tote hoping to find the hairbrush her mother had given her. Feeling the ivory teeth on her fingertips, she sighed in relief and pulled the item out.

Cole watched in disbelief as Ellenor completed one long stroke after another. Earlier that evening, the woman had sat huddled, afraid to speak. Now, she was moving around the campsite comfortably, drying her hair as if she were in a great manor curled in front of a hearth. Could a bath truly cause such a transformation? Regardless, he doubted she would be at such ease if she knew Jaime and Donald were far from asleep.

Cole watched as both of them stole appreciative glances. He almost called out to Donald, reminding him that he was supposed to be a happily married man. Jaime Ruadh, however, wasn't encumbered with a wife, and that knowledge irked Cole. Calling himself a fool ten different ways, he got up when she wasn't looking and switched the blankets.

Ellenor plopped the comb back inside the sack and quietly replaced it with Donald's things. Rallying herself, she maneuvered back to the other side of the campsite and lay down. It was surprisingly warm and soft and . . . clean.

Cole had exchanged the blankets.

Flipping over on her side, she stared in quiet disbelief at the sleeping Highlander just a few feet away. Why would he do such a thing? Then again, why did she care? Just this afternoon, she had been plotting her way to freedom.

A freedom that no longer seemed so inviting.

Chapter 3

Cole felt the early morning sun on his face and stretched. Immediately a twinge of pain shot up from his elbow to the base of his skull, proving he had slept on his arm. Extending his fingers above his head, the spastic muscle seizing in his neck began to ease.

He opened his eyes and grimaced. Bright sunlight was peeking through the trees. Daybreak had occurred nearly an hour ago. He had overslept. Cole bit back an expletive and told himself he shouldn't be surprised based on the amount of sleep he had had. If it hadn't been his nightmares keeping him awake, it had been the woman's.

He had watched her toss and turn for hours. She had an undeniable fierce streak of independence, and she certainly wasn't intimidated by him, his height, or his purported fierce scowl. But copious amounts of determination and doggedness had not hidden the fact that something tormented her. In her sleep, she had relived it again and again. It had torn at a piece of his soul he had thought long vanished. Terrified and vulnerable, she had trembled with fear. Cole had wanted to reach out and hold her, whispering that whatever she had experienced, whoever had hurt her, would never be able to do so again.

But he didn't.

Caring for Ellenor—on any level—would mean potentially opening himself to a pain he had vowed never to experience again. Fear had kept him closed off all these years, and his honor allowed him to justify it.

Stretching once more, Cole sat up and carefully craned his head to the right while trying not to reaggravate the sensitive nerve in his neck. He expected to see the woman still curled up in a ball.

Ellenor was not there.

He glanced over to the other side of the campsite, where Jaime and Donald were gnawing on some dried meat patiently waiting. Seeing their complacent demeanor, he assumed she was taking care of personal needs.

Sighing, Cole pushed himself to a standing position and grabbed both plaids. He walked over to his horse, and after fastening the rolled bundle to his saddle, he disappeared behind some trees.

When he reemerged, Jaime called out to him. "Ho there! I see you have finally decided to end your dawdling and allow us to continue our journey."

Cole fought the instinct to issue a quick retort. Too many times he had chided his men about their lazy morning habits and not expecting some amount of jesting would be foolish. The only thing to do was ignore the barb. "Your mounts ready?"

Both Jaime and Donald nodded and continued munching on their last bits of rawhide.

Cole grabbed a piece and looked around. "How long does it take a person to do their morning business, anyway?" he asked absentmindedly.

Jaime arched a single brow, grinned, and pointed

to the woods. "If you need more time, Commander, we'll wait."

"I'm talking about Ellenor," Cole retorted sharply.

Donald looked up at him, his brown eyes filled with incredulity. "You mean . . . the Englishwoman?"

"Aye, don't look at me like you have no idea who I'm talking about. Are we ready to go when she returns?"

Donald continued to stare at him in hushed astonishment. Jaime stood up, looking somewhat peaked, and answered, "The, uh, woman . . . she's gone."

Cole's eyes leveled on Jaime. "What do you mean gone?"

Recovering his voice, Donald rose and replied, "I caught her rummaging through my stuff around dawn and stopped her. The woman turned crazed, trying to scratch and kick at me. The wench even spit in my face."

White-hot fury surged through Cole's veins. He could see it now. Ellenor was innocently looking for something in her bag when Donald came upon her and caught her off guard. Instead of asking her what she was doing, he grabbed her and demanded explanations. She then fought him, clawing and kicking as she had in her dreams.

"*You* attacked *her*," Cole stated in a voice low, even, and accentuated with such coldness any normal man within hearing distance would have been taken over by fear. "Anyone can see how even being close to a man terrifies her. No other reason would cause her to lash out at someone your size. You grabbed her and held her against her will, and then when she forced you to let go, she ran into the woods frightened, helpless, and unarmed."

The sudden surge of emotion flowing through Cole was so powerful and so unexpected he had exploded without thinking how his comrades would react. Cole only knew that sometime in the night he had promised himself Ellenor would never be frightened of a man again. A vow he had not been able to keep.

"Wasn't it you who told us *not* to follow her if she ran off?" Donald challenged, the pulsing vein on his neck evidence of his own rising anger.

Jaime blinked. Cole was enraged and close to violence—a state Jaime could never recall his commander being in. He was suddenly referring to the Englishwoman as Ellenor and now he was accusing Donald of actually attacking her, scaring her. If the woman really was frightened of men, that fear did not extend to Cole.

Yesterday, she had appeared quite relaxed sitting and talking with their commander. Likewise, Cole had seemed surprisingly comfortable with the woman. More than once, Jaime had caught a small hint of a smile as if Cole was enjoying her sassy remarks. A strange bond had erected between the two of them and Donald was failing to notice it. If he continued to provoke Cole—even unwittingly—there would be bloodshed. And any blood spilled over an Englishwoman was something both inconceivable and unacceptable.

Pointing to the woods, Jaime said loud enough to catch Cole's attention, "She grabbed her bag and ran in that direction. She's been gone less than a half hour."

Cole immediately pivoted and disappeared into the dense forest. Jaime hoped his commander would be gone long enough for his anger to unwind and for Donald to realize that Ellenor Howell was no longer just any woman.

English or not.

Ellenor frowned at the small holes in the back of her bliaut. The thorns had caught at the hem during her mad dash from the campsite and now her already abused garment was one accident away from unwearable. Sighing, she started to loop the side of her gown and had just finished the first knot when she heard sounds of someone charging through the forest toward her. Alarm was just starting to pulse through her veins when she heard someone mutter something unintelligible and then curse all things English.

It was Cole.

Her heart began to thump wildly. Blaming a lack of sleep for her unwanted reaction, she ignored his call and concentrated on finishing interlacing the right side of her garment. She had just completed tying the last knot when Cole appeared before her.

She looked up casually, smiled, and then turned her attention to lacing the left side. "I'm glad to see you, McTiernay. I just need a couple more minutes and then we can return to camp. I am sure you are anxious to be on our way."

Cole's jaw dropped just slightly. His eyes were wide with astonishment. "I thought you . . . you were . . ."

"Running away again?" Ellenor asked, stealing a quick glance to see Cole's reaction. Satisfaction came in many forms, but seeing the dumbfounded look on his face would be a fond memory she would trudge up whenever she needed to smile.

All Cole could muster was a nod, unaware his hand was outstretched and pointing at her.

"I was," Ellenor answered honestly and then tied the final knot. She smoothed her bliaut as if it were her best gown and not a filthy garment she had been wearing for two weeks. "I changed my mind."

"You changed your *mind*?" Cole bellowed.

Ellenor smiled, knowing she had done it again. Shocking the massive Highlander was a small achievement, maybe even a petty one, but it did feel good. "You don't need to shout, and you don't need to look at me as if I have actually gone mad. Yes, I changed my mind. People do that, you know."

"Woman, you may not be crazy, but I must be for thinking you were in danger and needing help. God, help me, I actually was *scared* for you."

That made Ellenor pause. "Really?"

"Aye, really. I was charged to bring you back to the Highlands and I am going to do just that."

His words were like the water from last night's stream. Cold and awakening. Of course, he didn't care about her. All he cared about was his damn promise.

Ellenor swallowed and reminded herself that his honor was a good thing. Two days ago, she could barely stand being in the same room with a scrawny manservant. Now, she was traveling with three of the largest, most muscular men she had ever seen. And all because she knew she could trust him. "Yes, well, as you can see, I am just fine. You needn't have bothered coming after me. So in the future, save yourself from the effort."

Cole raked his fingers through his hair, trying to remain calm. He was failing. "Is this going to be typical every time we stop? You run, get lost, and then wait until I find you only so that you can try my patience before you make another attempt?"

"*No,*" Ellenor snapped. "As I said, I changed my mind. I have decided to go with you, Scot. *Willingly.*"

"And I am to just believe you? After you disappear into the woods screaming this morning?"

"I was *not* screaming," Ellenor denied defensively.

Cole cocked his head and outstretched one of his arms. "Well, you sure as hell were running," he countered, holding up a couple of pieces of her torn gown.

Ellenor stared at the evidence, proving her flight.

"Wouldn't you if you just spit in the face of some angry, towering giant accusing you of stealing? I may be English, *Scot,* but I am not an idiot. The smartest move was to leave. So that is just what I did."

"So you weren't afraid of Donald—"

"Afraid? Of your friend?" Ellenor asked with a snort as she bent down to gather up her bag and hairbrush off a nearby rock. She couldn't look him in the eye. He read her too well. "Not really," she lied and stuffed the item into the faded blue, mostly empty sack. Pulling out a ribbon of dark lace, she tossed the bag on the ground.

She put the ribbon between her lips and began to braid her hair, happy to have something for her hands to do. Just talking about what had happened made her nervous. She had not been afraid. She had been terrified, but she didn't want Cole to know. It had been an irrational fear. She knew that. She may not know his friends, but Ellenor held no doubt Cole would refuse to spend any time with anyone who could hurt another being just for enjoyment, especially a woman. Still, the instant Donald's hands had closed over her arms, she had been thrown back to the last time she had been vulnerable and exposed.

Cole studied her. Her denial was an obvious farce, but he decided not to pursue the line of inquiry. Instead, he returned to his original question. "No more running away. I find that hard to believe."

Taking the lace from her mouth, she let go a sharp grunt. "Believe it or don't believe it, McTiernay. It matters little to me what you think." After tying the end of the loosely braided lock, she swung it over shoulders and felt a soft thump against the middle of her back. By the end of the day, several tendrils would be flying around her face, but it was better than the pulling sensation of a tight braid along her scalp.

"Oh, but it does matter, *babag*. If I'm not convinced you won't disappear on me again, I just might decide to tie you up once more for my own peace of mind."

Ellenor's eyes narrowed at his continued Gaelic reference of her less than optimal state. The man was impossible. She didn't stink anymore, or at least not nearly as much. The semibath had helped, but whiffs from her chemise still laden with her odor had forced her into donning one of the two clean shifts she had in her bag. Her one other bliaut, however, she had saved. "If you must know, *Scot*, I made it to that poor excuse for a river and could have been long gone. I came back because I realized my original plans of joining an Irish monastery might have been a little impulsive."

"You're not serious."

"I most certainly am. I may have gotten lost last night, but I am—"

"A *convent*?" he asked incredulously.

Ellenor crinkled her brow, agitated that he found the idea so far-fetched. "Yes, well, I will admit I am not the ideal candidate for a nun—"

"Ideal? Hardly. Nuns tend to prefer quiet around them, and you, *preig*, are no nun."

His newest insult was the last straw. Ellenor opened her mouth to bark a retort but shut it just in time. Her understanding of Gaelic was the last thing she needed him to know. Besides, she did not talk too much. She just talked too much to be a nun. The benefits of living in a convent were exactly what she had desired. However, the prospects of actually *being* a nun had been more than a little daunting. "The vow of silence would have been difficult, but . . ."

"But what?" Cole asked with a huff. "Elle, your plan was doomed to fail with or without my interference.

Spirited females, no matter how much bribery money they bring, ruin convent reputations."

Time suddenly stopped. Her heart was pounding so fast it was difficult to remain upright. Cole had referred to her by name. Granted it was only Elle, and he didn't even seem to realize he had done it. Ellenor wasn't sure if she should say something or ignore the occurrence. Taking several deep breaths, she opted for the latter. "Well, then they should thank God in heaven you came along for I have decided to remain with your overly large-sized troop until we reach our destination. With certain provisions, of course."

"Provisions?" Cole exclaimed, rolling his eyes. "I may have lost my mind by agreeing to take you with me, but so have you if you think I am going to cater to any terms and—"

"There is really just the one," Ellenor interrupted in a low voice, taut with frustration. "All I want is for you to promise me that whenever we get where we are going, I will not be forced into marriage."

"And what if I don't make such a promise?"

"Then you and everyone else will regret it. That is a promise I will not only make, but will keep." Ellenor stared him dead in the eye, hoping he understood this was not a flighty vow made in the heat of an argument, but an earnest one. Whatever she needed to do, she would do it. She had killed and would kill again to keep a man from forcing himself upon her.

Cole returned her stare. He never flinched, but he must have understood because after several silent, tense seconds he said, "Then calm yourself, *babag*, for I doubt anyone will *want* to marry you, but you will not be forced into any man's bed without your consent."

"Do I have your word?"

"Are you sure a mere promise is enough to satisfy you?"

Ellenor gulped. "Anyone's . . . no. Your word, however, will satisfy me, Scot. Do I have it?"

Cole must have seen her growing nervousness for he suddenly became serious. "You have it. No one will force you to marry, be with, or tend any man not of your choosing, lass. You have my word of honor."

Ellenor felt rattled and she should have felt relief. Cole had just promised her the very thing she had thought only a monastery could provide. She gave her head a small shake and squeezed her eyes shut. *Remember,* she told herself. *Remember and see the world as it is, not the way you want it to be.*

Cole was not her friend. He wasn't even her ally. He was a Highlander who despised all things English and that included her. Pretending otherwise would only bring her pain—a lesson she refused to learn again.

Ellenor took a deep breath and opened her eyes. Brilliant blue pools framed in dark, deep brown lashes bored into her. She could detect no malice in their reflection, only a deep interest. Her beloved father used to stare at her with the same quizzical expression, as if she were a complete mystery he was unable to solve. He had often mentioned a desire to know what she was thinking, what motivated her, and most of all, the knowledge of what she would do next.

And that was how the Highlander was staring at her. Not as a woman, but as a puzzle to be solved . . . which bothered her most of all. For she was most definitely aware of him as a man.

Cole McTiernay was a Highlander full of pride and arrogance. He possessed an infuriating wit and she was tired of underestimating his cunning and ability to think ahead. His constant insults made him far from likable and he took no effort to disguise how much he enjoyed having the advantage. So why she cared what the massive Scot thought about her was beyond her comprehension.

But she did.

Before her father's death, she had been innocent of the evil lurking in some men. More than once, she had felt the harmless pull of attraction to a handsome or skilled knight who was paying a visit to her father. But those weak sparks had been nothing compared to the jolts that went through her moments ago when Cole had said her name.

Ellenor blinked and realized Cole was waiting for her to say something. Rallying, she licked her lips and asked, "If it is not for marriage, then why? Why are you bringing me with you?"

Cole shrugged. "You may ask, but I have no answer."

"Are you trying to be evasive, or do you really not know?"

"I have no idea," he said, and without another word, he turned and started marching back toward the campsite.

Ellenor stared at the disappearing figure in astonishment. For a brief moment, she thought to have seen a flash of the same discomfort in his eyes and wondered if maybe she was wrong. That perhaps he had seen her as something more than just a mystery.

She leaned down to pick up her bag and he saw the bottom of her bliaut. It was soiled and most of the hem was in shreds. Wrapping her hand around the sack, she swung it over her shoulder. She moved to smooth back the tendrils already coming loose from their braid when the palm of her free hand caught his sight. It was rough and callused from years of riding. Just like the rest of her, it lacked feminine grace. She was tall and awkward and, despite her efforts, still dirty.

Whatever she thought she saw in Cole's eyes, it wasn't desire. More likely disgust.

Cole jerked the reins sharply to the right to avoid another cluster of thistles. The purple-topped thorns littered the hills they were traveling, making the ride slow and unpleasant. Ellenor sat quietly in front of him, moving only to evade the tall bushes, but he had seen one or two scrapes where she hadn't been able to raise her legs fast enough. Unlike yesterday, the woman didn't say one word of complaint.

Proof he was in hell.

He had seen hell and experienced its many forms— loss, pain, horror, but never had he known torture in this particular form.

He had encountered many beautiful women in his life. A few were witty and some even endearing. They were also easy to ignore and forget.

Ellenor Howell, on the other hand, was impossible to dismiss.

At first, she had compelled his attention simply because she wasn't afraid of him. Intrigue had gradually set in during her attempts to gain freedom and the woman had actually shocked him with her unexpected moonlight bath. But it wasn't until this morning that he realized exactly how much trouble he was in.

The moment he had broken through the bushes and had seen her smiling at him, he should have turned around and returned to camp. Instead, he had stood dumbfounded, mumbling nonsense until building frustration had finally caused him to threaten her. But by all that is holy, how was he supposed to react?

He had suspected she would be somewhat pretty without the grime and crazy hair. But if he had known how pretty, he would have stopped last night's make-shift bath before it had even started. Hearing the water ripple and her moan in delight, he—like any normal man—had imagined her. The image had been of a typical woman of medium height, brown hair, and green eyes, pleasing to look upon, but far from compelling. Ellenor Howell was neither pleasing nor pretty. She was extraordinary.

She was tall, yet her face and body were formed with delicate bones. Her pale complexion, no longer hidden, only accentuated her green eyes, making them appear so large a man could feel his soul get lost in their loch-colored depths. Pale brown hair, the color of dark honey, hinted at a softness that begged to be touched. Together with gently lilting lips and a slim, but curvaceous wild beauty, Ellenor possessed all the features that drove a man wild. And he had been no exception.

He had forgotten everything. Her being English, his promise, her fears. Standing there, smiling at him with defiance and amusement shining in her eyes, she had been the most beautiful, desirable woman he had ever seen in his life. His whole body had come alive, yearning to kiss her and make her respond to his touch. Honor be damned.

That scared him the most.

He had been dead inside for a long time, taking comfort in not feeling anything. Having an emotional connection with someone—especially an Englishwoman—was not something he desired or enjoyed.

Jaime and Donald had also come under her spell. She had returned to the campsite with her hair brushed and in a new, much cleaner chemise, and both men had immediately reevaluated their unexpected travel companion. Her apologies for her behavior and promise for future restraint and cooperation had gone a long way in winning Jaime's favor. Donald, while not nearly as enamored, had softened noticeably.

Without a doubt, Ellenor Howell was trouble.

Unfortunately, that made Cole *in* trouble.

Home never seemed so far away. For the next four days, he needed to find a way to protect himself. *Four long days.* He doubted he could deal with any more than that and even those would be a torture he had never known.

Yes, he was in hell. And it was one of his own making.

Ellenor adjusted her position again for what had to be the tenth time in just as many minutes. All morning she and Cole had rode in silence with only the noise of the constant lifting of her legs breaking the monotony. Her body ached from the repetitive movement, but the pain caused by the thorn bushes covering the hills was enough to keep her doing it time after time. The burning sensation in her lower back from sitting rigid and so far forward that she was practically atop the saddle's pommel was so great she had to bite her bottom lip to keep from moaning aloud.

The leather seat was large and unusually slender, but it had been made with the idea only Cole would be riding in it. Yesterday's experience had proved that the only way she could sit comfortably was pretty much on his legs, either mimicking his straddle or sitting across them. After her reaction to him this morning, comfort was not an option.

Yet it was not her physical situation causing her the most turmoil . . . it was her emotional one.

Cole McTiernay had seen her greatest fear, and through a single promise, removed it . . . and then he had walked away. His oath should have given her a sense of peace. His indifference should have only added to it. Instead, it had only intensified Ellenor's confusion. Old instincts screamed to flee. Common sense warned her about the follies of reacting on primal desires, especially with this particular Highlander.

Still, she had to get control over her destiny. This required patience. By the time they reached their destination, she needed to have convinced not just Cole, but his two companions, of her cooperation. Then, she could exploit their resulting trust.

Ellenor had apologized for her outburst and received a chilly reception. Jaime's head nod had not been as cold as Donald's, but they both seemed to believe she regretted her actions. That gave her the hope she needed and Ellenor was positive that, by night's end, both men would feel significantly warmer toward her. That is, if she could pull off the next part of her plan.

Hunting, trapping, and catching food were not skills she possessed, nor ones she wanted to learn. However, she did have one secret talent that never failed in gaining admiration. She may not be able to find food, but very few could match her skills once it was caught.

Unfortunately, there was one flaw in her strategy. Her. It was not only Jaime's and Donald's trust she needed to gain. It was Cole's. And to get it, she would have to become vulnerable. The problem was, when it came to Cole McTiernay—she already was.

Nothing about him truly bothered her . . . and that bothered her the most.

His shoulder-length hair had once again been pulled back into a ponytail. He had not shaved this morning, which made his facial features appear more rugged and more what one would expect when conjuring the image of a warrior. With every breath, she inhaled the scent of wood smoke and leather that clung to his skin and envisioned herself being able to touch him, feel him, and know just what it was like to be held by a man.

"Elle."

Cole's name for her was deep and soft, sending shivers down her spine. She almost thought she imagined hearing him when he spoke again.

"Elle, stop it."

Immediately, her slumped back went rigid. How could she have been so stupid? Her mind had been totally consumed on him that she had not realized the slackened state of her body. She had been seconds away from sliding into his lap when he made her aware of what was happening.

Ellenor licked her lips. "Stop what?"

"Stop pretending that pommel is comfortable and sit back and relax. You're making *Steud* nervous."

"Oh, really?" Ellenor quipped. "I find that highly unli—"

Without warning, a large arm wrapped itself around her waist and pulled her back. The warmth from Cole's chest and legs seeped into her skin. Despite her best efforts not to, she relaxed against his body.

"Aye, really," Cole chuckled.

Watching her discomfort these past few hours had been difficult. At first, he was glad she was trying to keep the distance between them, but he had changed his mind as she silently endured what had to be a painful ride. He had reacted on instinct and told himself he would have done so for any woman.

And maybe he would have, but he hadn't been this close to a female in longer than he cared to remember, and he doubted if there was another woman in the world who could have made his pulse race the way Ellenor Howell did. It was like thunder in his veins.

Cuddled against him, her body seemed to mold itself

perfectly to his frame. Her cheek was nestled intimately in the hollow of his shirt, and the heat surging between them set his teeth on edge. His loins tightened, and any moment, she would know just how much she was affecting him.

"Ha. I have no doubt you selected a horse that is just like you," Ellenor scoffed, but she didn't move. She was finally where she had wanted to be all day. In his arms.

"And just how am I?" Cole asked, barely successful at keeping a moan from escaping. Something in her bag had to smell of lavender, for whiffs of the clean chemise she had donned this morning was driving him slightly insane.

Ellenor drew in a breath and then answered, "Impervious to nervousness."

It was only a partial truth. She wanted to say *unlike any man I have ever met.*

Cole possessed a hard and potentially ruthless element in him that made anyone nearby wary and on edge. Ellenor suspected he often tried to enhance the effect with a scowl. She had known him less than two days, but already his glowers seemed commonplace and easy to ignore. What was harder to overlook was the side of him that he kept hidden away. She had only gotten glimpses to his gentility, and each time, there, nestled in the act of kindness, was a sadness to him. It pulled at her heart. Whoever had hurt this Highlander had done so deeply. Worse, she knew whoever was behind the pain had been English. All men could be cruel, but she had witnessed firsthand just how unfeeling her own people could be.

Cole shifted his mount to the left without warning to dodge a hidden thorn bush and Ellenor instinctively grabbed his leg for balance. She reached down to lift her skirts and legs out of the way but it was too late.

Cole's quick maneuvering had avoided most of the bush, but one prickly arm still swiped her leg and grazed her hand.

The scrapes on her calf burned, and she could feel a trickle of blood roll down her leg to her ankle. Sucking on the raw knuckle, she decided to give up her attempts at being ladylike. Hiking up her gown, Ellenor pulled her knees to her chest, and then let the heavy emerald material settle around her legs, covering them with the exception of her feet. The tips of abused green slippers rested on the back of the horse's mane.

The new position was still surprisingly comfortable because of the animal's broad back and frame; however, it was also highly unstable. Cole realized it about the same time she did and once again wrapped his arm around her waist. This time he didn't let go.

Ellenor took a deep breath and tried to relax. Then his thumb grazed the bottom of her breast. Her heart began to pound erratically. Her response to his inadvertent touch was so strong she feared that any second he would realize the power he had over her.

"You can let go," she said with as much indifference as she could muster.

Cole's throat constricted. He didn't want to explore the reasons why, but the last thing he wanted to do was let her go. "Only if I want to watch you fall."

"I won't," Elle said too emphatically.

Cole released the breath he was holding. Relief filled him. Ellenor Howell was not impervious to him. She just *wished* she were. "Elle, be quiet and let someone help you for once."

"Trusting someone—especially a man—is a mistake I won't repeat. Now, let go of me."

"No," came the firm response and he gave her ribs a squeeze. When he eased up on his grip, his thumb slowly stroked her side as if to make sure he had not been too rough.

To Cole, the intimate touch was nothing more than a warning, but something inside Ellenor snapped. She tried prying his fingers off her, but they remained firm. Reacting on instinct, she waited for the air to leave Cole's lungs and then sent her elbow swiftly back into his sternum.

Cole gasped and released her as he tried to catch his breath.

Jaime urged his mount closer and called out, "Commander, you all right?"

Cole waved him back, nodding that he was fine. The pain throbbing in the middle of his chest was beginning to ease and he was breathing again. "Ride ahead and join Donald. I need to have a private word with our guest."

Jaime cocked an eyebrow, winked at Ellenor, and then urged his mount forward.

Cole looked down just in time to see the triumphant smile she had been sending Jaime. It lit up her face. She was radiant and he had never seen anything to compare. Possession hit him unexpectedly. He wanted to be the sole recipient of such beauty. His desire to see her smile at him hit him full force and he started to tickle her. If he had thought about it for even two seconds, he would have immediately squashed the idea. He hadn't tickled anyone—or been tickled by anyone—since he was a young boy, but the sudden need to see her squirming and begging for help was too great to be denied.

In one deft movement, he looped the reins around the pommel and began a merciless attack. What he had not been ready for was Ellenor's response. At first, she had been surprised but soon joined in on the assault, giving as well as she received. Minutes later, they were both laughing so hard tears were streaming from their eyes. Only sheer luck had kept either of them from crashing to the ground.

Unhooking the leather straps, he gave them a flick. Ellenor was now sitting sideways on his lap with her legs crossed and dangling. Her head rested against his shoulder and his arm was back in place, keeping her safe while he urged *Steud* into a lope to catch up to the rest of their party.

Softly, Ellenor whispered, "I . . . I . . . cannot believe I just did that. It has been a long time since I have really and truly laughed, and I honestly never thought to do so again. It's nice to know I still can."

Everything in Cole wanted to thank her in return. He wanted to shove his hands into her thick chestnut mass, pull her to him, and drink from her lips. He wanted to show her that laughter had never come easy to him, that conversation had always been forced and awkward. That she, for some mysterious reason, could make him feel things he thought were long dead. And that he was thankful.

Only one thing stopped him. He knew the fear it would cause. Ellenor trusted him and hell would freeze before he broke that trust.

Chapter 4

Sparks flew as another leg bone landed in the middle of the campfire. Jaime licked his fingers and leaned back against the large elm circling the small clearing. "I don't believe I have ever eaten as well while traveling."

Ellenor smiled, surprised at how the night had transpired. Cole had remained overtly silent on the edge of the campfire, choosing only to listen to their conversation. She had not made any headway where he was concerned, but both Jaime and Donald had succumbed to her cooking just as she had hoped. What she had not been prepared for was her own reaction. She had anticipated having to fake ease and comfort, but in reality, she felt both. "Just because you are away from home does not mean you cannot enjoy good food. Just wrap up the meat like I showed you."

Donald picked up the smooth stem topped by a rounded umbel of small, white, orb-shaped flowers. The woman was daft if she thought he was going to collect smelly bulbs just to improve how his meat tasted. "Yeah, well, I've never heard of using something that cures poison for cooking."

Ellenor chuckled under her breath, knowing he had

been eating "poison cures" most of his life. Almost everything cooked in a kitchen had been enriched with some kind of medicinal herb. "I've never used it as a healing remedy before. Tell me, does it work?"

Donald scowled. Truth was he had never known someone poisoned by an animal. He had just heard stories. "Yeah, well, I'm still not carrying the stuff on me," he replied, ignoring her question. He tossed the bulb far away from his side of the camp and then leaned over to procure the last bit of meat.

"Good Lord, Donald," she clucked, "you don't need to carry the flower with you. Just look for it when you are hunting that evening. They grow wild just about everywhere."

Jaime squeezed the leather mead pouch and swallowed some of its liquid contents. "Ah, now, Donald, I agree its smell is strong, but you cannot deny the flavor it has brought," he said, pointing at Ellenor. "Just think. If we could learn to cook half as good as the lass here, our army would grow so large not a soul would raise swords against our commander."

Ellenor's soft laughter caught the breeze and danced around the campfire. "Raise swords against Cole? Surely no one is so foolish. Cole can be extraordinarily patient . . ."

Donald and Jaime both paused midbite.

". . . but if pushed, he will defend his honor and those in his care. Surely, his glares alone convey how seriously he takes his responsibilities," she drawled, wondering what Cole's expression was. Probably a scowl.

Donald stared wide-eyed at Ellenor, trying to discern if she was being serious. Deciding that she was, he awarded her a genuine smile. "You know, lass, our commander has never had difficulties in developing and leading an army."

Ellenor cocked a single eyebrow and continued nibbling on the leg bone she had been savoring. "Not a revelation," she mumbled, licking her lips. "Only hearing the opposite would be unbelievable."

Donald paid no attention and proceeded with his original thought. "But he has never been considered by the fairer sex as someone who was tolerant, let alone patient."

Jaime sat straight up. His brown eyes sparkled in the firelight. He looked at Ellenor and then Donald. An enormous smile overtook his wild features. "'Tis right you are! Come now." He leaned closer to Ellenor. "You're a lass. Despite the commander's scowls and sometimes rough mannerisms, wouldn't you want him?"

Ellenor almost dropped the bone she was eating. "Wh . . . *What*?"

"Our commander. Wouldn't you want him for your laird? Some believe there is not a woman or child that wouldn't be scared of him, but look at you! You like him and you're *English*. I dare you to deny your feelings."

"You know," Donald chimed in, "Jaime Ruadh's right. You like him, so that should be good enough for anybody."

Ellenor's eyes widened. Jaime had been drinking steadily since they had stopped for the evening and he had not been alone. Donald had joined him as soon as he returned with the night's meal. She didn't know if it was the wine talking or if they were being serious.

She cocked her head to glance at Cole. As expected, his sullen expression gave no indication if he was interested in her answer. *Well, I can be indifferent too, Scot,* she mumbled to herself. She turned back toward Jaime and answered, "As hulking giants go, he is one of the more tolerable ones."

Jaime moved in even closer. "And what about me, lass? Do you favor redheaded giants as well?"

Ellenor bit her bottom lip to keep from giggling. She couldn't help it. The sappy grin on the man's face would make any woman laugh. But before she could respond, Donald threw a plaid at him, catching Jaime full in the face. "Don't mind him. No woman does."

Jaime tossed it back and then lowered his voice. "Now, tell me, lass. Are you looking forward to seeing our Highlands?"

Ellenor looked up at the night sky and then the beauty surrounding her. Trees hugged the nearby river, cutting off the view behind her, but to the north, the large crescent moon created a silhouette effect of the sizable mountains facing the small group. "I thought we were in the Highlands," Ellenor answered honestly. "Or at least at their edge."

Donald rolled his eyes with exaggeration. Grinning, Jaime hit his knee and shook his head. "Ah, pretty lass, those hills you are seeing are the Trossachs. They tell us that after tomorrow we will be in the midst of the grandest lands God has ever created."

Ellenor turned her attention toward the jagged rocky summit in the distance. *Good lord, if that was a hill, just how big were the Highlands? Did she really want to go somewhere that made that towering object look small?*

She snuck a peek at Cole. He was now leaning against a far tree with his upper body obscured in shadow. Firelight played across his long legs, reminding her of the afternoon's ride and how perfectly she had fit against him when he had held her. His eyes were focused on the hills they were discussing, but she knew he wasn't thinking of them. He was thinking about what lay beyond them. His home.

"And there is nothing to compare to McTiernay

lands . . . well, with maybe the exception of Fàire Creachann," Jaime continued.

"Fàire Creachann?" Ellenor repeated. Named after the Highland summits and the emerging dawn, it sounded beautiful. A scuffle caught her attention. She turned and watched as Cole disappeared into the night.

"Aye. If our commander is selected as laird, Fàire Creachann will be our new home."

Distracted by Cole's leaving, Ellenor found it hard to focus on the conversation. "I . . . I thought chieftains inherited their role."

"They do typically. But there are other ways."

Ellenor felt her heart stop. "Marriage? Cole's getting married?" she blurted without thinking.

"Hardly," came a quick reply from Donald. He stood up, brushed his hands on his leine, and grabbed his things. "I'm sleeping out on the perimeter," he said, indicating he was not going to elaborate and began heading out in the opposite direction Cole took.

Ellenor waited until Donald's dark figure disappeared completely before whispering, "What did Donald mean when he said hardly?"

Jaime shrugged. "Don't you know? You're a woman. Weren't you afraid of him? At least in the beginning?"

Ellenor thought back. It was just two days ago, but it seemed like she had known Cole much longer. Had she been afraid of him? "Honestly, I don't believe I ever was."

Jaime stared at her for a minute trying to assess if she was telling the truth. With a deep sigh, he said, "Well, you're one of the few. Most women claim they are either afraid of our good commander or repelled by his glares. I wish they could have been riding with us today."

"Why's that?"

"You made him smile, lass. Most believe his face isn't able to do anything but scowl. If more of his people could see him like he was with you, there would be no argument of who should become laird."

Ellenor casually arched her back in an effort to mask the indescribable wave of cheer flowing over her. She should probably be embarrassed that Jaime and possibly Donald had witnessed her and Cole's small deviation of decorum, but she wasn't. She had enjoyed the tickle fight enormously and was glad Cole had initiated it. "So if Cole isn't getting married and his elder brother is already laird of your clan, then how can he become a laird?"

Jaime leaned back and reexamined the English-woman once again. The woman was perplexing at best. Yesterday, her demeanor and appearance had been far from desirable. Then, she had combed her hair, cleaned her face, and donned a new undergarment, which smelled of Highland blossoms. It had been hard to believe such beauty had been hidden. And seeing it had only made him more suspicious of her motives. Women that beautiful knew their power and used it, often in very manipulative ways. But whatever she was after, it had not brought their small group trouble.

Just the opposite. It had created a miracle.

Cole had actually *laughed* today. Something in his many years, Jaime had never seen the commander do. Smile perhaps, or even grin when his young nephew did something particularly amusing, but laugh? Never. At that moment, Jaime had been convinced. Ellenor Howell was not an omen, but an angel, who had come to rid his commander of the nameless burden he had been carrying all these years.

Jaime coughed into his hand, hoping it masked the reason behind his delayed response. "Well, as I said, there are many ways to become laird, but in Cole's case the circumstances are somewhat unusual. With over ten years of war, the Highlands have lost many lairds and armies fighting. On top of that, a couple of years ago, several clans were nearly wiped out from disease. Together, numerous families and returning soldiers have been living in a nomadic state, existing by pinching food, cows, and horses. The neighboring clans can no longer sustain their numbers as well their own. It took some time, but these proud Highlanders are ready to come together and establish themselves as a clan under the name of a new leader."

"And that would be Cole."

"Aye, or another Highlander."

"Another Highlander?" Ellenor asked, surprised why anyone would consider someone else. "Is he as good as Cole?"

Jaime took a deep breath and exhaled. "Hmm. There are some men—like our commander—who are born to lead, and there are some men who could never lead a soul. Dugan, the other man being considered, is somewhere in between. He's a fine and able warrior, but does not possess the gift of forethought or strategy."

"Then why would they select this other man over Cole?"

"He's likable, for one thing. You seem to get along with our commander, but I meant what I said about that being a rarity among him and women. Then there's the fact that Dugan is one of them. He came back to a clan ravaged by illness and has been living amongst the nomads for almost two years, supporting them with food between hunts and raids. If he didn't lack the army Cole has, I doubt there would be the hesitation in naming Dugan laird. But he doesn't."

"But couldn't he get one?"

Jaime scoffed. "If he hasn't already started building more men around him than the few disreputable lads he has now, then he isn't going to without help." Seeing the puzzled expression staring back at him, Jaime sighed and explained, "Most of us, including myself and Donald, are much like Dugan. Not bad men, just bad leaders. But under the right training, we could learn."

"Right training . . . you mean, Cole."

"Aye. Like all the McTiernays, he has the gift. I was surprised when you mentioned his patience earlier, for you're right. The commander tolerates no laziness, and he is liable to give you a good slice for being careless, but for those who try, he has unparalleled patience. And that is why he has such a large army."

"Cole has an army? I mean, I thought you and Donald were his comrades."

Jaime's eyes lit up with merriment. "Lass, I have never met anyone with so many wrong assumptions. The commander has over three hundred men he can call upon. Over a hundred are dedicated to him alone."

The air rushed out of Ellenor's chest. That was over thrice what her father had maintained. "Good Lord! That's . . . that's . . . well, a lot. How can he afford to support such an army without being a laird?" she blurted out, as the question popped into her head.

Jaime shrugged. "McTiernay lands are fairly vast. Cole oversees the western edge, living off the land mostly, but if he is named laird, that will all change. We will go to live at Fàire Creachann and support not only ourselves but the new clan."

Ellenor encircled her arms around her bent knees. "I can tell by the sound of your voice that you hope to live there someday."

"Aye, you are right. And who wouldn't? It stands on a good-size portion of land stretching out into the blue waters of Loch Torridan, where you can glimpse the An

Cuan Sgìth, the strait of sea separating our homeland from its islands. Just before nightfall, the views of the glittering water and mountains are truly incomparable. And because Fàire Creachann is protected by sea on almost all sides, it is nearly impenetrable. The castle was abandoned long ago and is now in disrepair, needing much work, but it is an ideal place to begin anew. Lots of room, great land for farming, plenty of game . . . they would be fools to select Dugan," Jaime answered, his voice almost a whisper at the end.

"I take it Dugan has another place selected?"

Jaime nodded once. "The damn spot practically invites someone to come attack him. Only a fool believes himself to invulnerable, disregarding good advice and experience, ignoring the stirring hints and warnings of impending violence."

Ellenor froze. The skin on her arms became mottled as her grip tightened to a painful level. *Only a fool believes himself to be invulnerable,* Jaime had said. She had been such a fool. A fool who had been told and disregarded such a warning.

And she had killed someone as a result.

Cole returned just in time to see the blood drain out of Ellenor's face. Suddenly, his firm resolve fled. He had spent the past twenty minutes reminding himself on how all things English were abhorrent—even if they were incredibly beautiful. It hadn't worked very well.

Memories of Ellenor's laughter, her ability to see right through him, know what he was thinking, refused to be suppressed. The woman seemed to understand him at levels no one else did. Maybe that was the reason why she wasn't scared of him.

She had called him intolerable, but her eyes had

raked over him with a feminine desire that made his heart sing. He could recall not another woman ever looking at him with such incredible longing. Her eyes had roamed over every morsel of his body, lingering on his face in the shadows. It had been hard not to stare back. Then Fàire Creachann was mentioned.

He could see her standing on one of the battlements, tawny curls of her long hair swirling about, her chin proudly thrust into the wind. And though everything about her was English, the image in his mind said that was where she belonged. He forced himself to dismiss such fantasies and returned back to camp, thinking he had himself back in control.

Then he heard Jaime's assessment of Dugan and saw Ellenor's face go ashen. Whatever his friend had said, it had transported her back into another time. A time he suspected that was at the heart of her so-called madness. Terror filled her eyes and he could see she was about to flee, not from him, but from whatever haunted her. He knew what he had to do.

Make her mad. Boiling mad.

Odd though it would sound to others, anger was the best way to yank her back to the present. She needed someone safe to focus all those emotions onto, and a safe manner to do so. He was that safe place . . . at least for the next few days.

He braced himself as best he could for her snapping emerald eyes. Intense emotion brightened them, and their rich swirling color fed his inability to concentrate.

Stepping through the brush, Cole looked at Jaime and asked with unmistakable disgust, "Is the *babag* bothering you?"

Ellenor jumped, startled. "Stop referring to me as *babag*!"

"Or what?" Cole challenged, squeezing his palms into

fists, wishing she would look away, even if just for a second.

"Or I might just start calling you *sunndach*, Scot," Ellenor quipped proudly, refusing to budge her gaze.

Jaime raked his fingers through his red hair and said with unhidden mirth, "I've never thought of you as the cheerful type before, Commander, but aye, lass, it is a nice sarcastic accounting of his character."

A second later, she became fully aware of her mistake. Cole's face had hardened by several degrees. Jaime's mouth had dropped wide open as realization dawned on him. "Did you . . . Was that . . . Did I just hear you correctly?"

Ellenor wished she could disappear. In her anger, she had called Cole joyful and good-humored.

But she had said it in Gaelic.

Now they knew. Now *Cole* knew she understood everything he had been saying.

Her lids slipped down over her eyes. She had two choices. Be apologetic, deposing of herself of any remaining pride, or take advantage of her folly.

Ellenor chose the latter.

Ignoring Cole, she looked Jaime straight in the eye and then said in flawless Gaelic, "You mentioned assumptions, earlier, Jaime Ruadh. I just thought you should be aware you have been making a few yourself."

With confidence she didn't really possess, Ellenor marched over, picked up her bag, and sashayed past Cole, heading toward the river.

Moments later, she arrived at the same place she had washed her hands and face earlier. The river was the exact opposite of last night's trickling stream. It was wide as one of the taller trees and deep enough to fully immerse herself in. Plunging her hand into her bag, Ellenor pulled out one of three bars of soap she had been saving. She lifted the small mound to her nose and took a whiff. The fragrance filled her nostrils. *The overgrown giant won't be able to ever say I stink again*, she thought to herself.

All around her childhood home, flowered purple spikes of lavender grew wild. The art of making the carved scented soap mounds had been handed down in her family for years. Very few practiced the laborious craft of soap making and many had forgotten how, but her mother had taught her, just as her grandmother had taught her mother and so forth.

Ellenor flipped the carved purple and gray item over and felt a tear fall down her cheek. The initials EF were inscribed on the bottom. Ellen Frances. These were the last three her mother had made. There once had been four.

When she had been forced to move to her sister's, she had been given no warning, still she had managed to throw a few of her most precious treasures in a small trunk her father had crafted for her when she had been a child. Spying the trunk upon her arrival, her sister had announced that a woman crazed with madness didn't deserve such items as fancy dresses, gemstones, and a chest. Gilda had rummaged through the few things, angry Ellenor had not remembered to take a single Howell jewel. In a fit of rage, Gilda had thrown her a bag, two of her most worn gowns, a handful of chemises, a tarnished comb and brush, and a knotted ball of ribbons. Last, she had tossed the soap. One had broken into small pieces upon impact. At that moment, faking madness had gone from difficult to easy.

"Elle, are you all right?"

Ellenor jumped up, dropping the soap and the bag on the grassy bank. "Am I . . ." She paused midway through her question. She had been waiting for accusations, roars, bellows of deceit, not inquiries to her health. "What did you just say?"

"I asked if you were all right," Cole replied, pointing at her wet cheek. "Jaime can be thoughtless when he speaks, but he was not talking about you."

"Jaime?" she murmured, still puzzled. "Why aren't you angry . . ." Then understanding dawned on her. "You . . . you did it on purpose, didn't you? You *knew* I spoke Gaelic and was trying to trick me into revealing myself!"

"Trick you?" Cole choked. "Elle, I would first have to understand the workings of your mind, and *that* I have determined is impossible. I just noticed Jaime had in-advertently reminded you of some ghosts so I riled you some. It always works for me."

"You *intentionally* picked a fight?"

"Aye," Cole answered with a touch of self-satisfaction. "You cannot deny it worked."

"And you're not angry about my understanding your language?" Skepticism filled her voice and stance.

Cole stepped past her and knelt down by the water's edge. He cupped his hands and drank the cool water. "I've suspected you knew the Celtic tongue since last night. I watched you when my men were talking. Your face gives a lot away, *babag*."

Hearing his pet insult reminded her of why she was there. Ellenor pivoted, bent down, and grabbed the three pieces of soap. She stuffed two in the bag and stood back up, wagging the third back and forth. "You won't be able to say that for much longer, *sunndach*."

Cole's dark eyebrow arched mischievously, distracting her as he plucked the small item from her hand and began to unknot his leather belt. His mouth twitched with amusement seeing her stunned reaction.

Ellenor watched in horror as his dark tartan pleats began to unravel. "What are you doing?" she squeaked.

"You should know," Cole grinned. "I'm going to take a bath."

"You can't! I'm here!"

Cole grinned and shrugged his shoulders. "Didn't stop you last night. Turn around or watch, *babag*. Makes no difference to me," he replied, just as his kilt dropped to the ground.

Ellenor felt her jaw slacken in shock. He meant it. The man's blue eyes were practically dancing with pleasure, and her protests were only fueling his enjoyment. The only thing between her and his nakedness was his thankfully long shirt. He was baiting her, daring her to watch—something she both wanted and feared to do.

Suddenly, Ellenor was struck with inspiration. Without considering the ramifications, she grabbed the soap from his fingers and dove into the cold water. She held her breath and let her body adjust to the temperature before rising to the surface. Immediately her eyes sought Cole. The second she caught his sapphire glare, she knew she had succeeded.

The man was furious, but the weight of anger boiling in his eyes could not outweigh her glee. She waved at him and smiled. "Looks like your bath will have to wait until I am done, Highlander!" Then, she dropped below the surface again before he could retort.

Cole watched the wet copper locks disappear back under the dark swirling water. Terror had leapt through him a moment ago. She had plunged headfirst into the strong current and had not emerged until several seconds later. He was on the verge of diving in when she had finally broken the surface with a smile that could light up the night. There was no way she could have missed his fury at her reckless behavior. But did she care? The woman had actually *waved* at him. He should go ahead and jump in. Not to save her, but to throttle her neck.

He squeezed his eyes shut and clung to his remaining patience. A second later, he heard a soft thud and felt a light splash of water on his leg. Cole looked down and saw the familiar white material of her chemise. He picked the sopping item up and glanced at the water. Ellenor was not in sight. Panic again invaded his thoughts. "Elle," he called out.

No answer. "Elle!" This time he shouted her name. Her head popped up from the water. Two green eyes were frowning at him.

"Cole, don't wad it up like that. I threw it to you so you could lay it out over one of those bushes over there."

Cole stared at her. He could not believe what he was witnessing and hearing. Ellenor was holding her bliaut in front of her as she pointed to a cluster of thick juniper. He had no idea what she was going to do next, but he was not going to wait and find out.

He threw her chemise back into the water so that it landed practically in front of her. "Don't disappear again."

Ellenor was about to explode when she caught the warning in Cole's eyes. There was real fury in him and it stemmed from fear. The revelation made her own emotions shift between hesitant joy and sheer aggravation. Carefully choosing a response, she reached out, grabbed the sinking undergarment, and slid down in the water until she was submerged up to her chin. "I'm fine, Cole. I have swum in rivers all my life and never got a scratch." Pausing, she tossed the item back to him and again pointed to the bushes.

Instinctively, Cole caught the object. He was flummoxed. He could threaten her, but unless he really intended to jump in and physically force her to the shore, there was little he could do. He stepped over to the bush and splayed the flimsy material over the prickly branches. "You may be a good swimmer, but the water here is cold and the current is strong. Even a man can lose his footing and drown, especially at night. Now either put that thing on or throw it here."

"I plan to just as soon as you turn around."

Cole shook his head firmly. "No. I meant what I said. You're not to disappear out of my sight."

"Well, I cannot finish bathing with you looking at me. What if you turn around and I promise to keep talking?"

Cole let go a sigh and rubbed his face. He knew he wouldn't be able to watch her bathe, and her proposal was a solution to his predicament. He just wished he had come up with it. Resigning to her wishes, he gave a single nod, turned around, and prepared himself for a long speech about why he was so wrong and she was so right. Instead, a soft simple melody hit his ear. Ellenor was singing.

The lilting timbre of her voice was just like the rest of her, gentle, yet with some dark edges luring him in, like a siren driving him mad. The song was just as haunting. The words were soft and full of sadness about a woman who had overcome great evil only to die alone. *Was that how she felt? Alone?* The thought she might feel that way bothered him. He was about to turn around and ask when her bliaut landed in the grass by his feet, followed by her slippers. Both smelled of her lavender soap.

"Mmm, this feels wonderful. You should think about jumping in once I am done. It will do wonders for your bad mood, Scot."

Cole reached for the garment and threw it haphazardly next to her chemise. "My mood is not likely to change until I am home and you are no longer my responsibility, *English*. And if you recall, bathing was exactly what I had planned until you rushed in."

Ellenor's laughter rippled through the air, sending a shiver down Cole's spine. "Not true," she argued. "We both know that I had arrived at the river and was preparing to bathe first. And as far as rushing in, I had no choice. You're just annoyed that I surprised you."

"I'm not an—"

"Hold on, I'm going to rinse my hair."

A soft splash followed by silence filled the air. Cole raked his hands over his scalp, hoping the pain would distract him. The random splashes and her soft moans of pleasure were playing havoc with his ability to concentrate. His loins had been tight since seeing her slick and wet, holding her bliaut to shield her nakedness. Now the dark heavy garment lay alongside the white chemise. The only thing between the two of them was his self-control. Something that was rapidly slipping.

"Cole, are you listening to me?"

"How could I not be?" he grumbled, refusing to admit that he hadn't been.

"I said I had a problem."

Cole looked back and swallowed. She was standing low in the water so only her bare shoulders were visible. Cursing the direction of his thoughts, he reminded himself that she was bossy, brash, and far from his definition of a perfect woman. "I have no experience in helping women bathe."

"I don't need help bathing, Scot! And don't turn around again."

The hint was all he needed to discern the nature of her anxiety. "Let me guess. Your well-thought-out desire to seize an opportunity to surprise me didn't include dry clothes."

"My *plan* had been to undress on the shore, and whose fault why I didn't is rather pointless as it does not change the facts."

She was right, but the last thing he was going to do was admit it. The woman was already impossible. He reached for her bliaut, pretending to pull it off the bush. "Shall I throw these wet ones back in?"

The hard splash of hands hitting the water's surface echoed throughout the air, indicating his barb had hit its mark. "If you are going to be insufferable, then yes, toss it back in. But when I become ill and am miserable company over the next few days, I don't want to hear a word."

Damn, if she didn't somehow win every argument. Even when she shouldn't. "Woman, you could try the patience of a saint," Cole mumbled in Gaelic. Louder, he asked, "Don't you have another gown in your bag?"

Ellenor clenched her jaw, betraying her deep frustrations. Her other chemise, dirty and foul-smelling, was dry, but now that she was clean, the last thing she wanted to do was don a soiled garment. Unfortunately, there was nothing else. She was just about to agree to the suggestion when Cole threw his hands up in the air and growled, "Women! I'll get you a blanket." Then just before he marched off, he turned and pointed. "Stay near the shore and don't go under the water until I return. Understood?"

Ellenor beamed him a grateful smile and nodded dutifully. Grunting one last time, Cole turned and headed for camp.

When he arrived, he saw Jaime, alone, relaxing against a tree trunk, staring into the fire. His expression made it clear *who* was on his mind. The English minx was putting a spell on all of his men, not just him. If she returned wrapped in nothing but a blanket and Jaime was still here, there would be trouble. The mysterious feeling of possessiveness was growing exponentially.

"Jaime."

Jaime stirred and responded, "Aye, Commander?"

"Get your things. You're sleeping with Donald on the perimeter."

Jaime furrowed his brow. He didn't say anything. The commander's business was his own, but that didn't mean he had to be happy with the suggestion or hide his disapproval.

Cole shook his head. Jaime had jumped to the wrong conclusions, but there was no way Ellenor was returning here, undressed, with any man present besides himself.

Cole gathered the softer of the two blankets and returned. As she promised, Ellenor was staying near the shore, and while her shoulders were barely below the surface, she had not resubmerged her head.

He tossed the blanket on the grass close to the river's edge. "Wrap yourself up in that until we get back to camp. Then get dressed in the shift you had on yesterday, I don't care if it does stink. And do it *without argument.*"

"Aye, Commander," Ellenor teased, imitating his authoritative bur, and began to head toward the bank.

Cole was dumbfounded. The woman was completely unmoved by the seriousness of his tone and she should have been at least mildly terrified. His men certainly would have been. But then Ellenor Howell was as far from a man as one could get.

Ellenor hurried out of the water and wrapped the tartan around her shivering body. It had been a reckless decision to jump in the water and then undress. Reckless and wild and carefree. And it felt wonderful. It felt like her. She was Ellenor Howell again. Fearing nothing and no one.

The caution she had been exercising was not a genetic trait, it had been a learned one. She had been living in fear for so long, she had forgotten what she was like when unafraid. She had forgotten what it felt like to be happy. And it was all because of one large, scowling Highlander.

"Cole? I think I'm about ready."

Cole turned around and was suddenly swamped once more with desire. He had not been prepared for what stood before him. Swaddled in his tartan, only her neck, ankles, and feet were visible. Pale auburn hair cascaded around her shoulders like a velvet cape of soft waves. Her slim neck revealed creamy skin. He could almost taste her on his tongue, soft and wet and woman-sweet. But it was her eyes, dark, green, and large with golden flecks, that made it difficult to breathe. She was watching him beneath lowered lashes, and with every second that passed, he felt the lower half of his body tighten only further.

He had never been one to flirt and carry on with women. His brother Conor had teased him mercilessly about his inability to read a woman's thoughts, and that it would get him in trouble one day. That day had finally arrived. More than anything, Cole wanted to know what she was thinking.

"Can I have my slippers?"

"They're wet."

"I know, but I need them to walk."

Cole knew she was waiting, but there was no way he could come near her. Not right now. If she got even one step closer, she would be in his arms, finding out just how honorable he was. Suddenly, he needed the cool of the water and fast.

"My turn," was all he could grit out and began yanking off his shirt.

Ellenor's eyes shot wide open as his words registered. His leine began to ride up his thigh and she whipped around, causing the tartan to catch on a bush. Forced to turn back around to pull it free, she accidentally glanced up. What she saw, she would never forget.

There were men, and then there were men whom God fashioned to be perfect. Cole was made of the latter. He had tossed his leine on the riverbank and was slowly marching into the water, completely naked. Once he reached thigh level, he dove in.

Ellenor stood transfixed, unable to tear her eyes away. As a curious child, she had once hidden in the stables to find out what men and women did when they met in secret. She had learned much that evening, and until now, had a very low opinion of the male body. Grace and beauty were not words she would have attributed to the masculine physique, especially one of Cole's size, but then, she hadn't seen him move through the water.

There was a subtle power in the smooth, muscled contours of his shoulders as Cole stood against the strong current. His dark hair, now wet, gleamed in the moonlight, conforming to the firm, unyielding lines of his back. He looked like a sculpture brought to life.

Her eyes couldn't get enough of him, and then suddenly they had too much. He had unexpectedly twisted in the water and caught her staring at him.

Ellenor knew she should have turned back around or at the very least closed her eyes, but she was mesmerized by the intensity of his blue gaze. She shivered with heat, unaware the tip of her tongue was moving along her lower lip. He was watching her. And then suddenly he was gone.

The moment his head dipped beneath the cool dark waters, the spell had been broken. Ellenor sank against a dead log no thicker than her thigh. He hadn't even touched her, but in those few seconds, Cole had awakened a sense of awareness within her she couldn't explain. The blood was pounding in her temples. Her emotions were swirling out of control, and among them was a deep sense of shame.

Of all the idiotic, brainless things to do, Ellenor muttered to herself. *Why did you have to stare? Why did you have to look at him at all?* But even as she asked, Ellenor knew that if she could reverse time and redo those few moments over again, she would not.

Cole popped his head back out of the water and wished for the frigid temperatures of the winter Highland lochs. The tepid river water was doing nothing to relieve the masculine hunger in him. He had almost lost all control when he caught her looking at him. She had been captured, helpless to look away, just as he had been. A maelstrom was brewing in her bright hazel eyes, drawing him into the heart of its storm.

He had been seconds away from marching out of the water and pulling her into a kiss that would not have ended until they were both spent and fully satisfied. Instead, he had sunk deep into the water, letting the current take him downstream.

He was somewhere between joy and agony. His body demanded physical release but he knew it could only be achieved one way . . . and with one woman. Whatever was connecting them, drawing them together, was not going away, and pretending otherwise was not helping.

Cole reemerged and glanced toward the riverbank, hoping this time Ellenor would be looking away. His wish had been granted, but it did not bring the solace he needed. She was huddled in a ball, unmoving.

"Are your clothes still wet?" Cole asked. The question was inane, as the sopping garments had only just stopped dripping, but he needed to say something, and it was that or would you like to join me?

Ellenor heard the question and reacted automatically, relieved for something to do. She stood up and moved a step to her left to reach out and finger the outstretched garments; neither was close to being dry. She would be lucky if they would be only damp by morning. "They're still wet," she rasped out, wondering why he asked a question to which he already knew the answer.

Unwilling to chance even snatching a glimpse of him, Ellenor took a step backward to where she remembered tossing her slippers near the river's edge. Pain shot through her as a prickly thorn poked into the arch of her foot. Biting her bottom lip to keep from screaming, she plucked the tiny thorn from her flesh. She then reached down, grabbed her shoes, and slipped them on, grimacing at their soggy state.

Looking around for somewhere to sit, she opted for where she was standing as good a place as any other. Ellenor pulled her knees to her chest and wrapped the dark plaid of blues and greens tightly around her.

Silence filled the air. Only the light lapping of the water behind her could be heard. Panic flooded her. She hadn't heard any movement let alone sarcastic comments for several minutes. Was she alone? "Cole?"

Silence.

"Cole, answer me!"

"I'm here, *abarach*," came a deep burr.

She jumped, vastly relieved. Then as the meaning of his new nickname for her—brazen woman—broke through her conscious thoughts, her blood began to boil once again. He loved mocking her, and jumping into the river fully clothed had provided him plenty of new ways to continue. Sitting naked, wrapped in his tartan, wasn't exactly the ideal situation to argue back.

Nevertheless, Ellenor wasn't about to let his gibe go completely unchallenged. "I may be bold, Scot, but unless you want *me* to be watching *you*, then you, too, will have to sing so I know that you are all right."

Cole rolled his eyes. The woman obviously wanted to pretend that her earlier blatant stare had never happened. Fine with him. It wouldn't work, but it was better than discussing it. "I can't sing," he answered in Gaelic.

"Can't or won't?" she returned in his tongue.

"Doesn't matter."

The resolute tone was unmistakable. He was right. It didn't matter. She didn't necessarily need to hear him sing, she just needed to hear his voice. "Then talk, Highlander. Tell me of Fàire Creachann, your clansmen, and this man Dugan."

"They aren't my clansmen."

"Then you shouldn't be their laird."

Her counterstatement startled him. Cole doubted there was another person alive, save his older brother Conor, who would be as honest . . . and maybe not even him. Worse, she was right.

"But let's say you didn't mean that the way it sounded," Ellenor continued. "That you *do* feel an allegiance to these people, a desire to protect them and see to their welfare. Could this Dugan also lead these people?"

"In some ways."

"But not in all?"

"No, not in all."

"And could you? I mean, could you lead them in all ways?"

Cole thought about the question. He had never really considered it before now. His brother had tried pointing out some of his flaws, but he had only considered them as impediments to being *selected*, not as aspects of being a good leader. "I don't know," he finally answered.

The deep timbre of his voice spoke far more than his words did. Cole was a complicated man. "You may not believe this," Ellenor began, "because he was English— but my father was a great baron."

"Was?" Cole questioned.

"Yes. He died almost two years ago."

"I'm sorry," Cole murmured, and surprisingly enough, he really was. "Tell me about him."

"When I was young, I thought he was invincible and would have defied anyone who thought otherwise. No matter what occurred, in my eyes, he could do no wrong. My father was and had always been a great and caring leader our people adored."

"And was he?"

Ellenor bent her head and studied the dark threads woven tightly against each other. "He was."

"Then why . . ." Cole gulped, wondering if he should ask such as a sensitive question. "Then why are you so sad when you remember him?"

"Because while I knew he was a wise man, I didn't appreciate him. I didn't listen to him when he asked me to." She pulled the tartan even tighter around her. "But that is not the point of this conversation. Visitors were not uncommon to my home and I was silly and often flirted with anyone showing me any interest. Then one day, my uncle stopped by to meet with my father. I hated it when he came. He was . . ." She shivered.

"Not a nice man," Cole finished.

"No" was her simple reply, but it was enough to convey everything Cole needed to know.

"He was especially vicious one day. My father and he argued and he became very angry. He exploded, calling my father a liar and just as guilty of treason as he. I was hiding in the vestibule—listening. Unable to stand hearing any more, I jumped out, screaming how wrong he was. My uncle laughed and then told me that my father was dependent upon him for protection and funds. Without him, my father was nothing. Ashamed, I ran away."

"It's a rough day to learn your father is not perfect."

"Indeed. But just like you, he found me." Ellenor smiled against her knees and fought back a yawn. "And he *was* a great leader, partly because he believed all of his people—whether soldier, baker, or even daughter— could contribute and he found ways to make use of their best skills. He *could* have had a large army, but he didn't feel like he needed one. And the money he took from my uncle . . . he felt was of better use for his people than anywhere else."

A quiet stillness filled the air. Ellenor had been doing most of the talking, and Cole had enjoyed listening to the soft melodic rhythm as she spoke in his own language. An ability that must have taken years to cultivate, but how? He watched the slow rise and fall of her shoulders and guessed she had fallen asleep.

Quietly, he slipped out of the water and threw on his leine. He moved to check on her garments. Finding them still sodden, he quickly wrung the material and spread them on a bush closer to the river, hoping the steady night breeze would have a better chance at drying them out. Next, he collected her bag, his belt and tartan, and then moved to her side. Carefully lifting her, he gathered her close and turned toward the campsite. His hands caressed her back, molding her to him as if she were made for him, and only him.

She stirred only once as he laid her down still wrapped in his tartan. She opened her eyes and said in almost a childlike voice, "You would be a wonderful laird, Cole. And wouldn't it be great if Dugan could be your commander?"

"My commander?" Cole choked, letting her go. But before he could move out of reach, her arm whipped out and cupped his cheek. Her eyes were glazed, as if she weren't looking at him, but a dream of him. A sudden rush came over him and he wished that some-day she would look at him that way when she was fully awake—warm, sensual, and aroused.

"Mmm-hmm. It would make everyone happy. Your people happy, Dugan happy to have a place of impor-tance, and best of all, you could teach him how to be a great man."

And then Ellenor did the unthinkable.

She curled her hand behind his neck and pulled him down to a waiting kiss.

At first, Cole tried to ignore the soft full lips moving erotically against his. She was half-asleep and not aware of what she was doing, but his body didn't seem to care. His ability to resist suddenly crumbled, and with a moan, he invaded the sweet, vulnerable warmth behind her lips. He heard her groan softly and felt her grip tighten on his neck.

The kiss was a drug on his senses. His heart was beat-ing rapidly, his imagination was going wild, and he could feel his body trembling. Her lips burned against his, igniting flames that could burn out the aching emptiness inside him.

He turned onto his side and eased Ellenor onto her back, deepening the kiss. The blanket fell down to her waist and he covered her supple body with his own. His tongue swept her mouth, devouring her lips, and in-stead of pulling away, Ellenor responded. She arched into him, pressing her frame against the length of him.

It felt so good, so right, so wonderful, he knew he had finally found perfection.

Need tore through him, ripping away all of his carefully constructed defenses, leaving only the agony of knowing this kiss—this phenomenal, earth-shattering kiss—would be all they would share.

He was seconds from ending the thin barrier between them and discovering the rest of her secrets when a voice deep inside him made him stop. Cole wanted to ignore it, but he couldn't. Not this voice. It wasn't his; it was Ellenor's, yesterday, telling him that she didn't trust any man, but she trusted him. With a groan, he crushed her to him and kissed her one last time, wishing he could make time stand still.

With the last of his strength, he lifted his mouth from hers and looked down into emerald eyes still glazed with sleep. "Elle . . . God, Elle . . . what you do to me," he whispered, smoothing back her hair.

"You do the same to me, Highlander." Then Ellenor lifted her lips and pressed them softly against his cheek. "Good night," she whispered, closing her eyes and her body suddenly went limp.

Letting her go, Cole flipped onto his back and tried to steady his breathing. He didn't know whether to be grateful or insulted that she just slept through a kiss that would keep him awake every night for months.

Kissing Ellenor Howell was the least honorable thing he had ever done.

It was also the most manly.

Chapter 5

Cole stirred, refusing to open his eyes. The last time he had made that mistake, it was just in time to spy Ellenor tiptoeing into the trees in the dead of the night. She had wrapped the blanket around her waist, holding up the ends over her breasts. The extra material in the back created a deep and revealing swag. The memory-scorching view of her glorious honey-colored hair tumbling off her shoulder blades to the small of her back had sucked the breath right out of him and he had yet to recover. She had looked like a temptress and an angel seamlessly blended into one woman. A woman whose kiss had pierced his soul.

His body was becoming aroused, and he knew if he continued to lie still, it would only become worse, not better.

Rousting himself up, Cole had grabbed his sword and headed out after her. Minutes later, he wished he had stayed where he was. Ellenor had dropped the blanket and was wrestling with the thorn bush to retrieve her chemise. His throat had seized and suddenly he had been unable to breathe. Only in dreams did men chance to see such perfection and never was it quite as beautiful as Ellenor.

Unable to stop himself, his gaze swept over her, taking her in from head to toe and then back up again. Long, lithe legs, perfectly curved hips, the graceful line of her spine, soft ivory shoulders, a slender white neck . . . all pieces perfectly linked, beckoning to be touched. Kissed. Savored. And worst of all, Cole knew exactly how good it would be. He still remembered how she tasted and felt against his hands when he'd held her, all soft and vulnerable.

His body quickened at the memory, and he silently cursed his own weakness. Sheer willpower and a lifetime of suppressing emotion were the only things keeping his control from disappearing altogether.

God, how he wanted her. She just wasn't his to have.

Pivoting, he returned to camp and lay back down. Moments later, Ellenor returned dressed in her chemise and his blanket was once again around her shoulders. In her hand was her bliaut. He guessed it was still damp because she threw several more sticks onto the dying fire and then spread the gown on the log she had been sitting on earlier during dinner. Only once did she glance his way, just before she had settled back down to sleep.

Cole opened his eyes and stared at the night sky, watching his breath mist his view and then evaporate. The once rising moon was now setting, indicating it was hours later. Ellenor was still asleep but her breathing had quickened, awakening him from his already light slumber.

Her dreams had returned. The bad ones.

He wondered what he should do—if anything.

She was curled up into a ball with his plaid wrapped tightly around her, and every so often, a soft whimper would catch the breeze. The effect was like a knife in the chest.

Every male impulse he had cried for him to go to her, hold her, and comfort her. But his survival instinct forced him to remain outstretched, uninvolved, and silent. Physically he was distant, but emotionally he was still connected to her, and none of the walls he tried to erect had broken their bond.

After Rob's death, Cole had had no difficulty separating himself from those he loved. And while he was loyal to his men, respected them, and would readily die to save or protect any one of them, friendships were something he no longer shared . . . with anyone. So, why was he finding it impossible to keep his distance from this woman . . . this *Englishwoman*?

A groan followed by a loud cry caught his attention. Cole glimpsed at Ellenor and saw her struggling with the blanket, cursing at it as if someone—not the material—was pinning her down. Her eyes were opened, crazed with both terror and fury. She was starting to kick, tearing and clawing anything that was daring to restrain her.

The plan to keep away from Ellenor and let her fight her own demons instantly disappeared. This was no ordinary nightmare. Ellenor was once again reliving whatever had happened to her, only this time, she wasn't able to get free.

Without further hesitation, Cole knelt beside her and began to unwrap the maddening material from her body. The second her arms were liberated, Ellenor began pounding on his chest, screaming and repeatedly drawing out the word "No!" as he worked to release the rest of her limbs.

Finally free, Ellenor jumped up and held her hand out as if it clasped a dagger and not air. "I will kill you," she seethed, waving her fist in front of her. "Come near me again and I will slit your throat." With her chin, she pointed to the empty, wadded blanket on the ground and said, "See him? See that nasty beast. He tried to rape me and I did that to him. I doubt even the animals will want his rotten entrails. Come one step closer and I promise I will do the same to you."

Cole put both hands out in front of him. He needed to wake her up. In her struggle, she had ripped some fingernails and somehow gashed her wrist, causing blood to flow freely down her arm. "Elle. It's me, Cole. I won't hurt you."

Ellenor jumped back, still waving her fist. Her long hair slid off her shoulder and started swinging. "You're damn right, you won't. How could you?" she wailed. "How could you do that to your own baron? He was my *father*!"

Her sorrow-filled cry tore at his heart. Now he knew the nature of her demon. No wonder she trusted no one, not even her own people. "I would never hurt you, Ellenor. You know that. I am your friend. We are soul mates, you and I. *Shonuachars*. I understand your pain and would never add to it."

She had first mistaken him for one of the English soldiers who had attacked her so this time he had spoken in Gaelic. It seemed to have stunned her for several seconds. Then her eyes grew large as the glaze from sleep slowly disappeared and Cole knew she was once again awake, with him and in the present.

Her brows furrowed, and for the first time, Ellenor looked completely unsure of herself. She looked down at the blanket, the place she had dreamt killing the man who had attacked her, and then back at Cole. "You . . . you now know. You know what I did. What I am."

"Aye, I know." His voice was deep, soft, and without judgment.

"No, you don't," she whispered, still staring at the twisted plaid. "You can't possibly."

"You defended yourself. An action I happen to admire."

Ellenor's head snapped up. Her eyes narrowed accusingly. "You don't understand a thing. For if you knew all of what happened—what I did, you couldn't stand to see even my shadow," she said in a choked voice. "Do you know what it is like to loathe yourself? Could you possibly understand what it feels like to carry the burden of knowing that, because of you, someone you loved, adored, respected, was murdered?"

Cole stood there, mesmerized by flashing green eyes that challenged his comprehension of the very thing that ate at his soul. For the first time since Rob died, he had met someone who just might understand what he felt. The personal anger, the terror, the utter sadness that lived with him reflected in two shimmering pools staring back at him. "I can. That is the one thing I can understand."

She looked at him, and if possible, her green eyes became larger and she realized he had spoken the truth. Then suddenly, her rigid form went limp. Before she hit the ground, Cole grabbed her and held her close.

With her cheek pressed against his shoulder, Ellenor felt all the loss, the pain, the guilt explode within her. Tears began to fall, and for the first time since it happened, she cried. Slowly at first, and then in torrents, clinging to Cole as if he were the one safe place in a raging storm at sea. He never let her go.

When she could cry no more, he bent down and picked her up. Kicking her blanket back open, he sat down, cradling her in his arms. Scooting back a couple of feet, he leaned against a small boulder and settled her across his lap with her head on his chest. He could feel the soft, wet flutter of her lashes when she blinked.

She was no longer crying, but her mind was in the past, remembering whatever had happened.

"Tell me about it, Elle. I promise you. I will not judge."

His request met with several minutes of silence before she finally spoke. "I'm sorry. I didn't even know I could cry like that. When I should have wept, I couldn't produce even one tear. It was as if a piece of me—the piece that feels—had died along with everyone else."

"Was your father part of everyone?"

Ellenor nodded against his chest. "I found him, along with his murderers. They were in his room, robbing him of anything valuable. My father was on the floor. A dagger was in his chest. His eyes were open. Shock and pain stared back at me. His mouth was open, too, from when he had called out. That was what brought me to his room. But when I got there, he was already dead."

Cole forced himself to unclench and relax his jaw. Stroking her hair, he whispered, "I'm so sorry, Elie."

"I did it. It was my fault."

His initial impulse to her declaration was to refute it. Cole was positive it was not true; however, for some mysterious reason, Ellenor obviously imagined it to be so. "How so?" he asked softly.

"My father knew they weren't good men. He knew from the beginning. They were forced upon us by my uncle. My father didn't have many soldiers, but the ones he had were very loyal. When my mother died, they became fiercely protective of the rest of the family. My sister hated it. Said she felt like someone was watching her every move and pressured father into letting her marry. He finally agreed and Gilda selected Ainsley, someone very like herself. He's the greedy sort who is never happy with what he has. He enjoyed living well and demanded a dowry—one that my father could not afford. Gilda had made sure she was compromised, forcing my father to use the money my uncle gave him, not for soldiers as they had agreed, but on my sister."

"Unfortunate," Cole said, prompting her to continue.

"All was well, for a while. Then somehow, my uncle must have found out. He was furious. I couldn't understand why he cared so much. All my life I saw my uncle use people to get what he wanted, and he most especially liked using my father. And before you think badly of my father, he knew what his brother was about."

"Then why did he allow it?"

"He said it was because it suited him. My mother said my father was appealing to his brother's envy and that as long as my uncle believed himself to be better and more powerful than us, there would be peace. So, my father let him."

Cole scooted a couple of inches down into a more comfortable position and took a deep breath. Exhaling, he said, "Excellent strategy. Your father found a clever way to protect what he truly valued."

"I told you that you would have liked him. You think as he did. I only wish he could have fought like you," Ellenor said, her voice so small and weak she wasn't even sure she spoke aloud.

"These . . . men that killed your father, they came from your uncle?" Cole questioned. She had been sidetracked and he wanted her to fully explain what had happened, more for her sake than his. He was curious, but until she unburdened herself completely, she would forever have nightmares.

"A few weeks after my uncle left," Ellenor began, "he sent us three soldiers. I didn't realize why he was being so generous, but my father did. My uncle was cheating the king by skimming taxes."

"That explains why your uncle was willing to give your father money."

"I later discovered they had a standing agreement. Some of the money was to recruit soldiers who would eventually serve my uncle . . ."

". . . saving him the burden and expense of training," Cole finished as understanding finally dawned on him.

"My uncle came to see why he hadn't gotten his new recruits."

"That was the argument you overheard."

"Yes, but I didn't make all the connections until later . . . much later. When I started pretending to be crazy, I just wanted everyone to leave me alone. Then they did, leaving me only memories."

Cole knew exactly what she meant. Nightmares robbed one of sleep, but in the day . . . it bled one's sanity.

Unaware of how she touched him, she continued, "So when my uncle sent soldiers to 'support' my father, he of course wanted to order the men back, but I was naïve. I liked them. I was bored. They were fun. So I was relentless in begging my father to change his mind and he finally agreed, saying maybe it would be wiser to watch the fox, rather than wonder where it was. I didn't understand his meaning and I didn't care. I was just glad they were staying. One of them, Seth, the leader of the group, was enormously charming and funny and he flattered me continuously. After a few months of his company, I had actually imagined myself in love. My father must have realized I was being foolish and con-fronted Seth, ordering him and his two friends to leave. And they *would* have left," Ellenor scoffed.

"*Would* have? They didn't?" Cole asked.

Ellenor shook her head in shame. "I ran after them. I found Seth just as he was prepping his mount. He was eager to leave, mumbling how a knight of his caliber deserved a rich lord with a pretty daughter. I told him that I would go with him, that my father was wrong. I put my heart out there and he cruelly threw it back at me, calling me the least womanly, most unappealing female creature he had ever been forced to spend time with." She bit the last words, remembering the menacing way in which they were said.

Cole sat stunned for several seconds. *Had the man been blind? Could anyone be so foolish to spend time with this woman and fail to appreciate all she had to offer?* As soon as he asked the question, he realized he was just such a fool. Then again, Ellenor was not his to claim.

"Of course Seth was right," Ellenor continued, "but that just made his verbal onslaught even more painful. I wanted to hurt him—hurt him as he had hurt me. So, I lied. I told him my father was rich, much richer than my uncle, with hidden stashes of gold that would be given as a dowry to the man I chose to marry . . . a man that would never be him. Then I left, foolishly believing I had won."

Ellenor paused, remembering. "That night I went to apologize to my father. Just as I reached the door, I heard a scuffle and him calling out. It was one time and not very loud and his voice had been full of fear. I opened the door to see one of Seth's men collapsed in a chair with my father's sword through his back. Then I saw my father. He was on the ground with a knife in his chest. His eyes were facing towards the door, but I knew immediately there was no life in them. He was dead."

Her voice was fragile and shaking, but Cole knew she was only just getting to the heart of her nightmares. "What happened next?"

"I . . . I'm not sure. I cannot remember. I must have said or done something to alert them I was there, because the next thing I recall is Seth. He was on top of me. I was on the floor next to my father, lying in his blood, and Seth was straddling me, sneering, and saying awful things. His friend was nearby telling him to hurry up. He wanted a turn. I didn't know what they meant . . . and then I felt Seth's hand on my leg and I knew he was going to hurt me. I was reaching for anything to use to make him stop and that is when I felt the knife still in my father's chest."

Ellenor lifted her head up and looked Cole directly in the eye. "I had to kill him. I didn't mean to, but I am not sorry that I did."

"Your nightmares . . . is this what they are about?"

Ellenor turned her head slightly and stared blankly at the campfire. The flames were leaping into the night sky, both beautiful and deadly. "My dreams are about what I did next," she said flatly. All emotion—empathy, fear, regret—was gone from her voice.

"I sliced Seth's throat open. He didn't have a chance to even utter a sound. His friend leaned in close to find out why Seth hadn't responded and got the blade in his eye. He screamed for several minutes before he, too, collapsed, dead. That was when the servants came. They looked, saw what had happened, and dragged me free. They wanted to know what to do, whom to tell, and that is when I decided . . . no one. No one was to know.

"I buried my father, and then took the three men who murdered him to a hill. I rode out every day to inspect their decaying bodies, hoping to feel something as their flesh was mutilated by beasts and vultures—hate, anger, horror, even remorse—but there was nothing. Even now, when I think about it and envision them rotting—I feel not a single emotion."

"Then what scares you at night?"

"Me," Ellenor said simply. "I go and stare at them.

Then I leave and there is a river in front of me. I get off and let my horse drink. I reach down to dip my fingers into the water and see my reflection staring back at me. Except I am hollow, my own skin matches those of the men I killed. Pieces of my flesh are missing from animals feeding on it. Then the rippling image speaks, saying that I should be on that hill with them. For if I had not begged my father to let them stay, if I had not taunted those men, if *I had just listened*, they would have left and my father would be alive."

Cole lifted her head. He didn't say anything. Nothing he could say would erase her pain. Just as nothing she could say would erase his own personal hell. Regardless, in the semidarkness, his eyes held hers, silently promising that he understood.

Tears slipped down her cheeks. Cole brushed them away with his thumb. Then more came, and soon, her eyes were once again flooded. She collapsed against him, clinging to his chest, desperately needing him. She choked on a sob. "Oh, God, Cole. I miss him so much!"

Cole held her tightly against him, murmuring that he understood, that it wasn't her fault, and that her father would be proud of her. Slowly, she calmed. He continued to stroke her hair and waited until she was ready to talk once again. This time, she sounded much more like her confident self.

"For months, I made that trek. The servants kept the secret of my father's death, and I died a little more every day. Then my uncle came and quickly figured out that somehow my father had died. He told Gilda and soon both of them decided I should be married as quickly as possible. I wanted nothing to do with anyone, ever again. I know it doesn't make sense . . ."

"It does," Cole countered, his voice low and soothing. "You didn't want to be hurt again."

"I never thought of it that way, but you're right. I never wanted to care about anything or anyone again."

"And so if you couldn't keep people away, you decided to make them *want* to stay away," Cole added, with some levity.

Ellenor shrugged. "Madness seemed like a good plan. Between not bathing, throwing food, tripping, and many other creative tricks, I became the most unmarriageable lady in all of northern England. Word spread quickly about my ill behavior and no man was willing to marry me. And believe me, my sister tried. I have no idea how many suitors Gilda dredged up, but not a one was willing to wed me after ten minutes in my company. Until you, I cannot think of a single soul who could stomach my presence for more than thirty minutes without begging to be excused."

"But I knew you weren't mad," Cole stated, standing up.

Ellenor tilted her head to look him in the eye. "That's because you knew what I was doing and why. Maybe not the specifics, but you knew. I could tell the first time you looked at me."

Cole leaned down and gently clasped her face between his hands and said, "Elle, you will have your dreams again, but this time in the water, you will see me right beside you. And never again will you see yourself hollow or dead as those of your father's murderers, but as I see you. Beautiful and brave. Never be afraid again. Promise me."

Ellenor sat still, riveted by the almost imperceptible note of pleading in his face. The sorrow that always lingered in his eyes was still there, but so was an unquenchable warmth and limitless understanding. They spoke directly to her soul.

Then, as if he realized she could see through the walls he had erected around his heart, Cole threw up new ones. His face deadened, once again hiding emotions he wanted everyone to believe he did not have. But for those few moments, she had seen them all and she could no longer pretend he was just an honorable man. Cole McTiernay was much more.

She was in love with him.

She loved all of him. Physically, he drew her toward him and his compelling blue eyes had claimed her soul. He was strong, yet gentle, and in his arms, she was never afraid. She loved how he spoke in short sentences, how he laughed, how he never yielded to her whims, and how he was aggravatingly honest. She even loved his cold allusiveness, for she knew it was just a cover for incredibly deep and strong emotions.

But he would never know of her love for him.

Telling him was not an option.

Cole considered her a responsibility, not a woman. Loving him was heartbreaking enough. She would not expose her heart to the immeasurable pain of his rejection.

He squeezed her shoulder. "Promise me, Elle. You won't be afraid."

Ellenor swallowed and nodded. "I promise," she whispered. And she meant it. Somehow she knew the nightmare would return, but never again would it haunt her as it had. He had done that for her and she wished she could do the same for him.

Just before he could walk away, she grasped his hand. "Cole, someday, when you are ready, I want you to know you can tell me about whom the English took from you."

Cole waited for Ellenor to let go, but she didn't. She was waiting. When he refused to agree, she pressed, "Remember that distance avoids pain, but happiness as well. Until you can forgive yourself, you will never be the leader you want to be."

Cole thought about denying her allegation, but she would have recognized the lie. Still, he could not do as she asked. "It's my burden. Not yours."

"If not me, then who else? I have no expectations of you. You cannot destroy any hero worship for I have no visions of you being anything beyond what you are. Your secret will be safe with me."

Cole felt his mouth go dry. Never had he been so close to disclosing the events of that awful day. Not until now. And yet, he couldn't do it. "I don't think I can. Not even to you. I need my hate, Elle. It's all I have."

"If you need it, Cole, then keep it. But the day you no longer want to carry it with you, I will be there as you were for me tonight. Just keep in mind that whatever you have been doing, it isn't working." Then Ellenor let go and watched him return to his own blanket.

In a few days, they would arrive at his brother's home. Cole would leave and she would reclaim control of her future. Hoping he would be a part of it was foolish. He didn't love her.

For if he did, Cole would no longer need his hate, he would just need her.

Chapter 6

Trying to keep her teeth from chattering, Ellenor focused on the beauty all around her. They had crossed the Trossachs yesterday, and while the hills were inspiring, she had to agree with Jaime—the famed Highland mountains were the most glorious lands she could ever hope to see. Green and brown rocky giants were everywhere, seeming to grow larger with each one they crossed. The deep dark lochs cradled in their valleys only accentuated their splendor. Occasional farms located near the water came in and out of view, but Cole kept the small group moving, not saying whether he knew them.

His quiet, frustrating demeanor had started the previous morning. He had awakened before her and had begun dismantling the campsite, a clear sign he intended to begin the day's journey early. Breakfast had been quick with only a fast meal of dried meat and water, and though Donald and Jaime had chatted quietly, Cole had been aloof. Only once had he spoken to her and that had been a simple, to-the-point question. "Sleep well?"

Caught off guard by his abrupt tone, Ellenor had replied similarly, "Yes. You?"

"Well enough." Again, short and terse.

Ellenor was not fooled.

Nothing was directly amiss, but Cole's face had a lean look about it as if he had not slept at all. His critical expression made it clear he blamed her. She had stirred things up, and while she had finally summoned the courage to excise her demons, he had not. And he was paying for it.

After a full day of enduring Cole's aloof demeanor and another morning of clipped responses, Ellenor decided he could struggle alone. She could endure the lack of conversation, but not when it was accompanied with forced stiffness, as if the truth about her past reminded him that she was English and someone to hate. So when she awoke to more of the same, Ellenor decided to ask Jaime if she could ride with him and he had readily agreed. She had hoped Cole would intervene, but when he didn't, she had deadened her expression, refusing to let him know his indifference affected her.

At first, it had been unnerving being in the arms of another man. Her automatic fear of men had bubbled to the surface, and when it eventually subsided, a strange sensation was left in its wake, as if she were wearing someone else's clothes . . . and they didn't fit. To hide her anxiety, she struck up conversations on a variety of topics. Thankfully, Jaime obliged. It was during such a discussion when she inadvertently learned the truth about who had sent for her.

Ellenor had pointed to Cole riding ahead and the awkward item strapped to the back of his saddle. "Why is Cole the only one who carries a long bow?"

Jaime shrugged. "I find them cumbersome."

"And Cole?"

"He took it up a few years ago. And though he had never said why, I believe it is because our good commander found it unsettling someone was better with a weapon than he."

Ellenor shook her head incredulously. "Cole hates the English, and the last thing he would want to imitate is an English soldier."

"True, if the someone I was talking about was an English*man*, but it was an English *woman*. When Cole's eldest brother married an accomplished bow hunter, our commander forced himself to perfect the skill. And he has. With that long bow, he can hit any target, whether moving or far away, with deadly accuracy. And how about you, lass? Are you as skilled with a bow?"

"Oh, no. As I said before, I don't have a clue about most weapons, and never really had the desire to learn. Besides, my father never would have allowed it. It was hard enough convincing him to let me ride."

"And you ride exceptionally well at that," Jaime complimented.

Ellenor licked her lips. "You earlier hinted the woman Cole's brother married was English," she began hesitantly, knowing she shouldn't care if it was possible. "I didn't think Scottish chieftains married Englishwomen."

Jaime shrugged. "It does not happen often, but there is no law preventing the union. Anyway, Lady Laurel is only half-English. Her mother's people were Scottish, and well, ever since she met the laird, her heart belongs to the Highlands."

Ellenor had almost fallen off the horse when Jaime said the name. Laurel. It couldn't be the same person as her friend, but deep down, she knew it was. Laurel Cordell wasn't dead. Somehow, she had escaped and married a Highlander. Rumors of her supposed death had been false . . . and Ainsley had known. The man had let everyone think his sister was dead and had fed on the outpouring of sympathy. Then came the day he needed her to take his crazed sister-in-law off his hands, and Laurel, being the kind person she was, had agreed, sending Cole as a guardian and escort.

Now, everything began to make sense. Why Cole could so easily promise she wouldn't be forced into marriage if she didn't want to be. Why he would drag an unwilling Englishwoman into his beloved country and into his family home. Why on a dozen other mystifying things—including the reason he had kept the truth to himself.

Cole McTiernay wanted her to be dependent on him, all to keep her under control.

For a long time, Ellenor stayed warm on seething anger as they trudged farther north and higher into the mountains. Eventually, though, it became harder to ignore the cooler temperatures. The afternoon sun began to fade behind dark clouds and with its disappearance came a chilled wind that seemed to seep through her gown and nip at her skin.

She hadn't realized her shivering had caught Cole's attention until he rode up beside Jaime and with one deft movement lifted her from Jaime's mount onto his. Without asking, he tucked her against his chest—something she had been unable to make herself do with Jaime.

Ellenor tried to pull away but caved into her need for warmth and settled back against Cole. The resentment boiling in her had not simmered, but she was cold, and after yesterday's ride and being ignored this morning, she knew Cole wouldn't care. She was only punishing herself by keeping her distance.

Ellenor considered letting him know about her

discovery and her outrage, but decided that was too easy. He had intended the truth to be revealed at their arrival, and it still would be. Only now, Cole would be the one who was surprised—not she. Envisioning the look on his face when he realized she had bested him once again did a great deal to temper her anger.

Ellenor cuddled against his large frame and sighed. The knowledge her future was secure had not provided the feeling of euphoria she had expected. Safety was important, and when one didn't have it, it was hard to consider other things. Less than a week ago, she would have believed security alone could have made her happy, but that was before Cole. Now, she wanted more. Security wrapped in a lifetime of loneliness was far from an attractive future.

"Still cold?" Cole inquired. The wind had continued to increase, and up ahead, the dark rain clouds were releasing their mass. The temperature had dropped significantly. It wasn't quite cold enough to snow, but it would be a miserable, wet night.

"I'm all right," Ellenor mumbled, blowing into her cupped hands to keep them warm.

"We'll be through this pass soon and the mountain should block the majority of the wind. Once the horses are better protected, I'll stop and pull out the plaid for you to use as a cover."

It was the closest thing to a real conversation he had engaged her in for over a day. She didn't know why he had now decided to resume a dialogue with her, and fearing he might retreat into silence once again, she decided not to ask. Instead, she snuggled closer to him, marveling at how he could be so warm and unaffected by the elements. "I don't understand how you aren't cold."

Cole gave a halfhearted shrug and then, with an

arrogant grin, said, "As you have pointed out several times, I am a Highlander."

"You are many things I am not, Scot," she responded righteously just before adding, "including being an exceptional ass." She hadn't meant to reference his behavior for the past few days, but her irritation had slipped out. Ellenor held her breath, waiting for his response.

Cole surprised her and laughed out loud. Ellenor joined him and began to truly relax. She had feared admitting her past had changed their relationship and it was a relief he still welcomed her candor.

Ellenor nudged her chin toward the rocky peak in front of them. "Your mountains touch the sky. One can get drunk on such beauty." A large russet-colored animal with curved horns, shaggy pelts of thick hair, and forelocks so long it covered its eyes snorted as they rode by. "Even your cattle are suited to the weather. Think I, too, will be able to adapt?"

"You'll conform. Some things you'll find difficult and others easy, but aye, Elle, the one thing I have no doubts about is you flourishing in my world or any other. You are a survivor."

Ellenor squirmed. Cole's compliments were almost harder to take than his insults. "Easy. I doubt anything up here is easy."

"Perhaps, but then you have already conquered the hardest obstacle."

"And that is?" Ellenor prompted, wondering if he was serious or being sarcastic.

"Gàidhlig."

The language of the Gaels.

Ellenor blinked. Cole was right. She hadn't spoken a word of English all day. While Jaime understood her tongue, he was far from comfortable speaking it. It had been natural to converse in Gaelic and she had just continued to do it. The language was rich with unusual sounds, and though far from the easiest dialect she had ever learned, she had always loved how the syllables rolled off her tongue.

"I was curious. Why do you call me Elle and not Ellenor?"

"Do you mind?"

Ellenor considered his question carefully. Surprisingly, she didn't mind. She had never been given a nickname, nor had she ever wanted one. "No. It's certainly better than *babag*. Just no one has ever shortened it before."

Cole cracked a smile. He liked the idea that Elle was his name for her and not commonplace among her people. "Elle suits you better."

"Only you, though," she whispered, burying her face into his chest. "Everyone else still has to call me by my proper name." Then she remembered what his friends had called her. "Or lass. That works, too."

The relaxed expression on Cole's face instantly turned into a scowl. Yesterday's exercise in silence had done little to quell his memories of her nude in the moonlight, her soft lips pressed against his, or how she held him and trusted him with her fears. She was stirring emotions he didn't want to feel, so he had retreated, but Ellenor hadn't. Her willingness to comply with his unstated request for quiet during their ride had not extended to his comrades.

Donald and especially Jaime had become quite friendly with Ellenor in a very short amount of time, and last night all three had been infuriatingly friendly over dinner. Each time they called her lass, he had wanted to intervene. Yet if he had done so, it would have been the same as announcing Ellenor belonged to him. Something that could never be. She had to be just another woman.

Except . . . she wasn't. Not to him nor any other warm-blooded man. And after watching Jaime wallow in the pleasure of her company, Cole could no longer pretend otherwise.

Ellenor was exactly the type of woman that appealed to most men. Intelligent, witty, and surprisingly charming. She was gentle and nurturing and pulled at every male instinct to protect her from harm. That combination in itself was dangerous, but she was also beautiful. And seeing her unclothed, fighting a bush for her chemise, he had learned just how beautiful. If any of his men ever made the same discovery, he would most likely kill them. For not only did he feel compelled to protect Ellenor, he constantly battled his need to possess her.

Midafternoon the foul weather turned ugly and the damp mist in the air changed to raindrops soaking anything exposed. Cole and his men seemed oblivious. They had slowed only a fraction in their pursuit of the night's destination. Ellenor huddled within the blanket Cole had given her, which helped enormously, but she suspected only dry air and a campfire would be able to warm her bones. Neither of which were in the near future unless Cole planned to sleep in a cave.

A couple of hours later, Ellenor was thankful Cole had pushed the small group. The site he had chosen to make camp was probably the single natural dry spot in fifty miles. Two jagged cliffs of rock seemed to defy gravity as they created a semiroof and protection against the elements. Instead of tapering, both grew significantly wider until they met several feet over their heads, creating a patch of dry ground. The small foot-print required the four of them to be fairly close to-gether when sleeping, not sprawled apart as they had been, but they would be moderately dry and protected against the rain's accompanying cold wind.

Ellenor kept Cole's plaid wrapped around her, but began making dinner, the nightly duty she had as-sumed. She collected several small branches that had been piled against one of the rock walls from a previous traveler, keeping them dry. After bundling them to-gether, she asked Jaime to light the fire. He obliged before disappearing into the darkness in search of food. By the time he returned with two rabbits and a grouse, the fire was growing and Ellenor was beginning to feel the blood once again flow in her veins. How the Highlanders seemed to move about with only a shirt and a kilt for protection was a mystery to her.

Jaime once again braved the elements and fetched some wild onion and garlic before joining Donald and Cole to take care of the horses. Building a makeshift spit, Ellenor found an odd, bowl-shaped rock a little smaller than the size of her fist. It wasn't big enough to bake anything in, but she used it to capture the drip-pings and baste the meat while it cooked. By the time the men returned, the meal was done and, despite the weather, one of the finest all of them had enjoyed in some time.

Conversation had been light, as the storm grew in ferocity. The rain poured down and lightning lit up the night sky every few minutes. Pounding thunder fol-lowed. Normally, Ellenor could never have slept through such noise, but emotionally drained and physically exhausted from being cold, she could no longer hold herself upright. Leaning against Cole for support, she fell fast asleep unaware she was still holding the last leg of rabbit in her hands.

Carefully, Cole took the bone and threw it into the fire. He laid her down, but when he tried to withdraw, her clutch on his arm instinctively tightened. Worried he might awaken her, he caved in to his own desire and lay down beside her. Donald and Jaime didn't say a word but quickly followed suit. The party of four was soon asleep, oblivious to the storm as it finally passed over them.

Cole inhaled deeply. Ellenor's scent lingered in the air. The combination of flowers and woman was driving him crazy. The feel of her pressed up against him, innocent and vulnerable, was a bizarre mixture of bliss and pain. She had burrowed into his side in her sleep, seeking his heat against the chill of the night air. At first, it had been her head on his shoulder, then an arm across his stomach and a leg over his thigh. Finally, her whole body had melded to his side. He had welcomed it all.

She was delicate and soft, and memories of their kiss flared in his mind, sending waves of heat through his loins. Never had he experienced such an overwhelming desire to know a woman. He longed to touch, taste, and enjoy every inch of her body. He wanted to know what she liked, what excited her, and then drive her insane with need. If she had been someone else—anyone else—he might have indulged himself the pleasure.

But she wasn't.

She was an Englishwoman with a wounded soul, who was just beginning to learn how to trust and be herself again. He would fight armies to ensure she remained free from the hell in which she had been living. But that was only half the reason he kept his distance. One night with her and he would never be able to let her go.

Ellenor sighed and snuggled closer. Cole didn't move. He couldn't. All he could do was lie quietly and listen to his blood pound in his veins, thanking God his men had left.

The storm had been intense, but quick. In its wake came warmer air, proving once again that winter was over and spring had begun. Unused to being confined, Jaime and Donald had left to sleep in the open, where they had tied the horses. Cole had been tempted to go with them, but just as he was about to rise, Ellenor nuzzled her cheek against his chest and murmured his name in her sleep. All ideas of leaving immediately ended.

A few minutes later, she shifted again and Cole wondered whether he was in heaven or hell. With a small moan of pleasure, she had just resettled herself so that one of her legs was tucked between his and her hand rested on his torso, just underneath the opening of his leine. The steady rise and fall of her chest pressed her breasts against him, and he could feel the pulse in her neck pounding against his shoulder. His whole body tightened to painful levels with unfulfilled desire, but at the same time, he had never experienced such contentment.

It had been some time since he had tried to suppress his demons through sex and he couldn't recall ever wanting simply to lie with a woman afterward. Donald had told him once that he enjoyed the mornings best, because when he woke up, his wife was wrapped around him. Cole had thought his friend daft and stated unequivocally he would never feel the same. His bed was his own and he could not imagine ever wanting to share it.

And yet here he was, troubled that tomorrow they

would be home and Ellenor would never lie next to him again. His future loomed in front of him and it was darker than ever.

Cole's arm stole protectively around her. He thought about what lay ahead. Had Conor returned with a decision? Had he been named laird? Did he care? What would he do if Dugan were chosen in his stead? His men needed a home, something long-term. Something Cole had not really considered before Ellenor.

She was so focused on her future, what would happen, the control she would have over her destiny, it had made him begin to think about his.

Like all his brothers, he had a gift for strategy, an ability he applied liberally on the battlefield, but very little anywhere else. The reason had been simple. Life, beyond that of war and fighting, had provided only undesirable choices, and so he had avoided making one. And yet, being laird provided him an opportunity to make improvements not just in his men's lives, but also in those Highlanders who lived and loved this land as much as he did.

He had treated the decision-making council with indifference and Dugan with disdain. As a result, it might cost him something he didn't realize until now just how much he wanted. To be a leader. To make a difference.

Ellenor stirred once again. Cole moved his arm to let her move, but instead of turning to her other side as he expected her to, Ellenor sat up and immediately reached down to scratch her leg. With a look of immense contentment, she satisfied the itch. Then she arched her shoulders and threw her head back, causing dark golden waves to cascade in soft knots down to her waist. Yawning, she glanced around the campsite and spied that he was awake, too. A thoughtful smile flickered over her lips before she scooted over a couple of inches and tucked her blanket around her. Cole knew without asking that Ellenor was completely clueless about how she had been draped over him for the past few hours. She no doubt believed their close proximity due to the small area.

"Where are Jaime and Donald?" Ellenor asked sleepily, stretching once again before curling up to hug her legs.

Cole watched Ellenor teeter her chin on her knees and wished for an ice-cold loch in which to dive. "They left as soon as it stopped raining."

Surprise touched her pale face. "They're sleeping somewhere out there?"

"Aye."

"But they'll get wet!"

"Better than being cramped."

Ellenor shook her head and rolled her eyes. "Your men are far more unbalanced than I ever pretended to be. I'm glad you decided being warm and confined is much better than cold and damp."

Cole closed his eyes. If he had any sense at all, he would gather his things, leave right now, and join his men, but the little sense he had possessed fled days ago. Ignoring his inner voice, Cole asked, "What woke you? Another bad dream?"

"Uh-uh," Ellenor answered, shaking her head. "In fact, I don't think I have ever slept better. I only woke because my leg started itching." Reaching down to scratch her calf again, she saw the thorn-bush scrapes and wished for some water to clean them. "I need another bath."

Cole's eyes popped open. "*Another* bath?"

"Mm-hmmm. I hate being dirty, and after enduring filth for weeks, I could enjoy a bath every day."

Cole stared at her to see if she was teasing. His face

slackened in open shock when he realized she wasn't. "Good luck with that."

Ignoring him, Ellenor pointed out into the darkness. "Is there somewhere nearby where I can at least wash my face and hands?"

"Now?" Cole spit out.

Ellenor nudged his leg playfully with her foot. "No, of course not. In the morning. I want to arrive at our destination looking my best."

Cole's scowl deepened. He hadn't really considered people's reaction to their arrival. However, if she looked any better than she did already, Ellenor would have more than one open admirer, despite her being English. The last thing she—or he—needed was for her to make any more improvements to her appearance. "You look fine," he growled.

"Hmm, you woke up grumpy. Aren't you sleeping well?"

"Well, enough," he lied.

"Then why are you awake? Bad dreams?" she asked, parroting his own question back to him.

Cole answered her with another scowl.

"Ahhh, I see," Ellenor yawned without further explanation and settled back down, facing the crackling embers of the nearly dead fire.

After several seconds, Cole caved. "Just what do you think you see?"

"Fàire Creachann. Isn't that what's keeping you awake?" she asked, flipping over to look at him. "You have that pensive look one has when their mind won't stop swirling on a subject. I doubt there is much that can plague your thoughts, with maybe the exception of your men. You care a lot for them. So I'm guessing, you have been thinking about Fàire Creachann and whether you have been chosen. Don't you think you will be?"

Cole's blue eyes locked with her green ones. They were so open and full of belief that he was a good man—good enough to be laird. "I don't know," he answered honestly.

"Don't worry," Ellenor whispered, shifting to her back. "They'll pick you. Your scowl is not as terrifying as you would like to believe. It doesn't hide the depth of your feelings. You would do anything for those under your care. Even for a woman who's from a country you hate." Ellenor yawned and closed her eyes. "I'd pick you."

Less than a minute later, Cole could hear her steady breaths, indicating she had fallen fast asleep once again. He eagerly waited for her to move beside him and sighed with contentment when she finally did. He gently pulled her back into his arms and hugged her close, savoring the feel of her soft, limp form.

He was falling in love with her and he couldn't stop himself. Without even trying, she understood him like no other, not even his brothers, who had known him all his life. She recognized his inadequacies and still had unlimited confidence in him.

He had watched his eldest brother meet and fall in love. It had changed him. But those had been changes Conor had been ready for, even desired.

Love was not in Cole's plan.

To fall in love with anyone meant letting go of the past. To fall in love with Ellenor, however, meant much more. It meant embracing an enemy he had sworn to hate. It meant renouncing his promise to Robert. It meant living his life in the present and not the past. Something he did not know how to do.

Cole clenched his jaw. He had no choice. For his sake and hers, he needed to permanently distance himself as quickly as possible.

The moment they reached his brother's, he would leave.

* * *

Cole roused from his deep slumbered state and instinctively reached out for Ellenor. The space beside him felt oddly empty, as if she had slept in his arms for most of his life and not just one night.

In his youth, women had warmed his bed, but he found their company awkward and difficult once he had satisfied his physical need. He had learned quickly to meet elsewhere, enabling him to avoid spending an uncomfortable night with a woman who he had solicited for only one purpose.

Then he met Ellenor. If he rolled over and told her she had spent most of the night cuddled up to his side, she would deny it vehemently right after calling him a string of names beginning with giant and ending with Scot. Just the thought made him smile.

Cole propped himself up on his elbows and glanced around. Once again, she was nowhere in sight. *"How the hell does she keep doing that!"* he growled, throwing the blanket aside.

The sun was just starting to crest the horizon so she could not have been up for long, but the idea that Ellenor—that *anyone*—could maneuver around a campsite so quietly and not rouse him was more than disturbing. Skill and agility had not kept her from waking him; it had been sheer exhaustion. Nothing had ever plagued his ability to fall asleep as much as the simple knowledge of knowing she was nearby. And last night with her wrapped around him . . . it had been a miracle he had been able to fall asleep at all.

Snatching his belt, he cinched it around his waist and grabbed his sword. Small muddy footsteps trekked off to the right and down toward the rushing sounds of the river, engorged from last night's storms. He should have known. Ellenor had practically announced she was going to find a way to bathe at first light with her carefree "I feel dirty" comment in the middle of the night.

Cole stopped at the small clearing where Jaime and Donald were sleeping. He barked for them to pack and prepare to leave. After hearing them grumble a response, he followed Ellenor's trail into the thicket of trees lining the base of the mountain. He prepared himself to find her, walking toward him with her bag in hand, smelling of lavender and roses. But the vision at the riverbank was not one any man could have anticipated.

Ellenor was standing at an angle, fingering large, soft tawny curls that were just on the verge of being dry. Her eyes were closed and her head was tilted back, exposing the sensual curve of her neck. She wore a cream-colored, ankle-length chainse with a rich brown bliaut over it. A band of bronze needlework circled the long sleeves of the tunic and a braided belt hung low, cradled just above her hips. The gown was moderately worn, but it fit her perfectly, clinging to her curves just enough to make a man's mind go wild with ideas.

Lord, she was beautiful.

A slight breeze flickered across the water and captured a tendril of dark gold hair. It floated across her cheeks, causing Ellenor to catch the errant lock and tuck it behind her ear. The small graceful movement was purely feminine and reminded him what a gentle creature she was. Delicate wrists, slim fingers, everything about her was exquisite . . . and very provocative. And while her beauty was undeniable, it was her essence that had captured his soul.

Ellenor turned abruptly and caught him studying her. Her mouth curved faintly, lips, soft, pink, parting slightly, and Cole wanted so badly to kiss her he could think of nothing else.

Green eyes continued to hold his, and for a timeless moment, all he could do was look at her, drink her in, and memorize every inch. He reminded himself to breathe, but it did no good. His throat had constricted with desire to such a degree no air could be drawn in or escape. All he could do was stare.

His muscles tensed, his abdomen seized. Never had such strong, deep desire flashed upon him so quickly or forcefully. His heart was beating so furiously against the walls of his chest he actually felt lightheaded.

Get control, he ordered himself. *In a few hours, you will be home. Until then, stay calm and do nothing you will regret.*

Cole reined in his desire and squared his jaw. "Just where did you get that?" he barked, waving his finger at her gown.

Ellenor blinked, looked down at her bliaut, and then back up. "From my bag," she answered. "Where did you get your leine?" she asked, imitating his gesture.

"It's the same damn one I've been wearing all week!" Cole snapped, seeing her grin. Only then did he realize she had been teasing him. Hating to be on the defensive, he crossed his arms and asked, "And just what do you think you are doing coming down here by yourself? I told you the currents of these rivers are dangerous!"

Ellenor decided to ignore his caterwauling and respond as if he were being rationale and not roaring at her. "I took a bath. I left early so I had time to wash and plait my hair before we packed up and—"

"Left *early*? More like the middle of the night," Cole huffed. Her thick mane was nearly dry, proof she had risen well before dawn.

"—I didn't want to rush or have you wait for me," Ellenor finished, disregarding his sarcastic interruption. "I knew you had a lot on your mind, and you were sleeping so soundly I didn't want to wake you." It wasn't a total lie. She hadn't wanted to wake him, but his sleep had been far from sound. More like restless and agitated.

Ellenor looked down and tried smoothing out the wrinkles in her bliaut once again. "As for my gown? I was saving it. I know it's a bit crumpled, but still better than what I've been wearing. What do you think? Am I presentable?"

Presentable? Hell, no, she wasn't presentable. In that frock, every man they encountered would ogle her, imagining what it would feel like to hold and kiss such beauty. Those were his fantasies and his alone. They smacked of possessiveness, which also angered him. Not about to admit it, he grumbled, "Passable, maybe. You ready?"

Passable? Ellenor bit down on the inside of her lip . . . hard. "No," she mustered between gritted teeth and began to pace.

Her impromptu plan was falling apart. Almost two hours ago, she had awoken draped all over him. It had felt divine, right, as if that was where she was meant to be. His arm encircled her waist, and her face was nuzzled against his neck. Her mouth was just bare inches from his skin and it had taken all her will to break away and not press her lips to his.

She had wondered if Cole had even been aware of her presence. His breathing had been deep and steady, indicating he was asleep, but did he know she was sleeping beside him, curled against his torso with his arm around her? Or had it been an unconscious embrace any normal man would have welcomed?

A sense of self-preservation had come over her and Ellenor tried gently to pull away. Instead of letting go, Cole had turned on his side, drawing her closer to him. Any other man and she would have been screaming, clawing to get away. With Cole, it was not her body she needed to protect, but her heart.

Ellenor tried once again to disentangle their limbs. Succeeding, she held her breath and waited for him to wake. A handful of seconds passed before he grunted and then rolled to his other side. She was free. Then Cole had begun mumbling.

At first, his words had not been intelligible. Then suddenly they had become clear. It didn't take long to realize what Cole was dreaming. He had brutally lost his best friend at the hands of English soldiers. And while she couldn't discern the circumstances of his friend's murder, it was clear that it had not been in battle and Cole felt responsible. She had no idea how long ago it happened, but she guessed he had been young, not quite a man.

Just as Cole had slipped back into a deep slumber, he had whispered, "I promise, Robert, never to forget. They'll pay . . . every English *blaigeard* . . . will pay . . ."

Curling into a ball, Ellenor wrapped her blanket around herself, but still felt cold. Going back to sleep was impossible. Her mind was racing. She was beginning to understand why Cole didn't want to discuss what had happened, and she wasn't sure what she would say if he ever did. She just knew that she loved him.

Ellenor reached down and scratched her leg again. The irritation was caused by several scrapes she had received by thorn bushes in the evening's hastened ride to shelter. Dirt and sweat had only made the need to scratch worse. She needed a bath . . . and a plan.

Pulling on her slippers, Ellenor grabbed her bag and tiptoed out of the campsite and toward the sound of water. Glad to find a river and not a stream, she plunged in, welcoming the icy sensation. It did much to alleviate the stinging in her leg, but did little to end her chaotic thoughts.

Dinner conversation had been scarce due to the weather, but one sentence had cut through the noise. They were less than a half a day's ride from McTiernay Castle. In a few hours, she would be reunited with Laurel.

Their friendship had sprung from their mutual interest in Gaelic and had grown deeper as each understood the terrible emptiness resulting from losing one's mother. From almost the moment they met, they had conversed and chided and laughed as if they had known each other their entire lives. When Ainsley and Gilda decided to marry, Ellenor felt both conflicted and elated. She knew their marriage was based on escape and greed, but it gave her a new sister, a wonderful one with whom she could relate to in ways she had never enjoyed with Gilda. Then reality had reared its ugly head.

Her sister hated competition, and she was no match for Laurel. It should have been easy to marry Laurel off, but Ainsley discovered his sister was not going to sit by and be a pawn to his desires. Ellenor had begged her to reconsider, but once Laurel had been disowned, she had no choice but to leave for Scotland. Soon word came back that she had been attacked and killed. That had been four years ago. Ellenor had just turned eighteen.

Swimming slowly against the current, Ellenor headed back to shore to fetch the soap from her bag. She pulled the scented mound out and fingered its smooth sides. Being friends with Laurel had been so effortless, but four years was a long time. Laurel was now a wife to the laird of a very large clan. Did they still have anything in common? Ellenor wondered if she would be able to adapt and make a new life with a people and culture about which she knew so little. Laurel would be there, but would Cole? It was he whom she sought out for comfort and she didn't know how she would react if he wasn't there, by her side, telling her she was brave and a survivor.

News that Cole had been named the nomad's chieftain was most likely waiting for him. His departure would follow very soon afterward and then she would never see him again. She could ask to go with him, but Ellenor knew his answer would be a firm no. And even if Cole did for some unbelievable reason agree, being treated with indifference by someone she loved was a torture for which she did not intend to volunteer.

As memories of him holding her came to mind, a brilliant flash came upon her. She stood up, breathing heavily.

What if Cole *wasn't* indifferent? What if she bothered him just as much as he affected her? If Cole didn't like her, that was one thing, but if he did—

What she needed was a plan.

Ellenor grabbed her bag and pulled out the crushed velvet gown she had been saving. She smoothed out the material and fingered the intricate dark bronze stitching along the hem. Her sister hated the dark reddish-brown color, but combined with the off-white chainse, the russet shade flattered Ellenor enormously. She had never failed to get several compliments whenever she wore the ensemble. The moment Cole saw her in it, she would know.

Oh, how she had been wrong.

Initially, she had believed Cole's stunned reaction to be just what she had hoped. But the moment he spoke, demanding to know the source of her new bliaut, she was not so sure. His facial expression was that of an unemotional statue—completely unreadable. Cole either was fighting his reaction or had none to fight.

She needed a new plan and fast. Something much more definitive. Something that couldn't mask his true emotions for her. And most important, something she could not misread. But what?

Cole watched her pace back and forth for several minutes, muttering a stream of unintelligible words. Maybe he should have just said yes, that she was presentable, but he had been afraid she would have been able to see right through him and know exactly what her new look was doing to him. Instead, he had quipped some half-lie. Now, she was talking to herself and he was left with two choices. Either he could sling her over his shoulder and carry her back to camp, or he could wait until she was ready to talk about whatever was bothering her. Not in the mood to be pummeled and kicked, Cole opted for the latter and walked over to a large, waist-high boulder that must have fallen from the cliffs. He grimaced as he leaned back against the jagged surface. "Take your time," he said sarcastically.

Ellenor continued to move back and forth, waving for him to be quiet. Her mind was racing, but no ideas were coming to her. "I, uh, wanted to ask you something before we go back," she said, stalling.

Cole crossed his arms and cocked an eyebrow. "Aye. What?"

Ellenor took a deep breath and exhaled. *What?* Good question. What was it she wanted?

She looked at him. He was leaning on the rock, returning her stare. His legs were slightly apart and his arms were relaxed at his sides. He was a massive, self-confident giant, who despite his tousled hair and morning beard, had never looked so handsome. Nor so isolated.

His untroubled posture belied the haunted tension swirling in his eyes. Normally a bright blue, their color was much deeper. The same deep hue they turned whenever he was waging a mental war. Ellenor didn't know whether it was because of her, or their return home, or the impending decision waiting for them, but more than anything, she wanted to reach out and kiss him, let him know that she would forever believe in him.

"God help me," she mumbled and buried her face in her hands. *A kiss?* she mentally screamed at her psyche.

"I couldn't hear you."

Ellenor wrung her hands and resumed pacing. "Um . . . do you think I will be happy at your home?" she asked, wishing something more intelligent had popped out.

Cole arched a single eyebrow. "I do," he answered simply, wondering if Ellenor really was as nervous as she looked. "You and my brother's wife are of similar spirits and will no doubt form a bond that will drive my brother quite out of his wits. I only wish I could see it."

Ellenor came to a dead stop right in front of him. She had to have misunderstood. "What do you mean?" she demanded, her voice raspy with sudden fear. "Are you leaving?"

"Aye, directly after our arrival."

Ellenor felt her jaw drop. *"Immediately?"* she squealed and took a step closer. "But you . . . you can't!" Her eyes grew large and brimmed with tears. "I need you."

Her soft voice had been a bare whisper and it tugged at Cole's soul. "Oh, Elle . . ." he murmured and raised his hand to cup her cheek.

A tear fell and splashed against his thumb. He brushed it away. He should have removed his hand, but he couldn't. Not with her looking at him like that.

Fear swam in her green pools along with a profound sense of loss. A wave of despair washed over him as he saw his own life reflected in her eyes. The years of emptiness, the loneliness, the past and the future with no one to share happiness or pain. No one to care whether he lived or died except his men. No one who would ever know the piece of him that wasn't a commander. No one to recognize just the man. A man with ghosts.

Suddenly, his need for Ellenor was too much. Cole curved his hand around her neck, pulled her close, and gave in to the need to kiss her. She was warm and damp, and God, so alluring as he brushed his mouth lightly, persuasively, across hers.

He heard her gasp and tried to pull back. He'd meant only to give her a gentle kiss and end it, but then her arms wrapped around him and she groaned, opening her mouth to him, changing the gentle caress to one that was far deeper. All thoughts of ending the kiss were pushed aside.

Cole lessened his grip and began to stroke her spine. Ellenor moaned and arched her back, quivering with untutored passion. There was something completely satisfying knowing he could make her react so genuinely to him. It ignited his own feverish need with an intensity he hadn't known he possessed.

With a soft, low growl, Cole pulled her roughly up against him so that her body was molded against his. He deepened the kiss, sinking his soul into this one brief moment of sheer pleasure.

The embrace was far different from the one they had shared when only he had been aware of what was transpiring. An awake Ellenor was wild, undisciplined, following his lead, tasting him, meeting him stroke for stroke. The result was a soul-stripping, demanding, and far more blatantly erotic kiss. It shocked him, and yet he was not about to let it end.

Her mouth slanted over his lips, her tongue mating with his repeatedly, until Cole was consumed, breathless, and mindless with need. He knew he was in danger of losing control, and yet, he couldn't get enough of her. He invaded her mouth, thrusting his tongue deep, swallowing her moans of satisfaction.

Her chest was heaving with the effort to breathe, and Cole wanted to taste more of her. His mouth began to rove from her lips across her cheek to her earlobe, suckling it between his teeth. His hands made their way from her lower back, to her stomach and up to touch her breasts. They were the perfect size, and with one flick of the hand, they could be free, accessible for verifying what he knew to be true. That they, along with everything else about her, would taste exquisite. Suddenly he was ravenous.

Cole returned his lips to hers, silencing any potential words of protest, and let his fingers slip beneath the collar of her chemise. With a slight tug, a perfect cream and pink mound sprang free. His hand moved over to touch the softness awaiting him. He thought for a moment she would pull away, but instead, Ellenor lost the ability to stand. Catching her, he moved a leg between her thighs to balance her weight, allowing him to focus on the new delights he had just found.

Blood surged through his veins, and every muscle in his body became tight as he began to touch her in ways he knew would give her pleasure. She shivered but did not pull away. He needed no further encouragement. His lips trailed down the column of her throat to the soft, sensitive flesh just above the swell of her breast. Finally, he laved the pink bud, tantalizing it until it had swollen to its fullest.

Ellenor's head tipped back. A small cry was caught in her throat. Her nails bit into his shoulders as she clutched at him. Then she began to move. With each swirl of his tongue across her nipple, she rubbed herself gently back and forth against his straddled thigh, letting him feel the sultry heat emanating from between her legs.

Cole was so hard, he feared he would burst, but nothing was going to drive him away. Not even the pain of knowing he would never again be able to touch her and know such pleasure. He was going mad with conflicting needs to cease his torture and to extend the experience for as long as possible.

"So soft, so sweet. Never have I wanted another woman more," he murmured, lifting her, pulling her against him, letting her feel all of him.

"Please, Cole," she begged. "Please, I don't know what is happening. Just don't leave me . . . promise me you won't go." And then she planted her lips once again on his.

It was the most incredible kiss Cole had ever experienced. And very few things could have made him break it off, but Ellenor's sweet request was one of them. He released her lips and cradled her to him, pulling her sleeve back over her shoulder. For the rest of his life, when he smelled lavender he would think of her and how it felt to hold an angel in his arms.

He would also remember what it felt like to let her go.

"No, Elle, I can't. That's the one thing I won't do."

Ellenor felt as if she had been pushed into a very deep, very cold loch. She was drowning in misplaced trust. How could she have been so naïve?

Slinking out of his arms, she hugged herself and felt the weight of cold reality flow over her, deadening her body that just seconds ago was more alive than she had thought possible.

Ellenor glanced at him. His face once again looked as if it had been carved out of stone, completely unreadable. *No one*, she told herself, *no one is that devoid of emotion.* Especially after *that* kiss.

It had been magical. Everything a kiss should be. For a few blissful moments, all had been forgotten, the world had drifted away, and it had been just her and him. Then she had asked for more. That was when Cole had retreated to the impenetrable place of protection.

Understanding filled Ellenor and her own expression relaxed into a smile. The only reaction Cole gave was a slight rising of the eyebrows, but it was enough. Enough to confirm what she knew in her heart. He was not indifferent to her. Far from it. He had peeled away the deep parts of her, and she had done the same to him. And it scared him.

Cole had been honest when he had said he needed his hate, and Ellenor wondered if he knew just what it was costing him . . . her . . . them. And suddenly it didn't matter.

A week ago, she had wanted to run away from all men. She had not realized at the time avoidance would give her no solace. He had made her feel whole again. With Cole, she was no longer afraid of her future, her past, or the possibility she had changed so much, she was no longer herself. Cole had given her that gift and she had fallen in love with him. And based on what they had just shared, Cole felt something, maybe not love, but something for her. He just hadn't been ready. *Well, prepare yourself, Highlander, for I am not about to let you go.*

Ellenor leaned into Cole and gave him a peck on the cheek. "Thank you. Now I know."

Cole pulled back and crossed his arms. Ellenor walked over to her things, trying to move and act as casually as possible. As she had hoped, it piqued his interest. "Know what?"

The question had not been loud, but clipped. Her reaction was rattling him, just as she had intended.

Ellenor swallowed and convinced herself it was all

or nothing. For if she didn't try, she would lose him anyway. "That kiss," she said, tossing the few items scattered on the ground into her bag. "I know you promised I would not have to marry, but we both know that unless I am being imprisoned or made a slave, eventually I will have to face the possibility. Now I can," she said with a shrug of her shoulders, rising. "And I can even look forward to it. I'm not the same person you met just a few days ago. I had forgotten who I was. Now I remember."

"And just who are you?" Cole demanded, his voice lower, softer, and darker.

"I'm not someone who will waste my time pining after a man who doesn't want me. I'm obviously attracted to you, but I want a man who would fight heaven and hell before walking out of my arms, just as I would do for him."

Ellenor tossed the bag over her shoulder, turned, and began to head back toward camp. *And that is just what I am doing*, she whispered to herself. *Fighting hell for you.*

Chapter 7

Cole watched Ellenor run into Laurel's expectant arms, evidence of his latest blunder. There was not an inkling of surprise in Ellenor's demeanor. Just the opposite. The moment they came through the gatehouse, she began searching the courtyard, her expression one of eager delight. Not until then did it dawn on him that Ellenor knew exactly who had sent for her. She had certainly dropped enough clues. Her behavior had been eerily calm and there was a surprising scarcity of questions for someone in her supposed ignorant position. Unfortunately, his mind had been too preoccupied on their kiss and her parting comment to notice any of the signs.

He should have turned around, gathered his men, and left the second he realized Ellenor was more than happy being reunited with Laurel. Instead, he found himself stealing a final few minutes to watch her.

The two women hugged, pulled slightly away, smiled, and then hugged again. Then they started chatting. Ellenor pointed at Laurel's protruding stomach, and Laurel fingered Ellenor's hair, indicating that it was now much shorter than it once was. The two laughed and went on for several minutes. They had obviously been very close, and time had done nothing to dampen their friendship.

For once, Laurel did not outshine the woman next to her. His sister-in-law's classic features of long blond curly hair and blue-green eyes were nothing compared to Ellenor and her wild beauty. Maybe it was because Laurel was large with child, but Cole suspected he would always prefer Ellenor's tawny looks, athletic frame, and curvaceous figure.

A sudden rush of unexpected envy washed over him. Laurel would be the one Ellenor would turn to now, not him. And in the future it would be someone else. A husband. The thought was almost unbearable and the need to leave immediately rose again to the surface.

He was just about to head out when Laurel waved at him to come over. Cole grimaced, took a deep breath, and nodded. He swung his leg over his mount's massive hind end and hopped down. He threw his reins to Jaime and pointed to the waiting stable master before making his way across the yard.

Ellenor met him halfway, and before he could say a word, she frowned and lightly nudged his shoulder. "Stop scowling," she hissed under her breath. "Laurel will think you are upset with her."

Cole cocked an eyebrow in surprise, knowing Laurel would be more shocked if he *wasn't* scowling. "*I'm* practically grinning, *abarach*," he replied. Seconds later, he produced a genuine smile seeing her reaction. Ellenor hated being called bold, especially because she thought he meant it as an insult. In reality, he liked her audacity, but he would never tell her so. "*Your* scowl, however, could scare the most impudent of recruits."

Ellenor's jaw dropped in preparation for a scathing response, but Laurel chimed in before she could utter the unladylike phrase. "My, Ellenor, what have you done to our Cole to make him give you such high compliments?"

Ellenor swiveled to correct her friend, but she was quickly silenced by Laurel's wink.

Laurel reached out and grabbed Cole's forearm, entwined it with her own, and began to walk toward the massive tower at the far end of the yard. Ellenor fell in step, her eyes not on their destination, but on Cole.

"I take it Conor is not here," Cole said coolly. "Is he just out for the afternoon or has he yet to return from Fàire Creachann?"

Laurel shook her head. "He is still north, and therefore I must ask you to stay. With Conor gone, I need help. Your brothers, Craig and Crevan, are away at Laird Schellden's, and Clyde has gone south for training, leaving just you."

"What about Conan?" Cole demanded and immediately felt a sharp prod in his back from Ellenor. "I mean, he's here, isn't he? Can he not assist you until Conor returns?" he asked more softly, suddenly comprehending what had just occurred. Without a word, Ellenor had told him to correct his tone and he had surprisingly complied.

"He's here," Laurel sighed, "but Father Lanaghly just returned with a new set of maps, so pulling your brother away from his studies would be near impossible. Besides, I had assumed you would *want* to stay until Conor returned with news." Laurel shifted to face Ellenor. "That is why I am so glad you are here. First, I have missed you enormously, but mostly I can use your assistance until I no longer have to waddle around here like a fat bird begging to be on someone's dinner plate. And since you get along with Cole so well, it only makes sense he stay and help."

Ellenor's jaw visibly dropped. Cole twitched with the

realization Ellenor was in even more shock hearing
Laurel's request than he was. Whatever the two women
had discussed, it had not included a plea to make him stay.

Laurel unconsciously rubbed her protruding stomach, and images of Ellenor, large and beautiful with
his child, flooded Cole's mind. He imagined her curled
up in front of the fireplace in his room, her hair dish-
eveled and wild across his chest as she slept in his arms.
In his mind's eye, he was whole . . . he was happy. He
was in love.

In reality, he was a fool.

His feelings for Ellenor had been building, not dimin-
ishing as he had hoped. He should have realized emotions this powerful never dissipated. He loved Ellenor,
but he would not make her happy. Not in the end. She
needed someone whole, someone who lived for her and
not for a ghost.

Cole abruptly stopped in the courtyard, capturing
the attention of both women, who had continued to
chatter away. "Lady Ellenor, I suspect we will see each
other later. Lady Laurel," he began ominously, "you
and I have much to discuss about what constitutes a
treasured item and any future attempts to have me run
your errands. Until then, if I am to stay, there are things
to which I must attend." And with a nod he pivoted,
and headed toward the stables.

Laurel waited until Cole was out of sight and then
turned her enormous sea green eyes to Ellenor. She
sent a quick, playful elbow into her friend's side and
asked in wonderment, "Good Lord, what have you done
to him?"

Ellenor's brows shot up. "*Him?* Nothing. It's not possible to do anything to him. You have one large rock for

a brother-in-law," Ellenor snapped and crossed her arms. "And that '*Lady Ellenor*' he so casually dropped was the *first* time he has ever used my name."

Laurel gave Ellenor a look of blatant disbelief and restarted their trek toward the tower. "No need to pretend. I know you like him. He likes you, too, by the way. A lot. And as for him calling you 'Lady Ellenor' . . . well, you will have to search your heart for another reason because he holds no ceremony with me. It was not I who prompted the gentlemanlike remark, I assure you."

"*Gentlemanlike?*" Ellenor choked out. "For days he said that I smelled or told me I was brazen . . ."

"I'm sure you did smell, and unless you are a completely different person than the one I once knew, you *can* be surprisingly bold."

"But to be called names like *babag* and *abarach*?"

Laurel cast Ellenor a sideways glance. "And as your sweet docile nature is still firmly in place, I am guessing you never once called him a name or two, however appropriate."

That got Ellenor to pause as she remembered two of her favorites, Elmer and Scot. She was just about to admit to it when she realized the enormity of the tower in front of her. "Good Lord, how many stories is it? And please tell me my room is not on the top floor," she murmured as her eyes journeyed down and then back up the stacked stones stretching into the sky.

"There are seven stories and I thought the same thing when I first saw the Star Tower," Laurel laughed, remembering her own awe upon entering the courtyard. The tower's battlements were still one of her favorite places to go, especially on a clear night. "It is where Conor and I sleep. You'll be staying in the North Tower." She pointed to the large round structure anchoring the other end of the curtain wall. "The only one who bunks in there right now is Conan, but he mainly stays up on the top floors amidst his books and maps."

Ellenor took a moment to look around. She had been so focused on Laurel she had not taken in the castle's size. Six round towers supporting a sizable curtain wall formed a large D-shaped inner yard. Two at the ends of the straight ravine wall, two at the bends, and two on either side of the guard gate that was further fortified by a single well-sized barbican. Along each wall were several buildings, some Ellenor recognized from their size as the Lower Hall and Great Hall, stables and chapel. Others were not as obvious, but definitely in use as people shuffled in and out of them. All of them were aware of Laurel's presence, looking in her direction with expressions of curiosity about the identity of the newcomer.

One man stood out more than the rest. He had curly ginger hair and a beard that was several shades darker. He was not short, but neither was he overly tall. His shoulders were extremely broad, giving him a somewhat squat appearance. On the surface, his size and portly status made him appear out of place, but he walked as if he ruled all those he saw.

Laurel waved her hand at the grim-faced Highlander. The man returned the gesture before disappearing into a small building. "That's Fallon, our steward. I will introduce you to him later. He can be a little disagreeable, but if you can handle Cole, you will have no problems with him or Fiona."

Ellenor's brows shot up. "Fiona?"

"Our cook," Laurel said with a sigh and proceeded toward the Star Tower's large arched-shaped doorway. "She's the best in the Highlands, but oh, what we have to endure to have good food. Let's talk where it is more comfortable."

Laurel leaned into the large bog oak door and stepped inside the portico. It was empty. She headed to a corkscrew staircase and began to climb, using a thick rope as support. Ellenor followed, noticing that the burst of energy Laurel had exhibited earlier was beginning to wane. "I think you should lie down."

"Aye, I should, but don't you dare let anyone know I admitted such a thing," Laurel huffed and rounded the fourth story. "Here we are."

Ellenor trailed Laurel around a narrow hallway and into a large bedchamber of muted golds and greens. Three arched windows overlooking a deep ravine provided ample light to showcase the room's splendor. A small fire had been lit, making the air feel warm and welcoming, encouraging those who entered to sit down and relax. Just to the hearth's side was a large wooden tub with steam rising from it.

Ellenor gasped in delight as Laurel nudged her toward the warm slice of heaven. "As soon as the sentry returned with word of your impending arrival, I had a bath drawn for you and pulled out a few gowns in case you would like to change. Don't worry. These don't belong to anyone. I had a suspicion Gilda wouldn't burden you with many personal things and you might need some new clothes. So I had a couple of things made for you based on my memory and my old figure, so I hope they fit. If not, my friend Brighid is a genius with a needle."

Ellenor fingered the deep burgundy and gold bliaut and soft new chemise. It had been a long time since she had had such nice things. Brushing off a tear, she mouthed the words "thank you" and hugged her friend again.

Minutes later, Ellenor sank into the hot water and felt

the weight she had been carrying temporarily lift from her shoulders. The calm lingered about her as if she had not a worry in the world. Then Laurel scolded her stomach, telling it to stop hitting her. The silly comment was a soft reminder that much had changed in the past four years. "Tell me everything, Laurel. I feel like my life has been in a strange state of suspension and I have only just realized it. How did you come to live in the Highlands, fall in love, and be with child?"

"Be with child?" Laurel chuckled. "This will be my *third* child. At least I hope it's only one!"

Ellenor's eyes grew enormous, demanding explanation. Laurel complied, detailing her wild courtship with Conor. She described how they met during her escape from being attacked, how she fell in love with the harsh but bountiful northern country, her children, and the many friends she had made. Throughout it all, Ellenor could hear the love in her friend's voice for her husband. A week ago, a love that strong would have mystified her; now it was something she understood far too well.

Hours passed. The tub was removed and a nice young girl helped Ellenor style her hair for the evening. Throughout it all, she and Laurel talked. Conversation slowed from the flurry of all that had happened to a nice pace about current life and the stresses of being the wife of a chieftain. They had just started discussing the wonders of motherhood when they were interrupted by three short staccato-like taps on the door.

"Come in, Brighid!" Laurel called out, recognizing the distinctive knock. A petite woman with a delicate oval face and almond-shaped brown eyes entered the room. Her unruly brown hair was partially covered by a skewed triangular-shaped piece of off-white linen. The kerchief was tied behind her neck and was barely able to contain the mass of curls beneath it. She didn't wear a bliaut, but a skirt and leine-like shirt. Over them was the McTiernay plaid, belted across her waist with the ends thrown over her shoulder as a shawl. The mass of material should have made her look bulky and weighed down, but somehow, the woman's small figure was still distinguishable.

"I am so sorry it took me so long to get here . . ."

"The babes?" Laurel inquired, hoping her children had not been the cause of her friend's delayed arrival.

Brighid shook her head and turned to close the door. "No, I was with Donald, so this better be good. My husband was being unusually affectionate and he was giving me an earful about the new . . ."

Brighid stopped midsentence as she realized Laurel had company. Her jaw was slack and her expression was a mixture of horror and embarrassment. Ellenor took pity on the woman. She stood up, gave her a friendly smile, and completed her sentence. "The new English wench Cole was tricked into retrieving. You must be Donald's beloved and perfect Brighid."

Brighid's eyes widened further as she assessed the newcomer. "Good Lord, you are pretty. Donald forgot to mention just how—"

"Brighid, this is Ellenor Howell," Laurel interrupted as she waved to Brighid to come in and relax. "She's the childhood playmate I spoke to you about, and Ellenor, meet Brighid, a close friend and, as you have already surmised, Donald's wife."

Ellenor bobbed her head in acknowledgment, inwardly grimacing as she imagined what Donald had said about her and his bruised groin. "Uh . . . I'm very sorry about your husband. He grabbed me and I didn't realize where I was kicking—"

"Sorry! Don't be!" Brighid interrupted, waving her hands for Ellenor to sit back down. "Whatever you did, *please* do it again and regularly! I love that contrary beast enormously, but never has he been quite as open with his compliments as he has been this past hour. In fact, he was quite sore you called for me, Laurel, and I was, too . . . at first. Now, I think I am going to have a much better night for it, so thank you."

Laurel tilted her head. "I accept your thanks and plan to accept Donald's tonight at dinner. I assume he is coming."

"Aye, even if I have to drag him. Aileen and Finn will be there as well." Brighid twisted one of the empty hearth chairs so that she could converse more easily with both women and then fell into it unceremoniously. She wagged her finger at Laurel. "I thought you promised the laird you would rest."

"I am resting so don't hound me and now that Ellenor is here . . ."

Ellenor sat up a little in her chair. "What do you mean, *now that I am here*?"

"Just that you, more than any one here, is well versed in the management of a keep," Laurel explained. Then, in a more serious tone she added, "With Conor gone and this little one growing larger by the day, I am hoping you are going to help Fallon run things until I am able to move about once again."

"I am?" Ellenor quipped. "I mean I would love to help you . . . but won't people think it a little presumptuous to have an Englishwoman—"

"Then find someone else who knows how to run a castle." Laurel sighed, closing her eyes. "This baby is a lot easier to carry than two, but the past couple of weeks it has been a great deal more painful. It kicks my ribs constantly. I can only seem to manage standing up for short periods of time before it hurts too much and I have to lie down."

"Then shouldn't we fetch the midwife . . ."

Laurel waved her hand, dismissing the idea. "No need. Hagatha comes every few days and says it is just the way the babe is positioned. Best thing to do is lie down whenever I can. That is why I need help to run this place."

"Surely there must be someone else. I mean . . . I can't! I'm English and I don't know anyone and—"

"*And* besides me, you are the only one who has ever maintained a keep and managed staff."

"But what about that steward you pointed out?"

A scoff came from Brighid. "Fallon is the best, as is Fiona and all of the McTiernays . . . but they are *McTiernays.*"

"What Brighid means to say is that while they are wonderful and exceptional at their duties, they are stubborn, hardheaded, and will bicker endlessly and get nothing done if there is not someone guiding them to do otherwise."

"But there have to be others . . ."

Laurel shook her head. "Glynis won't be back for a few more weeks until she has finished helping her husband plant the crops, and Aileen is busy with her two babes and the twins."

"Well, what about you?" Ellenor asked Brighid in desperation.

Brighid threw up her hands and leaned back. "I am probably the *worst* choice Laurel could make. I don't have the right temperament, and with Donald home, I have my own cottage to oversee. I've seen what Laurel has to do keeping things running here and it is a full-time job, not to mention it requires dealing with Fallon *and* the laird."

"Conor isn't that bad," Laurel piped in.

"Aye, he is. *And* so is Fallon, not to mention Fiona. So bless you, Ellenor, for not only knowing how to maintain a keep, but being willing to do it."

"There is absolutely no one else?" Ellenor squeaked. A week ago, she had refused to associate with anyone. Running a keep meant meeting, talking, *interacting* with a variety of people—most of them men. She was still adjusting to being around just two or three huge Highlanders, let alone dozens of them. She was not prepared for such a responsibility and promptly said so.

"Don't go scaring her, Brighid. It won't be that bad. It won't be for long. Conor should be home any day and Fallon is a tame housecat compared to Cole. As far as being around people . . . well, you'll manage. I'll ask Cole to help you," Laurel finished with a yawn, unable to fight sleep any longer.

The blood drained out of Ellenor's face. Her mind started racing. How was she going to manage? What was Cole going to say? She muttered his name and then suddenly brightened. She had told Cole she was moving on with her life, and maybe seeing it happen would make him realize what exactly that meant.

Brighid watched Ellenor's expression go from dread to anticipation. She had considered returning to Donald once Laurel fell asleep, but seeing the Englishwoman's dramatic shift in demeanor while whispering the name of the most difficult of McTiernays, Brighid changed her mind. She wanted to know more about this newcomer.

Donald had described Ellenor as difficult and stubborn, troubling the commander more than he could recall any other person ever doing. He also had said they had argued constantly and Cole had actually *lost* some of them.

Brighid suspected she was going to like this Englishwoman.

Cole McTiernay was a complicated man. He never spoke, and when he did, it was clipped and to the point. It had taken almost two years for Brighid to appreciate what Donald found so admirable about his commander. Since then, she had hoped someday Cole would meet someone who could crack his hardened heart and teach him how to let others see the man he truly was. Who would have thought that person would be an Englishwoman? Then again, who else could it have been? Cole lived in the past, and maybe only someone who represented that past could bring him into the present.

Brighid stood up and indicated for Ellenor to follow. Once outside the room, they quietly as possible closed the door and descended the twisting stairs. Just before they reached the bottom, Brighid explained where they were going. "Laurel fights sleep, and I thought it best to leave and talk elsewhere. We could go to the Lower Hall, but at this hour, soldiers will start to come and go . . ."

The thought of dozens of huge men eating and being boisterous sent a wave of panic through Ellenor. She wasn't exactly afraid of men anymore, but neither was she capable of ignoring the instinct to stay away from them either. "If you don't mind, is there somewhere . . . more private?"

Brighid pursed her lips, thinking. After a moment, she murmured to herself, "Why not?" and then turned to Ellenor. "How about the Great Hall? No one should be in there since the laird is away and I know Laurel won't mind. And the laird did say we were to ensure she got her rest . . ." Brighid added, clearly rationalizing the unorthodox suggestion. Then, without waiting for good sense to intervene, she tugged on Ellenor's gown and said, "Come, it's this way."

Ellenor accompanied Brighid across the courtyard, which seemed to be growing more and more crowded as the time came closer to the dinner hour. Most of them enormous men, who by their appearance, were soldiers that had spent the day practicing the art of war. As Brighid predicted, most were mulling around the Lower Hall waiting for food and ale.

Skirting around a cluster of them, Ellenor ignored their strange looks of curiosity and open admiration and silently thanked the Lord none had reached out and physically stopped her. Finally, they reached the Great Hall.

Ellenor entered the cavernous space and stood still in open admiration. Along each of the long walls were generations of detailed tapestries of great battles, people, and the Highlands. She took a step and heard the sound echo in the empty room. A high stone vault, made more elaborate by the addition of ribs, created the ceiling. Underneath the fresh rushes covering the floor was not dirt as she assumed it would be, but wood, indicating that there were rooms beneath. To the left was a sizable fireplace to heat one end of the room, and to the right, along the east far wall, was a canopied fireplace, already lit, with several chairs situated around its heat. Similar to Ellenor's day room, the Hall—despite its size, grand decorations, and current empty state— felt warm and inviting.

Brighid headed for the chairs without hesitation. The ease of her action indicated she had been in this grand room multiple times and truly did feel comfortable being there without the laird's or Laurel's accompany.

Sinking down onto one of the dark cushioned chairs, Brighid waved her finger for Ellenor to do the same.

"Oh, before you do, hand me that, will you?" she asked, pointing at a semifull pitcher of mead.

Ellenor passed it to Brighid, who poured the contents into two wooden drinking cups sitting on a small round table between the hearth chairs. Picking up one of the cups, Ellenor sat down and sipped the sweet honey drink, sighing with pleasure. "After that trip, this is excellent."

Brighid grinned mischievously. "Someday I am going to have to make that trip myself. The most unexpected people come from the south."

Ellenor smiled at the roundabout compliment. "I am glad to know your husband was wrong in his assumptions."

"Wrong?"

Ellenor nodded, kicked off her slippers, and pulled her feet up underneath her. "Mm-hmm. He swore you and I would never get along."

Brighid rolled her eyes. "Donald should've known better. Laurel's half-English."

"My being English was only *part* of it. I hate to admit this, but at the time, I smelled rather awful." Ellenor chuckled. "You will be glad to know your husband considers you a woman of quality who, according to him, would *never* associate with anyone who intentionally refused to bathe, kicked men where they oughtn't, and most especially, pretended to be deranged."

Brighid's eyes flashed with curiosity. "I'm tempted to ask about the kicking, but I think I am better off not knowing. It's hard to imagine a woman besting my husband, and if I knew any more, I might burst out laughing when I saw him next. And you've met my Donald; he wouldn't take too well to that."

Ellenor smiled. "He is very lucky to have married a woman who understands him so well."

"It seems he knows me better than I thought. A woman of quality, eh?"

"I promise you those were his words."

Brighid shook her head in disbelief. "What is almost more unbelievable was how vocal he was in front of you."

Ellenor finished swallowing her mead and waggled a finger back and forth in the air. "Uh, not exactly. To be fair, he was talking to Jaime Ruadh and he had no idea I could understand Gaelic."

"Now *that* makes more sense. Laurel said you could speak our language, but I confess I didn't believe it. Most outsiders consider our tongue too difficult to learn."

Ellenor's brow furrowed in confusion. When not warring, the men and the women who lived on either side of the Scottish border conversed often. Granted it wasn't English or Gaelic, but a form of Scot; nonetheless, each culture had learned to barter with the other. "Surely that is not true. I know my father spoke with several Scottish farmers and—"

"Not in *Gàidhlig*."

"No, but—"

"Ellenor, most *Lowlanders* cannot understand our speech, let alone converse in it. Donald can only speak broken Scot, and I know not one word of it, never having been south of the McTiernay mountains. And yet you speak our language as if you have lived in the Highlands your entire life." Brighid leaned forward and asked, "Are you truly English? Or are we going to find out that you, too, have Highland blood in your veins?"

Ellenor winced at the hope in her voice. "Not a drop in me, I'm afraid."

Brighid took a deep breath and exhaled, openly still skeptical. "Then how did you learn Gaelic? And so well?"

Ellenor shrugged her shoulders. "I don't really know. I used to sneak into the village abbey and listen to all the strange languages being spoken by the visiting clerics. Then one day an abbess caught me spying. She must have realized I had some kind of ability, for instead of throwing me out, she began teaching me what she knew. Now I can speak and write several languages. They just come naturally to me. As for Gaelic, in the village I overheard the smithy speaking to Laurel and the sounds were so different, intriguing . . . well, that is how we met."

"*Several* languages, you say," Brighid murmured, tapping her finger on the edge of the cup. "Conan will be quite envious."

Not understanding Brighid's inference, Ellenor shook her head and said, "Unfortunately, understanding your language is one thing. Knowing your customs is quite another."

"I wouldn't worry about that as much." Brighid reached up and pulled the kertch off her head. She shook her brown curls free and tossed the white fabric onto the nearby table. "See that? It's a custom that married women wear those things. Some love them, claiming it keeps their hair out of their eyes, but I find them binding and uncomfortable."

"Then why do you wear it?"

"Thanks to Laurel and her willingness to defy certain customs, I usually don't. I did today because, as you might have guessed, Donald is somewhat of a traditionalist and I wanted to make him happy on his first day back. Tomorrow, I will return to making *me* happy and enduring his grunts of disapproval."

Ellenor's smile widened and she tipped her head

back. "Laurel disavowing customs. That sounds like her. My older sister, who is much closer to her in age than I, considered Laurel thoughtless with her rebellious ways and hated the fact that I'd rather be with Laurel than her. What can I say? She knew how to have fun. Gilda still doesn't."

"Oh, really," Brighid said, her eyes sparkling with interest. She propped her elbow on the edge of the side table and rested her chin on her palm. "Do tell. For it is hard to imagine our Lady of the Castle not perfect at anything."

"Well, she has always been a good mistress and she taught me much of what I know. My sister—"

"No, no, no," Brighid interrupted. "I want to hear about Laurel's wild and unladylike days."

Ellenor bit her bottom lip. "Hmm, well, you know that she hunts."

"Aye."

"And has a serious love of knives."

"I know that she can throw them."

"Fine. Then how about midnight swims. In the nude."

Brighid's jaw dropped and Ellenor began relaying stories of their midnight rendezvous. Soon, Brighid couldn't control her laughter. "Oh, tell me more!"

After a while, both were sharing outrageous escapades from their childhood and they found themselves laughing so hard their stomachs hurt.

"Oh, how is it that we have only just met, but it feels like we have been friends forever." Brighid sighed, holding her ribs as the laughing pains subsided. "I never would have believed to have so much in common with a noble who grew up in England."

Ellenor took a deep breath and wiped away a happy tear. "Ah, I think Laurel and I are English oddities. Many titled women are like my sister, unfortunately. It's a shame really. I cannot recall Gilda ever once giving way to hysterics as we just did. She will probably die never knowing how good it feels."

"Meeting you is going to make it all the more difficult to leave this place."

"Leave?" Ellenor sputtered, sitting straight up and looking her new friend in the eye. "What do you mean? Why would you be leaving your home?"

"A few years ago, Donald and Cole fought together and have been close ever since. The McTiernays are a well-known clan in the Highlands and also a very large one. The laird's army is substantial, but in the past few years, several men, including Donald, have chosen to follow Cole. As a result, Cole feels responsible for the families and wives of his men."

"Wives like you."

Brighid nodded. "And children, sometimes parents and brothers, and such. Cole has not yet erected himself a permanent home, but if Donald's right and Cole becomes a chieftain . . . have you heard about that?"

"I have and he will."

The solemnity of Ellenor's answer caused Brighid to momentarily pause and reassess her new friend before continuing. "Uh, well, then many families will be relocating. Part of me is thankful to see my husband more often than pockets of time, but it does mean leaving all that I have known . . . and new friends," she added, stretching out her hand.

Ellenor reached out, clasped Brighid's fingers, and was about to echo her sadness, when the Hall's doors swung open and a serious stout man Ellenor recognized as the steward entered. He took two steps before stopping to fiddle with his gray and red beard and stare at her with scrutiny. Ellenor felt as if she were a semiplump pheasant being visually plucked and found to be unsatisfactory.

Instinct took over. She let Brighid's hand go, rose smoothly to a standing position, and clasped her hands together in a relaxed, but authoritative way. Behind her, Brighid whistled softly, "Good Lord, it's like watching Laurel."

Fallon renewed his march. He stopped directly in front of her, gave a curt nod, and then said "Milady" as if it created an ill taste in his mouth.

Ellenor arched a single brow and said, "What can I do for you, steward?"

Fallon blinked twice. The woman spoke Gaelic and she knew who he was. He had not been prepared for either. He had also not been prepared for her reaction to his assertive entrance. He had witnessed the woman's unmannered arrival this afternoon, and seeing her jump off a horse and run into her ladyship's embrace, he had assumed her unknowledgeable about decorum and proper behavior.

For the past hour, he had been avoiding the newcomer, waiting for Laurel to awaken and make some last-minute decisions about the night's event. He had planned to retire before ever having to say a word of false welcome. But when he finally had met with Laurel, she had refused to answer his questions. Instead, she had directed them all to this woman. He didn't like dealing with outsiders, and after four years of working with a Lady of the Castle who understood her role and performed it superbly, he absolutely dreaded going to a haughty, inexperienced Englishwoman for anything.

Fallon licked his lips and said, "I was directed by her ladyship to seek your counsel on tonight's meal."

Ellenor heard Brighid suck in her breath and fought the urge to turn around and tell her to hush. Knowing that Brighid would not be able to curtail any further gasps, Ellenor pointed to the doors and proceeded toward them, indicating Fallon to join her. "I think it might be better if we spoke outside."

Fallon nodded almost imperceptibly, and before turning to follow Ellenor out, he gave Brighid a long hard stare that only caused her to erupt in a fit of giggles. "Milady," Fallon began as soon as they were outdoors, "Lady Laurel instructed all questions concerning keep activities be directed to you."

Ellenor suddenly wished she hadn't left the Great Hall. She needed a place to sit or at least lean against. Laurel had been serious about having her help out, but Ellenor hadn't thought that meant today. She didn't even know where anything was, how things worked, what kind of help Laurel did and did not want. "I, uh . . . is Laurel unwell?"

"Not that I am aware of, milady. She indicated she would be attending tonight's dinner in the Hall, but you would be helping with final preparations. There is an issue dealing with the birds and the ovens, and an even larger difficulty in getting all who are supposed to be present to attend."

Ellenor took a deep breath and reminded herself that she had been dealing with such problems for years and it mattered little how well she knew these people or their customs. A fowl was a fowl and people were people . . . or so she hoped.

"Let's start with the birds and the ovens. And keep your explanation brief."

Fallon opened his mouth and closed it, shocked. He waited for a few seconds before trying again. This time with more respect. "It's the cook. Fiona," he began. "She refuses to prepare any birds for evening, saying the ones left are rotten and not fit for her kitchen."

"Is she correct?"

"What do you mean?" Fallon asked, throwing his hands up in the air as he always did when frustrated.

Ellenor instinctively jumped back. "I mean is the meat indeed rotten? And if so, what other food can be made ready in time?"

Fallon's thick brows bunched together, forming a fuzzy bridge along his forehead. "How would I know? Fiona's the cook!"

"Then listen to her and ask her to prepare something else for dinner. There has to be something. Tonight is just close friends, correct?"

Fallon nodded, rubbing his scalp.

"Then whatever she prepares shall suffice. Laurel says she is an excellent cook and I am assuming not just at roasting birds. Tomorrow I will inspect the meat myself and . . ." Ellenor paused, realizing that the timing of this problem was just a little too coincidental. From what Brighid and Laurel had insinuated, the famed McTiernay cook had an obsessive need to exert control over her kitchen. "And Fallon, you might also inform Fiona that she and I will meet each morning to discuss the day's meals and identify any problems *before* they occur. I suspect your good cook knew the meat was rotten long before now. For some reason, she wanted to create a different meal, so let her—tonight."

Fallon gasped and his eyes widened to saucer size. "Aye, milady." This time his voice held a distinct level of admiration.

"You mentioned a second problem. Are there really clansmen who are refusing Laurel's request?"

Fallon winced. "I might have overstated that a bit. I should have said *Conan* is refusing to come."

"Who's Conan and what reason did he give?"

"Um, he's one of the laird's younger brothers, and

the reason he gave was that he had more important things to do. I was to leave him alone and have someone bring his meal to him."

"I think I remember Laurel mentioning Conan now. Something about a new set of maps."

"Aye, milady. Father Lanaghly brought them yesterday and the young McTiernay has refused to leave his study ever since."

Again Fallon threw up his hands in aggravation and again Ellenor jumped back just in time. "Let me handle Conan. Could you tell me where he is?"

Fallon pointed to the North Tower. "Top floor. And, milady, Conan and women . . . well . . ." He paused and then shook his head giving up. "Never mind."

Ellenor didn't understand why Fallon had become so nervous, but she couldn't imagine Cole having a brother who would hurt her. "Don't worry about me."

"I'm not. I mean I was, but now that I think about it, it's Conan who should be warned, not you."

Ellenor was about to ask just what he meant when Fallon coughed into his hand and said, "Oh, and there was one last refusal."

"*Another* brother?"

Fallon nodded. "Cole. Same reason Conan gave. Too busy."

Ellenor crossed her arms and closed her eyes. The man had to be the most stubborn creature alive. Cole wanted to leave. Fine. He wanted to be miserable and alone. Again, fine. But until then, she was not going to let him run and hide from her under such weak excuses as being too busy. Even if it was true.

Taking a deep breath, she opened her eyes and smiled warmly at the steward. And as sweetly as possible, she said, "He'll come, Fallon. After you meet with

Fiona, find Cole and explain to him that if he doesn't attend tonight's dinner, all will learn about Elmer."

"Did you say *Elmer*, milady?" Fallon asked, clearly confused.

"That is correct. Elmer. Trust me. He'll come."

The North Tower did not have as many stories as the Star Tower, but the ones it had seemed inordinately taller than most. Pausing by the big oak door hiding the fourth-story room, Ellenor caught her breath and tried to prepare herself for whatever physical or mental affliction Conan must have to cause such consternation among his friends and family.

She gave the thick door a solid knock and waited. Finally, a short and exasperated "Enter" bellowed from the other side.

Ellenor pushed the thick-planked door open and almost stumbled over a stack of papers, scrolls, and boxes filled with more writing and pictures. The room was crammed with stacked chests and boxes, all with various writings in them. "Good Lord, it must have taken years, decades, to collect all this stuff," she muttered aloud.

Bright blue eyes shrouded by a wavy mane of shoulder-length brown hair popped around from one of the corners, quickly glanced her up and down, and with a snort, disappeared again behind a makeshift bookcase.

Ellenor rolled her eyes, wondering if Highlanders thought it was their God-given right to be rude. The man only came into view for a few seconds, but it was clear whatever Laurel, Brighid, and even Fallon had been intimating did not involve a physical impairment.

She skirted around the various sundries and found him alone, bent over a massive workbench studying what looked to be a map. There were several other similar items strewn over the table, each with rock weights to keep them from recurling. "Are you Conan?"

Silence followed. Ellenor shrugged. She knew he was. The dark coloring, blue eyes, and oversized frame all screamed McTiernay. Ink covered his fingertips and the sleeves of his leine were rolled to his elbows. He didn't wear a sword, but she did see one teetering against the stone wall within arm's reach. Like his brother, Conan was enormous and powerfully built, and yet, despite their numerous physical similarities, Ellenor thought Cole a much better looking man. There was something lacking in Conan that Cole had. A type of confidence one gained only with experience.

"I asked you a question."

The dark head snapped up at the light reprimand. His royal blue eyes darkened a tad before narrowing. "I have no need for pretty women with empty heads consuming what little space I have. So unless you can read French, be gone." Immediately he turned and started searching for something in one of the chests.

Ellenor moved over to the bench and peered at the large rendering of what she had been told was the European coastline. Nothing about the map looked any different from the dozen or so she had seen at the abbey. "I cannot see why this is so interesting. It depicts nothing different from any other map, except that it seems a little older. A little more worn perhaps."

"I thought I told you to leave."

"You said anyone who didn't know French should leave," Ellenor corrected.

Conan pivoted and leveled his eyes on her, giving her a long stare. "Women are unable to know such things. Now go, and don't *touch* anything." Then with a quick shake of his head, he dismissed her with a deprecating scoff before adding, "And find Fallon and tell him I'm hungry."

Ellenor stood silent, shocked for several moments. She had just grasped the nature of Conan's problem with the rest of the human race. He was an ass. Sharing that fact with him would be pointless, as he had no doubt been told by numerous others. He didn't care. To him, he was surrounded by ignorance and women were the worst offenders.

Left with few options—walk away, return the insult, or stay and prove him wrong—Ellenor opted for the latter.

Pulling a stool over to the bench, she sat down and scanned the illustration. "This isn't French. It's Latin."

Conan dropped the few things in his hands and moved over to reexamine the document. "Latin?" he asked incredulously. "Are you sure? What does this say?"

Ellenor followed his fingertip to a paragraph above one of the elevated markings and said, "It says *caveant consules.*"

"*Caveant consules,*" Conan repeated. "What the hell is that supposed to mean?"

Ellenor swallowed her chuckle but could not hide her grin. She had suddenly gone from being a brainless female to a fellow man, where swearing in front of each other was not only done, but expected. "It means 'Consuls beware.' The Roman Consuls were—"

Conan cut her off with the wave of his hand. "I know. I know. Roman officials. This map is old, but it certainly does not date back to when Roman consuls were in power. So why would someone write *that* on a map and here?"

Ellenor shrugged her shoulders. "Who knows? Maybe they were raiders who attacked wealthy travelers in the area. Maybe it was just a dangerous journey. Maybe the map was a re-creation of an older one when there *were* Roman consuls. There could be dozens of reasons."

Conan grimaced and leaned over another drawing right beside the one he had been studying. "Is this Latin? It looks French."

Ellenor moved closer, but made sure they did not come into contact. "Uh-uh. It's Latin as well. The languages can be confusing as some words are very similar such as this one—*abundans*—is very similar to the French word, *abondants*. But this word here clearly makes this phrase Latin. In French, the word approach is *approche*, but you can see this is *accedo*. Definitely Latin. Basically, it's telling the reader to approach this reef with care. I assume it is shallow."

"Fascinating," Conan mumbled, sinking into a nearby chair. "Latin, huh? No wonder I have had trouble translating these damn things." He rubbed his scalp and reassessed the unfamiliar woman who had entered his private domain. "Just what other languages do you know? How did you learn them? And *who* are you, by the way?"

Ellenor's light laughter filled the room and Conan found himself intrigued by the mysterious beauty. "I am Laurel's friend from England."

Conan's mouth opened slightly and he bobbed his head in memory. "The one she tricked Cole into fetching?"

"The one. My name is Ellenor."

Conan whistled. "She didn't say you knew our tongue." *Hell*, he thought to himself, *our Laurel didn't mention several things about the Englishwoman, including how beautiful she was or how intelligent.* "How many languages do you know anyway?"

"Only a few both spoken and written."

"And *Gàidhlig*?"

"I can only speak Gaelic as I have never seen it scribed."

That knowledge restored a little bit of Conan's pride and he felt himself breathing easier around her. Until today, he had never encountered anyone who was possibly smarter than he was. Even more disconcerting was that the person was a woman. Women were supposed to be docile and weak, requiring support and nurturing. They needed men, and men needed offspring. That was how it worked, or at least mostly. Laurel was definitely an exception to that rule and it seemed the second Englishwoman he had ever encountered was one as well.

"Anything else you know? Mathematics, science, or are you like Laurel, a hellion with a knife and bow."

"Nothing like that, I assure you. My passions are few and they do include reading. I was fortunate my father didn't mind and allowed me to converse with several travelers when I was young." Ellenor pointed at the door with her thumb. "I think it is time you and I made our way to the Hall. Your lady requests your presence for dinner and I promised Fallon you would be there. So unless you want to tell Laurel that her pretty, empty head is not worthy of your undeniably important task of interpreting a map, then we better leave."

Conan's jaw dropped, but no quick retort came out. He finally shook his head in disbelief and followed her out the door and down the stairwell. "If only I had known you would be a scholar *and* had the power to tame Fallon, I would have leaped at the chance to bring you back. I almost feel ashamed of knowing you were forced to travel with my brother."

Ellenor couldn't help herself and laughed out loud. Smooth, this young Highlander was not. "Cole was quite the honorable gentleman."

"Honorable I believe," Conan smirked, stepping out of the tower and into the inner yard. He looked up. Dark clouds were on the horizon. The wind was starting to pick up, indicating another storm would arrive some time that night. "Heroic maybe, but gentleman? Ha! I don't think Cole has ever behaved in a courteous, gallant, or any other 'gentlemanlike' manner to a single woman. And you're English!"

Ellenor stopped to turn around. Long dark gold strands of her hair swirled around her face but she ignored them. Her dark green eyes pierced his blue ones and she said, "Cole is . . . who he is, but he was actually very helpful and I will always be grateful that he came for me. He understands people better than most realize."

A flicker of desire stirred inside Conan. Ellenor was proving herself a truly exceptional woman. Someone who could look past all of Cole's harsh qualities, and admire the traits that truly made a man what he was, was a very rare find. Anyone who could do that *and* read several languages was someone to pursue. "Be careful, Lady Ellenor, or I just might ask for your hand in marriage."

Ellenor turned and started once again toward the Hall. She tried to suppress her laughter, but couldn't. It finally erupted and its infectious sound caused Conan to join her and all those in earshot to smile.

All but one.

Chapter 8

Cole had just returned from seeing his men and was dismounting by the stables when he spied the happy couple leave the North Tower and move toward the Great Hall entrance. Jealousy, white-hot and savage, raced over every nerve. His body tensed with possessive anger, made only stronger knowing he had no right to feel that way. Still, no stab wound had ever hurt quite as much as seeing another man desire Ellenor.

Conan, who treated all women with disdain, was practically falling all over himself. He was like a lost puppy dog, lapping up whatever crumbs she left behind. And who could blame him. Ellenor was stunning.

Dressed no longer in the worn brown bliaut, Ellenor wore a deep crimson gown. The sleeves were gathered at the elbow with gold thread that matched the embroidery around the hems. The rich jewel-colored garment was simple, elegant, and with her long hair being tousled by the breeze, she looked like an angel sent from the heavens. Tonight's dinner was going to be a more painful experience than he had anticipated.

He needed a drink first.

Throwing his reins to the stable boy, Cole stomped

toward the Lower Hall, intending to join Jaime in a few swallows of ale before succumbing to the inevitable. Fate, however, had other plans.

Laurel stepped into the inner yard and spied him before he was even halfway to his target. She shot him a questioning look as if she knew where he was going and intended to intercede. With one hand, she captured her hair to keep it from blowing in the wind, and with the other, took his arm for support. "I am glad you returned for dinner tonight. I had thought you might try to avoid the gathering."

Cole bit his tongue. That had been exactly what he had planned to do. He had promised to stay until Conor returned, but that hadn't meant sharing evening meals and being constantly available to Laurel's whims. Laurel had servants for that. Then Fallon came with his message from Ellenor. It had been brief and in the form of an ultimatum. *Come or I will embarrass you.* The woman had no idea whom she was challenging.

"I'm here tonight, but don't expect this to happen again."

Laurel's blue-green eyes popped open wide to enhance the look of innocence. "I can promise you, Cole, I do not. I am just glad you came this evening. It means a lot to me, and I am sure Ellenor will appreciate your presence as well."

Cole grunted, pushed the doors to the Great Hall open, and waited for Laurel to enter. They were the last ones to arrive and join the small party. Cole immediately felt out of place in the warm and friendly environment.

Finn, Conor's commander, who had also been in the training fields, had arrived just moments before. He was kissing his wife, Aileen, hello when Laurel spied them and moved to the side of her best friend and confidante. Finn was soon shooed away by the two women and gladly joined Donald, who Cole guessed was in forced attendance because of his wife, Brighid. The bubbly petite woman, who somehow had caught Donald's eye, typically preferred Laurel's company. Tonight, however, she was standing by the large canopied hearth with Ellenor and his brother Conan. They were all giggling over something.

The happy scene was almost perfect. Only his presence marred the room's social climate. Then Conan, with all the casualness of a Highland cow, stretched and attempted to put his arm around Ellenor's shoulders.

Cole's world, which was spiraling down a deep pit of torture, suddenly righted itself again.

At the first touch, Ellenor leaped and spun around, almost toppling into Brighid. Cole had no idea how Ellenor would have justified her reaction if he hadn't been there, for the moment she regained her balance, her green eyes latched on to his and in one graceful movement began walking toward him as if he was the cause of her bizarre conduct.

"Cole! You came!" she called out in sincere relief and seconds later embraced him in front of everyone.

The feel of her warm body pressed against him sent shock waves of possession and need through his veins. His arms moved of their own accord, encircling her, holding her close. Her sweet scent drifted all around him, binding him to her, reminding him of the smoldering passion waiting to be ignited with a single kiss. "Aye, Elle, I came," he whispered into her hair, his voice raspy with need. The desire he had tried so hard to suppress heated his blood to nearly uncontrollable levels.

Ellenor pulled back slightly but not enough to break his hold and looked up, smiling. Cole doubted anything could have disarmed him more than the soft, loving curve touching her lips. And he was the cause. Whatever tactics she might have used to persuade him to come this evening, Ellenor did truly want him here. With her.

Taking her hand, he escorted her back to the main table, sat her beside Brighid, and then moved to where Finn and Donald were pulling up chairs to settle down and eat. Conversations had continued, but none reflected the topic on everyone's mind.

All had witnessed Ellenor's flight into Cole's embrace. Even more, they had seen his welcoming response, and none knew what to think. Women just didn't venture near Cole. They certainly didn't display affection, and they absolutely did not seek reassurance from him. He never offered comfort . . . to anyone. That he did just now was more than enough proof that Cole had deep feelings for the young Englishwoman and she for him. The question was, what were they going to do about it?

Everyone settled down at the table and began to eat. Ellenor was introduced to the few guests she had not met. Typical questions arose from her knowing Gaelic to how she and Laurel became friends, but not a soul broached the topic of her and Cole. But as soon as discussions broke off into smaller groups, Brighid finally could hold her tongue no longer. "You and Cole seem to get along pretty well."

Ellenor swallowed some mead and considered her answer. She shrugged, hoping it came off relaxed and indifferent. "Sometimes."

Brighid picked up a piece of meat and popped it in her mouth, eyeing her new friend. "Uh, *sometimes* is not what I saw a little while ago. In fact, I would go so far as to say it was—"

"Friendship," Ellenor declared, interrupting. "What you saw was simply friendship." She then turned her attention to the food on the table and tried changing the subject. "I know now why Fiona didn't want fowl. She needs the grease and lard from the pig for her cooking. All she had to do was say so."

Brighid shook her head. "Whatever are you talking about? Wait, no, on the other hand, I don't want to know." She lowered her voice and said, "Cole, Ellenor. That is what we were discussing and don't switch the topic again. What is going on between you two? I didn't think it possible for him to be so . . ."

"What? Understanding? I think a lot of people don't realize just how much Cole sees and how much he cares about what is going on in their lives."

"Are we still talking about Cole? The one who believes his sole appointment in life is to train soldiers and fight the English—and by the way you *are* English."

"As everyone keeps reminding me. But I find it interesting that the subject only comes up whenever Cole and I are mentioned in the same sentence," Ellenor quipped and then bit down on a piece of bread soaked in gravy. She moaned. Fiona might be one crabby soul, but the woman *could* cook.

Brighid clucked her tongue, unwilling to concede defeat. "Jest all you want, but I saw the look of happiness on your face when you were hugging him, and I also got a good look at the one on his."

"Happy to see a friend?" Ellenor piped in, hoping if she persisted with the light banter, Brighid would drop the subject and let things be.

"Uh, no. More like a man who wished all of us had disappeared and he had this room *and* you all to himself."

Ellenor looked around and confirmed no one could hear their conversation. Aileen and Laurel were laughing practically nonstop and Finn, Donald, and Conan were speaking so loud and clanking mugs, daggers, and whatever else was in their hands so often, one would have thought a huge party was taking place and not a small dinner gathering. Cole was participating as well, but just as her gaze kept stealing toward his, his blue eyes kept finding their way to her.

Brighid yanked Ellenor's arm and got her attention. "Listen, Ellenor, I mean it. Cole is, well, like family and he's Donald's commander and probably going to be my laird very shortly. I want to know what exactly happened between you two. Did he? I mean, did you?"

Ellenor reclaimed her arm and hissed, "Of course not!"

Brighid stared in disbelief and was about to argue when full comprehension dawned on her. "But you wished he had. Good Lord, you are in love with him!"

Ellenor stood up abruptly, smiled at the group, and grabbed Brighid's forearm, tugging her off the stool. "I'm cold. Let's talk over by the fire."

No one, except Cole, paid them any attention. She saw a brief look of concern and sent him a quick smile before focusing on Brighid, who was not being deterred. "You are in love with him! You wouldn't have dragged me all the way over here unless it was true. And he loves you!" Brighid reached over and crushed Ellenor in her arms. "I can't tell you how relieved I am. I mean, you and I, whatever happens, we'll know that there is at least one good friend nearby to—"

Ellenor pulled free. "You are both right and wrong. I do love Cole, but he *doesn't* love me."

Brighid waved her finger toward the entrance. "I don't believe you. I saw him return that embrace."

Ellenor looked at Cole, who was staring at the two of them. Again, she tossed him a brief smile and snatched Brighid's wagging finger. "Lord, you are obvious."

"Me!" Brighid retorted, freeing her finger, only to

point it at herself. "I wasn't the one who threw herself at one of the most emotionally distant men the world has ever created."

Ellenor rolled her eyes and plopped into one of the hearth chairs, dropping her head into her hands. "I know, but what am I supposed to do?"

Brighid sank into the chair next to her and said, "That man responded—no, he *welcomed*—you. He is starving for what you have to give him. How could he not be in love?"

"Simple. I asked him to stay and he refused. He wants to leave, never see me again, and forget I ever existed. And he's going to, as soon as Laurel's husband returns."

"And you are going to just let him?"

"I wasn't going to," Ellenor bristled. "I had planned to find a way to make him stay, but then Laurel did that for me this morning. And my next plan will never work. I can't do it."

"Do what?"

Ellenor toyed with the deep blue fabric covering the chair's arm. "I had thought to make Cole jealous. Make him realize that if he didn't want me, others would. But you saw how ridiculous that is. Conan barely touched me and I went flying across the room making an idiot of myself. The only person here who is jealous is me, and not of another woman, but of a dead man whom Cole holds more dear than a future with me. There. I've said it. Now you know."

Brighid's rich brown eyes went very large. She slumped back in her chair and muttered, "Oh, my. I don't know what to say other than Cole has an even colder heart than I thought."

Ellenor shook her head and stared into the hearth. Only two of the three pits were lit and the dark shadows in the empty niche echoed what she felt inside. "You're wrong. Cole feels things deeply. He just doesn't want anyone to know. He uses his code of honor to mask his reasons for keeping himself apart."

"I hope he knows what it is costing him."

Ellenor's gaze floated to Cole across the room. He was talking and the corners of his mouth were turned up as if he was smiling, but when he glanced her way, she could tell his laughter had not reached his eyes. They were a deep startling blue, but they were not dancing as she had seen them do with her.

The doors suddenly burst open and a cool wind swept through the room. All rose to their feet just as a large, burly man with scraggly auburn hair and matching beard entered the room. Laurel cried out, "Hamish! Is Conor here?"

Ellenor watched the Highland giant gently squeeze Laurel hello and shake his head. "He did send me with news, which is why I made my way here when the stable master said you, Finn, and Cole were gathered inside."

Cole stepped forward. His expression was blank, with the exception of his eyes. Tension swam in their piercing gaze. Hamish grabbed Cole's extended forearm and said, "Talks continue, but Conor wanted me to ride back and ensure Laurel was in good health. I am to tell you he will return in a week's time with word."

Ellenor didn't hide her bafflement. "They *still* haven't made a decision!" Her harsh whisper echoed throughout the room.

Hamish's gaze moved to Ellenor in perplexed wonder. He glanced at Cole and then at Laurel and back to the mysterious woman who was defending Cole.

Laurel took pity on the soldier and patted his arm. "Hamish, this is Ellenor Howell, an old friend."

Ellenor curtsied, giving Hamish an excellent view of her cleavage. He swallowed and tried to act unaffected by the surprising beauty in his laird's Great Hall. "It is a difficult decision, one in which everyone feels very strongly. However, the laird is making progress. He must be or he wouldn't have sent me here to give you word." He spoke the words to Cole, but his eyes never left Ellenor's.

"I take it then you haven't been a part of the talks," Cole surmised, his voice level and calm, belying the true depth of what he was feeling. Only his white knuckles gave him away.

Hamish finally wrenched his gaze free. "Very little, and I cannot tell you which way the group is leaning, Cole, but the laird wanted me to assure you that it will not be much longer. That is all I know."

Laurel let go a deep sigh the whole room was holding. She grabbed Hamish's arm and said, "Please join us. You must be famished after such a ride and the weather is beginning to act foul again."

"I might grab a side of meat, but then I must see to a few things before I return."

"You aren't leaving to go back in this weather, are you?" Aileen asked, moving to stand by Laurel.

"Nay, I'll go in the morning, leaving me just enough time to reunite with a certain someone and say hello," he said with a wink.

Brighid leaned over and whispered into Ellenor's ear, "I didn't know Hamish was seeing anyone. Did you?"

Ellenor rolled her eyes and elbowed Brighid lightly in the ribs. "How would I know? I don't even know who he is."

Hamish marched toward the table and wrenched a hind leg free from its hinge. Just as he did, his gaze fell upon Ellenor and his bushy brows furrowed. "I don't think we know each other, lass. You are far too beautiful for me to be forgetting such an encounter."

He dropped the leg, brushed his hand on his kilt, and walked toward her with what Ellenor guessed was supposed to be an enticing swagger. It was almost comical. "Really?" Ellenor retorted.

Out of the corner of her eye, she saw Cole inch his way toward her. He may deny wanting her, but the fact was he did. And the look on Cole's face indicated he was about to prove it to everyone present . . . violently. Jealousy was one thing, but not if in the end it caused him to leave and not return.

Turning back to Hamish, Ellenor said impishly, "Maybe we can meet another time . . . when you don't have to *reunite with a certain someone*." She ended with a lopsided grin.

Instantly, Cole stopped his forward movement and visibly began to thaw. Ellenor almost thought she saw a genuine smile begin to cross his face, but just before it truly appeared, it vanished again.

Conan began to half-cough, half-cackle into his fist. Finn pounded him on the back as he tried to swallow his own mirth. Laurel, Aileen, and Brighid didn't even try to hold back their laughter as they erupted into giggles. Even Hamish broke into infectious howls, causing Ellenor to join him.

Laurel finally caught her voice and explained, "Hamish, I should have warned you about Ellenor. She is a friend of mine from England who has agreed to come and stay with us. As you can see, she is delightful and has a keen wit and unusual grasp of our language."

Hamish surveyed Ellenor appreciatively. His thick red-brown beard parted as an enormous grin appeared across his face. "Ah, lass, if only you and me had more time. When I return, maybe it will be *you* I will seek to be with."

Laurel witnessed the sudden flash of hatred in Cole's

eyes at the same time Ellenor did. With a hard smack of her hands, she got the room's attention. "Thank you all for coming this evening and welcoming Ellenor into the McTiernay clan. Thank you, too, Ellenor, for helping me stage this small party. We all are blessed with your willingness to help me until this babe is born. Unfortunately, I must leave this gathering now before I fall asleep most ungraciously, leaving you men to carry me back to my room."

"Not me!" Finn cried out, laughing. "Last time a man carried you to the bedroom, the laird suddenly appeared and the poor wretch almost died."

Laurel rolled her eyes. "And thank *you*, Finn, for that wonderful reminder. Conan, for right now, I am putting Ellenor in the North Tower and would ask that you stay in either the West or East Towers for the time being."

Conan nodded in agreement and said with a mischievous smile, "Ellenor can have my room. It has been tended and—"

"She'll stay in my old room." The announcement had come from Cole. His voice had been level and without inflection, which somehow left the feeling it was not to be questioned.

Laurel clucked her tongue and said, "Well, then I guess that is settled. Conan, would you mind escorting me to my room, and Cole, please show Ellenor exactly which room you wish her to have."

The sarcasm dripping off her last statement was obvious to all, just as her ploy to have Cole be Ellenor's escort and not Finn, Brighid, or any of the others present. But before Cole could ask one of them to do the honors, both Aileen and Brighid grabbed their husbands' arms and began shuffling them out the door as quickly as they could muster, offering good nights and final words of welcome as they disappeared into the night. Hamish followed with a large meat bone in hand.

Cole glanced back at Ellenor, who was now standing by the hearth, looking both mystified and beautiful as the fire created a halo effect about her. Lord, she was gorgeous. And dangerous.

He had made a fool of himself declaring she would stay in his room, but the idea of Ellenor sleeping in another man's bed was not something he could handle. At least not yet. He needed time, space, distance away from her so that he could once again focus on what was important. His men and his vow.

"If you are ready, I will show you now before I retire. Otherwise, I'll send Fallon to escort you to your room."

Ellenor swallowed, still shocked at how the night had ended so abruptly. A few minutes ago, she was professing her love for Cole to Brighid. Now she was suddenly alone with him. Unable to think of what else to do or say, she murmured, "I'm ready."

Cole pivoted and left Ellenor to follow his lead.

Cole leaned his shoulder against the massive bedroom door. It gave under the pressure, opening to a large interior room lit only by the faint torchlight coming from the corridor. The windows were shut, but the ever-growing storm wind was howling just on the other side, giving the room a ghostly quality.

Ellenor hugged her arms and briskly rubbed them for warmth. From behind, Cole said, "Sorry. I should have realized there wouldn't be a fire. Maybe you should stay in Conan's room."

Ellenor bit her bottom lip. She would rather sleep in a Hall chair than in Conan's room. The idea seemed intimate and therefore inappropriate. The thought of being in Cole's bed, however, was not only appealing, it gave her a sense of hope she desperately needed. "I think I see some wood. If you don't mind, would you light it before you leave?"

Cole stepped around her and knelt down by the hearth. He threw several new logs in, followed by some kindling. Standing back up, he grabbed a stick and went out to the corridor to light it. He came back in with the wooden tip on fire. He lit a candle on the small table next to the bed before igniting the logs and the once gloomy room was transformed with soft light.

Ellenor expected Cole's bedchamber to be sparse, but instead it was filled with a medley of odds and ends that obviously had meaning to Cole. Across the hearth was a thick beam of wood serving as a mantle. On it was a beaten wooden sword used in training when boys first learned how to wield a weapon. In addition, there were several cups, an old leather belt, and a faded plaid hanging from a nail. A large thick rug lay in front of the fireplace and to its side was an oversized padded chair well worn from years of use. To the right of the fireplace was a muted tapestry of two dark-haired boys playing near a loch. Ellenor wondered if one of the boys was supposed to be Cole.

Two chests, one small and one significantly larger, were on either side of the door. The larger one had an etched crest of an eagle clutching a tree branch. Across the room, there was a small table with a couple of arch chairs and a long settee under the window with three pillows lying haphazardly on one end. Next to it was the bed, which was like everything else, large and sturdy. The rushes that covered the floor were fresh, proving Laurel had the staff come through periodically to keep things clean and ready for use.

Cole shifted his weight and Ellenor realized he had been waiting for her reaction as she took in his room. He was exposing a piece of himself she suspected few saw. Suddenly, his offer to have her sleep here meant more to her than if he had given her the grandest room in all of Scotland.

Ellenor turned to face the fire, unable to look at him. "I can't believe how scared I am."

"Scared?" Cole asked, perplexed by her admission.

"Mm-hmm. Scared. I'm standing here in this warm inviting room, and I'm scared. I haven't slept in a place where I have felt safe in so long . . . Even my home, before I was forced to leave, didn't make me feel secure. Faces, reminders were everywhere . . ."

Cole swallowed and moved closer. "You don't have anything to worry about here, Elle. I made you a promise to never let harm fall on you again. Know that just by being here, on these lands, you are safe, even if I am not by your side."

Ellenor nodded her head and rubbed her arms again to keep from crying. "Thank you for letting me stay here, Cole. I don't think I would have been comfortable anywhere else. Somehow, knowing this was your room makes me feel safe. Like you are still sleeping just a few feet away."

A calloused finger slipped under her chin. "Then why are you crying?"

"I don't know," she replied, brushing away a tear. "I'm just overwhelmed, I guess, but I am glad you made me come."

Cole cocked a brow and took a step back. "*Made* you come? Elle, I don't know exactly when you figured out Laurel was the one who had me come for you, but the moment that happened, I doubt there is a force in all of Scotland that could have *stopped* you from coming."

Ellenor tilted her head back and sighed in acknowledgment. "You are probably correct, and though seeing Laurel again was wonderful, I am still worried. She expects so much and I am an outsider, and English, and . . ."

Cole framed her face between his hands and looked at her, his eyes piercing and alive with desire and pride. "You've been in my home for less than a day and already are conquering the hardest of souls. Even Conan, who hates all women."

Ellenor smiled. "Conan doesn't hate women. He just gets frustrated with those who are less knowledgeable."

"That's about everyone."

"True . . ."

"Everyone but you."

The intimacy of Cole's touch was proving too much. If she didn't break free, she was going to throw her arms around him and make a fool of herself. "I like Conan. I do, but he makes me nervous."

"And does Hamish?" Cole asked, releasing his hold before moving to the mantel. He unhooked the faded plaid and draped it around her shoulders.

Ellenor tightened the material around her and huddled inside it, pretending it was Cole wrapping his arms around her and holding her tight as he did in the Hall. "Hamish? No. Yes. Maybe . . . I don't know. He was so large and comical; it was hard to know if he was serious or trying to get a reaction. But he sure got one out of you."

"The man was out of line," Cole replied crisply and fell into the single hearth chair.

Ellenor, also wanting to sit down, decided to curl up on the rug in front of the fire. She crossed her arms over her knees and laid her head on her elbow, watching Cole mentally stew over the night's events. His expression had changed and she knew his mind had moved from Hamish's flirtatious actions to his brief but disappointing message. And despite the concern etched on Cole's face, Ellenor couldn't help feeling content. This was what she had always wanted. A home and a good man with whom she could be completely herself. "They will choose you, Cole. They will."

Cole's eyes snapped to hers. Surprise that she had read his thoughts and understood what bothered him swirled in the cobalt depths. "They might not. In the end, it doesn't really matter."

"You don't care?"

"No."

Ellenor tossed off the blanket. She stood up, pointed a finger at his chest, and said, "Elmer Ludlow of the clan McTiernay, I don't believe you. I think you do care—a lot. Those people need you and you know it. Without you, they won't survive. Stop pretending to be indifferent and admit what's really bothering you. That if you are chosen, it was because of circumstances and not for wanting *you*."

Cole stared at her. He should have been angry or, at the very least, annoyed at being chastised by an English-woman, but he could think of nothing but her. Thoughts of his future, her past, and all the reasons he should stand up and leave vanished. Only memories were left, tantalizing ones of how good it had felt to hold her, all soft and vulnerable pressed up against him. Of her silky hair and her naked breasts, perfect and round filling his hands. Of how her lips moved against his, un-tutored, full of genuine passion, eagerly responding to him as if she had been made just for him, only him. And he was mere inches away from knowing such exquisite pleasure again.

His body quickened at the thought and he silently cursed his own weakness as he caved in to his need and tugged her onto his lap. "I told you to stop calling me Elmer."

"I fully intend to," she whispered. His nearness pulled at her senses, flooding her with strange feelings she had only discovered that morning. Her heart was racing so fast she could barely speak.

"When?"

His blue eyes had become disturbingly dark, blazing with hot, intense, sexual magnetism. Primal energy danced dangerously in front of her, and she could not look away. She wanted to, but her body was responding to his gaze in ways for which she was unprepared. Everything about him . . . his strength, his pride, his principles, even his blatant desire for her . . . all of it captivated her and she could not break from its spell. "Someday . . ." Ellenor managed to mumble, and before she could say anything more, he brought her mouth down to his with an intimate aggression that seared her senses.

From the moment he entered the tower, Cole had known he wasn't leaving without kissing her one last time. But he had thought it would be a safe kiss. He would try to leave and she would meet him halfway out the door, standing sweet and innocent and full of untutored passion. It was something he was supposed to be able to have, enjoy, and control.

This embrace, however, was far different.

Ellenor's scent had taken over his every breath and Cole thought he was going to drown in the rose and lavender fragrance. His mouth was voracious, his tongue stroking, probing the warmth of her lips, seeking the very thing that made her full of life. It should have frightened her, made her recoil from his touch, but instead, her fingers clenched around his shoulders, and pulled him even closer.

He groaned in response, drinking hungrily from her lips as if the years of loneliness that lay in front of him could be ended with this one last taste of her spirit. How could such a woman want him? But she did—of that he had no doubt.

When Cole's mouth broke from hers, Ellenor's heart stopped and only started beating again when his lips slowly began to trek across her cheek, lingering as he nibbled the line of her jaw, her ear, and finally her neck. His tongue swirled around the base of her throat and below.

Ellenor could not recall feeling so alive, so beautiful, in her entire life. Each time Cole touched her, she was filled with a restless yearning for more, but knew not of what.

She had known all about the physical act of making love for years, but the idea that a man's touch could lift her to an unworldly realm was new and incredibly powerful. It was a world of passion and awe and beauty, and it could only be found and shared with one man. One Highlander.

Cole inhaled the scent of her and knew she was already moist, just as he had already become hard, so hard he hurt. With only a kiss. He knew he should stop; the pain would only increase if he continued, but he didn't care. He needed to hold her for just a little while longer. Pleasure unlike he had never known was in his arms and he wasn't ready to let it go. At least not yet.

She arched her back, and her thick dark golden mane tumbled behind her shoulders. His slid his fingers beneath the weight of it, relishing the silky feel. Nothing could be so soft and yet, here it was, made for him to touch and enjoy.

His hands started to explore the curvature of her spine and then her rib cage. He spread his thumbs just wide enough to barely graze the sides of her breasts. The simple touch reminded him of their perfect size and how good they had tasted. Trailing his lips to her shoulders, he slowly moved the sleeve of her gown down, exposing her skin to his mouth and tongue. She sucked in her breath and then moaned with satisfaction. It was like the sweetest music to his ears and he wanted—needed—to hear more.

Cole covered her mouth with his once again, drugging her senses, as he lifted her body so that she was stretched across his lap. His fingers found and caressed the sensitive skin at her nape before moving lower. Pushing aside the curve of her hair, he lowered her sleeves before finding the ties to her gown. He tugged at them. They parted, freeing the treasures hidden beneath their burgundy folds. Moving the lacy edge of her chemise aside, pert, perfect breasts were thrust into the air, hardening as the cool night air teased her overheated skin.

He swallowed and the aching hunger that had been driving his emotions and actions suddenly swelled to new levels. "God, Elle," he groaned, his voice thick and husky, "you are so incredibly beautiful."

Ellenor arched her back, twisting, her body begging to be touched. Cole complied. He bent down and closed his mouth over hers for a long, searing moment, and then unable to wait any longer, cupped her breasts. His thumbs trembled as they brushed across her soft skin. A light sigh of relief escaped her lips as her nipple tightened against his palm.

Capturing one hard little nub, he squeezed it gently, relishing how she shuddered in response. He let his fingers caress, massage, and knead the flawlessly shaped mound under his callused hand. Then he moved to the other nipple, stroking it, teasing it, until it strained for release.

Ellenor gripped his shoulders. Her body was screaming for more of his touch. His fingers were tormenting her with their light stimulating caresses. She needed his mouth on her, tasting her as he did before. "Please, Cole, touch me."

"I am, love," he whispered and brushed his mouth against hers, switching his massage to her other breast.

"No," she moaned. "Touch me," she begged, only half aware she was voicing her uninhibited request, "like you did before."

Cole knew exactly what she wanted, what her body longed for, and reveled in the thought he could make such a beautiful, strong woman weak with need for him. "Tell me. Tell me exactly what you want, Elle, and I will give it to you. I don't want to scare you."

Scare her! He was torturing her and suddenly she knew why. Even while she had forgotten her distrust of men and her fear of their touch, Cole had remembered. He was holding back. Something she didn't want him to do. "Kiss me with your mouth," she purred. "Here." Reaching up with her hands, she clasped them around the back of his neck and pulled him down to her awaiting breast.

Cole took the nipple into his mouth and gently held the bloom between his lips, flicking his tongue over the sensitive flesh. It was firm and ripe and her impassioned response caused him to lose restraint. He began to suckle, drawing more of the pink bud in his mouth. She was trembling and her quakes were going through him as if they were shivers of his own. Some of them might have been. Ellenor was everything he could ever want in a woman. Spirited, spontaneous, and so passionate she set his body ablaze. And he had only grazed the surface of what she had to offer.

Ellenor's fingers dove into his hair and then down his back. Pausing to embrace his shoulders, she could feel his muscles flexing beneath her hands. Her palms turned hot. Her heart was racing as his mouth continued to weave its magic spell.

"I never thought," she moaned, "it could be like this. I thought I would never . . . I didn't know I could feel this way . . ." Cole covered her mouth with his own, preventing her from further speech in another soul-scorching kiss. In one effortless move, he swung her up into the air and removed the rest of her gown. Then, he unhooked his own belt, letting his kilt fall to the floor as he headed toward the bed.

She whispered his name, a sound so full of longing his heart ached in response. He was teetering on the biggest mistake he would ever make and it would be days before the building pain in his loins would ease, but it would be worth it. Tonight would have to last a lifetime. Ellenor would learn just how beautiful it could be between a man and a woman, and he would have the memory of sampling heaven, even it was only a piece. To know more would force her to be a part of his life. He was not fit for any woman, especially her. He had committed himself long ago to another path. She knew that, but still she trusted him, wanted him, and it was driving him over the edge.

Easing her back against the pillows, he traced her lips with his tongue, trying to be reassuring, calming her in case she was scared. Ellenor ignored the soft touch and leaned forward, kissing him with a kind of abandon that let him know she trusted him, completely, totally. He could go wild with this woman and she would go with him, even help him to get there.

Cole felt his leine move upward and realized just in time that she was tugging at it, trying to get it off him. He captured her fingers in his own and said, "No, love, tonight, is just about you."

Ellenor squirmed. "I want to touch you, feel you. Please, Cole, let me . . ." she whimpered. Her green eyes had turned translucent, and for a brief moment, he wondered if he was going to be able to withstand the pain of never having this again. Then he didn't care.

He swung his leg over hers and leaned down, his mouth finding the sweet, scented curve of her breast. He teased the already taut dusky pink nipple until she called out with pleasure. He smiled against her skin and, with a deep groan of satisfaction, whispered, "Love, you haven't felt anything yet."

The sensations rippling through Ellenor were on the verge of overwhelming her—there were so many of them. One hand held both of hers above her head, his thumb tenderly circling her wrist. It was a gentle caress and yet it said so much. His mouth was the opposite. It was voracious, plucking at one nipple, holding it, sucking until she was writhing with the need for more. Her lower body was on fire, aching to know his touch. Then, his fingers started stroking her inner thigh, softly, creating waves of both pleasure and agony.

Up and down his fingertips went. First one thigh and then the other, each time getting closer to the heat of the fire that threatened to consume her. She was begging him to stop and yet crying for him to continue. She was shaking as his hands finally drifted higher, brushing her hair. Then finally his hand covered her mound, and for a moment, time stood still.

Cole could hardly breathe. His mouth hovered above hers. His body was stretched over her with only his leine between them. The one last piece of protection to remind him he could only go so far. His other hand was where no man had ever gone before. Moisture beaded between the soft folds. This unique, surprising woman was ready for him. Her forest green eyes pleaded with him to continue, weaving a spell around them, making it impossible for either of them to back away.

Cole's palm rubbed back and forth, and when he felt her hips begin to rock against his hand, straining for a more intimate touch, he parted her with one finger and slipped into her heat.

Ellenor heard the blood pounding in her veins. Her knees trembled. The added stimulus of his finger was almost too much, and Ellenor closed her eyes in wonder. His touch was so gentle she couldn't believe the pleasure streaking through her. It almost seemed indecent to have a man know her this way. Almost. Her body had a mind of its own, seeming to understand what was happening and reacting naturally. Her legs opened wider and her hips arched, praying for more. One finger twirled at the entrance. It was cruel and divine and she was about to scream, when it plunged into her canal. All breath left her body. Never could she have imagined a man touching her there, being inside her, could cause such eçstasy. She was flying and he had only just begun.

Being inside her was like dipping into hot, sweet honey and Cole wanted more. Ellenor was so wonderfully responsive. She opened up to him, allowing him access to all of her. What he felt was incomparable.

He had been with many women in his life. Sometimes he just wanted to feel something other than an all-consuming hollowness. Other times he was there simply to satisfy a basic need. But nothing he had done had ever filled him emotionally as much as merely touching Ellenor. And nothing ever would again.

He needed to learn all her secrets, sear them into his memory, and never forget this moment. Gradually he moved his finger deeper into her tight channel. She moaned a soft whimper and it nearly pushed reason aside. Forcing himself to move slow, he eased his finger in farther before withdrawing it and delving in again. She was so incredibly hot, and all of it was for him.

His fingers continued to penetrate, drawing forth her wet heat, stroking the flames until she was half mad, ready for one more. Then he added a second finger and increased his tempo—in and out. Ellenor heard herself cry his name. She wrenched her hands free from his grasp and clung to his shoulders, over-whelmed, aroused, and unable to rationalize what was happening. The world was spinning faster and faster, driving her over the edge. No longer quivering, her body was shaking as it split into pieces. Desire scorched through her, igniting sensations that had no name. Stars erupted from behind her lids and suddenly every muscle went tense. A second later, her frame relaxed.

Cole held her gently, stroking her hair, murmuring unintelligible words into her ear. It was a while before Ellenor realized she was still holding her breath. The heat of the sweet, hot flame that had scorched through her could still be felt as her body continued to trem-ble. The feeling was unlike anything she had ever experienced.

It scared her. She had lost complete and utter con-trol. She had given it all to Cole, trusting him without reservation. He had shown her what it was like between a man and a woman, allowing her to experience what pleasure it could bring, how it could bind two souls to one another forever. And they were bound now. She loved Cole with every fiber of her being and would until the day she died. And she was positive he felt the same about her.

That was until he sat up and raked his hands through his thick hair.

Ellenor reached up and kissed the back of his neck, letting her hands slide up and down his arms. "Where are you going?" she murmured. "Lie back down with me. It's my turn."

Cole knew he shouldn't have started what he couldn't finish, but he hadn't been able to stop. With a supreme act of will, he shifted away from her. "No, Elle." The deep sadness to his tone said more than anything else.

Ellenor recoiled slightly and then shifted so that she was in view, getting ready to demand exactly what he meant. Then she saw his eyes. Deep blue troubled pools filled with a hunger that matched, even exceeded, her own. That knowledge shook her. He wasn't denying her . . . he was denying *himself.*

Ellenor reached out and traced the long white scar down his jawline. Cole trembled but he didn't pull back. The man was desperate for what she had to offer. Not just her body, but her love and understanding. Stark need was etched into every line of his face, but so was the control and self-discipline that governed that need. The man was not ready yet to let go of his past completely, but he was getting closer. He just needed more time. More time to release his ghosts and come to her.

Standing up, she walked over and collected her chemise. Donning it, she moved back to the bed and sat down in front of him, hoping the simple gesture would show she had no more expectations tonight. She would put no more pressure on him to give more. That what he had offered was enough for now.

Ellenor cradled his face in her hands and said, "I love you, Cole. More than you realize, but if all you can give me right now is just a piece of your heart, then that will be enough for me."

Cole swallowed. She meant it. She loved him. Her hazel eyes were windows into her soul, and there, spinning in an eddy of love and hope, was what she felt for him. No one had ever looked at him that way. It shook his core, and his own feelings for her began to swirl in a maelstrom. He only knew he needed to protect her more than ever, that she was the most important thing in his world.

And that protecting her meant he needed to lose her.

Cole gathered her hands and pulled them away from his face. His cheeks felt as if they had been burned with her warmth and understanding, and he didn't deserve them. "I can't do this, Elle. I just can't."

Ellenor felt as if she had just been slapped. She only wanted to give him comfort, but instead of being grateful, he was erecting emotional walls once again. He wanted to keep her out, completely out. If she had a piece of his heart, then it was a piece he had never intended for her to have. She couldn't believe it. Not after what they had just shared. "What do you mean you can't do this?"

The soft, shaken whisper tore at his soul. "God, Elle, I want you so bad I am minutes away from throwing you back on that bed and losing control."

"Then do it!" Ellenor cried. Tears started to form as it dawned on her what he was really saying. They had not gotten any closer tonight. If anything, he was farther away. "Don't you understand? I want you, too! I love you. It's real and it's rare and I know you feel the same way about me."

Cole clenched his jaw and closed his eyes.

Ellenor leaned forward and brushed her lips against his, leaving behind the cool salty taste of her tears. "I will never love anyone else like I do you. Never. Please don't do this."

Cole's eyes flew open. He steeled himself against the green despair looking back at him. He would have new nightmares to join his others when he slept, but he knew the pain she was feeling now was nothing compared to what it would be if he stayed.

"Never is a long time, Elle, a long time."

Ellenor pulled back and stared at him, shaking her head in disbelief. She could look for a million years and never find another man to equal him, and by the agony swimming in his eyes, he felt the same. "I don't understand. I don't understand how you can walk away after we just . . ."

Avoiding her eyes, Cole stood up and walked over to where his belt and kilt lay on the floor. He picked them up and began quickly folding the material around his waist. "Elle, I told you before that you and I had no future. You wanted something tonight. You needed to know you could enjoy a man's touch and not fear from it. I gave that to you. Do not misunderstand what happened. You are still chaste. You can still marry."

A low fury began to boil in Ellenor's veins. "Do *not* try to dismiss what happened tonight as pity and do *not* try to make me believe that it meant nothing to you. I may not be experienced, but I am no fool. You want me, and I am standing here saying that I want you, too! All of you!" She ran over and put her fingers on his hands just as they were about to cinch his belt. "I want to know what it's like to see the world explode in your eyes and know that it was because of me."

Cole stopped and looked down. "And if I do that, Elle, if I bed you tonight, then that will leave me with no choice but to marry you, *and I will not do that.* Do you hear me?"

Ellenor flinched, letting go. Cole resumed his dressing. "Why?" she threw at him. "Because I'm English?"

Cole's head snapped up. "What? God, no, it's me, Elle! Me!" he shouted, grabbing her shoulders. "I can't be the man I need to be and love you as well. Can't you understand that? I *can't* be both."

"So you choose hate."

"I made the choice long before I met you. I made it on the deathbed of my best friend. Robert couldn't be here and I must do for him what he can't do for himself. I will avenge his death."

Ellenor spun out of his hands and went to stand in front of the fire. "And what does that mean, Cole? When will Robert's death be avenged? When can you stop hating and start living? When are you going to live your life for just you and not for a ghost? Your friend was a *boy* when he died, Cole, not a man. Would you ever burden someone as he did you? Never. A man doesn't do that because it's *not honorable.* So how is it so honorable that you uphold a promise made when you were only a boy yourself. It's not fair to you and it is certainly not fair to me."

Cole watched as Ellenor turned to face the flames. The light of the fire flickered through the thin material, reminding him of what was partially hidden. He steeled himself, bent down, and collected his sword. "Fairness has nothing to do with this, Elle. I never lied to you."

"If you leave, I won't hold on to you. I *won't* be you, Cole. I won't suspend my life for someone else. I'm *going* to be happy. I'll find someone. I'll have a family. I may not love him as I do you, but I swear I *will be happy.* I know now that I deserve that much. You taught me that. I thought I had taught you the same."

Cole hooked his sword and pivoted toward the door.

He opened it and stepped outside. Just before he allowed the hinge to swing shut, his hand reached out and held the wooden planks open. "After Conor arrives, you won't see me again." He paused, drinking in the sight of her one last time. Her back was still turned to him. Her tawny tresses tangled down her slim back. She was a goddess, and it was killing him that she wasn't to be his. "I wish the best to you, Elle. I mean that."

Chapter 9

Ellenor opened the door to Laurel's day room and grimaced as all four of the women gathered immediately went silent. Only old Hagatha, Laurel's midwife and unusual friend, dared to look her in the eye. The woman was built like a cauldron, round in the middle and made of iron. No effort was made to tame her wild, slightly graying red hair. She wore a man's leine underneath her plaid arisaid, which was tied off with a large leather strap. Living several hours north of the castle, she came down once a week to check on Laurel's progress. Five days ago, she had decided to stay until the next of the McTiernay line was born, which could be any time.

Laurel grew larger and more exhausted every day, enjoying only snippets of rest before being roused again by little kicking feet attacking her rib cage. Hagatha was not as nervous as the first time Laurel was pregnant, but the midwife was taking no chances. Lady McTiernay was ordered to rest often, and the old woman kept a tight rein over who visited and when. Laurel practically had to order her to allow Ellenor to be one of those deemed acceptable.

Ellenor guessed Hagatha was more bark than bite, but didn't want to put it to the test. She suspected that if the midwife was pushed, her bite could be deadly. Still, the two had made a truce of sorts. Hagatha called her *stìorlag*, hinting she was excessively thin, and Ellenor let her, even though it was only true by comparison.

The relationship went from hostile acceptance to welcomed ally the day Hagatha accidentally—or so she had said—witnessed a contest of wills between Ellenor and Fiona. Fiona lost and the midwife had decided that maybe another English exception could be made.

"So what is the topic of the afternoon?" Ellenor asked lightheartedly to all four women. Brighid, Aileen, and Laurel glanced elsewhere, guilt shadowing their expressions. Hagatha was the only one of the four who refused to look away. The damn old woman had the nerve to stare blatantly back, happily acknowledging what everyone knew. The topic of the afternoon, day, night, and week had been Ellenor. More specifically, Ellenor and Cole.

Since the night of Laurel's small party and Hamish's arrival, there had been only one conversation buzzing about the castle. Too many guests and servants had witnessed Ellenor run into Cole's arms and his returned embrace. His disappearance to the training fields had not helped squelch murmurings either. Ellenor had had no choice but to ignore them and continue to swear that nothing should be read into what had happened.

At night, however, when she was alone, she stopped pretending and cried. Only when her eyes could make no more tears could she finally fall asleep. However, slumber was not her friend. Dreams would shift between those with happy endings where Cole declared his love and those of her old and alone, still wishing for him to hold her once more. Every morning when she woke, tired and drained, she swore to herself that would be the last time she would dream of him. Today would be the day she started over. Today she would prove to him, and to herself, that she could be happy without him. *Would* be happy without him.

"The same topic, I see." Ellenor sighed and floated into the room. She sank into the large armchair Laurel had brought in so that all could sit and visit comfortably while she dutifully stayed in bed resting as much as possible. "Can you four find nothing else to speak of? I mean, whatever did you do for conversation before I arrived?"

Aileen snorted and said whimsically, "Well, it was significantly more boring. Her being with child"—she thumbed at Laurel—"has made the laird overly agreeable so we haven't even had a good juicy fight to enjoy."

Laurel threw a pillow at her friend. It missed, not even coming close to its target. Brighid rolled her eyes and tossed it back on the bed. "I suspect our tongues would be far less active if you were to confess."

"What more do you want me to confess? I have told you all that I love Cole. I do. He's the one that doesn't love me. He has stated quite clearly he has a life and it does not, and will not, include me."

Hagatha twirled the small piece of pine she was gnawing. "You, *stìorlag*, have it all wrong."

Ellenor gave the midwife a side glance and then stretched out with a sigh, crossing her legs and staring at her entwined thumbs. "Really? How's that."

"It's not a man's job to catch a woman," Hagatha said, pulling the stick out of her mouth. "It's the woman's job to catch the man."

"I cannot think of a single Highland man I have met

that would like to think his wife had caught him and not the other way around."

"Of course not! That's why all the brainless women remain unmarried. But I thought more highly of you, *stìorlag*. Maybe I was wrong."

Ellenor stopped twiddling her thumbs and furrowed her brows. "I know what you are getting at, old woman. You think I should trick Cole into coming back to me. Find reasons to go out into the fields and sashay around, maybe even flirt with the other men to make him jealous. I've thought of it. I've even considered that it could have a good chance of working."

Brighid nodded in agreement. "Cole is the possessive type. All the McTiernays are."

"I don't want Cole that way."

"Pride," Hagatha scoffed. "Well, I guess, lass, then you don't really want him."

"The same could be said of Cole!" Brighid declared, rallying to her friend's defense.

Laurel drew a deep, audible breath and tapped her blankets, a clear indication she wanted to change the conversation to a less sensitive subject. "Are the twins asleep?"

Ellenor nodded. "As are Gideon and his brother," she said, answering Aileen's unspoken question. Maegan is watching over them and will let you know when they awake."

Laurel relaxed. "So if the twins aren't running you ragged, it must be Fiona. Is she giving you any more trouble?"

Ellenor waved her hand. "Fiona? No, not a bit. We actually had a long discussion this morning and we each taught the other a new trick."

Aileen's mouth dropped. "You have to be jesting."

Ellenor smiled and nodded her head. "I doubt Fiona

would admit it to anyone, but if you want proof, stop by the kitchens tomorrow morning. There you will see Norah, learning from the best."

Laurel's brows drew together, forming a skeptical expression. "Norah? The smith's daughter?"

Ellenor grinned, unable to hide the pride of her accomplishment.

Aileen leaned forward and said, "Norah has been trying to get into those kitchens for three years."

"And she should have been. The girl's a damn good cook," Hagatha huffed, aiming her criticism at Laurel.

Laurel threw her hands up in the air and said, "Fiona and I have an agreement. She works with me on the menu and I stay out of the workings of the kitchen. It has worked well for four years and I wasn't going to spoil what was hard won between Fiona and me for Norah. Even if she is good."

"Well, she has accepted the idea now," Aileen said suspiciously. "But the question is why?"

Ellenor met her direct stare and said, "I bet her this morning that I knew something about cooking she didn't. She bet and lost."

Brighid squinted her eyes and asked, "And what would it have cost if *you* had lost?"

"I would have been the one in the kitchens working as her helper." Ellenor kicked off her slippers and tucked her feet underneath her. "But I didn't lose. And now Cole will have a decent cook who knows a thing or two about running a kitchen when Conor comes with word Cole was selected."

Laurel's eyes widened and bobbed her head approvingly. "That was brilliant, Ellenor. But might you be just a little overconfident about Cole?"

"I don't think so. He will be selected. Dugan sounds like a nice man and able soldier, but he cannot bring half of what Cole can. Those clansmen and women know this. They will choose him. They just want to make Cole stew for a while and give him time to think about what kind of laird he wants to be. They've proven their point. An army alone doesn't make a man laird; he also needs the support of his people. Cole knows this, and soon after becoming chieftain, they will recognize he is a leader who cares very much about the welfare of his people. They will be very glad of their choice . . . especially since the meals at Fàire Creachann will be second only to those of Fiona's."

"Nice speech, little English. I hope it's true," Hagatha huffed.

Ellenor was about to reassert her opinion when a loud banging came from the door. Brighid rose to answer the urgent call. It was a boy, shaking and breathing hard from running. "Milady," he said panting, his eyes finding Laurel. "We need help!"

Cole slipped into the smithy and stood in the shadows looking out into the courtyard. He had come here often the past few days under the guise of ordering more supplies for his men. All the while, he hoped to spy a glimpse of Ellenor.

She would dart across the yard, sometimes with Fallon, other times with Brighid, usually to the bake house, the buttery, or the storeroom. In the past week, he had seen her visit almost every building in the yard, including the Warden's Tower, housing the soldiers assigned to protect the castle. The smithy was the one place she had not ventured. Here mostly swords, spears, and other weaponry were made. Odd requests for items such as pots, bridles, and miscellaneous needs came in, but none from Ellenor.

Today she was going from the kitchens into the Star Tower. She looked exhausted and Cole was tempted to visit Laurel later and let her know that Ellenor was being overworked. The pale brown gown she was wearing was new and it matched the color of her hair. Usually, she pinned it back or plaited it, but today she had left it long and loose so that it caught the sunshine as it moved.

For the first couple of days since their parting, he had half expected, half hoped to see her make an excuse to visit the training fields, bring food to his men, or at least casually walk about the inner yard the afternoons his and Finn's men conducted contests at the castle. But she had stayed away, honoring his request. And the fact that she could burned at him, eating him whole.

The clanking of metal being shaped abruptly stopped and Cole turned around. The smithy handed him a long, thick double-edged blade. Its red tip was turning gray as it cooled. Cole swung the large sword, nodding at its balance. "'Tis good work."

The smithy nodded and pointed across the yard at the Star Tower. "I wonder what has those two hurrying so?"

Cole followed his finger to see Hagatha and Ellenor rushing toward the stables with a young boy in tow. Neal, the stable master, was ready for them, handing Hagatha the reins to her horse and helping Ellenor mount a large chestnut meant to carry soldiers, not a small woman. Before Cole could step out and stop them, Ellenor grabbed the young boy by the arm and whipped him up in front of her. With a flick of the reins, both women were loping through the gatehouse and out of sight.

The old smithy shrugged his shoulders and went back to his bench, laying the sword down beside several others that were in one of varying stages of fabrication. "Never would have thought to warm to an English-woman, even if she could speak my words," he uttered, regaining Cole's attention. "But after what she just did for my Norah, I guess I have to. Isn't hard to look at either, is she?"

"What did Lady Ellenor do for Norah?"

The old smithy eyed Cole. "Don't you know? Well, I suspect she was going to tell you tonight at dinner."

Cole didn't know how to tell the smith that he didn't eat dinner in the castle, with his men, or anywhere in which he might encounter Ellenor. "Tell me now. I don't like surprises."

Grimacing, the smith studied Cole. Finally, with a grunt of resignation, he wiped his brow and said, "My Norah is a good cook, has a natural talent in the kitchen. That Englishwoman—"

"Lady Ellenor," Cole inserted forcefully.

"Uh . . . Lady Ellenor," the smith quickly corrected, "somehow found out about my Norah and, well, con-trived a way for the laird's cook to teach her all about running a kitchen. Says that when you're to leave for your new home, Norah's to come with you and keep your men happy. Her ladyship believes good food will help you win over the hearts of your clansmen up there." The withered man looked absentmindedly at nothing as if lost in thought and then shrugged his shoulders. "Couldn't hurt. I know I'm susceptible to a fine meal."

Cole's jaw turned hard. A good cook was hard to come by and harder to keep. His brother had learned this the hard way. But Ellenor had assumed too much with Norah. It was not her decision whom he took north and gave duties; it was his. He would decide if he wanted a cook and who it would be. She was staying away from him physically, but if Ellenor thought she could worm her way into his life by such attempts, she needed to think again.

"Have that ready for me tomorrow," Cole ordered the smith and left for the stables. He was going to find Ellenor and order her to cease all plans dealing with him and his life.

The ride out to the far end of the training fields took less than an hour but felt much longer. When the message came that Jaime Ruadh had been seriously hurt, Ellenor had immediately prepared to leave with Hagatha. That Cole might be at the fields had not occurred to her until they were well on their way. Even so, she knew she still would have come. Jaime had been one of the first to be kind to her and she needed to know he was going to be all right.

Arriving at the scene, both women were directed to a cluster of trees. Jaime had not been alone. Almost a dozen men had been hurt, all with deep cuts requiring stitching, something Ellenor had no idea how to do.

Hagatha quickly began dolling out instructions. Ellenor listened and watched carefully, committing all she heard to memory. Those with medicinal knowledge were uncommon and skills in stitching wounds were highly coveted. She had been welcomed into the McTiernay home and had tried to make herself useful these past few days, but she was no fool. Ellenor knew that as soon as Laurel was able to assume her role as Lady of the Castle once again, she would. At that time, Ellenor would have very little to offer beyond friendship. She was no great weaver and her services in the kitchen weren't wanted or needed. Seeing to injuries may be one of the few areas she could be of true assistance.

"There," Hagatha said, showing her how to hold a wound closed and make stitches simultaneously. "Now, get me some of that paste I showed you how to make." Ellenor handed her the bowl. "Pack it on like so. Now help that man, and do the same while I speak to the commander."

Ellenor gathered her gown and moved to the soldier Hagatha had been pointing toward. It was Jaime. He smiled at her. "Hello there, lass. You are looking finer than sunshine. I always knew you were bonnie, but—"

"Shhh," Ellenor whispered, soothing his brow. At the same time, she was wiping away the blood all over his chest and arm. He winced and she jerked her hand back. "Jaime, am I hurting you?"

"Nay, lass," he lied and tried to smile.

"Liar," she murmured back and began her ministrations once again.

Several cuts covered his back and arm from falling into a thicket of thorn bushes, making it difficult to find the main wound. Finally seeing the tip of the deep gash along his side, she followed it down. The leather belt strapped around his waist had been sliced and blood soaked his kilt along his hip and upper thigh.

Ellenor swallowed. She had been getting so much better. She could be in a man's presence and no longer jump at being touched. She had stopped searching for Cole anytime a man she didn't know was near. But this was different. She would have to pull down Jaime's plaid at least partially to cleanse and tend the wound. In doing so, she would be touching a man in a way that made her instinctively want to retreat and run away.

She squeezed her eyes shut. *You can do this, Ellenor,* she told herself encouragingly. *This is Jaime Ruadh. He's your friend and needs your help.* Gathering her confidence, she reached out for the cloth, but before her fingertips encountered her goal, her forearm was caught in a fierce grip. It was Jaime holding her back. "No, lass, the commander would kill me for sure. Have the midwife come and tend me."

Ellenor shook her head. "She's with someone else."

"Then I'll wait," Jaime growled through gritted teeth.

Suddenly, the fortitude Ellenor was seeking came upon her. She jerked her arm free and said unequivocally, "No, you won't. Now lie still and let me know if you need something to bite upon."

With a quick flick, she spread open the plaid and carefully began to wipe away the blood. The injury was bad, more so because of its location than its depth. Grabbing a needle and thread, she burned the tip in the fire and pressed the wound closed. Quickly she made the stitches, looping, spacing them just as Hagatha had shown her.

Jaime groaned and Ellenor, who had entered a concentrated state, was reminded that this was a man, who had feelings. "I'm sorry, but it has to be done. Talk about something. Anything to focus your mind elsewhere."

Jaime grunted and said, "All I can think of is the commander and how he is going to kill me."

"Why is that?" Ellenor asked absentmindedly, her attention on her task.

"If he finds out you tended me, I'm a dead man, that's why."

"Your head is playing tricks on you. Cole will be glad you are all right and will recover."

"My hip is injured, lass, not my head, and the last thing the commander will be is glad. Have you not wondered why Donald and I haven't been to see you since you arrived?"

"I saw Donald the first night. And as for you, I assumed you were busy."

"Not too busy to look in on you. I wanted to make sure you were adjusting well, that the clan hasn't been treating you as an outcast. The commander wouldn't let me."

"Well, you can calm yourself. I have been treated very well." Ellenor was glad of the conversation. Her stitching had reached the midway point between his hipbone and pelvis. Jaime flinched and she fought not to do the same. "So what is all the nonsense about Cole?"

"God, you are beautiful. I had no idea how much, but the commander did. He must have and that is why he has kept all his men away. He wanted you all to himself. And God, I would, too, if I had a woman half as bonnie as you."

His words were slurred and Ellenor knew he was about to pass out. She wished he just would. It would make things much easier. "You are mistaken, Jaime. Cole doesn't want me and I am as free as any other maiden," she said, finishing off the last stitch. She tied it and bit off the end. Grabbing the bowl of ground ivy and oak, she applied the paste liberally to the wound and then began to smooth the mixture to the other various cuts covering his body.

She finished and was about to go the next man when Jaime reopened his eyes and said, "He may have freed you, but you never freed him."

Ellenor opened her mouth to deny his accusation, but it was too late—Jaime went limp and was out. She then turned and looked at the next man needing attention, forcing her mind to put aside what Jaime had said.

Later. She would think about it later.

* * *

Cole stepped away to view the damage he had seen upon arriving. He should walk the area again with Finn, Conor's commander, but the second his eyes had locked onto Ellenor, they could look nowhere else. She was in the distance, bending over Jaime. Her long hair hung around them like a golden veil. Her hands roamed his chest and then moved lower, finding his injury. He watched as Jaime tried unsuccessfully to stop her. When Ellenor pulled his kilt back to examine his wound, Cole saw no desire on her face. Only concentration was in her expression.

Ellenor's fear of men was subsiding.

He hadn't realized until that moment how much knowing she kept all men physically at a distance had been keeping him sane. Ellenor was not about to eagerly accept a man's touch, but she was fast approaching the time when she wouldn't shrink away from it. Then, she would do exactly as she promised. She would find a way to be happy and he would forever lose her. And the idea was eating away at him.

Finn called out. Cole broke his gaze and wandered to where Finn was standing talking to another soldier. "A small brush fire caused the cattle to charge the farm. Two of the fields were lost, but thankfully the cottages are still standing and the women and children are unharmed. That wouldn't have been so if your men hadn't reacted so quickly getting the herd to veer course."

Cole pointed to Hagatha and Ellenor. "How many were injured?"

"Four, severe. The others have minor cuts. Hagatha tells me all will survive, though they won't be moving quickly for a few weeks."

"That's good news."

"Aye."

"I see Ellenor is assisting. Strange to see that. The few times she and I have crossed paths, she seemed tense, as if she thought I might grab her. I guess it's just me," Finn ended with a shrug.

"You need help?" Cole asked, changing the subject.

Finn shook his head. "You go to your men and have the injured ones brought back to the village to be cared for."

Cole nodded and proceeded up the hill. The rest of his men now blocked his view as they huddled around those injured, getting reassurance from Hagatha and Ellenor that all would live. Cole knew their concern was just an excuse. Almost all of his men had been injured once or twice and they knew the wounds their comrades received were serious, but nonlethal. They were there to watch Ellenor.

Jaime had blathered on about her for days. And short of cutting the man's throat, Cole had been unable to stop him. Donald had been just as bad, but in a different way. Each time Jaime offered up a story of their journey, Donald would grunt and reaffirm it was true.

Only once did Jaime ask Cole directly if he liked her. Cole had been lying down, feigning sleep, but he had heard the question and refused to answer it.

Minutes passed and Jaime spoke again, this time to no one. "No, I suppose you wouldn't admit it even if you did. And it's not because of what happened to Robert or that she's English. I've never said this to you and probably wouldn't have the courage to do it when you were awake, but I think you're afraid that she just might be able to make you happy. And you don't know how to handle happiness. So I hope you figure out how to handle true misery for that lass is too damn pretty to stay single around here. And, Commander, I'm just as susceptible as any other man."

Cole knew then what he had to do. Ellenor might not be for him, but she was not for his men either. His only choice had been to confine his soldiers to the training fields and away from the castle. He had hoped space and time away from Ellenor would dull his feelings enough so that if his men ever did meet her, he would not care if they became smitten.

Time and space had not helped, he realized, breaking through the gathering. They had only made things worse. His men were ogling her as if they had never seen a woman before. Jealousy coursed through his veins and an unjustified anger boiled within him, threatening to erupt.

"Hell, I thought Jaime Ruadh to be exaggerating," he heard one of his men murmur aloud.

"I don't think she is English," said another. "A lass that bonnie has to be from the Highlands."

"Only the English could be such fools and let that angel go."

"Aye, we're not that foolish. Are we, lads?"

Cole could stand no more. "Get back to work!"

The crowd instantly began to disperse and Cole spied Ellenor standing by one of the men, a bloodied cloth in hand. She looked exhausted and was staring directly at him, unmoving. Without a word, Cole walked up to the clearing, grabbed her hand as he moved by her, so that she fell in step beside him. When they were no longer in sight of the others, he swung her into his arms. His fingers threaded her thick mane and pressed her cheek to his chest. Her arms curled around his waist and held him close.

"What happened?" she mumbled into his leine, refusing to let go.

"A fire startled the animals. My men charged them to save the farm."

Ellenor nodded against his chest to let him know that she had heard. Suddenly, the lack of sleep the last several days had caught up to her.

Cole had seen her fatigue and could feel it even as she clung to him. Bending down, he sat upon a soft pelt of grass and leaned back against a rock with her cradled in his lap. "You've been working too hard. As Laurel's friend, you don't need to prove yourself."

Ellenor bobbed her head. "Yes I do. Everyone works hard and so must I if I am going to stay."

"Aye, contribute, but no one expects you to collapse from exhaustion."

"It's not the work. I cannot sleep. Every time I close my eyes, I'm haunted by you." Ellenor suddenly pulled back, realizing what she had just admitted. "I shouldn't have said that. Forget it."

"No."

"You must. I don't want you out of guilt or pity or concern over my welfare, and that's what it would be if you came back. What I just said changes nothing between us. Tell me it changes nothing."

Her eyes darted back and forth peering into his, searching for agreement. "It changes nothing," he whispered, and then pulled her back against his chest, rocking her in his arms. She took a deep breath and sighed, her body relaxing as it gave way to slumber. Cole stroked her hair and, after several minutes, said, "I lied. It changes everything."

Cole carefully stood up and carried her back down the hill. Hagatha had already departed, after getting a promise that one of the men would see Ellenor safely back. The moment Cole emerged from the shadows, he could feel the weight of all his men's eyes bearing down on him. They had questions and now they had answers.

Cole threw back his head and waited for one of his men to retrieve his mount. Carefully resting Ellenor on the front edge of his saddle, Cole braced himself and swung his leg over the animal's back before gently pulling her limp body back into his arms. She shifted but remained asleep as she unconsciously nestled against his shoulder.

Cole released a deep breath he had not realized he had been holding. The sinking sense of panic haunting him since the moment he had left her room was dissipating, and in its place was the unfamiliar feeling of hope. Something he had thought never to know again.

The last few days had been a living hell. The type of dreams that had been haunting Ellenor had been visiting him as well. Visions of her rising nude from moonlit waters, seductively hovering over him as he slept, or blatantly kissing him to painfully arousing levels—all had been torment. But the worse nightmares had been those scenes of her laughing and playing with two children. Both boys and both with his coloring, brown-haired and blue-eyed. She would gather the giggling figures in her arms and then look up in his direction and smile. The warmth and sincerity of her gentle expression washed over him, bestowing upon him all the joy and peace he had sought his whole life. But then, just as he was about to step forward and embrace his family, another man would walk before him and take all that was supposed to be his.

It had gotten to the point he dreaded going to sleep in fear of having another dream and seeing another man enjoy what he had so foolishly discarded. Even the days had become long and miserable. Activities he had always found diverting—physical contests, mental challenges of strategy and wit, or simple pleasures such as a swim—no longer held his mind off his troubles. His thoughts always turned to Ellenor. He needed to know if she had been similarly inflicted.

That began his daily visits to the smithy, where he would wait until she passed by, looking for even a hint of reciprocal misery. He had seen her tired, and once angry, but mostly, she had been busy and happy and it had ripped at him.

But he hadn't lost her. She had been crying inside as well, needing him just as badly as he needed her. And this time, he wasn't going to let her go. His ghosts still ate at him and he wasn't half the man Ellenor deserved to have, but no longer did it matter. He didn't have to be.

The last morning of their journey, she had said all she wanted was a man who loved her. Who would fight heaven and hell before leaving the comfort of her arms, and after this past week, Cole knew he would never leave them willingly again. More so, he would fight any living being who tried to take her away from him. And that included Jaime Ruadh or any of his other doe-eyed, besotted men.

Cole pressed his mount into a soft lope, holding Ellenor gently to him to cushion the thud of the horse's hooves. The afternoon sun was setting and a breeze had been whipping about all day. The moment the sun's heat disappeared behind the mountains, the wind would be cold, chilling all unaccustomed to its bite.

Veering up the path toward the barbican now in site, Cole began to make plans. First, he would carry her up to his room. Then he would fetch some food and drink and leave orders for them to remain undisturbed. Returning to her side, he would rest beside her, and when she awoke, he would beg for forgiveness, kissing her until she accepted. And this time those kisses would end with both of them deeply and completely satisfied. Diving into the cold loch at all hours of the day and night were over.

Cole entered the yard and headed for the stables. Hopping off *Steud*, he slid Ellenor into his arms and turned eagerly toward the North Tower. He took two steps and stopped.

It had been a good plan. Unfortunately, its existence was short-lived.

"Conor," Cole acknowledged woodenly. "You've returned."

Chapter 10

Ellenor yawned and stretched her arms way above her head, arching her back and pointing her toes. She felt refreshed, and for the first time in days, didn't feel tired upon waking. Opening her eyes, she relaxed her muscles and exhaled.

A bird was chirping near the window. She twisted her head on the pillow to look in its direction. Her eyes popped opened and she sat straight up. By the amount of light pouring in through the open shade, it was middle to late morning. She had overslept.

Throwing the covers aside, she jumped up and began a wild search for her slippers. A lot of the Highland women refused to wear shoes, but that was one custom Ellenor didn't anticipate adopting. She noticed Laurel still protected her feet and wasn't alone. Several other Highland women wore some kind of footwear, including Brighid.

"Where could I have put them?" she asked herself, peering under the bed. Standing back up, she tried to recall her nightly ritual and almost lost her balance.

The reason why she could not find her slippers where she always left them was very simple: she hadn't taken them off. Cole had. The last thing she could remember was making a complete fool of herself right before committing an even more idiotic act of falling asleep on him.

Ellenor sank onto the mattress and buried her head in her hands. "What was I thinking?" she moaned. "The man must think me an *òinnseach* if there ever was one."

Only one memory of their encounter saved her from complete disgrace. Cole had agreed that nothing had changed between them. None of her unwitting actions had made him pity her. She would rather suffer alone than endure life with a miserable man at her side. She wouldn't do it, and thank God, she had avoided that situation.

Rubbing her scalp brusquely, Ellenor sat back up and got off the bed. She washed her face, quickly plaited her hair, and donned a new chainse and bliaut. Yesterday's gown was over the chest, covered in dried blood—a cold reminder of yesterday's horrific accident. She would ride out and see Jaime and the rest of the men to make sure all were recovering, but first she had her chores, of which she was extremely behind in executing. Both cook and steward would no doubt give her an earful for being tardy, but she would just have to endure it.

Dashing down the stairwell, she exited the structure and headed straight for the Star Tower. When she had climbed to the fourth floor, her chambermaid pointed to the floor above her. "Her ladyship is still asleep."

Ellenor sighed in relief, glad Laurel had not been waiting for her arrival.

Moving to the door once again, the chambermaid again bobbed her finger upward and whispered, "Her ladyship's in the solar."

Ellenor gave the young girl a strange look and then shrugged her shoulders. Maybe Laurel was missing her husband and wanted to be close to his things. Ellenor certainly understood the compulsion. Everything in her room reminded her of Cole. Especially the bed. Even after several days, the pillows still held his scent, both a comfort and torturous reminder.

Descending the staircase, Ellenor began to contrive counterarguments in preparation for the confrontation she was about to have with Fiona and probably Fallon. Both were going to enjoy lording her tardiness over her. Swinging out into the inner yard, Ellenor aimed straight toward the kitchens, intending to get the worse of the two out of the way. Mentally rehearsing a small speech, she didn't see the enormous soldier emerge from the armory. She collided directly into the giant.

Grimacing, Ellenor gave him a withering stare and then swiftly moved around him. She took two steps and then a bellowing sound erupted from behind her. "You!" the hulking soldier hollered. "Look where you are going or next time you might find yourself flattened or even worse, dead."

Ellenor came to an abrupt halt, pivoted, and marched back. The hairs on the back of her neck were standing upright. The insult was unappreciated, but after she had spent the past week issuing constant reminders about not yelling in the courtyard, especially in the morning, Ellenor was in no mood to be reprimanded for *her* actions.

"Cum do theanga ablaich gun fheum!" she ordered, waving her finger at him.

Conor stared at her in complete shock. The woman had actually called him an idiot and told him to shut up in his own home. "Listen here, *amaid!*" he began at the top of his lungs.

"You big, giant oaf of a man," she hissed, cutting him off. The Highlander rivaled Cole's height and had similar dark hair, but instead of blue eyes, his were a cold gray that held no compassion. "Is it impossible for you

Highlanders to do anything but holler? You will stop it right now or I will wallop you until you cannot speak for a week, you overgrown *thòin*."

Conor felt his mouth drop open in astonishment. Only his wife ever spoke to him in such a manner, and then she had learned to do it in the privacy of their bedroom and *not* in public.

Ellenor ignored the dumbfounded look and pointed to the Star Tower. "Your chieftain's lady is asleep right now, in one of those rooms above your head. Do you have any concept of how hard it is to ensure she gets her rest? It's been damn near impossible. And every time she hears one of you soldiers bellowing, she uses it as an excuse to leave her room. I have two sleeping babies, a grumpy cook, and a sour steward, so what I *don't* need is another overgrown giant underfoot. So if you have any brains to match those large muscles, turn about and do you duties, soldier, *without* disturbing her ladyship! Or I promise, I will tell the laird when he returns exactly what you and your fellow men . . ."

Out of the corner of her eye, she saw Conan pop out from the North Tower. He was waving to her but she ignored him, focusing on the mammoth in front of her. His gray eyes no longer possessed the frigid coldness they had just moments before. Now, mirth reflected in the silvery depths, causing her ire only to deepen.

Conan arrived at her side, but before he could utter a word, Ellenor cut him off. "Just a minute, Conan. I am having to remind one of Cole's men—"

Conan chuckled, and unable to help himself, he grabbed Ellenor by the waist and swung her around. "He is not one of Cole's men."

Ellenor punched his shoulders. "Conan, put me down."

"But I have been waiting all morning to see you! You are just the one who can help me," Conan said happily, finally letting her back down. "Besides, someone had to properly introduce you to my oldest brother and our laird. Conor, meet Ellenor, a superb scholar and extraordinary wit. Ellenor Howell, meet the fiercest of all the McTiernays, Conor."

Ellenor gulped and squeezed her eyes shut, considering the idea of just going back to bed and staying there until next year.

Conor watched the young beauty with amusement as she slowly reopened her eyes. She was still holding on to Conan's arm for balance, unaware of the effect it was having on his younger brother. Conan wasn't the only man who had fallen under her spell.

When Hamish had returned with news that an Englishwoman had been invited by his wife to stay at the castle, Conor had not been thrilled. His loyal guardsman, on the other hand, had been very vocal about how eager he was to return and spend time with the exceptionally bonnie visitor. Seeing her last night and again this morning, Conor could see why. Her lithe body, long hair, and angelic face were unforgettable combinations. Years of experience had taught him that unmarried, pretty women caused trouble among the ranks. And Ellenor was just that . . . trouble.

He had been prepared to find her later this morning and send her back from wherever she came. What he hadn't planned on was liking the Englishwoman.

Few things could quickly earn his trust and support. And that list dramatically dwindled to naught if insulted. The Englishwoman stumbled across the one exception that would not only keep her on the premises, but make him one of her allies. Any woman who was willing to dress down a man twice her size to ensure that his wife and child were well was worth tolerating, even if she was exceptionally pretty.

Conor pointed to the kitchens behind Ellenor and said in an exaggerated whisper, "I believe you were headed there before I started all my bellowing."

Ellenor felt the sudden rise of color filling her cheeks. The man had the same satisfied look Cole did when he thought he had bested her. Well, this McTiernay needed to learn that she never backed down from a challenge. Even when she ought.

She cocked a brow, dipped her head in respect, and just before she turned to walk away, broke into a friendly smile, and said in English, "I *was* headed there, but only because I had not known you were home. I am sure you have your own ways of running things when Laurel is unavailable and I certainly wouldn't want to interfere. The kitchens are all yours. Welcome home . . . laird." Then she casually retook Conan's arm and said, "I believe you wanted to show me something. Seems my morning and afternoon are now completely free."

Cole closed the door to the Lower Hall and weaved his way back to his chair. The long narrow, rectangular room was well lit with large arch-shaped windows and fires burning in both braziers located at opposite ends of the hall. Most of the tables were still erected with benches and stools scattered from where many of the soldiers had enjoyed last night's dinner. The high table was at the far end of the room close to the fire with several worn, padded high-back chairs askew around one end. His drink was sitting in front of one of them, just where he had left it.

He had been nursing a mug of ale when Conor started bellowing outside. At first, he had ignored the commotion. It wasn't typical of his brother to yell at someone first thing in the morning, but then again, it wasn't atypical of him either, especially since Laurel had entered the later part of her pregnancy. His anxiety over her welfare spilled over to everything. Cole wondered if he would be the same.

A loud gasp coming from a servant standing near the entrance caught his attention, and he realized it was not just anyone challenging Conor. It was Ellenor. And the scolding she was issuing was going to get herself thrown off McTiernay lands, if not belted across the cheek. Cole had never seen Conor hit a woman, but then no woman had ever dared to tell him to shut up right before calling him an ass, an idiot, and a few other less than flattering terms.

Cole immediately headed toward the door intent on rescuing her. He had just stepped outside when he saw Conan swing her about the yard. A surge of jealousy coursed through him.

He had never seen his younger brother smitten with any woman, and it mattered little that Ellenor didn't reciprocate Conan's interest, Cole was still resentful. She was his. Granted no one else knew that yet, but it didn't dampen the sense of possession swelling in him seeing another man's arms around her, holding her, discovering just how good her hair smelled.

Balling his fist, Cole took another step toward the three of them, prepared to play hero and save her from the humiliation she was obviously experiencing. Then she spoke and the world stopped for a brief moment.

Ellenor had done the near impossible. She had stunned Conor into silence and, at the same time, quelled his own need to pummel Conan.

Cole crossed his arms and rocked back on his heels, his face breaking into an enormous grin. Finally, someone else knew what it was like dealing with her. The woman was bold and audacious, driven by a fierce competitive streak, and living with her would be forever frustrating. But seeing the dumbfounded look on Conor's face as she turned and strutted away was worth all that he would have to endure.

Cole poured himself a mug of ale and waited for Conor to join him. They had met briefly the night before when his brother had imparted the council's unusual request, giving him until this morning to think over his decision.

Accept the terms or decline lairdship. And there were many reasons supporting both choices.

Cole took a swig of the dark beverage just as the entrance doors swung wide open, banging against the walls. He glanced at the stomping figure approaching. It was Conor, who had gotten over his stupefaction and was struggling for composure. Cole couldn't tell if his brother was mad or in awe.

Marching over to where Cole was sitting, Conor grabbed a mug, poured himself some ale from the pitcher Cole had been using, and plopped into the big chair at the end of the table. "That woman . . ." he growled, pointing his finger toward the courtyard.

"Aye, she's that," Cole agreed and took another swallow.

"Is the most aggravating, infuriating woman . . ."

"Aye, and you have not seen anything," Cole cautioned and tipped his mug before taking another swig.

"Laurel says you were the one who brought her here. Must say I was surprised."

Cole glanced at his brother. "Don't bother mocking me. I've seen how successful you are when Laurel wants something. I was still refusing to go when I found myself halfway there. But in my defense, your wife had failed to mention it was an Englishwoman I was collecting from her brother."

"Sounds like you have had quite an experience with the wench."

Irritation flickered briefly in Cole's eyes and he reached for a bowl in the middle of the table. "She stank and saw everything as a challenge. She was annoying, but *never*," Cole asserted, grabbing a slice of bread left over from the previous meal, "was Ellenor Howell a wench."

Conor leaned back in his chair. "Toss me one of those," he said, eyeing the bread. Cole pitched him a slice. Conor easily caught it. "Well, she's still bossy," he said, taking a big bite. "And based on what I just saw, it seems you taught her how to look like a woman again, maybe a little too well."

The idea took Cole by surprised and he began to cough on a piece of bread. He cleared his throat and downed the rest of his ale. "*Taught* her? Hell, I didn't teach her anything. She *decided* to act crazy and then *decided* to be normal."

"And which one is that? Crazy or bossy?"

"The latter," Cole answered with an appreciative grunt. "She will rise to anything perceived as a challenge. You experienced what happens when she feels like she's being outwitted. That woman doesn't back down from a fight . . . ever. She will drag herself back up and come at you until you yield."

Conor's eyebrows arched in surprise. "*You* yielded? I don't believe it. You lost an argument to an *English-woman* in a battle of wits?"

Cole's face briefly hardened before relaxing. He poured himself another mug of ale and leaned back in the chair, stretching his feet in front of him. "*You* lost," he said, pointing to Conor with his mug, "not me. Although there was a time or two I might have let her think she won."

Conor stared incredulously at his younger brother. Cole ignored him. He wasn't exactly sure why he was keeping his feelings for Ellenor to himself. It would be a short-lived secret as he intended to announce their engagement that night. Still, in this setting and after Conor had just experienced the bolder side of Ellenor's nature, Cole wasn't ready to open himself to the ridicule he no doubt would receive. Payback was hell and he had done more than his share of teasing when Conor had announced his wedding plans to Laurel. Cole knew the moment anyone in his family learned of his intentions to marry Ellenor, the peace he was typically afforded by them would instantly disappear.

Conor pointed in the direction of the North Tower. "I think our younger brother has also been outsmarted a time or two. And unlike us resentful old men, he admires her for it. Maybe she admires him back."

"Conan's a boy," Cole said with a little more bite than he had intended.

Conor leaned forward and poured himself some more ale. "To you and I, maybe. But to women, Conan looks like a man. A damn smart man who pretty much irritates and is irritated by all women. Except that one. What do you think? Maybe he has finally found someone who can stomach all his nonsense?"

Cole leaned back and narrowed his gaze. Conor returned the stare without expression. It was hard to know if his older brother was goading him, or truly thought Ellenor and Conan would make a good couple. "Ellenor's not for Conan."

"Well, she is certainly not for you," Conor concluded and stretched out to put his feet on the table. "She's English."

Cole eyed his brother's ankles and shoved them out of view. His brother was definitely goading him, and worse, it was working. "Aye, she's English. And she's actually *proud* of it. But that has nothing to do with whether or not she's right for me."

"Damn!" Conor cried out. He leaned forward and slammed his mug on the table. "You *like* this woman. I should have known last night when you rode in with her asleep in your lap. I just assumed you had somehow gotten stuck with the duty, but hell, I bet you would have punched me or any other man who dared to take her away from you."

Conor cleared his throat and Cole wanted to ram his fist through it. Then he realized that Ellenor, in a way, already had. Cole stretched casually and said, "Before you get too proud of yourself, you might want to remember the mess you're in."

"What mess?"

"Who do you think has been running this place while you've been away? Your wife has been in bed per Hagatha's orders, Aileen's been busy with the twins, and Glynis is good at what she does, but you know she can't handle Fiona or Fallon. It's been Ellenor, and I do believe her parting comment had something to do with it being your responsibility now."

The color drained from Conor's face. "Good God, not again."

"What do you mean? I thought you and Laurel used to argue endlessly about whose responsibility it was to manage the castle."

"We did fight. Hell we still fight all the time. But on running this place . . . well, I am not ashamed to admit that I eventually lost and was glad to have finally admitted defeat. Fallon is a great steward. Glynis is capable of overseeing the maids, and Fiona . . . well, she's the best cook in the Highlands. But dealing with the three of them . . ." Conor raked his scalp. "This Englishwoman was actually managing things?"

"Aye, and very well."

"Damn," Conor muttered, rubbing his course chin. He hadn't shaved in a couple of days and the growth was now evident. "Do you think she meant it?"

Cole smiled and shook his head, unwilling to prolong his brother's distress. "Doubt it. Elle likes Laurel too much. She just wanted to shut you up. And she did. If it turns out I'm wrong, I'll ask her to continue for you. But she can only do so for a while. She'll be leaving for Fàire Creachann with me."

"So you've decided then. You are going to accept."

"Aye, I have. But I have a few unusual requests of my own."

Ellenor leaned against the flat wide worktable and watched as Conan searched an overstuffed chest for another scroll. "You cannot leave yet. You have to stay, and as my newfound absolute favorite lady, you cannot refuse me."

"High praise coming from a woman hater."

Conan glanced back briefly and then continued his rummaging. "I don't hate women. In fact, I enjoy what they have to offer. It's not my fault that rarely does the enjoyment extend beyond the bedroom." He pulled something out. "I think this is it."

"You are incorrigible, you know that?"

Conan raised a single brow and grinned, his expression one of mockery. "This coming from the Englishwoman who just called my eldest brother an idiot? And in the middle of a crowd of McTiernay clansmen, nonetheless."

Ellenor grimaced. "Not my proudest moment."

"Don't worry about it. If Conor was going to throw

you out, he would have done it by now. Besides, I thought it was great. Between you and Laurel, I just might have to reconsider my position on the fairer sex."

"Someday you are going to find someone who is going to make you rethink your whole approach to women. You might find yourself endearing—"

"But I am," Conan said, leaning against the bench, pasting on a devastating grin.

"Huh, maybe a little, but then I am not interested in you."

"Not yet," he said softly, leaning closer.

Ellenor poked him in the chest and pushed him back. "Not ever."

Conan frowned, but Ellenor could tell that he wasn't really hurt by the rejection. He shrugged and began uncurling the map in his hand. "That's because you're still in love with Cole."

"What makes you think I am in love with Cole?"

"That wasn't a denial. And I hate seeing you get hurt. You are wasting your time on him. He doesn't allow anyone to get close. Not friends, not family, and certainly not an Englishwoman. Any man who refuses you doesn't deserve you . . . but then, why listen to me? I'm the incorrigible woman hater who needs to rethink my approach to women."

Ellenor rolled her eyes as Conan opened out the parchment and laid it in front of her, weighting the edges. "This is the last one," she mumbled and started reading the various hand markings along the sides. "It's not very old."

"No, in fact I think it is a recent depiction of the European coastline. Most of it I can understand, but these markings right here, I think they have something to do with the unusual depth in the area."

She shook her head. "It's Latin again. *Sinus Cantabro-*

rum is just the name of this region. The Ocean of the *Cantabri*."

Ellenor could sense Conan's frustration. He didn't just have a love of maps, he actually wanted to see and visit the places he was studying. Conan devoured all things written, but most especially those items that told him what to expect, details on the weather or how to best travel in the foreign lands.

"Then what about these markings on the side. They are not in Latin."

Ellenor took a deep breath. "No, they are French, but they, too, are meaningless and have no relevance whatsoever to the map."

Conan shook his head, unwilling to give up. "But what about these notations right here. They have to be of some importance. They definitely describe the waters in this channel area. What is meaningless to you—like dark blue or turbulent—is not meaningless to me."

Ellenor sighed. "You really need to learn French."

"Aye, but until I do, what does it mean?"

"You're not going to believe me," Ellenor murmured, knowing he would not relent. Looking down at the manuscript again, she read, "To my wife, who fell over on these stormy seas of hell. A better coffin for which she could not dwell."

Conan's jaw dropped. "You are not serious," he said. "What about the tag below it?"

"Hmm, in a way it, too, does describe the waters. Though indirectly."

"I knew it! What does it say?"

"It must have been made by a different man because he adds, 'I curse these warm, foul summer days. I curse these dark calm waters, but mostly I curse my own luck.

The blessed coffin lapping all around me, my wife has yet to find."

"You cannot be serious."

"Well, the handwriting is messy, but I am not making it up. But it does say the seas are dark and calm in the summer."

"I guess there is that."

"Then again the man may have just been trying to be poetic."

"Thanks."

Ellenor exhaled and moved away from the bench. "Well, I have to go if I am going to get things ready for tonight."

"Why? I thought you handed off all your responsibilities to Conor now that he has returned."

Ellenor tipped her head back and scoffed. "Laurel told me about what happens when Conor runs things around here."

"Aye, it's awful, but there is an up side. Just think of the work we could do . . ." Conan said, waving his hand at the various papers and items scattered all over the room.

"I wanted to teach your brother a lesson, not punish Laurel and everyone else around here. Now I really must go. With the laird back, I need to talk with Fiona and Fallon about a small celebratory meal. You *are* coming, and if you want me to help you ever again, don't make me come up here and get you," she warned with a grin and approached the door.

"Ellenor?"

She paused and turned around.

"Ellenor? Wear the McTiernay plaid tonight."

Ellenor hesitated. "I cannot. I am a guest of your clan's, but I am not a member of it. I have no right."

"You do if a McTiernay asks you. Promise me."

She gave a firm tug on the latch. It freed and she

swung the door open. She looked back and said, "I'll think about it."

Laurel pressed her palm against her stomach and gave it a good shove.

"Sit still," Ellenor chided, moving Laurel's head back so she could finish pinning her hair.

"I cannot. I am being kicked mercilessly and it hurts. My ankles are swollen. My back aches and I look like a stuffed pheasant."

"Then stay up here and rest," Ellenor goaded, knowing that her friend desperately wanted something fun to see and do.

"Never! Besides I have to be there as Conor's wife. Are you sure all will be prepared? I still think you should have delayed this celebration for a day or two to give you more time."

"Nonsense. The food will be ready. The Great Hall is set, and the wood for the bonfires is being piled up right now."

"But what about the game? I could have made sure we had enough if I could have only gone out to hunt with the men."

Ellenor threw her hands up in the air in exasperation. "What's more important? Another type of meat or your baby?"

Laurel pursed her lips. "The baby, of course."

"Then stop your complaining. We need to finish making you look beautiful. I want your husband's eyes to be completely on you. Hopefully, then when he does see me, he will have totally forgotten about how I insulted him. Somebody," Ellenor said, tugging a particular braid a little stronger, "should have warned me he had returned."

"I *told* you he wasn't angry!"

"Yes, well, now it won't matter," murmured Ellenor as she fastened the last hairpin. She handed the polished silver dish to Laurel. "There. You look stunning, even for a stuffed pheasant."

Laurel looked at her reflection and nodded in approval. Her deep teal bliaut was accented with cream beading along the hems. Most of her gowns had been adjusted as best as possible for her ever-growing figure, but this was the one bliaut that had been made for her extended form and went all the way to the floor. Lightly fingering the small interwoven braids, she said, "You are going to have to teach Aileen this trick you did with our hair. It is quite becoming."

"I'll ask someone to send her up here to the solar. Is she still in your bedroom?"

Laurel shook her head, laying the dish down on the table in front of her. "No, she and Finn are going to meet us in the Great Hall." Getting up, she shook her finger at Ellenor, indicating it was her turn to sit down.

Ellenor took several steps back in protest. "I am done primping tonight."

"Just one or two more gold threads," Laurel encouraged.

"No, I don't need them. They just blend in with the color of my hair and the pins scratch my scalp all night."

"You are right about your hair. How about some deep blue thread to match your gown."

"Blue strings in my hair? No, Laurel. It was hard enough accepting this gown as a gift, but no more. You have done enough."

"It wasn't I, it was Brighid. She's the one gifted with the talent of embroidery," Laurel said, gesturing to Ellenor's shallow, curved neckline and sleeves.

"Brighid is amazing," Ellenor agreed, afraid to look

in the dish one more time. The reflection staring back was of another person. Someone beautiful, in a stunning gown, pretending to belong to a clan when she had no right.

The soft, velvet material of deep, almost midnight blue complemented almost every aspect of Ellenor, from her long, thin frame, to her wispy chestnut hair. The sleeves were split along the arm, exposing just a hint of the creamy, diaphanous chainse underneath. The gold looped belt drooped over her hips, accentuating her small waist and emphasizing the intricate golden designs stitched along each hem.

The only adornment she wore was attached at the shoulder. An old luckenbooth of the McTiernay crest held the heavy plaid in place. The material was of dark greens and blues with lines of gold, red, and burgundy, and it hung down to where it just barely touched the floor. The rich dark colors of the gown and plaid made the green in her hazel eyes pop with intensity, capturing the attention of any onlooker.

When Conan asked her to wear the McTiernay plaid, Ellenor had placated him by saying she would consider it, but she knew before his study door had closed her decision would be no. She was a visitor here. Welcomed by most and tolerated by the majority, but for an Englishwoman to don this proud clan's colors and wear them as if they were her own was just too self-indulgent. She would lose the little respect she had gained, and she wouldn't have blamed them.

Then, while she was preparing Brighid's hair, a knock had come at Laurel's door. A maid entered and handed Ellenor a folded plaid. On top of it was a rare, old pewter pin of the McTiernay crest—an eagle clutching a tree branch of Highland mountain ash. Ellenor was just about to refuse the items when she noticed the small rip at one of the corners. This request had not come from Conan. Cole had sent her his plaid to wear, and somehow, not insulting him was far more important than possibly losing the clan's respect.

Laurel walked over and picked off the couple of stray hairs caught on the soft material, and then fingered the dark silver pin. "I have seen this pin only once, in his room during a rare visit. Of course, Cole said very little, but he did say this belonged to his mother and his mother's mother. She gave each of her sons something to hand to their wives, to pass down to the next generation. I know this means a great deal to him."

Ellenor swallowed. "It wasn't a gift. I am sure it is just a loan to make me feel accepted and not so out of place tonight."

Laurel arched an eyebrow and shrugged her chin. "I don't recall Cole ever considering someone's comfort before, but then, until now neither has he been in love."

Ellenor shook her head. "Cole doesn't want me. I'm English, and I don't fit into his life."

"Conor said he carried you all the way home and up to his room."

"Because he had to! I fell asleep . . . and . . . and it changes nothing!"

"Conor seemed to think you and Cole were going to get married."

"Your husband is very much mistaken." With hands on hips, Ellenor took a deep breath and stared at the ceiling, forcing her tears back. "I actually thought I could win Cole, Laurel. Fight for his love and make him realize just what we could share together. But Cole has room in his life for his men and for Robert, nothing else."

"Robert?"

"Yes, a ghost. And after yesterday, even if Cole *were* to

ask me to marry him, I would refuse. It would be for all the wrong reasons—pity, guilt, or lust. Cole would never ask me to be his wife simply because he loved me, because I made him happy, completed him . . ."

Laurel was tempted to ask what happened yesterday, but decided it might be better if she didn't. Instead, she walked over and stroked Ellenor's arm. "That's how you feel about him, isn't it? And you want him to feel the same way about you."

Ellenor nodded and brushed a tear from her cheek. "But what I want and what I can have are two different things." She took a deep breath and pasted on a smile she hoped would someday become genuine. "I'm content with what I have and that is more than enough for me. It is much more than I deserve."

"I will not pretend to understand your reasons, but if you don't want to marry Cole, that is your choice. Let me simply caution you about wanting the undying, ever-professing love of a man—it rarely exists. Men like Cole do not sing love songs and speak eloquently of their feelings, but they do feel deeply. I thought you understood that. Someday I hope someone will, and if you can see Cole happy with another woman, to have someone else hold him, bear his children, and grow old with him, if you can do this and still be at peace, then your decision is indeed wise. If not—"

Laurel was interrupted by a sharp rap at the door. She called out for her visitor to enter, and Ellenor was face to face with the man she had called an ass, an idiot, and a few other things. Laird McTiernay. She had successfully avoided him all afternoon while dashing about making last-minute preparations for tonight's feast. Now, he was peering down at her, using his height to intimidate her. At first, it worked . . . until she realized what he was doing. Then, it had the opposite result.

Ellenor backed up a step and raked her eyes up and down and snorted. "You are a lucky man, laird. Laurel agreed to marry you. Not too many women want a hulking giant for a husband." Stepping around him, Ellenor smiled to herself and headed toward the door. "I'm going to check on the twins. I'll meet you inside the hall."

Laurel waved in acknowledgment. Ellenor closed the door but not before Conor's laughter erupted from the other side. "Good God, Cole has picked himself one. If I looked for years, I couldn't have found someone better for my brother. Who would have thought it? And she's an *Englishwoman*!"

Ellenor grimaced. She was going to have to do a lot better job at hiding her feelings. Just as she was about to walk out of earshot, she heard Conor say in complete awe, "Lord, wife, you are beautiful. Once again, I will have to fight the urge to pummel every man who looks at you."

She leaned against the stairwell wall for a second and then headed to Laurel's chambers on the fourth floor. They were empty and provided the privacy of a good cry. She had never been a jealous person, but hearing how much Conor loved his wife, witnessing the admiration and approval in Donald's eyes when he had seen Brighid, hearing the love in Aileen's voice when she spoke of Finn . . . these were things she wanted to have and never would.

Ellenor had no idea how long she cried, but a sudden shout reverberated up from the inner yard followed by several others. It was dark and the bonfires had been lit. People were packed around them as drinks from the buttery began to be passed around. She was late.

Wiping her eyes dry, she pinched her cheeks and walked out of the room and down the stairwell. She hadn't gotten two steps out the tower door when several men engaged in a jovial shoving match slammed into her. Barely escaping injury, she tried to wind her way through the throngs of people. They were celebrating, and after hearing bits and pieces from the crowd, she knew what about—Cole had been named the McTiernay laird for the northern nomadic clans.

Eager to find him, she continued to weave her way across the inner yard. Most clansmen she encountered ignored her. She had nearly reached her target of the Great Hall entrance when a large arm suddenly wrapped itself around her waist and lifted her into the air.

"Damn, if you aren't the bonniest thing my eyes have ever seen. I have been gone a long time, *bòidheach*, and I want to be welcomed home properly!"

The arm belonged to a soldier but not one she recognized. "Put me down!"

"Nay, woman. I'll put you down when I find a space where you and I can be alone."

The man was drunk and slurring his words, but his grip was firm and he was walking away from the Hall and toward one of the nearby dark corners. Panic flooded her and she was suddenly back on the floor of her father's solar, pinned down on the floor with a man's hand on her legs. In her mind, Cole came and saved her, killing the beast who held her. But Cole was nowhere in sight. No one she knew was.

The man pressed her against the wall so that her feet dangled a foot off the ground and held her there by her waist. She would have screamed, but his lips were over hers, smothering all attempts to yell for help.

Ellenor began to thrash and kick and bite anything she could find that was soft, fleshy, and capable of feeling pain. The man yelled and suddenly she was in the air. A sharp pain shot through her back as it collided with the ground. As fast as she could, Ellenor whirled onto her feet and disappeared into the shadows. The instinct to run far from everyone and everything was nearly overwhelming. Her mind raced, trying to find a place she could be alone and in complete control of all things around her, but before she could think of one, another thick male arm slinked around her waist, pulling her once again into a hefty chest.

"Mmm, you smell good," the raspy voice said, twirling her around.

Shaking, Ellenor closed her eyes and pleaded, "Please, let me go."

Immediately he did as she asked. Her feet touched the ground and Ellenor felt the weight pressing down upon her suddenly lift. She looked up at the grisly face beaming down at her and returned the smile.

The man backed up a foot. "Ah, lass, for one as bonnie as you, I'd do anything. I'd fight all the men here tonight for one of your smiles. Tell me your name, love, and I promise to be yours forever."

Ellenor was about to turn around and try running again when another man's voice stopped her. "Seamus, be warned. This is *Cole's* Lady Ellenor."

Her eyes darted to the source of the deep authoritative voice and realized it was Jaime, but before she could sigh in relief, he gripped her arm and firmly tugged it, compelling her to follow.

"Jaime Ruadh, please let go."

Jaime firmly shook his head no. "In this crowd, I could lose you again."

Ellenor's feet could barely move quick enough to keep up with him. "Could we slow down? Where are we going?"

"We are looking for Cole. He's somewhere out here searching for you and I am pretty sure that if he doesn't find you soon, men are going to find themselves hurt if not worse."

"Why?"

That stalled Jaime. He paused to look back at her, his face full of incredulity. Sliding his grip from her arm to her hand, he again started his mad march through the courtyard, pushing anyone aside—male or female—who got in his way. "Because Cole saw that man grab you, and unless we find him and he sees you are unharmed—"

"He *saw* that?" Ellenor interrupted. "Why didn't he help me out!" For the first time since the encounter, Ellenor started feeling less scared and more angry.

Her voice caught the attention of several onlookers, all of whom looked past Jaime as if he weren't there. Ellenor shouted, "Look out!" but Jaime was already moving as one large heavyset farmer began his attack. A second later, the farmer was in the air and fell to the ground with a hard thud.

Without wasting another second on the drunken group, Jaime grabbed Ellenor's hand again and proceeded toward the Lower Hall. Along the way, he tried to explain. "Cole was in the Great Hall, watching through the windows for your arrival. By the time he spotted you, it was too late. I don't know what he saw, but he began to bellow out orders. Donald is right now gathering men in the Lower Hall, and unless you can be found, *unharmed*, Cole is going to demand blood."

Ellenor remembered the promise he had made to her. That she would be safe behind McTiernay walls. He must have thought he had broken an oath, the one thing Cole held more dear than all else. His honor. She had to get to him and explain it wasn't his fault. "Oh, Lord, where is he?"

"Somewhere hunting that man down."

Just a moment ago, she had wanted that very thing.

For Cole to find the man who had attacked her and kill him, but now that it was actually about to happen, Ellenor wasn't sure of anything. "Then why are we headed to the Hall? We've got to find Cole."

Jaime shook his head, beads of frustration forming on his brow. The closer they moved to the Halls and the kitchens, the thicker the crowds became. Shoving people out of the way was slowing their progress. "Before Cole does anything, he will meet with Donald. We need to get there before he does."

Ellenor could see the rooftop of the Lower Hall and sighed in relief. They were almost there.

She was just about to point and say it looked like they made it in time when suddenly someone snatched her arm sleeve to get her attention. Instinct caused Ellenor to pull free from Jaime's grasp and turn around. "Brighid?!" she yelled.

Her friend, who had looked stunning just hours ago, was still wearing her new deep rose bliaut, but most of her curly hair had sprung lose from its constraints. "Thank God I found you," Brighid gushed. "All these people I never thought it would be possible. You *must* come with me," she said, her words tumbling out in heavy breaths. "Now."

Ellenor pulled back her sleeve and pointed to where Jaime was waiting impatiently. "I cannot. I absolutely have to get to the Lower Hall—"

"No," Brighid huffed. "You must come with me now."

She clutched Ellenor's forearm and pulled, but Ellenor stood firm. "I must get to the Lower Hall. We will talk later—"

Brighid gave her a narrowed look, her vexation evident. "You are coming with me! Right after Cole started yelling, Donald, the laird, and all the men left. And a minute later, Laurel went into full-blown labor. We found out she had been having pains all day."

That got Ellenor's attention. She felt Jaime tug on her sleeve, but she gestured for him to wait. "What? Why didn't she say something?"

"When Laurel gave birth to the twins, it took a long time. A *real* long time, and she just figured this would be the same. But it seems this bairn is coming soon. Hagatha is worried. She said something about it not being right and Laurel asked for you. She's scared and needs you *now*."

Ellenor stared for a moment at Brighid's pleading brown eyes and then glanced back at Jaime. His patience was waning, and there was true fear of what would happen if they didn't arrive in the Lower Hall soon. She looked back at Brighid. "Has Conor been told?"

Brighid shrugged her shoulders. "The men had left when the pains started coming in earnest. I don't know whether she told him or not. My guess is no; otherwise he would never have let her come down for the festivities."

"Where is she?" Ellenor asked, hoping she wasn't still in the Great Hall.

"We had a couple of servants carry her to her room and I went looking for you."

Ellenor nodded in acknowledgment. Turning back to Jaime, she said in an even, decisive voice, "Jaime, return quickly to the Lower Hall. Find Cole and Donald and let them know that I am well but that it is urgent to find Conor. His wife is in labor and there are complications. We will tell you as soon as we know more."

Then without waiting for Jaime to agree or argue, she turned and followed Brighid to the Star Tower. Away from the kitchens and fires, the crowd was not nearly as thick, yet several times, she and Brighid were stopped by one or more drunken men, barely able to stand. Ellenor, now prepared to be unexpectedly accosted, felt herself elbowing sternums, kicking groins, and aiming for knees with more ease than she would have thought possible. Finally, they reached the Tower's entrance.

Hurrying up the stairwell, Ellenor heard Laurel cry out and rushed into her friend's day room. Inside were Aileen, holding Laurel's hand, and Hagatha, who was at the end of the bed, her face tense and bothered. Laurel was in bed with her eyes closed, her bliaut discarded and her chemise wet along her chest and arms from perspiration.

Walking straight toward her friend, Ellenor nodded at Aileen on the other side and whispered, "Laurel, I'm here. Brighid found me. You have us all now."

Laurel reached out and found Ellenor's hand, but before she could say anything, her back arched and the veins in her neck bulged as another pain struck. After a few seconds, a gush of air came out along with a holler of, "Oh God, something is wrong."

Ellenor reached up and brushed Laurel's hair back off her forehead and murmured, "Nothing is wrong. You're just having a baby. Just think, when this is done, you will have a beautiful child to hold and love."

Hagatha moved the chemise up and placed her hands on Laurel's distended stomach, pushing at various spots. When done, she shook her head at Aileen. Laurel's best friend, who seemed confident in any situation, was crying. Fear ripped across her face and one word, barely audible, escaped her lips. "No . . ."

Alarm seized Ellenor. "What does she mean, no? No to what? You aren't saying Laurel is dying, are you? I mean . . . she can't be."

Hagatha stared down at her hands with a look of helplessness. "She said her mother died in childbirth. I should have known to be more careful, but I thought with the last one, I thought . . ."

Ellenor grabbed the old midwife's shoulder and yanked on it. "You thought what?"

"I didn't think it would be a breech. She said the baby was kicking her ribs. I assumed the baby was down."

Ellenor licked her lips, struggling to understand what the old woman was trying to say. "So you are saying the feet are down."

Hagatha nodded, still looking at her hands.

"Then pull the feet. Can't you do that?"

"I can't reach them."

Now Ellenor understood why Hagatha was staring at her hands. They were big for a woman. Knowledgeable and skilled, but large. Too large to reach in. At that moment another pain struck Laurel and Ellenor knew something had to be done and now. Her friend could not last much longer this way. No one could. "I can do it," she heard herself say.

"You?"

"Yes, tell me what to do," she ordered and shoved her sleeves far above her elbows. She quickly washed her hands in the basin and then sat at the foot of the bed. If she was going to do anything, it would have to be now and quick before Laurel seized again with pain.

Hagatha blinked and then got herself together. "You have to reach in and find the feet."

Ellenor took a deep breath and then watched Laurel as she moved up and inserted first her fingertips and then her hand up the canal. Laurel twisted, but seemed only half-aware of what Ellenor was doing. "I'm in. I feel . . . I think I feel the bottom."

Hagatha took a deep breath and exhaled. "It would be better if the baby could be turned. Can you turn the

child around? Find the shoulder and press and see if
the bairn responds."

Ellenor began to probe. Never could she explain to
anyone what it was like to touch a new life in such a way.
She found the shoulder and gave it a small shove. Immediately it responded. Hagatha, whose hands were
doing what they could from on top of the stomach,
sucked in her breath. "I think you did it, *stiorlag*."

Ellenor smiled and was about to remove her hand
when she touched a small ropelike thing around what
felt to be the baby's neck. "I think there's another problem," she said and then proceeded to explain what
exactly she was feeling.

"You must unwrap the cord and quickly. If another
pain strikes, the baby will choke."

Ellenor carefully eased the slimy thick cord from
around the slender neck. She pulled free just as Laurel's
back went rigid. Instinct must have told her to bear
down, for she did with all her might. A second later a
head appeared. Hagatha told her to keep pushing.
Laurel took one last breath and suddenly the shoulders
appeared, and a second later, a baby girl slipped into
Ellenor's waiting hands.

Hagatha reached over and took the little red and
white thing and gave a quick thump to the back. A
small, defiant holler filled the chambers. Ellenor had
never heard a sweeter sound.

Quickly the baby was cleaned and swathed while
Aileen and Brighid helped Laurel don a clean chemise
and change her bedding. By the time, Hagatha placed
the squirming child into Laurel's arms, Ellenor finally
returned to the present.

"Oh, Laurel, she's absolutely beautiful."

Laurel looked down at the mass of brown hair and

stroked the small cheek. "You saved our lives, Ellenor. How will I ever be able to thank you?"

"You came and got me when nobody would. You saved me first."

Laurel turned her head and said, "That reminds me. What happened? I was so worried about you! Cole was so angry . . . something about saving you."

"Shhh, I'm fine. A man grabbed me and I just had to convince him to let go. I didn't even get a scratch," Ellenor quietly reassured her friend.

Suddenly she realized that it was true. A man had held her and wanted to hurt her, but he hadn't. Not because of Cole. He hadn't been there to save her. She had saved herself, not just that time, but many times tonight. She had been surrounded by men who were bigger and stronger than she was, but time and time again, she had forced them to keep their distance. She hadn't needed to learn how to trust everyone else; she had needed to learn how to trust herself again. Isolation did not bring about control. That was the façade. Friendship made one stronger. And love could heal any wound. Cole had given her the means to finally feel whole again. Suddenly the urge to do the same for him was overwhelming.

"Laurel," Ellenor whispered. Laurel's eyes were on the small little hand gripping her pinky. "I have to go. I will tell Conor the news, but if I am ever to experience the happiness you have on your face right now, I need to find Cole. I cannot wait one more moment."

Laurel nodded, smiling. "Go. Go and be happy. He loves you, so don't let him get away."

Ellenor brushed back a tear of joy and said, "I won't."

The words were still lingering in the air when she vanished into the corridor and down the stairwell.

Just as she was rounding the last turn, she ran into something large and solid. It was Conor.

"Oh, laird . . ."

Conor grabbed her shoulders and his gray eyes pierced hers. "My wife?" he choked.

Ellenor threw her arms around him and squeezed him hard. "She's fine! You have a beautiful baby girl. Both are eager to see you." She waved her hand for him to proceed by her.

Conor paused and said, "If you are looking for Cole, he left shortly after Jaime arrived and said you had been found unharmed."

Startled by the news, Ellenor leaned against the cold stones for balance. "What do you mean 'left'?"

Conor stared at her for a second as if debating on what and how much to say. "I don't think I have ever seen my brother so mad as he was this evening. When you didn't come back with Jaime Ruadh, he nearly exploded and demanded he be allowed to go up and see you and verify for himself. He actually threatened me."

Ellenor erected herself, her brows bunched. She shook her head in disbelief. "But that doesn't sound like Cole. He's . . . he never . . . well, he's always so damned composed."

"Up until he met you, I'd agree."

Ellenor gave Conor a slight smile. "I don't think most people realize just how much he keeps inside. He's not as detached as he wants everyone to think. Unfortunately, I seem to bring his more volatile emotions out."

Conor chuckled. "Strong perhaps, but I wouldn't say volatile. Regardless, you definitely have an effect on him. As soon as we met, I knew he had changed and quickly deduced you as the cause. I wasn't sure whether you would be a good influence on him, you being English and him a new laird."

Ellenor swallowed. "And now?" she asked, afraid to ask the question, but more afraid not to know its answer.

"Now I think you are just what he needs. You unlock his soul. If you are lucky, you meet the one person in this life who can do that. I assume you feel the same way about him."

Ellenor felt a tear fall. "I do."

"It's the middle of the night, and if it were any other brother, I would tell you to wait until morning. But I think Cole needs you now just as much as it looks like you need him." Conor stepped back out of the tower and waved for someone to approach. "He went down to the loch to cool off, but I doubt it worked. Seeing you will help more than any cold dip ever could." Then he turned and ordered a soldier she didn't recognize to take her to the stables and escort her to the loch.

Ellenor turned around to say thank you, but Conor had already disappeared back up the stairs, eager to see his wife and new child.

Chapter 11

Cole could hear the horse's hooves pounding the earth long before he could see them. Whoever was approaching didn't know anyone was near, didn't care, or came specifically to find him.

Cole stepped out of the cold water and threw on his leine, muttering. He had intentionally ridden nearly an hour to the farthest end of the loch for assured peace. He had needed time to think. Jaime had said·Ellenor was unharmed but still in a state of shock when Brighid had found her and demanded she help Laurel. Once the upheaval of tonight's events passed, Ellenor would no doubt retreat into her shell.

He needed a plan. Hell, he needed several plans. He had just become laird, and Cole suspected Dugan would soon challenge him. Time was critical to thwart any threat the man was almost certainly concocting. That left little choice but to leave first thing in the morning.

The original plan had been to explain the situation to Ellenor and suggest in his absence to prepare for a wedding—hers. But he never got the chance. Ellenor had been attacked at the one place he had promised her safety. Cole knew her instinct would be to run, and Jaime finding her had been a miracle. But once she had time to think, Cole feared she might resurrect her old ideas and once again shun men—even him. He needed time with her, the one thing he didn't have. The two most important things in his life claimed his immediate attention, and each could be satisfied only at the expense of the other.

He had to decide between Ellenor and his clan.

Grabbing his sword, he stepped behind a tree and waited to spot the rider. The air was clear. The clouds that had been lining the night sky with thunder and lightning had moved north, allowing the stars and nearly full moon to shine below. With so much light, Cole could see for miles, but then so could an enemy. With the threats he had made earlier after witnessing Ellenor's fight for freedom, it was possible more than one man would want to find him and try their hand at teaching him a lesson. He hoped one particular soldier would. However, if he was smart, the man who had dared to lay hands on Ellenor would never cross paths with Cole again.

Waiting patiently, he saw the figures of two riders. One pulled off and headed away, but the other continued at a full gallop. Cole eased his grip on his sword. Whoever they were, an attack was not on their mind. It had to be news from the castle.

He picked up his tartan and gave it a quick whip to scatter all the leaves and dust clinging to it. Quickly folding it around his waist, he belted the garment, secured his weapon, and then approached the rider. He had just broken out of the line of trees hugging the water's edge when he recognized the messenger. Ellenor.

As soon as she saw him, she pulled the reins back hard, slowing the monstrous beast she was riding. She slid off the animal's back, but instead of moving toward him, she stood still, staring at him, as if her feet were held to the ground.

She was covered in blood.

Cole felt his whole body go instantly cold. The second rider had not been a friend. The bastard had attacked her. Cole began running. A torrent of icy terror ricocheted through his veins and twisted his heart. His feet couldn't move fast enough.

When he reached her, all he wanted to do was pull her into his arms and hold her, never letting go. Instead, he stroked her cheek. "Elle, love," he began, trying but failing to keep his voice level, "where are you hurt?"

"Hurt?" She looked down at her stomach and hips, where his hands were gently probing. "Oh, that's Laurel's blood, not mine. She had a beautiful baby g—"

Cole seized her mouth midsentence and began to ravish her lips, letting her feel the fear and anger tearing through him. Ellenor answered his embrace with one of her own. She slid her tongue into his mouth, moaning at the taste of him. He drew her closer until her whole body had melted against him. A raging hunger was building inside him. It was consuming him and it would not be contained with mere touching and another icy swim. Cole wanted nothing more but to lay her down where they stood and make sweet love to her.

Nothing . . . with one exception. Before he enjoyed the pleasures for which he had too long been denying them both, he needed to make sure she understood what it would mean. She was his. She had been his since the moment their eyes had met, and he had been a fool to imagine otherwise.

He finally mustered the ability to lift his head and break off the kiss.

Ellenor sucked in air and sighed, smiling. Believing

he was about reclaim her lips, she stood on her tiptoes and reached up to wrap her hands around his neck. Diving her fingers into his loose, damp hair, she tried pulling his head back down toward hers. He resisted. "Cole," she whispered, rocking against him, seeking his mouth again.

"Ahh, *abarach*, how can I resist you."

Ellenor nipped at his lower lip and purred, "Don't you dare try, Scot."

Cole closed his eyes. If she ever learned what that soft, hoarse sound did to him, he would never win a single battle in their marriage. His hands stole up her arms to her shoulders and gave them a slight push, once again breaking off the embrace. "Elle," he began, his mind racing to find just the right words.

Ellenor followed his lead, leaned back, and severed the intimacy of their physical connection. She blinked. Cole was not just pausing . . . he was stopping. But it did not make sense. She had recognized the urgency in him, the tension in his arms, the tautness in his back and shoulders. He had wanted her and had been fighting to control his desire. She had felt it.

Her green and gold eyes widened with hurt, but only for a moment before narrowing. No longer was she going to let this man dictate the course of their futures. She pressed a finger into his chest and said through clenched teeth, "No. Not again. You are *not* doing this to us again. I don't care how stubborn you may consider yourself to be, but this time I am not letting you just walk away and say it won't work between us. Or pretend that what is between you and me is something we can move past and forget." Ellenor took a step closer until they were almost touching and looked up, staring him directly in the eye. "I may not be beautiful like Laurel, but some do consider me desirable."

"Very," Cole acknowledged, but before he could add that Laurel couldn't touch her beauty, Ellenor spun around and began to pace.

"When I first met you, I was terrified and it wasn't just of men. Never again did I want to be out of control of anything . . . my surroundings, my body, but especially my future. So I had devised a plan that would enable me to avoid everyone, believing isolation would keep me safe. Then we met."

Cole took a step forward and reached out, wanting to reassure her that none of what she was saying was necessary. He already knew. "Elle . . ."

Ellenor came to an abrupt halt and leveled him with an icy stare. It stopped him cold. She nodded, assured that she would be allowed to finish and resumed her pacing. "At the beginning I mistook my attraction to you to be nothing more than trust. With you, I was safe. You are strong, have an inflexible sense of honor, but most importantly, you despise the English."

Cole's brows bunched, having long ago stopped perceiving her as an *English*woman but as *his* woman. "I don't despise the English," he lied.

Ellenor waved her hand dismissively. "Oh, yes, you do. And if a Scottish warrior had murdered Laurel in front of me, I can promise you my feelings would be just as strong against your kinsmen." She paused and her eyes met his. "And I would have wanted to hate you, but I wouldn't have been able to, just as you do not hate me. You don't, do you?"

"I don't think I ever have."

"I never hated you either. I needed you, though. When you took me from my sister's home, I once again was being forced into a situation that I neither understood nor controlled, but I had you. I trusted you, and after we first kissed, I knew then that I loved you more than I thought it possible to love another being. I was going to fight for you, make you understand what we shared was special, unique, but . . . I didn't. I couldn't. The truth was I didn't think I deserved to love you or have your love in return."

Now *that* surprised Cole. His expression must have revealed his enormous shock, which created a similar reaction in Ellenor. "Did you never wonder why I never tried to stop you from walking out on me or plead for you to come back?"

Cole hadn't wondered. He had just assumed it had been her pride holding her back from begging him to stay where he didn't want to be. It had never occurred to him that she had welcomed his retreat.

Misreading his silence, Ellenor continued. "I never once doubted you would be selected laird. No matter how good, qualified, or *friendly* any other choice might be, any clan that *could* have you, would have you."

Again, she surprised him. Ellenor had said as much before, but all during times when he had needed to hear such encouragement and be reminded that the future he had never aspired to have, but suddenly wanted, could be his. But he had assumed incorrectly. Her professions had not been to bolster his confidence, but because she truly believed in them.

Ellenor stopped her quick-paced strides. "And though I knew you would be selected, I also knew some might contest you, especially if given cause. As laird, the woman you select to be your wife would have to be strong, capable, and seen as honorable to your clan. Until tonight, I didn't believe I could be any of those things for you. I needed you, but while you might desire me, you never needed me in return. We both know that neither you nor I could be happy with one of us being dependent upon the other. So I let you push me away. I coveted the few embraces we shared, but I never let myself hope for more."

Ellenor moved in close and placed her hands upon his chest. "But I learned something a little while ago. A man grabbed me and tried to kiss me and touch me. I called out, but no one could hear. No one came. *I* fought back. I am unharmed—not because anyone saved me, but because I saved myself. Then, before I could be afraid of what happened, I had to save a new life fighting to get into this world. Feeling that small little babe in my hands, everything became clear. Isolation protected me only from the pain inflicted by others, but it intensified the pain I inflicted upon myself. I am not afraid anymore. Not of men, people, or the uncontrollable state of my future. So you see, Cole, I don't need you anymore."

All during her dialogue, Cole had been experiencing a series of emotions—astonishment, anticipation, and a level of joy from knowing his future would be with this woman, who had recognized who he was and loved him despite his shortcomings since almost the beginning. Then his world plummeted and with five small words shattered into pieces.

Cole, I don't need you anymore.

He refused to accept it. She had admitted she loved him. Whether or not she needed him, be damned. She was his, and he was not going to let her slip away just when he realized how much she meant to him.

Ellenor licked her lips and took a deep breath. Everything she had said until now had been easy. The whole ride out, she had rehearsed just what she wanted to say. Right until this part. The part where she had to convince him that he loved her, that she could make him happy, and that he should marry her despite his past and hers.

She risked looking up. His eyes swept over her face,

probing into her very soul, robbing her from further speech. His hands moved to gently cup her cheeks and then he spoke. "But I need you."

His voice had been soft, raspy with suppressed emotion. Unshed tears brimmed in his eyes and Ellenor felt her fears drift away. This man was hers. He loved her. "Marry me?" she asked, just before pulling his mouth down to cover hers.

He kissed her hard and deliberately, searing her lips to his, excising all the fears that had been coursing through him the past few minutes. Again and again, he took her mouth, his own tongue rough and insistent. And each time she responded. Her hands moved to his shoulders, stroking him wild, and he became intensely aware of the sensual hunger building in him. Soon he would lose control. And while the ground was not where Cole had intended to teach her all the pleasures between a man and a woman, there was no way he would be able to withstand the long trip back to their room.

Ellenor could feel Cole easing their kiss, but she also sensed he wasn't ending it. Instead, it turned into one much softer, and if possible, even more consuming. The soft caress held so much love and tenderness it nearly choked her. Then without a word, Cole lifted her into his arms and began to head toward the loch. Laying her head upon his shoulder, she succumbed to the desire to touch him and reached into the opening of his leine and began to stroke his chest.

Cole could feel his arms trembling. Things almost seemed too perfect, and he was suddenly afraid that she still might not know how he felt about her. "I love you."

Ellenor's hand froze. He had spoken the words so quietly, with the barest hint of sound, and yet it was as if he had said them directly to her heart. And she knew what Cole had just said was true. "I love you, too," she whispered.

Cole's grip tightened as he used his shoulder to hold back a tree branch while carrying her through the narrow path. "You do need me then?"

The question puzzled Ellenor almost as much as the rock-hard tension in every part of his frame. She almost said "no" and reminded him about her earlier claim— that she no longer needed anyone—and then it hit her. Cole *hadn't* understood. She considered telling him that it was because she *didn't* need him that she could live her life fully now and truly give herself to him. But she suspected he still wouldn't understand, not yet.

Ellenor nuzzled her head back on his shoulder and whispered her answer. "Forever." And she had meant it. She would always need him and his love.

Immediately, Cole's lungs released the breath he had been holding. He stepped past the last of the foliage that protected the bank of the loch and gently placed Ellenor on her feet. "Don't move," he ordered and planted a quick kiss on the tip of her nose.

Ellenor watched with curiosity to see what Cole planned to do. She had assumed he had been intending to retrieve his horse so they could return to the castle. But when he had put her down, his eyes had become sapphirine fires, nearly burning her with smoldering passion. A long ride back was not what he had in mind.

When Cole reached to strip the plaid blanket from his mount, she guessed his intentions and wrung her hands in anticipation. Her fingertips felt spots of dried blood on her palms she had missed in her hasty cleanup. She looked down at her fingers and the bright moonlight revealed just how bloody her wrists and arms were, but even more so was her gown. She had been so focused on finding Cole she had not realized just how grimy and soiled she had become helping Laurel.

Ellenor glanced at the small ripples sparkling on the loch. Its enticing bank was just a few feet from where she stood. Making a decision, she reached for the strings binding her bliaut and pulled. When Cole took her into his arms, she was not going to be covered in someone else's blood. Last time, he had kissed and tasted and teased her all over, and Ellenor wanted nothing preventing him from doing so again.

Stepping out of the caked garment, she kicked off her slippers and removed the diaphanous chemise made specifically for the once gorgeous outfit. She dropped a toe into the cool water and shivered, despite the unusual warmth in the air. Fed by the Highland mountaintop snows, the water was significantly colder than that of the rivers she had bathed in during the journey here. Taking a deep breath, she forced herself to wade in, unaware of the two eyes following her every movement.

Cole had seen her naked before. He had even seen her wet, emerging from a river after bathing. He had tasted her skin and knew just how sweet it was, but it still had not prepared him for what he had just seen. Maybe it was the knowledge that this time he wouldn't have to hold back, or that she loved him, or that all that beauty was truly and forever his, but watching her undress and then gracefully glide into the dark waters of the loch had created a storm of need within him that had been unlike anything he had ever felt.

Cole quickly laid out the plaid on the thick yellow grass just beginning to show new spring growth. Walking to the water's edge, he yanked his belt free, ripped his leine over his head, and dove in.

Ellenor heard the splash and stopped rubbing her

skin. She turned toward the sound but saw nothing but ripples of disturbed water. A dark head suddenly emerged and she instinctively screamed and tried to retreat. Cole's arms stole around her waist and pulled her close. His mouth kissed the valley between her breasts and Ellenor suddenly felt very vulnerable. Last time, Cole had kissed her to a drugged state in which she had been aware only of him.

Ellenor pulled her arms in front of her. Cole chuckled and traced his fingertip across her lower lip. "I love you, Ellenor."

Ellenor's heart quickened. The sensual touch, the raspy sound of his voice that echoed her own longings, his eyes gleaming dark and hot—everything about him was weaving a spell about her. Her skin no longer felt cold, and an incredible warmth began to course through her blood and pool in her lower body.

Slowly, she lifted her arms and circled them around his neck. Cole sucked in a quivering breath as she pressed her soft round breasts and belly against his own desperate yearning. He closed his eyes and fought the overwhelming need to plunge inside her. The coldness of the loch's dark waters was doing very little to help ease the strain. He was afraid to touch her. One more sensation could prove to be too much.

Ellenor drew closer, burying her fingers in the softness of his hair. She felt another shiver run through him and relished the newfound knowledge that she could excite and make this huge Highlander moan with need with just the mere touch of her flesh. Feeling both strangely powerful and safe to be her wild, adventurous self, she let her right hand drop from his hair to his neck, and with a featherlike caress down his spine, dip into the dark waters. Then her fingertips wandered over the dent created by his taut muscles before tightening around the round curve of his cheek.

Suddenly his hardness nestled between them grew longer and became very rigid. Cole groaned, "You're killing me."

Ellenor wondered if she had done something wrong, but before she could ask, Cole slid his body down until his lips were level with her nipples. "It's dangerous to touch a man like that, love. I can barely control myself."

Ellenor raked her fingers through his hair. "Then don't," she whispered and placed a loving kiss on his temple.

He lifted his head and gazed into her deep green eyes. There was no mistaking the yearning in the misty pools. Every nerve, every impulse ached to respond to her beseeching request and fulfill his own desire, which had been building since the day they met. But unless she was there with him, crying out with shared pleasure at the moment of their joining, it would be a hollow gratification. And that would be an even greater pain than the physical discomfort he was experiencing now.

He placed a soft kiss on the inside of one breast. "First, you," he replied, and then trailed his lips all around the soft mound until he reached its peak. Laving it with his tongue, he took the already hard nipple into his mouth and teased it. His teeth lightly tantalized the pink berry until Ellenor squirmed with growing need. He held her close, massaging the muscles of her back and buttocks.

He finally freed the pink bud, and the moment the air touched the sensitive flesh, Ellenor cried out and arched upward, offering herself to his hungry mouth, hoping he would comply. Cole smiled and then roamed the valley between Ellenor's breasts until he reached the other creamy mound. He found the nub already taut and waiting for him.

Ellenor was holding her breath, unable to speak, yet wanting to shout for him to take her in his mouth and love her as he was doing before. Slowly, his tongue traced circles around her nipple, until it flicked over the rosy peak. Ellenor gasped and clutched his shoulders. "Cole," she moaned. It was half plea, half demand for him to do more.

Finally, he captured the throbbing nipple in his mouth and held the bloom between his lips, stroking the sensitive flesh with his tongue. Ellenor cried out and Cole began to suckle. Over and over, he stroked the hardened peak until it quivered, and then he gently pulled on the swollen nub with his teeth.

Cole shook with building need. He wanted to taste all of her, know her, feel her body react to his touch. With his mouth still warm and hot on her breast, his thumb skimmed across her other nipple one last time before sliding down under the water. Slowly his fingers trailed across her hip until he found the soft triangle of hair between her legs. He laced his fingers through its softness and tested her gently with one finger.

Ellenor cried out softly as a deep tremor shook her. She lost control of her legs and felt herself sink into the water before big, warm hands lifted her and carried her to the shore. The last time Cole had touched her like that, he had created a storm of sensations and she had lost control of her body. She wanted that again, but this time she wanted him to lose control with her, and purred her desire in his ear.

Cole almost lost his footing. He had already been shaking, and her nibbling on his earlobe had doubled the intensity growing in his loins, but when she had asked if he would like her to touch him, he had almost fallen. He wasn't quite sure how he had managed to stay upright.

He made his way to the waiting plaid blanket and then gently eased her down on to the makeshift bed. He began to lower himself along the length of her and stopped halfway. The ground, which had never before seemed so hard, suddenly felt too severe for the soft beauty in his arms. "Are you comfortable?"

Sensing his concern, Ellenor raised an eyebrow mischievously as she slid her palm down his chest, across his belly, and lower until her hand cradled his sex. "Now I am." She grinned.

"No, Elle . . ." Cole groaned in protest and was about to stop her, when she started moving the velvety skin up and down over his inner, rock-hard shaft. Instinctively, he pushed himself forward, deeper into her palm, and growled the word "yes" as she kneaded and stroked his flesh. Her semidamp hair had spilled around her head and her eyes glowed with desire as she increased the tempo of her caress. He knew he was about to lose control. Either he lie back and surrender to the climax building within him, or he had to stop her hands before he exploded.

Cole sucked in his breath slowly through his teeth and gathered all his will to pull her hand away. She was about to object when he kissed her heavily, silencing her protest and ending any other thoughts besides him. This time his hands did the roaming.

His thumbs grazed across her nipples and the curve of her hip lifted, pressing into his thigh. His mouth left hers to trail kisses down the side of her throat, until his lips found the softness of her breast and encompassed a pink bud. He began to suckle. She cried out, opening herself to him.

Ellenor lost all power over her body. His velvet tongue was both torture and exciting. And his hands were everywhere, lightly caressing, barely touching. The sensual assault was causing her to writhe and twist with a physical need she could not describe. She didn't want him to stop what he was doing, but her body was screaming for more. All she could do was cling to his shoulders and say his name. "Ohhhh, Cole."

Cole released her breast. It was swollen like its mate. Crushing them against his chest, his mouth found hers again with a hungry urgency. And his sweet Ellenor kissed him back, rubbing her hips against his thighs, her body desperate for more. His already aroused shaft tightened even further and the pain from holding back was mounting. He needed to be inside her. She was almost ready.

Reaching down, Cole stroked her from breast to thigh, enjoying her smooth, satiny skin. As he moved his fingers upward, she opened herself to him and arched her hips, hungry for his touch. His heart was pounding as he stopped just shy of the sultry heat that emanated from between her legs. Only his thumb moved in slow torturous circles as he waited.

Ellenor couldn't take any more. She needed him to touch her soon or she would perish. "Please, Cole," she begged.

"Please, what, love?"

"Touch me . . . I need you, please."

Cole moved then, cupping her gently before easing one finger into her damp heat. Ellenor tipped her head back and a small cry escaped. She could hear the blood pounding in her veins as Cole moved within her, adding one then two more fingers, spreading her narrow passage. Every nerve ending in her body was alive and begging for release. She closed her eyes and forgot everything except for Cole and what he was making her feel.

His fingers probed and stroked, sliding in deeper, exploring her with a level of possessiveness that made her tremble. Then he teased the small female flesh and Ellenor no longer was in her body. The world exploded, just as it had before. This time, though, Cole didn't hold her and rock her back to Earth.

He was hovering, waiting until she was semiaware of what was happening. "Love, I can't wait any longer," he groaned in obvious pain.

Ellenor blinked, trying to understand in her partially drugged state. "Wait? For what?"

"To be inside you, wrapped around me, letting me feel you tremble with need." And to make sure she understood just what he was saying, he lifted her buttocks and pulled her against him, letting her feel all of him.

Ellenor felt his length. It was hard and impatient as it pulsated against her thigh. He was also huge and suddenly the idea of him being inside her didn't seem possible . . . or enjoyable.

Cole settled himself between her legs and watched as the fear of what was to come flashed in her green eyes. He had never bedded a virgin before and doubt swam before him as he fought the fierce desire to bury himself in her. He wanted her to enjoy the experience, not cringe with fear. "Love, I promise to go slow. We were made for each other," he whispered against her lips, kissing her back into a state of euphoria. He could feel her tension leaving and began to penetrate.

Feeling him inside her, Ellenor's body clenched in reaction. Cole slowed his entrance but continued pushing against the natural resistance of her wet, tight passage. His breathing became harsh, uncontrolled, and ragged with need, and Ellenor suddenly understood the pain his own patience was causing him. Unwilling to deny him the pleasure he had just given her, Ellenor sucked in her breath and surged her hips upward, sliding his hard shaft in one swift thrust into her, letting it fill her completely.

He was inside her now, throbbing with incredible need, but the desire to quench his physical yearnings ended with her soft wrenched cry of surprise. Holding her closely to him, he whispered promises of never hurting her again. That she meant everything to him and nothing else mattered as long as she loved him.

Ellenor held on to him, listening to his promises and calming down. The unexpected sharp pain of his entry was subsiding and her body was starting to accept him, despite his great size and length. She twisted slightly and the sensation it created caused her to tremble with reawakened desire. She wanted him to move, do something. Her body was screaming for him to finish what he had started.

Cole gripped Ellenor's hips to steady her rocking movements. She groaned in protest. "Tell me what you want, love." As badly as he wanted her, he wasn't going to do anything until she was ready.

"I want you," she moaned, pushing against his hands, wanting him to move within her.

Cole almost shouted to the heavens in joy as he began to craft a slow pace. Each time he pulled out, Ellenor arched her hips, ready to take him deeper inside, and Cole's ability to control their lovemaking soon gave way to a primal need that had been waiting for this moment, this woman, since he first understood the urgings of a man.

Wrapping her legs around his waist, she surged to meet him with each deep thrust until she was crying out at the wonder of it. Her nails bit into his shoulders. She hadn't known she could feel like this. His fingers had only introduced her to this world where sensual heat and passion overruled all other sensations. Suddenly her breathing came short and fast, and she felt herself quake with pure, unadulterated joy.

A second later, Cole's body peaked and went into hard tight convulsions. His arms clenched around her, and with one final deep fierce thrust, he gasped, "Oh, God, Elle . . ." He clung to her with his face buried deep into her hair as he filled her with the gift of life.

For several minutes, he held her, unwilling to let go as his body slowly calmed from the miracle they had shared. He had taken her, possessed her, claimed her, as he had never done with any woman before. He had let go of every bit of control, and in return he had made her his own. She was now a part of his heart and soul.

Long minutes passed, and Ellenor felt Cole's heavy weight ease as he rolled to his side, pulling her close to his frame.

She didn't think it possible to love him more, but she did.

Toying with the crisp dark hair on his chest, she sighed with complete contentment and said impishly, "I am assuming your answer is yes then."

Cole cocked a brow and stared at the star-filled sky. He had no idea what she was talking about, but he couldn't imagine denying her anything at that moment. "To what I am agreeing to, I have no idea, but aye is my answer to whatever desire you have."

Ellenor gave his shoulder a playful swat and balanced her chin on his chest. She looked at him, and when his eyes locked with hers, she caught her breath. A liquid fire still burned in the blue depths, matching the deeply sensual expression etched along his mouth. She traced the deep scar along his jaw and felt the growing tension within him. He appeared relaxed, but with a few small encouragements, she guessed he would be more than willing to join with her again. First, though, she needed to make sure just what role she was going to play in his future. "My asking you to marry me."

Cole's eyes widened with the memory. Her question had been a shock, but also a balm to his bleeding soul. He had reacted, not answered. Besides, he had wanted to ask *her*, not the other way around. "I think it was I who asked you."

Ellenor propped herself on her elbow and shook her head. "No, I asked you, Scot, and I would like to know your answer."

Moving to sit up, Cole pulled her across his lap so that she straddled him. "Now how would it appear for our clansmen to learn that it was their lady and not their laird who prompted our marriage?"

"It depends. To the women, you would appear quite clever, being wise enough to solicit and then accept such a request."

"But the men?"

"Well, you Highlanders are a proud lot," Ellenor started, "but I would think even the men would praise your ability to make an Englishwoman ask for your hand and not the other way around."

Unable to squash the temptation, Cole bent his head and placed several feather kisses along the line of her jaw. "Aye, those answers would work," he whispered against her skin, "but what if someone discovers that I *had* intended to ask you, but I waited too long, causing you to propose first?"

Ellenor tipped her head back to give him better access and moaned, encouraging Cole to continue. He nibbled at her earlobe and she lost the ability to think. "Umm, that would be a problem," she muttered.

Cole's mouth lifted. He cupped her cheek and then slanted his lips across hers. She immediately responded, opening her mouth to him, welcoming the hot glide of his tongue against hers. The passion building between them would quickly be unstoppable, and Cole knew it was too soon to take her again. He had never intended to ride her so hard, and in doing so, it would be days before she would be ready for any more lovemaking.

He lifted his head and grinned at her. The gleam in his eyes was full of tenderness and love, but a touch of humor was mixed in there too. "Then we agree. I asked you to marry me. And I am still waiting for my answer."

Ellenor's jaw opened slightly and then closed again. The man was impossible. And the sight of his dimples were making it difficult to counter his preposterous suggestion. Deciding to treat him in the same torturous way, she pushed him back down onto the blanket and covered his body with hers, recapturing his lips in a wild kiss that held nothing back. Cole instinctively returned the embrace, thrusting his tongue into her warm mouth with an almost violent need. Rolling her over to her back, he crushed her body to him. Ellenor responded and began to rhythmically flex and arch her hips into his growing shaft.

Cole broke free and pulled her into a spoon position against his frame. She was already quivering with need. He kissed her hair. "We will be married as soon as I return," he whispered, sounding hoarse.

Ellenor tensed. "Return? Why not tomorrow? I don't—"

"My men and I are leaving in the morning, as soon as the sun rises."

Ellenor felt her heart begin to thump wildly. He was leaving her. He was going to Fàire Creachann without her. "I can come with you. We can marry when Father Lanaghly has time to visit—"

"No." Cole's voice left no room for argument. "When

I take you to our home, it will be as my wife, not as an Englishwoman and not from handfasting."

Ellenor froze. He still had not let go of who she was. "Then tomorrow. Why can we not marry in the morning and then leave for Fàire Creachann?"

"I must take care of things before your arrival. Until I do, you won't be safe. Here, with Laurel and Conor, my mind can be at ease."

Ellenor didn't respond, but she didn't argue either.

Cole stroked her hair and contemplated telling her the full truth of their situation. Knowing she would discover it herself soon enough, he decided to forewarn and prepare her for what lay ahead. "Beyond the men I bring, I command no loyalty. I was chosen as laird because of my army. I have been given a year to gain my clansmen's trust."

Ellenor flipped to her side and stared quietly at his chest. Lifting her gaze, she said, "Then I guess you have a few decisions to make, beginning with if you are going to accept the offer."

The shock of her statement hit him full force. He had never really considered the option of declining the lairdship. Oh, he had the chance, but truth was, he wanted to be chieftain and not to just anyone, but to those Highlanders. They were a proud group of clansmen who had wandered too long without a leader to guide them. He wanted to build these clans back into the force they once were and he knew he could do it.

Ellenor traced one dark eyebrow down to his cheekbone and finally his mouth. "I'm guessing that not only have you accepted, but you would again even knowing all the problems that must be handled by doing so."

His eyes caught and held hers. "Aye, I have."

"Then your next decision is an easier one."

"Which is?"

"What to do about Dugan Lonnagan."

Again, surprise registered on his face. "That I have already decided."

"Do you think he might resist the decision? Maybe even try to fight you?"

A small smile touched his lips before fading. "Eventually, aye. And it will cost him his life. Dugan is no leader, but he is a good man and a seasoned soldier. Scotland should not lose such men."

"So what are you going to do?"

Cole took a deep breath and exhaled. "Make him my commander. He cannot refuse without looking foolish, and his honor will force him to be loyal, at least at first."

Ellenor nodded, understanding his logic. "And you hope that, in time, it will not be his honor, but his allegiance that keeps him by your side."

"Aye, but until I know you will be safe amongst our combined forces, you are to remain here, helping Laurel and preparing for our wedding."

"And how long do you think that might be?"

"One month, perhaps two."

The undefined timeframe was disconcerting, but Ellenor knew there was no other way. Throughout their marriage, there would be many things in which she could beg and plead and get her way, but knowing which decisions were not negotiable would save them both many hurtful exchanges. "Then I will wait and hope that your new commander quickly realizes just how lucky he is to be serving under you. Until then, remind me once more of what our life will be like once we are married."

Cole almost denied her appeal, believing it would cause her too much pain. But the expression on her face brokered no excuses, and he knew then that he wouldn't be able to deny her. His body was already responding to the passion smoldering in her eyes.

He reached for her and she gladly surrendered to his claiming. The urgency and demand for physical release would soon be too much. Until then, Cole intended to take his time with his lovemaking, crafting a slow sensual dance. He wanted to taste and touch every inch of her body, savor every sensation, and remember every moment of the next few hours.

A month was a very long time.

Chapter 12

Cole surveyed the mass of crumbled rocks. They were strewn haphazardly around the base of the corner tower that would someday house his room, as well as Ellenor's and eventually their children's. The majority of stones, erecting the keep and surrounding structures, were still in place and secure, but they lacked the wooden beams and slats that fit into the notches and crevices for floors and ceilings. Until they were in place, Cole could not invite the clan, let alone Ellenor, here to live.

He had known progress might be slow. Restoration was hard work, but at the rate the men were progressing, the day he would be able to marry Ellenor and bring her to Fàire Creachann with peace of mind was far into the future. And that was unacceptable.

From the moment he had left her side, a pervasive loneliness had filled him. Until Ellenor, he had chosen a solitary life, and therefore hadn't expected such a deep feeling of loss. He had left a piece of himself behind, and it would be weeks before they could be reunited.

Cole pointed to a young lad who was moving the

stones from one pile to another across the yard. The purpose eluded him. "You, what's your name?"

The skinny boy came to a dead stop, holding one broken and apparently very heavy stone in his hands. His eyes grew large and he gulped before answering. "Tyrus, laird."

"How old are you Tyrus?"

"Nine summers last month."

Cole pointed to the rock the boy was struggling to hold but refused to drop. "Who instructed you to move these rocks and why is no one helping you?"

"I, uh, the commander told me to do it and that I shouldn't ask questions."

Cole felt his jaw clench and gestured for the boy to drop the heavy burden. A resounding thump was heard moments later. "Did Dugan explain why the rocks were to be moved away from where they are needed?"

Tyrus looked confused. "Commander Dugan didn't instruct me to move the stones. It was the other one. The one with no hair."

"Leith?"

Tyrus nodded. "He told all of us that we were to refer to him as commander and do what we were told. That if we didn't, he would see that our families were barred from the keep and your protection."

"I see," Cole replied.

Dugan's longtime friend and right-hand man had either slowed progress or impeded it since the day Cole had publicly accepted the title of laird. Leith was power-hungry and spineless, a dangerous combination. He had been hiding behind Dugan's name in his efforts to disrupt improvements, and Cole had yet to determine if Dugan was an active player or an innocent dupe. Either way, Cole was beginning to wonder if his decision had been a wise one.

Three weeks ago, a small group of pseudonomadic leaders swore their allegiance and that of their people to a single clan under Cole's leadership. Dugan and his longtime ally had surprisingly done the same.

Immediately afterward, Cole took the four commanders of his now combined army—Donald and Jaime, and Dugan and Leith—and assigned new responsibilities. Donald would oversee three dozen elite soldiers, half from Dugan's men and half from his own army, each handpicked by Cole. These men were to protect him and what he held most dear. Dugan would oversee everything else with Jaime and Leith as his seconds. Cole would determine the clan's needs and it would be Dugan's responsibility to see that they were addressed.

Dugan had been shocked by Cole's decision, knowing it was both a great honor as well as a test of ability and trust, but he had readily accepted it.

At first, he heavily leaned upon his old friend and longtime confidant, Leith, believing Jaime's real assignment was to be a mole for Cole. Within the first week, though, the effects of Leith's abrasive personality could no longer be ignored and Dugan put aside his distrust and enlisted Jaime's help with managing the majority of the newly combined army. That sparked in Cole the first glimmer of hope.

In Dugan's position, he had several choices to make. Through those choices, Cole was going to decide if his commander's oath of allegiance was sincere or a method of reprisal. And after three weeks, Cole was no closer to deciphering the truth. Each time Dugan made a decision for the good of the clan and his laird, he would follow it with another—usually through Leith—that would indicate his position was one of slow, methodical revenge.

Cole looked down at the young lad still staring wide-eyed at him with a mixture of fear and awe in his expression. He was skin and bones like so many of the families for whom he was now responsible. Digging into his sporran, Cole pulled out some chunks of dried beef and tossed them to the boy. Tyrus caught them readily, but before he could speak, Cole issued an order. "I want you to go to the training grounds. Do you know where they are?"

"Aye, laird."

"Good. Find Dugan and tell him that I want to see him immediately. Can you do that? And that beef is yours to eat along the way. But be quick."

Tyrus didn't need to be told twice and ran toward the path that led to the mainland outside the walls and cliffs of Fàire Creachann.

Almost two hours later, Dugan rode into the yard with Leith right behind him. They dismounted and Dugan did a double take when he saw Cole. Correctly interpreting his laird's unwavering stare, Dugan whispered something to Leith. The bald man nodded, issued a blank look to Cole, and then grabbed the reins to both horses before heading to the stone enclosure designated as a makeshift stable. Only stalls and a roof were missing.

Dugan reached Cole's side and said, "Young Tyrus said you wanted to see me."

"Aye," Cole replied and swung his arm open, gesturing for Dugan to walk through the keep's archway. Both men marched up the stairs to the second level and entered one of the few rooms in Fàire Creachann with a floor, a roof, and windows.

Cole moved to the decanter of ale and filled two mugs. He handed one drink over to Dugan, who accepted it. "What's on your mind, laird?" Dugan tried again, following Cole's example and easing into a chair.

Cole downed a few swallows and leaned back, carefully considering his next few words. "This room is the only place in Fàire Creachann that a man can get away from the cold."

Dugan's eyes narrowed in question. "There is also the Lower Hall."

"Aye," Cole agreed, "but the windows have yet to be mounted and the draft is monstrous when a storm blows off the sea."

"I told Leith to get shudders attached. I'll find out why it hasn't been done."

Cole took a deep breath and swirled the remaining contents in the cup. "Do you remember when I first arrived at Fàire Creachann and you and I walked the whole of what was to be our home, our protection?"

"Aye."

"And do you remember what you said?"

"There was much work to be done, too much, perhaps."

"And then you made me a promise, Dugan, a promise which you have yet to fulfill."

Dugan's fist tightened around his mug and his jaw became rock hard. Cole's words had the effect of a strong kick to the groin. His instinct was to retaliate by driving a fist into his laird's jaw. The only reason he didn't was—although painful to admit—the man was right. He had not kept his promise. The keep, the towers—hell, not a single building had been restored and made usable in the past few weeks. And blaming others—more specifically Leith—would not be an acceptable excuse.

Cole watched Dugan wrestle with his emotions. It was possible he was acting, just as it was possible he was truly angry over the situation. "After three weeks, rebuilding has not taken place and repairs, even little ones like the shudders you mentioned, are nonexistent. And now I am to decide why. You never believed Fàire Creachann the best place for this clan. So are you trying to sabotage my efforts to erect a stronghold here? Or are you oblivious to the nonexistent progress being made? Either way, I am left with an unpleasant decision. Remove you from my army and risk the fallout from the clan, or publicly dishonor your work, making it impossible for my men, and future recruits, to respect you."

Dugan took a deep breath and counted several seconds, flexing and relaxing both fists. "Leith was—"

Cole leaned forward and cut him off. "Leith is not the problem. You are."

Dugan narrowed his gaze and stared Cole straight in the eye for the first time since the discussion started. "But I assigned *him* the responsibility of resurrecting this place," he said coolly, angry that he, and not Leith, was being admonished.

"And *you* are responsible for the actions of your men. That includes Jaime and the soldiers in training *and* Leith."

Dugan looked away and stood up abruptly. He walked over to the windowsill and looked down. Leith was near the stables laughing with two other men. He was relaxed and resembled the man Dugan remembered. Leith had fought alongside him in numerous battles, rejecting assured death. They had been best friends for years, sharing dreams and hoping for a better life. But in the month since the council chose Cole, they had not laughed together. Their friendship had not been able to create a bridge between their vast differences of opinion. Instead, Leith sought new relationships and all with one thing in common—those were opposed to Cole being laird.

Dugan knew his friend was not happy, and not knowing what to do, he did nothing. He had allowed Leith to fester and ignored the malcontent he was brewing among the clansmen.

"Pride can be an evil thing, laird," Dugan began, his eyes still directed to the scene below. "And in my desire to save mine, I failed to see how others around me interpreted my actions. It was not my intent to ignore my promise. I swore to you Fàire Creachann would be habitable and thriving again, and it will be." He turned toward Cole and looked him directly in eye. "This time I will personally see to it."

Cole gave a slight nod and placed his mug beside Dugan's. "Come, let us see just what has been done and discuss where to start next."

Dugan nodded and followed Cole down the staircase and back out into the yard. They began their trek around the castle, but throughout the walk, multiple clansmen came up to Cole with a wide range of questions. Some dealt with minor issues or work needs; others were less simple, requiring resolutions to conflicts or determining which clansman's needs took precedence over another's. Each question, Cole answered quickly and decisively. Some replies gained him gratitude, but many others garnered scowls and grumbles. But Dugan noticed one thing in common across all the clansmen who walked away: they respected Cole. They might not have welcomed his decision, but Dugan could see that they all believed their laird to be fair, impartial, and dependable.

For the past three weeks, Dugan had truly believed he had been doing Cole a favor by accepting the position as commander in his ranks. Dugan had assumed that his presence alone would mollify the clansmen and bring a sense of unity. He had been a fool.

On a battlefield with a sword in his hand was where he felt comfortable, maybe even invincible, but these past few weeks had proven to Dugan that, without question, he had not been ready to lead anyone, especially a wary people who needed clear and decisive leadership. He would have been their friend, and consequently, far from impartial and, therefore, far from consistent. These people did not need friends. They needed someone who could plan ahead, predict needs, and proactively address them. In time, Dugan knew he would learn such skills, but only if Cole kept him as his commander.

Dugan made one final vow. This time to himself. He would earn Cole's trust and never again give the man a reason to doubt his integrity. To do so, he knew his loyalty had to shift from that of Leith and his friends to that of his new laird. Dugan hoped they, too, would learn to appreciate Cole and his wisdom and become loyal clansmen. Regardless, Dugan would no longer protect Leith and his antics. Either he stopped, or he would be forced to leave.

"Put that baby down!" Brighid scolded, running over to Ellenor and taking the infant out of her arms. She cooed at the six-week-old babe, whose enormous silver eyes were still on the shiny strands of dark gold hair locked in her fist. "No, no, no, Bonny, your mother has spent a significant amount of time getting your soon-to-be aunt's hair just so." After finally prying the child's fingers loose from Ellenor's hair, Brighid quickly gave her over to her mother before full-blown wailing ensued at the loss of her new toy. She then issued Ellenor another stern stare. "See? *That's* why I told you not to pick her up. Once you do, only her mother can console her."

Laurel bounced her daughter gently, and immediately the babe quieted to her normal placid state. "I don't know what I am going to do with both you *and* Brighid leaving. The twins are growing and getting into mischief all the time and now with Bonny . . ."

Brighid nodded with some sadness and picked up a simple tiara. Situating it on Ellenor's head, she said, "I will miss the children very much. Donald doesn't want to start a family until he is assured the new clan is established, and it was comforting looking after yours every once in a while."

Laurel scoffed. "There are plenty of young girls in the village who would leap at the chance of looking after the children. It is *I* who will miss you. Two of my four best friends gone! With Hagatha refusing to visit more than once every couple of weeks, poor Aileen will be the only one around with whom I can vent my frustrations."

Aileen waved her hand dismissively and adjusted Ellenor's bridal gown on Laurel's bed so that she could finish with the final stitches. "Don't let her make you two feel guilty. Laurel knows how much I enjoy hearing the trials and happenings around this place." Aileen bit off the end of the thread and studied the fixed hem. "There, I don't think anyone will ever know the twins played tug of war using your gown as a rope. We're lucky they were pulling down along the lower hem and not along the sleeve, interfering with Brighid's beautiful work. You really outdid yourself this time."

Ellenor attempted to turn around and look, but Brighid pulled her head firmly back in place and continued to fiddle with the headpiece, fastening small flowers along the edge. "I was inspired. There," she exhaled with satisfaction and picked up the polished silver dish, handing it to Ellenor.

Looking at her reflection, Ellenor couldn't believe the miracles her friends had created since that morning.

The gentle waves of her fawn-colored hair had been transformed into buoyant curls cascading down her back. The locks framing her face were kept in place with pins, giving her a soft ethereal quality. The headpiece of simple twisted pewter and scattered blossoms finished the look. "Oh, Brighid . . . I don't think I've ever looked prettier. Cole might not even recognize me."

Brighid winked. "Oh, he'll recognize you, and if he has the urge to pluck the eyes from all the other men staring at you, then I have done my job."

A knock came at the door. Aileen went to answer it while Laurel moved to inspect Ellenor's hair. She smiled approvingly. "I wonder if Donald knows just what a talent he has for a wife, Brighid."

"Oh, he does." Brighid blushed. "He doesn't want anyone to know how much he dotes on me, but I suspect after being apart for six weeks, he will outdo himself tonight. The only man in the Highlands who might be more affectionate this evening is Ellenor's Cole."

A loud snort followed by a "Ha!" filled with skepticism erupted from the doorway, where a very thin girl stood. Her thick, umber-colored hair was plaited down her back and her pale blue eyes flashed with indignation.

Ellenor stood up and studied the twelve-year-old, trying to appear cross with her. Maegan was precocious and outspoken with her opinions, which was probably why she had so quickly endeared herself to Ellenor these past few weeks.

A few days after Cole's departure, Ellenor's daily routine began to change as Laurel became stronger and resumed her duties. Ellenor still helped, but no longer was she directing work, ensuring peace, and making decisions. Her life was on hold. She couldn't take on many responsibilities or assume an integral role in the castle's duties because of her impending departure.

Too many times she found herself bored, with very little to do, which was far from palatable. That was when she had met Maegan.

Taking a walk along the river that flowed behind the rear curtain wall, Ellenor had believed she would be alone with her thoughts and tears. But someone had beaten her to both. A young girl sat crouched on the grassy bank with her knees tucked to her chest and her forehead bent down on her arms. She was so slender her whole body shook with each sob. In between snivels, Ellenor convinced the girl to tell her why she was crying.

Her best friend was Clyde, the youngest of the McTiernays, and two months ago, he had left for the Lowlands. He was to train under his elder brother Colin and wouldn't return for at least two years. As a child, Maegan had followed Clyde and his friend, Kam, everywhere. After realizing they couldn't entice or even scare her into leaving them alone, they finally gave up and let her tag along on many of their adventures. Her small physique enabled her to carry out many of their more inappropriate schemes against the villagers. And despite the age difference, the three of them became inseparable.

Being a year older than Clyde, Kam had left last fall. Then Clyde followed at the first signs of spring, leaving Maegan all alone. She had acted like a boy for so long the other girls her age made fun of her and Maegan wasn't interested in becoming domesticated. She just wanted things to be as they were.

Ellenor had invited Maegan to help care for the twins that afternoon, and having nothing better to do, Maegan had accepted. Within a week, Maegan's outspoken personality had wormed its way into the heart of not only Ellenor, but Laurel, Aileen, and Brighid. The girl never held her tongue for anyone or for any reason.

And seeing Maegan's current disgruntled stance and the exaggerated roll of her sky blue eyes, it seemed Ellenor's wedding day was going to be no different.

Ellenor waved her into the room. "If you expect any of us to react to your grand entrance, you are going to have to be a little more specific. 'Ha' is rather nondescriptive," she chided and directed the young girl to one of the hearth chairs.

Maegan ignored Ellenor's suggestive gesture, instead heading straight for Aileen and the wedding gown she was holding. It was a deep cranberry bliaut with small seed pearl beads along the neck and down the openings of the sleeves, and Maegan had never seen anything more beautiful. She reached out to fondle the soft velvet material.

Most Highland women wore linens or wools, but years ago, Conor's mother had convinced his father to make an annual journey to Aberdeen to purchase the exotic cloths from faraway lands. After marrying Laurel, Conor had resurrected his father's act of love. Each year, he would purchase material and compel Laurel to expand her wardrobe. She capitulated, with the stipulation that she could use some of the rich cloth as gifts for her closest friends. As a result, both Ellenor and Brighid would leave with an enviable wardrobe as well as many linens, curtains, and other items to help them set up their new home.

"This . . . this is beautiful," Maegan murmured softly. "Oh, milady, do you think when Clyde comes back, I could wear something like this?"

Laurel nodded and chuckled at the irony of the request. Maegan professed to dislike all things delicate and feminine, but she was on the verge of becoming a woman. In a few years, she would shed her tomboy ways and begin to ask how to entice a man's eye, but Laurel hoped it didn't happen too soon. Maegan was special, and Laurel hoped to preserve some of the girl's spirit into adulthood. Until then, she was going to be a handful, especially since she had only aging grandparents at home to guide her.

Laurel laid a sleeping Bonny down on the middle of the bed and watched the little girl's chest rise and then fall, followed by a sweet sigh of contentment. She was a fighter and only speckles of her strong-willed personality had begun to show. It was hard to think that the small infant had almost not made it into the world.

Ellenor snapped her fingers, trying once again to get Maegan's attention. "When you came in, you were upset about something . . ." she prompted.

Maegan stopped stroking the soft, dark garment and turned around, the glint in her eyes returning. "The laird didn't want you to know . . . yet," she qualified before continuing, "but the soldiers who arrived this morning . . ."

Ellenor's brows drew together in confusion. "Cole's men," she clarified.

"Aye, but *he* wasn't among them."

Brighid stepped forward. "That's not true. I saw Donald ride in myself."

Maegan rolled her eyes. "Aye, *your* husband is here. But what was supposed to be hers is not." She then crossed her arms and added definitively, "When Clyde and I marry, he isn't going to be a single second late for our wedding."

Ellenor licked her lips, strolled over to the window, and looked out. The McTiernays always married at sunset, and that was less than an hour away. She had been concerned she might be late with all of Brighid's and Laurel's nitpicking, but never had she considered it would be Cole who wouldn't be there.

For over six weeks, she had waited for him to return

and tell her that today was the day. In the meantime, she and Brighid had toiled over her wedding gown, hoping with each hour, news would come. Weeks passed and hope wavered on misery. Thankfully, Donald had ordered Brighid to remain behind with Ellenor until their new home was prepared. Without her friend's daily support, Ellenor suspected she might have tried to make the journey north on her own. Then three days ago, a rider from Cole's army had finally come with a message. Cole would arrive with a dozen or so of his men on Saturday. Ellenor was to prepare an afternoon wedding, and before sunrise the next day, they would be married.

Laurel and Fallon had worked tirelessly to prepare for the event, leaving Ellenor and Brighid to pack their belongings. By Saturday morning, only Cole's tapestry remained to be bundled, but before Ellenor could take it down, Aileen had hustled her out of her room, barring her from the North Tower until after the ceremony.

Ellenor hadn't argued. She hadn't contested anything. She couldn't. Her mind had been on only one thing. Cole and becoming his wife.

Now all was ready for the ceremony with one exception. There was no groom.

Ellenor turned from the window and pasted on a determined smile. "So you're not going to *allow* Clyde to be late, are you?" she asked Maegan.

Maegan shook her head and flopped onto the hearth chair. "No, I won't. Besides, Clyde wouldn't be late. He's already learned his lesson about making *me* unhappy. Told me himself that it was more painless to let me have my way than to fight me."

Ellenor wagged her finger at the young girl and said, "But what if you change your mind? What if another man snags your heart and he is not as compliant as your Clyde is?"

Maegan produced a loud snort. "It may take you Englishwomen a long time to find the man you want, but us Highland women are much better at it."

"Us Highland *women*?" Brighid laughed at how the twelve-year-old considered herself among her peers.

"Aye," Maegan confirmed, not recognizing the humored looks being shared around her. "I have loved Clyde since the day he saved me and nothing is going to change my feelings."

"And does Clyde know of your love?"

Maegan squirmed and drew her lips tight in thought. "I think so. I mean I told him the day he left that I would wait for him. That should have been clear enough."

Brighid made a face, but Ellenor cut her off, warning her not to laugh. "What is it about Clyde that makes you think you love him enough to wait—possibly years—to marry him?"

Maegan cocked her head to the side. "Well, he is handsome and very strong. He can hunt for our food. And I am sure that he can be whatever makes a good husband. And if he doesn't, his brothers can teach him. But mostly, because he is my one true friend. He knows everything about me and I him. I know things that even *Kam* doesn't," she finished matter-of-factly.

Ellenor raised her brows and glanced around the room. Aileen shrugged and Laurel nodded. All silently agreed that, as answers go—even from a twelve-year-old—that was a good one.

"And *that* is why I know *my* Clyde would never be late. It's also why I know he would invite all the world to our wedding."

Ellenor bit her inner lip to keep from letting go a harsh remark. Maegan meant well, but her opinion was young and naïve. "Well, I hope there is enough room in the chapel for the whole world, and as for Cole and me, well, I am glad he requested to minimize the attendance and refrain from inviting neighbors."

"Aye, as am I," Brighid interjected. "Large parties can be wonderful events, but they take time to plan, there is the journey here . . ."

"Not to mention the cost of their stay," Laurel added.

Ellenor nodded. "Besides no one likes to travel only to leave the next day, and that is exactly what would happen. Cole needs to return as soon as possible, and if others came, he would be obligated to stay and participate in events and talks." She paused and waited until she had Maegan's full attention. "He was right to limit who comes and I fully support his request," she finished in her most I-will-argue-with-you-no-longer voice.

Properly chastised, Maegan crossed her arms and huffed. Unwilling to totally concede, she said, "It's not just Cole I don't understand. You, too, Ellenor, are a mystery."

"How so?" Ellenor asked, adjusting one of the pins holding the tiara so that it wouldn't poke her scalp when she bent over.

"Well, there is your *present,* for one thing."

"What about it?"

"It? *It* is not a present. It's a . . . it's an insult. Clyde would nev—"

"Enough, Maegan!" Ellenor hissed. "Enough about Clyde and what he would or wouldn't like. Clyde is still young, he is not a laird, he has no responsibilities, and most of all he is *not Cole.*"

Ellenor's sudden bristly manner did not faze Maegan in the least. "But a *boy?*" she scoffed. "Clyde would laugh at me for weeks if I tried to give him a *boy.*"

Ellenor closed her eyes and prayed for patience. She loved her little friend's tenacity, sometimes even applauded it, but today, at this moment when her future was in doubt, Maegan's persistence was not welcome. "The *man*," Ellenor started, moving to face her challenger directly, "whom I have enlisted just so happens to be the one person who could help Cole the most. He is trying to rebuild Fàire Creachann with very little skilled help. Henri is a trained, experienced mason, and as a favor to me—"

Maegan rolled her eyes and stood up, cutting Ellenor off. "Well, I just hope that Clyde doesn't grow up wanting me to get him another boy. Because I won't. I don't care how much he needs him for whatever."

Brighid hustled over to Maegan and poked her into standing up. "Go check on the twins," she ordered.

"But they—"

"No, go check," Brighid hissed, shooing her out the door. The young girl was smart, but she was also incredibly dense when it came to realizing when she should just be quiet. Maegan hadn't felt the growing tension in Ellenor but everyone else had. Wedding nerves had been bad, but with the news of Cole missing, the anxiety building in Ellenor was incredible and Maegan was not helping. "And if you come back in here with any more comments about Cole missing the wedding, I'll personally sew your lips shut."

Ellenor watched as Brighid shut the door and then sank into a chair. "Is she right? About Cole and Henri?"

Laurel shrugged and picked up the wedding gown, carrying it toward Ellenor. "You and Maegan are both right. Boys don't like to share their most coveted toys with other boys, no matter what their age, and you, Ellenor, are definitely Cole's most coveted treasure. But he is also a man and a laird and he needs Henri. Eventually, Cole will be glad, even if not immediately, for the mason's help. Now turn around and let's get this on you."

Ellenor did as instructed, glad for the nonemotional,

honest answer. Somehow, it calmed her more than a simple "no" or "of course not" ever could have.

Brighid's brows furrowed as she watched Laurel slip the deep crimson vision over Ellenor's head. "Shouldn't she wait to dress until Cole arrives?"

Ellenor shook her head and slithered into the garment. "No, Laurel is right. Sunset is almost here and I think it is time to finish dressing and head down towards the chapel. I want to be there waiting when Cole arrives."

Ellenor removed her gaze from the dark night sky and refocused it on the few remaining friends still in the chapel. "I'm fine, Brighid, really. Please convince your husband that you and he should go. I would feel much better knowing that Cole and I haven't robbed you of your own reunion."

"But . . . what are you going to do?"

"I'm staying," Ellenor answered calmly.

"Here? In the chapel? You can't!"

"*I'll* stay with her," Maegan growled.

Ellenor took a deep breath and exhaled. It had been almost six hours since the last bits of sun disappeared behind the horizon. After which, it had taken three hours to convince everyone in the chapel to return to their homes. Finn had forced his exhausted wife, Aileen, to retire, and finally Conor made Laurel go to bed under the guise that someone should be awake in the morning. Brighid and Maegan, however, had doggedly refused to leave. And because Brighid would not leave, neither would Donald.

"And if you would, please take Maegan home. I doubt her grandmother realized it would be so late when she agreed to let her stay." Ellenor reached out and clutched her little friend's hand. "I need you to go, please."

"I'm not going!" Maegan shouted.

"Yes, you are," Ellenor returned quietly. "Father Lanaghly will be with me. I won't be alone."

"How can you even *want* to stay and wait for a man who didn't even show up to his own wedding?"

Ellenor tapped the padded bench beside her and waited for Maegan to sit down. Gathering the small thin fingers in her hands, Ellenor tried to think of an explanation the young girl might understand. "When Clyde left, you knew he might be gone for a long time. Years. Much could happen in that time. Things you cannot control. What if it causes him to be away even longer than you thought? Are you still going to wait?"

Maegan stared at her fingers. A teardrop fell. "I would wait forever."

"Then you understand why I have to stay."

Maegan turned and embraced Ellenor. Letting go, she sniffled, wiped her eyes with her sleeve, and shook her head as if the small gesture erased her lapse into tears. Then she mumbled something about the ingratitude of men and marched out the chapel doors.

Brighid quickly hugged her friend and whispered, "I'll leave and take care of Maegan, but the moment Cole arrives, I want to know." Standing up, she issued Donald a cutting stare as if he had any control over the situation.

Donald glanced at Ellenor, giving her one last look of apology, saying once again with his eyes that he had no idea where Cole was. He should have arrived hours ago.

Ellenor watched the couple leave. As soon as the doors closed, she pivoted in the pew and stared at the altar. Father Lanaghly moved to sit beside her. She gave a sideways smile at the older priest. His deep brown eyes, usually merry, were full of concern, and Ellenor reached over and tapped him reassuringly on his knee. He stroked his white beard as if contemplating a difficult speech. Ellenor knew what he was going to say. A second later, the kind man confirmed it. "You, too, should retire, milady. A chill is rising in the night air and the fires are turning to embers. Soon it will be cold."

Ellenor shook her head and remained seated. "No, Father, I am going to remain here. When Cole arrives, I will be waiting for him, ready. For I will be Cole's wife before sunrise. He promised."

Father Lanaghly inhaled deeply and sighed. He stood up and shrugged his shoulders. The possible reasons for Cole's delayed appearance were limitless and varied, but the majority of them said if Cole were going to arrive, he would have by now. Still, if his future bride needed to believe Cole would come, Father Lanaghly would not tell her otherwise.

Turning around, he grabbed a stick and thrust it into the embers. After a minute, it began to burn and he moved to relight some of the candles. He then tossed several more logs into the hearth, and after a few crackle-filled minutes, the blaze grew and the small chapel began to warm once again.

Once done, he went to stand beside Ellenor, who had moved to look out one of the large arched windows overlooking the dark ravine below. In the distance, the sinking moon highlighted majestic mountains that jutted out into the sea. Ellenor pointed to them. "See those? Every night I look at them and wonder if those are the mountains of my new home. I hope so. They are truly magnificent, don't you think? So beautiful."

Father Lanaghly nodded thoughtfully. "I cannot fathom your reaction, milady. I was watching you this evening to see if you were suppressing any anger while amidst your friends, but that is not the case. You are calm when most women I have met would be more than a little angry by now. But not you and I cannot help but wonder why? You have every right to be mad and no one would blame you. And yet, you are not."

Ellenor stretched her shoulders and looked up. The chapel was a simple one with few decorations. The one exception was the large round, arched ceiling. A traveling artist had created the masterpiece, and though it had been many years, the bright colors and vibrancy of the heavenly mural was still very beautiful.

Walking over to the hearth, she stood in front of the fire with her backside to the flames and thought how to answer. "When Cole came to get me from my sister's home, I had no choice but to go. Cole had made a promise to Laurel to bring me back, and my feelings about the matter were of little consequence—especially when we first embarked. I felt like I had no control over anything, and it . . . it scared me. What took me a while to realize was that I *did* have control, not over all things, but I was not powerless over myself. I had a choice about how I behaved, and for at least the beginning of the trip, I chose poorly."

Father Lanaghly nodded silently in understanding.

Ellenor moved her gaze once again to the dark horizon and spoke softly, almost as if it were more to herself. "Cole and I have strong personalities, and if we are to work, we must be friends. The best kind of friends. We need to know that when things happen, there is at least one person whom we can count on—each other. It's the greatest gift we can give to each other. So," she said with a half smile, looking back at the dark brown eyes studying her, "when Cole arrives, he will know that I have faith in him—in us."

Father Lanaghly stared quietly at the young Englishwoman. When news had traveled that Cole was to wed, he had ended his visit with a friend and immediately journeyed to McTiernay castle. He had married Cole's parents as well as their first two sons, and he had been surprisingly eager to marry their third.

He had been curious to meet the young woman, wondering what prompted such a radical change of heart in the most unemotional of the McTiernay brothers. Upon meeting Ellenor, he had thought well of Cole's choice. She had been kind, helpful, and very pretty. He had assumed she brought out the need to protect in Cole, and she, being a foreigner, had wanted his protection. But it wasn't until just now did he ever consider that only something much more meaningful could have convinced Cole to marry. This woman understood him. "I wonder if Cole knows just how lucky he is to have found you?"

A light, sincere laughter filled the chapel. "Of course he does, Father. What else could have made him overlook my one serious fault of being English?"

Chapter 13

Cole gripped his reins, waiting for the portcullis to slowly rise. Flames from lit scones flickered against the stone walls, leading the way through the gatehouse and into the dark inner yard. Just beyond the iron bars, he hoped Ellenor was still waiting for him. There was a chance—a good one—she wasn't and he couldn't blame her. Laurel and Brighid probably had her sequestered, protecting her from more disappointment. And yet, Cole could not see his Ellenor crying in some corner, wallowing in self-pity. More likely, she was spitting mad, pacing the floorboards ready to launch at him the minute their eyes locked. That he could handle. At least he hoped he could.

For weeks, he had been waiting to be reunited with Ellenor. He had dreamed of it every night, and when he was awake, she constantly invaded his thoughts. Countless times, he had almost sent for her, but until he could provide her a home and protection, he had forced himself to wait.

Three weeks ago, he had made his displeasure about the forward pace of reconstruction—or lack of it—abundantly clear. Dugan responded by working alongside

Leith to rebuild Fàire Creachann, and finally, a few basic rooms had been made livable and shelters had been erected. It was not much, but now most of the clansmen working on the keep had a place to sleep that protected them from storms and foul weather. Most of all, it was enough for Cole to get Ellenor and bring her home.

Cole had not been alone in his anticipation. Donald, plus the handful of his married soldiers who had left wives behind, were also eager to travel south and return with their families. So a message had been sent. They would arrive on Saturday and there would be a wedding.

Saturday had ended three hours ago.

Riding hard, stopping only to sleep, the journey from Fàire Creachann to McTiernay Castle took forty-eight hours. Thursday morning the group had just begun the trip south when a messenger had caught up with them. There was a problem, requiring his immediate return. Unwilling to delay anyone else from greeting their loved ones, Cole ordered the group to continue, telling Donald that he would join them as soon as possible, but that he would be there. Unfortunately, the problem was neither small nor quick.

Fàire Creachann was heavily fortified, not by man, but by nature. Situated on top of a sizable headland that jutted 300 feet above the sea, the castle could be accessed by only one of two ways. Clansmen could ride on top of the strip of land that connected the promontory to the rest of Scotland, or they could travel via a tunnel inside the strip. Cole had ordered the tunnel to be sealed until its safety could be verified. Several young boys desiring a retreat away from adults and supervision hadn't listened. A cave-in had occurred.

Wagons carrying heavy beams were crossing when part of the ground gave. Screams were heard for several minutes, then nothing. Left in charge, Dugan had immediately issued orders to get the wagon out of the way and start digging. He also sent for Cole. The situation called not just for the laird to reassure his people, but a critical thinker who could develop a plan quickly and decisively.

Cole had returned, assessed the situation, and began barking orders. Clansmen and soldiers worked tirelessly for hours and into the night, but finally, late the next morning, more than twenty-four hours after the collapse, the boys were rescued. Bumps and several bloody scrapes covered them, but they were alive.

And Cole was very late.

The whole ride toward McTiernay Castle, Cole reviewed his decisions in his head, and for each one, he would do the same thing again. He loved Ellenor and she loved him, but could she be happy as a laird's wife? Especially if it were a struggling clan whose demands upon their leader were constant and numerous?

Cole had tried telling himself that his delay was auspicious, that it gave them both a chance to realize if such events could be weathered or if they would be a source of constant battles and tension. But he also dreaded learning the truth, because he knew, deep down, that if he ever lost Ellenor, he would be losing a piece of himself.

Finally, the iron barrier was high enough to allow entry. Cole kicked his mount in the hind legs and directed the animal toward the stables. He slid off the back, threw the reins at a semiconscious stable boy, and dashed across the yard toward the North Tower and his old room. He bounded up the stairs and hesitated only a moment before pushing open the door. It was dark with only faint starlight coming through the window to guide his movements. The embers from the fire had died, and with the exception of a soft fragrance in the air, the room felt cold and empty. He reached the bed. It had been turned down and something was scattered all over it. Petals from flowers. There was no sign of Ellenor.

Cole scooped some petals in his hands. They were dry and crumbled easily. Sweeping them aside, he sank onto the edge of the bed and bent over, clutching his head in his hands. Memories of the last moments they had shared together flooded his mind, and suddenly, Cole knew that it was not as it seemed. Simple dismissal was not Ellenor's style.

Cole rushed down the tower stairs and headed toward the Star Tower, hoping his brother would be able to tell him where Ellenor was waiting and just how mad she would be when he got there. He was nearly at the tower's archway when he spied candlelight flickering to his right. Pivoting, he changed direction and hastened toward the chapel entrance, wondering if Ellenor was there. And if she was there, why had she refused to leave?

Ellenor was afraid to open her eyes. She didn't want to learn that the tender kiss against her cheek or the strength in the fingers softly enfolding her hand were only parts of a fading dream. "Cole?" she whispered.

"Aye," came the husky reply.

Her lids fluttered open. It was Cole. He was bending over her. He had finally arrived. She wrapped her arms around his neck and hung on as he lifted her onto his lap. He tilted her head back and she gazed into his eyes. Pain, worry, and fear lurked in the deep blue depths. She tucked back a stray lock of his dark hair. "I knew you would come," she whispered. And then she leaned forward and kissed him in a way that left no doubt about her feelings. Her embrace was tender, but passionate, and Cole took full advantage of the offering.

They kissed away the weeks of loneliness, the hours of worry, the fear of unfulfilled promises. Ellenor once again found the man whom she could trust with her heart and soul and Cole clung to the softness and intimacy only she could give him. No longer did fear accompany the intensity or depth of their need for each other. Never again would they be alone.

Ellenor felt a shudder pass through Cole as he reluctantly eased himself away from her. "I love you," he whispered.

"I know. I love you, too."

"I have to explain, tell you why I was—"

"Shhh," Ellenor said, stopping him with a finger softly pressed against his lips. "You need say nothing."

Cole kissed the fingertip and then tugged it away from his lips. "I don't know whether to be grateful or concerned," he said warily.

Ellenor gazed into his eyes. His love for her was abundantly clear, but equally clear was the fear of which he had spoken. He couldn't believe that she wasn't angry, at least on some level, about his late arrival. Taking his hands in hers, she said, "I have faith in you and therefore in us. I know you would have been here if it were not for a very good reason. And if I needed proof"—she paused, fingering his filthy tunic—"all I would have to do is to inhale deeply. You . . . well, you stink."

Cole laughed and hugged her tightly to him. "And you smell wonderful. How did I get so lucky?" And before she could respond, he closed his hand around the back of her head and brought her mouth down to his.

His kiss was surprisingly gentle as he urged her lips apart. She allowed him into her moist warmth, tasting

him with her tongue, recalling what it was like to be with
him. Suddenly, she needed to touch Cole everywhere—
his throat, his chest, his abdomen—she needed to explore every inch of him. The full force of her hunger
must have broken over Cole for she could feel the increased tempo of his pounding heartbeat, hot and
heady and compelling. Her body stirred in response, remembering. He groaned and crushed her hips against
him, letting her feel his desire, knowing it would build
her own need for him to uncontrollable levels.

Ellenor was seconds away from ripping their clothes
off when a simple, but penetrating cough followed by
an "Ahem" filled the room. Embarrassed, she tried scut-
tling off Cole's lap and down the pew, but he wouldn't
let her. The most Cole would allow was for her to turn
around in his arms. "Hello, Father. I think we are finally
ready. Care to do the honors?"

The old priest grinned and his brown eyes were dancing again. "Why, of course—"

He was interrupted by another, much louder,
"Ahem". Conan stepped around the priest and entered
the room. Ellenor took advantage of Cole's shock and
jumped off his lap. "How did you know I returned . . ."
Cole muttered in disbelief.

"Between the stable boy and the guard from the gate
going around announcing your arrival, I believe most
everyone knows and will soon be here wanting to witness the miracle of your wedding," Conan teased. Then
he looked at Ellenor. Her hair was askew and flowers
were entangled in golden knots, but she still looked
beautiful. "So, if you don't mind waiting just a bit
longer, Ellenor, there are a few more of us McTiernays
that want to witness this event. We all still find it hard to
believe Cole actually found someone who wants to be
his wife."

"Ha!" Cole exclaimed, pulling Ellenor protectively into his side. "The only thing more ill-fated is *you* getting married."

Conan nodded and chuckled in agreement. "True, true, marriage is a blessed curse meant only for some and thankfully I am *not* one of them, but I am truly happy for you, brother. You have a most beautiful bride and with the exception of marrying you . . . a most intelligent one. Take care of her."

Conan had barely spoken the words when Brighid came barreling in followed by Maegan and Laurel. Magically procuring Ellenor from his grasp, they gave Cole several dirty looks before declaring Ellenor needed to leave and would be back shortly. It was *his* turn to wait.

A half hour later, the resentment Cole had been feeling regarding Ellenor's hastened absence and the discomfort of bathing in a tub in the kitchen instantly vanished. Most of the town had risen in the predawn hour to witness the nuptials, and their gasps as Ellenor reentered the chapel likened his own.

Ellenor looked exquisite. Her hair was down and the flowers had been removed. Only the simple tiara remained. The luckenbooth that had once belonged to his mother held the McTiernay plaid over one shoulder. Never had she looked more beautiful. She was a dream, an *aisling*, and she was about to be his.

Cole didn't know when or why he had become so lucky; he just knew he was.

Ellenor laid her head against Cole's shoulder as he carried her up the winding tower staircase. The simple reassuring movement of his muscles filled her with a sense of peace deeper than she had ever known. The night, which had started so uncertain, had ended with merriment and celebration. Instead of the morning light marking the end to the festivities, it only gave them new life. Those clansmen who had retired disappointed awoke to news of a wedding. They had quickly joined the feast, putting aside all but the most basic of chores and necessities.

The McTiernay clan didn't show any signs of slowing or ending the party, so when Cole swung Ellenor into his arms and left to celebratory cheers, she was surprised, but thankful.

"I cannot think of when I have ever been so happy," Ellenor sighed.

"I can think of only one time."

Ellenor's lashes flew up as she moved her head to look him directly in the eye. "And when was that?"

Cole paused and held her gaze. "When you first told me you loved me."

Doubt flooded Ellenor's expression. She had expected him to reference the last time they were together, not the final day of their journey from England. They had kissed and it had been magical. Then directly afterward, Cole had announced that the concept of they, as a couple, could never be. "Are we remembering the same moment? Because if I recall correctly, I wasn't exactly in a good mood the first time I said I loved you. And you were anything but happy."

Cole twitched his lips and resumed his march up the stairs. "Stunned more like it, but I *was* happy. To think that a woman like you could feel that way about someone like me . . . well, it still is a miracle. And for a brief moment, it gave me hope."

"But then why were you so cold? So distant?"

"Hope that I might someday marry, but not you. You scared me. But it was too late, those words changed my future. At the time, I might not have realized or accepted it, but that's understandable." He paused at the door and nudged it open with his knee. Walking inside, he gently put her down on her feet and started to walk away.

Ellenor caught his arm and stopped him. "Understandable?"

"Aye," Cole answered, brushing his knuckles down her cheek in a soft caress. "A man like me hopes to find someone who can tolerate him enough to start a family. And honestly, I had long ago resolved myself to bachelorhood. I thought I liked my freedom."

"And didn't you?"

"It wasn't freedom I was clinging to, it was loneliness, and you, with those simple words, forced me to really look at what I was choosing."

"Then why didn't you say something sooner?"

"I thought you deserved better than me."

Ellenor shook her head in incredulity. "Never. Never will I ever want any man other than you. I will always love you."

Cole took a deep breath and exhaled. She still scared him. Losing her would cost him his soul, but he would not lose her from walking away. "And I love you, Scot," he said with a smile. The love reflecting in the dark green depths of her eyes was bright and clear, and he knew it would never dim.

Ellenor grinned and playfully smacked his shoulder. "Scot! I'll have you know that I am a legitimate Highlander now and will not tolerate such insults."

Cole returned her grin and pulled her to him, gathering her closer to his chest. "I'll never get enough of you, do you know that?"

"Aye," Ellenor whispered, lacing her fingers in his thick hair, pulling his lips to hers.

His mouth came down and she kissed him with a kind of wild abandon that came from torturous weeks of waiting. She could feel the heat from his large hands splayed over her back, holding her close. Thinking about the last time they had held her, touched her, memorized her, caused her pulse to race. It was followed by hot little ripples of pleasure as she discovered the hard bulge under his plaid. She instinctively and sensuously moved against it.

God, she wanted him and knew she always would.

She made a small hungry sound deep in her throat and pressed as close to him as she could get.

Cole broke the kiss and held her tight, stopping her body from rubbing against him. Any more sensation and their first coupling as husband and wife would be standing up, her pinned against the stone wall just a few feet away.

He raised his eyes to look down at her. The passion reflecting back at him caused his own throat to tighten.

"God, you're beautiful," he whispered.

Ellenor smiled playfully. "I know. It's a shame really that your looks don't compare. I think it's the dimples," she teased and reached up to stroke his right cheek.

"Liar." Cole laughed, grabbing her hand. "You've liked them since we first met. You kept staring at them. Face it. You're jealous."

"Jealous? Why should I be jealous if I am already beautiful?"

Cole kissed the tip of her nose. "Don't know, love. You have no reason to be. I just know that you are."

Ellenor narrowed her eyes at him, but they lacked the fire needed to portray true anger. She took the end of her plaid and swatted him. Cole laughed and began to loosen his belt. Ellenor moved toward the chest housing her garments, kicked off her slippers, and pulled on the strings binding her gown. She heard a hard thud and glanced behind her to see what it was. It had been Cole's heavy leather belt. His plaid was right beside it. Cole was riveted, sitting on the side of the bed, watching her undress. She quickly returned to the task, suddenly feeling apprehensive. She slipped the bliaut over her head. The thick velvet material caught the chemise underneath and the thin gown rose up her leg almost to her buttocks. A nervous giggle escaped. She waited for Cole to say something. When he didn't, Ellenor assumed he was waiting for her. She forced herself to turn around, hoping that he would take her into his arms and dispose of the chemise himself. Instantly, she knew that was not going to happen.

Cole had fallen back onto the bed and was fast asleep. His knees were bent and his feet were still against the floor, unmoved from where he had been sitting. Only sheer will had enabled him to stay awake these past several hours. But there was only so much will a body could produce, and even the promise of a wedding night could not overrule basic needs.

Ellenor went over and picked up his legs. Her goal had been to carefully move them on top of the bed, but immediately she realized two things. First, his legs were incredibly heavy, making the effort to move them hard, cumbersome, and far from gentle. And second, it didn't matter. The man was out cold. She could probably scream and he would remain comatose. Ellenor doubted anything short of several hours' sleep would change Cole's deep state of unconsciousness.

She finally maneuvered his body so that it was completely on the mattress, but he was lying at an angle preventing anyone else from sleeping comfortably. Ellenor tried unsuccessfully to move him, but succeeded only in getting him to twitch. Shrugging, she curled up against his side, cast a leg over his large frame to keep her atop the bed, and then finally managed to pull the plaid over them both.

She placed her chin on his shoulder and said, "Some might not believe this, but I promise you, Cole McTiernay, I could not have asked for a better wedding night. You kept your promise and I vow to keep mine. I will always love you, Highlander." Then she planted a kiss on his cheek and nestled next to him, falling into the most peaceful sleep she had had in weeks.

Cole awoke and rubbed his face. It wasn't often he slept hard, but when he did, it always left him unsettled upon awakening. And this time he must have fallen into a deep slumber for he wasn't quite sure where he was. It almost felt far too comfortable to be real . . . and far too real to be a dream. He turned and his chin encountered a head, which quickly mumbled something derogatory. Instantly, the haziness of sleep vanished and clarity of where he was and whom he was with came into full understanding.

He had returned just before dawn and married Ellenor. In the morning, he and she retired to celebrate . . . and that was the last of his recollection. Cole raked his scalp, hoping for more, but none came. The movement must have disturbed Ellenor, for she flipped over to her side and cuddled up against him, her head on his shoulder and her leg flopped over his. Her shift had gathered around her hip and he could feel the soft skin of her leg against his own.

Her shift!

Cole's fingers curled into a fist and he clubbed himself in the forehead. He hadn't even touched her. "Late to your own wedding. What kind of man . . . what kind of *husband* . . . falls asleep on his wedding night?" he chided himself under his breath.

"The best kind." The reply was half sigh, half hum, followed by soft, sensual kisses on his chest along the stretched opening of his leine.

"I . . . I didn't mean to wake you." Cole knew he sounded just as clumsy as he felt. Distant, uneasy, these were things he had felt multiple times in the presence of a woman, but never embarrassed or awkward and suddenly he was both.

Ellenor pushed back the edge of his leine, giving her access to his shoulder and neck. "I'm glad you did, husband," she mumbled between kisses.

Cole closed his eyes and grimaced. "I'm not really that yet, am I?"

Ellenor paused her attentions and propped herself up, so that she could look down at him. The light in the room was faint. The moonlight, which typically poured into the bedchamber via the window, was obscured with clouds, leaving only near-dead embers to illuminate Cole's face. "Oh yes you are. We may have enjoyed our wedding night before we were actually married, but we had one, and you cannot get out of this marriage now, Highlander."

Cole narrowed his eyes mischievously and flipped Ellenor over on her back. He lowered himself slowly on top of her, bracing his arms on either side of her head. Her soft curves molded perfectly to the contours of his muscular body and Cole growled his pleasure. "Ah, Scot, that's the last thing I would be wanting to do," he purred and then began nibbling at her neck.

Ellenor closed her eyes to the sensation, wanting to scold him for calling her Scot, a name he himself had challenged. Before his mouth could capture hers in a full kiss she knew would leave her breathless and unable to think, let alone speak, she whispered, "Call me Scot again, and I'll start calling you Elmer." She then lifted her head, hoping to catch him full on the mouth, but Cole had arched just out of reach.

"I was going to start calling you *sonuachar* but I don't know now. I'm not sure I want a soul mate who enjoys correcting me as much as you do."

Ellenor squirmed, trying to get out of his grasp, but he kept her firmly underneath him. She knew her attempts were only causing him to become more aroused. "I'd better be someone you're happily married to. I waited hours—no weeks—for you. *You'd* better be worth it," she ended, pointing a finger into his chest.

Cole grinned. He loved her spirit and her inability to yield, even when she was outsized, outmuscled, and even outmaneuvered. He needed her like he needed the air, and right now, he needed to make Ellenor his wife in every way. "I don't know if I am worth it, love, but I promise you I will do everything I can to make you think so."

Before Ellenor could say another word, Cole kissed her.

Edging his knee more deeply upward, he lodged it between her thighs and planted another kiss while he removed the last of their clothing. The moment they were both free, Ellenor pressed eagerly against him and her hands roamed freely over his chest, back, and then lower. He lost the power to think. Ellenor's natural, unrestrained response to their lovemaking challenged his sanity. Every muscle in her body was tight with sexual tension, demanding he pull her close and drive himself into her. Cole refused to do that, but he knew his need for her was too great to wait much longer.

"Cole." Her voice was a velvet murmur. "Later. Be slow and gentle later."

The fire inside him suddenly raged out of control,

searing away any remaining desire to hold back and take his time. Nothing mattered except being as close to her as he could be. A moment later, they were one.

Nothing had ever been so good.

Cole blinked and stared at the wooden beams that served as the support for the fourth floor of the North Tower. He had never felt so incredible, so loved, so *good*. And the best part was knowing that tomorrow it was not going to end. This time when he left, Ellenor would be at his side. She was now his in every way. And he was hers.

She had opened walls inside him he had thought were forever shut, and in doing so he had become vulnerable again.

Robert had been his friend. His best friend. They had shared many of the same dreams, believed in the same ideals, and aspired for similar glory. They had understood each other in ways few friends ever did. And when Robert died, a piece of Cole had died with him and what hadn't perished had gone numb. Until Ellenor. She had done the impossible. She had reawakened his heart and, in doing so, had become his soul.

He had fallen in love with Ellenor just after they met. And after all these weeks, he was still falling. Every moment together she consumed him a little bit more. And now, Cole knew living without her would not be hard, it would be impossible. The depth of his love and need for her no longer terrified him. In its place, he could find only peace. He finally had what he always wanted but never thought he would possess.

Ellenor stirred beside him, but she didn't awaken. They had made love all night, catching an hour or two of sleep in between bouts of insatiable need. It seemed impossible, and yet, each time one or the other had shifted, they had instinctively reached out for the other. That was all it took. One caress, a simple kiss, even a hushed murmur, and both would find themselves willing captives in a whirlpool of desire.

Even now, his body was responding to her soft backside pressing into his hip, inviting him to touch and explore. Any moment he would lose the ability to keep from ravishing her body once again.

A beam of light suddenly flashed across the ceiling, indicating that the sun was on its descent. Cole frowned. It couldn't be that late . . . could it?

Cautiously, he rose, taking care not to rouse her, and plodded to the window. He leaned forward and looked down at the activity below. The yard was busy with typical late afternoon activity, but few soldiers were in sight. Today's training must have taken place in the fields. Soon, however, the men would arrive and begin massing for dinner in the Lower Hall.

Cole's stomach growled and he realized that it had been a long time since he had eaten. Over thirty hours and he was starving.

He glanced back at Ellenor, who had slowly invaded the vacated space on the bed, but she was still unconscious. If he left now, he might be able to get back with some food before she awoke.

Cole walked over and grabbed his clothes. He threw on the leine and then exited into the corridor. He softly shut the thick wooden door behind him and quickly pleated and belted his plaid. He listened for traffic on the stairwell, and hearing none, he quickly descended the tower.

The best place for food and drink was the kitchens. It was also the best place to find some of the most inquisitive personalities in the McTiernay clan. The head cook was a crotchety old soul and she thrived on gossip. He wouldn't even have to participate to fuel her passions. Cole decided to try his luck in the halls, hoping that some food had already been laid out in an effort to prepare for the soon-to-be arriving crowd.

The second he cracked open the Lower Hall door, the smell of fresh breads and meats floated over him and his stomach growled in approval. He stepped inside and headed for the closest table. Grabbing a pitcher of ale and a platter of what looked to be a mixture of fowl and beef, he quickly turned around and headed back out, ignoring the smiles and looks of the few servants setting tables and benches in preparation for even more food.

As soon as he turned around, Cole knew the trip back would not be as blissfully uneventful. Brighid was waving at him from across the yard and heading his way. There was no way he could carry everything back to the tower before she reached him. He took a deep breath and exhaled, hoping that whatever she wanted to discuss would be quick. And painless.

No such luck.

"Hello, *laird*."

Cole raised a single brow to the greeting. It was the first time Brighid had referred to him as laird, and he couldn't tell if she was being sincere or sarcastic. He suspected a little bit of both.

Brighid grinned. "You are, are you not?"

"Aye," Cole replied and glanced down at the young skinny girl with reddish-brown hair standing beside Brighid.

Her pale blue eyes caught his attention right before she rolled them in an exaggerated fashion. She elbowed Brighid in the ribs and said, "Don't pretend you weren't just reminded of the fact. I heard Donald give you clear instructions about referring to Ellenor as milady and this one as laird. I also heard what you told him—"

"Hush, Maegan, and I mean it. Not another word," scolded Brighid. Then she mouthed the words "Clyde's friend" to Cole.

Understanding was instant. He had heard about "Clyde's shadow" but had never met the boisterous girl that followed his youngest brother everywhere. All knew she was wild, outspoken, and driven to the interests of boys, and most clansmen pitied Clyde in tolerating her. Not Cole. Clyde was young and by far the most charitable of his brothers, but he would have ended this shadow business long ago if her company were undesirable. Few understood that his baby brother, while relaxed and comparably mellow to his elder siblings, kept close company with only those whose level of candor was typically considered rude. And this girl, if anything, was honest. Brighid could lecture her, but he suspected it would do no good.

Cole swallowed a chuckle and changed the subject. "We leave tomorrow. Donald ready?"

Brighid tucked back a stray piece of her curly brown hair. "Aye, and so are the rest of the men."

"Ha!" came a short huff. "Like you know. You and your husband have been just as busy as they have," Maegan said to Brighid, waggling her thumb toward Cole. "The question is, will *he* be ready? It looks like he's got enough food to disappear for days."

It was Brighid's turn to roll her eyes. She looked at Cole and gave a quick shrug of the shoulders to say, "Sorry, I have no control of her tongue." Grabbing Maegan's shoulders and forcibly turning her around, Brighid gave her a little shove and said, "Tomorrow then, laird." Then caught the arm of the girl and began to lead her away.

Just as he pivoted toward the North Tower, he heard Maegan squeal. "Ouch. I didn't say anything, but you and I both know she hasn't told him. And I *still* think Ellenor is crazy for thinking a man—especially that one—would be happy to find out he's getting a *boy* for a wedding present."

Cole almost dropped the food he was holding. He hadn't once considered the possibility of Ellenor being pregnant, but she could be, and based on what he'd just heard, she was. All this time, she had been waiting for the right time to tell him and he never gave her the chance. Every time she was awake, he was practically attacking her, leaving neither of them the energy to speak afterward.

Cole bounded up the stairs. By the time he arrived at their bedroom door, his hands were shaking so badly he could barely hold the food. Taking a deep breath, he forced himself to calm down before entering. Finally he pushed the door open with his knee, and his eyes searched the room, landing on the bed. Ellenor was still asleep.

He placed the items on the small table near the hearth chairs. He untied his belt and tossed his plaid onto the floor chest, but left his leine on, hoping it would give him some fortitude to resist her delectable body. Cole then sank down on the edge of the bed and leaned over to kiss her lightly on the cheek. Ellenor moaned and stretched, offering him her other cheek. Cole obliged.

Her eyelids fluttered open and her arms wrapped themselves around his neck. "Hmm, come here," she purred.

"I love you, Elle."

"I know. You've been showing me just how much," Ellenor murmured as she planted small kisses up and down his neck.

Cole gritted his teeth. Her honey-soaked voice was hard to resist and the bed's cover had fallen to her waist, exposing her perfectly sized breasts. For a moment, he forgot his intent and almost succumbed to her caresses. He steeled himself once more. "I mean it, Elle. I love you more than I ever thought it possible to love anyone, and I always will."

Ellenor leaned slightly back but did not let go. Her brows drew together in confusion. "I know that. I love you, too."

"I'll always be there for you . . . and our children," Cole prompted.

Ellenor sat up and smiled brightly. "Of course you will be and . . . is that food? I'm famished." She bounded out of bed and grabbed her shift, stuffing her arms through the sleeves as she moved toward the platter of meat. She poured herself a drink and pulled a piece of pork loose, popping it into her mouth. "This is delicious. Have some."

"In a minute," Cole replied. He was still sitting on the bed, unable to move.

An hour ago, he was so hungry he could hardly think of anything but eating. Since then, his appetite had disappeared and wouldn't be returning until Ellenor told him about the pregnancy.

"Mmm. Fiona cooked this just right. Tender and juicy . . . are you sure you don't want any? It really is wonderful."

"Not yet."

Ellenor shrugged her shoulders and ate another piece. "Well, thank you for getting this. I didn't realize how hungry I was. Did you see anyone when you were out? Donald?"

Cole shook his head. "But I did run into Brighid."

"How is she?"

"Tired."

Ellenor grinned. "And happy, I bet."

Cole's patience was wearing. He was giving her the opportunity to tell him about the baby, but she was not taking it. "You can tell me anything."

Ellenor plucked another piece of meat and sashayed toward the bed. Once at his side, she yanked her shift up to her waist and straddled his lap. She gave his shoulder a slight push. Cole conceded to her will and lay down. Ellenor then dangled the piece of meat in front of him and he seized it with his mouth.

Slowly she drew back her fingers from his lips. "The only thing I want to tell you right now is how incredibly strong and handsome I find you."

Cole's eyes twinkled. "What about virile?"

"Well, I hope so," Ellenor returned with a wicked grin.

She was leaning seductively over him and was about to plant a kiss on his lips Cole knew he would not be able to resist. He quickly stopped her by framing her face in his hands. "Anything, Elle. Anytime. Even now."

Ellenor slid off his lap. He had asked one too many times and now her dark green eyes glittered with suspicion. "No, do you have something to tell me?"

Cole propped himself up on his elbows. This wasn't at all how he had expected this conversation to take place. "That girl who likes Clyde. Maegan?"

"Aye, I know her."

"Well?"

"I think of her as a little sister."

"Well, your little sister was with Brighid when I ran into her on the way back with the food. When they turned to leave, the girl mentioned something about a wedding present . . . and a boy . . . ?"

Ellenor squinted her nose and stomped her bare foot. "Maegan!" she muttered. "You and I are going to have a talk." Then toward Cole, she said, "That was my *surprise.* I was going to tell you in the morning, but since she already told you about Henri, I guess it doesn't matter." She threw up her hands and went back to re-straddle his legs.

Cole must have misunderstood. "Henri?"

"Mm-hmm," Ellenor answered and resumed her passionate assault on his neck. "Henri Jenuard."

A man, Cole thought. *Not a baby . . . but a Frenchman.* He must have muttered the last word aloud for Ellenor corrected him. "A French mason to be more specific," Ellenor mumbled, nibbling on his ear. "He's going to help . . . you . . . rebuild Fàire Creachann."

Fighting his instinct to return the kiss, he pulled her back into view. "Why?"

Ellenor blinked. "Why?"

"Aye, why?"

She shrugged her shoulders. "Because he owes me a favor."

"Favor? Men don't do favors."

"This one does. If not for me, he would not have had my father's commission for part of our home—of which he did a wonderful job *and* which led to his first serious commission in France. So when Father Lanaghly mentioned he encountered a mason named Jenuard less than a week's ride away . . ."

Cole's face was not one of gratitude. Maegan might have been right. A man might not have been the best wedding present. Ellenor did the only thing she could think of; she leaned in and kissed him full on the

mouth. Cole let her. She murmured against his lips.
"Just meet him. Get to know him."

"Oh, I will," Cole answered. *Aye, I am going to get to know Henri very well.*

Ellenor's mouth was moving seductively against his lips. His mind was losing the battle and his body was winning the war. He made one last promise before surrendering to their mutual need.

And Henri Jenuard is going to get to know me.

Chapter 14

They had been riding north for three days, and before the morning sun was overhead, Fàire Creachann would be in sight. Cole stared at his wife, riding a few horse lengths ahead with Brighid . . . and the Frenchman. The man irritated Cole and never more so than when he and Ellenor burbled back and forth in that feminine-sounding gibberish. Cole had heard the language before, but it wasn't until lately that every smooth, musical word sounded like a dance of seduction.

Ellenor told him he was being ridiculous, but she didn't see how Henri looked at her. How the men watched her as she moved. And who could blame them? She was breathtaking and becoming more so every day. She had rediscovered her confidence and sense of self-worth, and now her beauty, previously obscured from onlookers with fear and doubt, could be seen by all—not just him.

Donald coughed into his hand, regaining Cole's attention. "You want me to send a rider ahead, notifying them of our arrival?"

Cole shook his head. "There should be no need." He

wanted to wait and see if Dugan had posted a sentry to lookout for their or anyone else's arrival.

Laughter rang out from ahead.

"My wife finds your *present*," Donald grated, "amusing. I find him to be annoying."

"As do I."

Henri was more than annoying, he was clueless. The first day of riding, Cole had sent the man an untold number of contemptuous looks, ranging from disapproving to blatant hostility. And the *ùmbaidh*—the few times he even recognized Cole was looking at him— would just smile, give a wave, or say something friendly as if he were acknowledging a good friend. It was as if the man lived in his own private world. Consequently, Cole had avoided any chances to get to know the mason better. He could learn all he needed to just from watching him.

The man was tall, but slight, had strait raven-colored hair that he was continually pushing off his face, brown eyes so dark they almost seemed black, and a thin beard that refused to grow in certain patches around his jawline. To Cole, Henri was weak and unappealing, but there was no denying something about the man attracted the opposite sex. As they were preparing to leave McTiernay Castle, several clanswomen had clustered around the mason's horse, moaning about how much they would miss him. Why, Cole could not fathom.

There was something questionable about a man who always smiled. No one was that happy. And no one ever needed to talk as much as he did either. Henri's Scot was adequate, but his Gaelic was barely tolerable. He understood the Highland language well enough, but he couldn't utter a syllable without adding the galling flourish of his own tongue. Cole intentionally cringed whenever he spoke. But did that stop Henri from talking? No. And when he wasn't grating everyone's nerves with awful Gaelic, he was speaking French to the one person who could understand him. And Ellenor encouraged him. She listened, smiled, and in Cole's mind, laughed far too often. He knew the idea of her happiness belonging to him was ridiculous, but Cole couldn't help the surges of jealousy that overcame him each time the air tingled with the sounds of her delight. He doubted his reaction would be conquered anytime soon, if ever.

The only thing that had kept him sane these past few days was the physical distance Ellenor maintained between her and those around her. Her comfort level being around men had grown significantly in the past several weeks while he had been away, but she still allowed only him to come close enough to touch her. Others would approach, maybe even lean in to whisper, but she would always withdraw just enough to keep contact from occurring. With Cole, though, she was just the opposite. If he was near, her hand would find his, her body would rest gently against him, and each time she would smile, just a little, but it was enough. Cole knew her actions were unconscious, but they calmed him as no words could have ever done.

The pass between the steepening mountains was narrowing and Donald gestured that he was going to ride ahead. Cole nodded, but chose to remain behind in case someone in the group needed help as they traversed the winding path. Ellenor wouldn't need assistance. On a horse, she was probably more at home than on foot in this wild country, but he still liked to watch her ride.

He had been appreciating the view for almost an hour when a soldier approached on his left. Cole scowled at him for interrupting his favorite pastime. "Laird, Donald requests you ride up and meet with him."

Cole clenched his jaw and nodded. Urging his horse into a gallop, he dashed ahead of the small group, aware that Ellenor would have questions when he returned. He hoped he had answers.

Half an hour later, he reached the seaside of the Torridon mountains, where Donald was waiting for him. Cole searched for the sentry that should have been posted nearby. No one was in sight, and at the high vantage point, Cole could see the edge of his land and it was clear no rider was on the way.

Donald pursed his lips and asked, "Should we send someone now?"

"Your men still in place?"

Donald raised a single eyebrow and Cole flashed him a quick grin, acknowledging the question was needless. The men—Cole's personal guard, trained and led by Donald—were exactly where Donald told them to be. Flanking the group on all sides, they were positioned to see and notice not only things inside the traveling group, but outside it as well. Passersby, even when far away, would not go unnoticed.

"Send a couple of men to the fields," Cole ordered.

Donald nodded, and within minutes, two riders were ripping down the slope of the mountain headed to a valley in the distance.

Ellenor pulled on the reins to halt her mount and looked up. The day's beginnings had promised warmth and sunshine, but a cold wind had steadily increased over the past hour, bringing with it gray clouds that covered the sky. The thick wet mists hid the tops of the great, colossal beasts they were climbing, giving what some felt an ominous feel about these mountains. Ellenor could not agree. The Torridon peaks were majestic. Instead of frightening her, they pulled her toward them as if they knew her, and were glad she had found her way home.

She waited until most of the group had moved past her before entering another narrow trail forged between the enormous crags that seemed to grow steadily less tame and more crowded with each turn. The pattern of traversing the harsh but beautiful terrain had become routine. Forced in some places to ride single file through the pass, the group would convene and mass together in the next valley, often stopping and allowing the animals a chance to rest and drink. Despite their group's makeup of women, children, and a few farm animals, their traveling pace had been quite steady and uneventful.

The journey, usually a two-day ride, had turned into just over three and supposedly, by morning's end, Fàire Creachann would be in sight. Ellenor hoped that was still true. Cole had unexpectedly ridden ahead, galloping at a pace only a highly skilled rider should attempt. He hadn't said anything, but Ellenor suspected something was not right and she worried for him. A man had only so much fight in him, and if the clan didn't start cooperating, Cole would leave when his year was up . . . and she wouldn't blame him.

Ellenor leaned to her left to stretch her side and then shifted to her right. She was now trailing most of the group and the viewpoint was much different. Tempted to fall back even farther, she changed her mind when an exclamation followed by several gasps and a couple "oh my's" floated by her. She immediately prodded her mount forward to see what exactly had caught the attention of those riding near the front.

As she weaved through the boulders fallen from a landslide occurring years if not decades ago, a long brown and green slope came into view. The land stretched outward until it met the deep blue of the sea, which seemed to welcome its touch. The shoreline jutted out to the lapping waters sporadically, and at the end of one narrow neck of land that extended far into the sea was Fàire Creachann. Even from a distance, it seemed magnificent.

Ellenor felt the touch of a leg gently pressing against her and knew immediately it belonged to Cole. "It's . . . it's incredible."

"Aye," Cole answered, understanding her awe. "Even your Frenchman is impressed."

"He's not *my* Frenchman, he's *yours*," Ellenor countered, hoping Cole caught the rolling of her eyes. She knew he was still far from excited about Henri's presence, but she maintained—if only inwardly—that once Henri had arrived and demonstrated his value, Cole would be thankful the mason had agreed to come.

"Elle, if he was truly mine to command, he would still be back at my brother's entertaining the women there, instead of my woman the past three days."

Ellenor bit her bottom lip to keep from grinning. Fact was she liked the idea of Cole considering her his woman. Yes, it was a touch possessive, but it also said that he cared. She pointed to Henri, who was doing nothing to hide his enthusiasm or appreciation for what lay ahead. "Well, at least he's excited."

"Aye, the little man is nearly falling off his seat."

Ellenor sighed and was about to protest when Henri suddenly pulled back and joined them. "Laird, just how old is Fàire Creachan?"

"Not old. The keep is three no more than four generations old. Most of the other structures were built in the past few decades, but few were ever completed. Since its desertion, whenever neighboring clansmen or nearby farmers needed stone, they came here."

Henri licked his lips and nodded absentmindedly. His mind was racing with possibilities. "I'm surprised no one wanted to finish the place and live there until now."

"Many have and tried."

Henri cocked his head to one side, reevaluating the view. "The pass? Or the cost?"

Cole gave a quick shrug. The mason was a menace, but he had to admit to some level of astuteness. "Both."

Henri's already large smile widened further. "Well, then, Fàire Creachann's luck has changed for it now has a laird with means and a master mason who is eager to overcome its challenges!" he cried out and kicked his mount in the side. The animal reacted and leaped into action.

"The man is a danger to not only himself but others," Cole mumbled.

Ellenor watched as the thin body bounced uncontrollably on the overly large steed. She knew Cole had offered that particular animal to Henri because of its enormous size and ungainly footing. Used primarily for plowing and farming, the horse was rarely ridden. And because he was ignoring her warnings to ride slowly, Henri was going to be in pain tonight. "Ha. I bet you secretly admire the fact that Henri has never complained. Not once."

"Let me be clear, Elle. I don't admire that man and never will. He could not lift even a boy-sized sword above his head, let alone swing it with any accuracy, which makes him more of a menace than anything else."

Ellenor kept her gaze locked on the bouncing rider and bobbed her head a couple of times, feigning agreement. "I guess I misunderstood the amount of progress your men made during these past several weeks."

"We'll see if a little Frenchman can do more."

"If he can?"

Cole nudged his own mount forward. "The most he can ever earn from me is my respect."

Ellenor moved in beside him. "Coming from you, that will be more than enough. And despite what you think, Henri likes a challenge and considers you one. Just give him a chance," she appealed softly.

Cole scoffed, but he didn't say anything more. The two riders Donald had sent ahead had come back into view and they were signaling.

The training fields were empty.

The soldiers were gone.

Ellenor could feel the rapid rise of tension in Cole and knew very little, if any of it, was caused by Henri's presence. No, something else bothered her husband. So when Cole urged his mount to a faster pace, she did not join him. Whatever demons were on his mind, her husband wasn't ready to share them. Only Donald dared to ride with him, leaving the guard to ensure the group reached the plateau safely.

Ellenor focused her mind and gaze on her new home. The ride toward the promontory looked deceptively trouble-free, but after years of going unfarmed, the land had grown wild again. Rocks and various-sized holes were hidden beneath heather and tall grass, forcing her as well as the others unfamiliar with the territory to maintain their slow pace all the way to the village.

Located on the mainland on the other side of the narrow strip of land that connected Fàire Creachann to Scotland, the village was larger than she had anticipated, but also less developed. Efforts to erect cottages, homes, and shelters had just begun. Most families had only crude attempts at shelter, which would suffice for summer, but in a few months, they would have to have something more substantial. Even these hardy Highlanders could not face a winter here without protection.

The villagers were peaceful, but not overly friendly. Ellenor received a couple of head nods, but no one directly said a word to her. Instead, they continued with their business. Ellenor felt more like an interloper than a welcomed mistress and she suspected it was because that was exactly how they viewed her. She took a deep breath and exhaled, telling herself patience and time would turn them around.

"Milady?"

Ellenor recognized the voice. She turned and saw several of the soldiers and their wives who had been riding with them. She knew most of the women, but only a couple of the guardsmen had dared to talk to her during their journey. Liam had been one of them. "Liam, are you thinking of staying?"

"Aye, milady. The beginnings of what will be our cottage are just across the way, and my wife wants to get settled before the rain comes in. I suspect the others are wanting the same. After we see to our families, we plan to ride out to the training fields."

Ellenor glanced at the rolling hills toward which Liam was gesturing. They grew in size until they collided with the western edge of a sheer slope that jutted straight into the sky. Its southern border held a gentler incline and contained zigzagging paths, etched out by climbers and riders trying to cross the mountain's summit. Somewhere between here and there, several hundred of Cole's men were training, unaware of their return.

Ellenor quickly said her good-byes and then joined

Brighid and the handful of remaining soldiers to proceed across the headland.

Most of the strip was fairly wide and stable, but one small stretch narrowed considerably. On impulse, Ellenor stopped, jumped down, and looked around her, letting the rest of the party go by. The day was overcast and the waters far below were churning from a distant storm making its way toward land. As the waves hit the rocks below, the water turned into a white spray, soaring high into the air. The rhythm of the pounding sound mixed with the seagulls' cries was hauntingly melodic. Again, she felt as if she were being beckoned home.

"Coming?" Brighid called to her.

"Aye," Ellenor answered and remounted.

Fàire Creachann was situated on an egg-shaped tip of land, which was large enough to encompass two, maybe three McTiernay-sized castles. The sheer drop eliminated the need for a stout curtain wall for protection, but a rock fence that looked to be predominantly waist-high surrounded most of the jagged plateau.

The connecting strip of land did not enable a rider to easily cross from the mainland to the castle. Instead, it dead-ended straight into the headland's rocky cliff thirty, maybe forty, feet below its edge. There a gateway stood, severely foraged over the past several decades for its stone and iron. But connected to the gateway was a short but steep tunnel constructed from stone, which to Ellenor's quick inspection, looked to be untouched. Most likely because if one did begin to dislodge any of the carved rocks, the whole thing would collapse, making it near impossible to enter and pillage other supplies.

The tunnel was actually the first of a series, each wide enough to allow approximately four riders through simultaneously. And while the tunnels' height allowed her to ride through comfortably, Ellenor suspected that

Cole and some of the taller Highlanders had to crouch a little when mounted.

Brighid, who was riding ahead, exited the final semi-dark passageway and let go a soft cry. Ellenor nudged her horse to continue up the steep incline until she emerged onto a semiflattened piece of land, mostly green stretching out in all directions. Scattered everywhere were unfinished structures that had been completed at one time or another. Only the five towers located at critical edges of the upland were still standing. One tower was a little larger than the rest. It was rectangular shaped on one end and round on the other, had a new door, and looked to be the focus of most of the recent construction. Ellenor suspected it to be the keep.

Makeshift stables and a smithy had been erected along one rock wall between two towers. Cole's horse along with several others were being tended to by some boys who looked to be no older than twelve. Farther along the wall, on the other side of the tower, were the remains of an enormous building, serving as the Great Hall. Much of its stone had been pilfered and it would take time to resurrect the structure to its former glory. Next to it was a place for a kitchen. There were stones missing but not as much since it was nestled between the Great Hall and the storehouse, which also looked fairly untouched.

Down farther and across the plateau was an enormous well, answering the question about their source of fresh water. Around it were several crude, newly erected structures serving as living quarters. Ellenor hoped one of them was not intended for Brighid.

The only other buildings were a nearly complete hall-like structure made of wood and next to it a small shelter that was a fusion of wood and stone. Smoke was rising from its roof, and Ellenor hoped it was a kitchen and that a decent meal was being prepared for them. Regardless, the building's existence was a sign of progress. While it would take years to build Fàire Creachann into what it could be, Cole had already done much to begin turning it into a home and a place for people to gather. They had all summer, and with Henri's help, by winter no one would be without housing.

The soldiers that had continued to ride with them had headed straight for the stables and were now disappearing into the hall. A few clansmen were in sight, although nothing close to the numbers she had expected. They were purposely ignoring her and Brighid. Ellenor was about to remark about it when one figure caught her eye. She pointed.

"Looks like Henri," Brighid said, acknowledging Ellenor's gesture. "I guess he did make it here all right. He rode off so crazily I thought we might find him broken and bruised on our way here."

Ellenor nodded in agreement. "He appears to be trying to blend into the scenery." The slight mason was clasping both his hands behind his back and wandering about the well looking at everything . . . and nothing. Something had happened and Ellenor suspected that whatever it was had much to do with Cole's rising tension before he departed ahead of the group. She thought back and suddenly knew what it was.

Ellenor dismounted and waved one of the stable boys to her location. "I just realized we were not—"

"Look."

Ellenor pivoted and saw several men exit the hall. Donald was among them.

Brighid hopped down and joined Ellenor's side, letting go a long, low whistle. "Whatever has happened, Donald is furious."

Ellenor looked at the man, trying to see what Brighid perceived as anger. He was facing partially away so she could only see the side of him and his mass of red-brown hair hung down, obscuring his expression. "Are you sure?"

"Aye," Brighid responded. "His legs are rigid. And look at his hands."

Ellenor did look. Donald's arms were crossed, but his hands were balled into fists. "We weren't greeted."

"Maybe they thought—"

"No," Ellenor interrupted, "I mean we weren't greeted in the mountains. *Someone* should have seen our approach and ridden out to welcome us. No one did."

Brighid turned and stared at Ellenor, her brown eyes large and incredulous. "I didn't realize . . . but you are right. No wonder Donald is mad."

Ellenor handed the reins to the lad who had just arrived. She gave him a big, friendly smile. "Would you take our horses back to the stable and ensure they are rubbed down and fed?"

The boy shrugged his shoulders, but took both sets of reins and headed back. Brighid was about to set his attitude straight, letting him know just whose horse he was tending, but Ellenor indicated for her to remain silent. "Let's find out what has happened. You talk with Donald. Tell him that you need to know where you are to be sleeping. Meanwhile, I'm going to find Cole."

"What are you planning to do?"

"First, I intend to remind him how glad he is that he married me."

Ellenor cracked the already opened door to the newly built hall a fraction wider and stepped through. Sparsely furnished, the building looked larger from the inside. The location of the hall must have previously had a similarly sized room, for one wall was made out of stone and in the middle was a large working hearth made to warm a spacious area. Cole was staring into the flames flickering against the cavernous walls of the fireplace, unaware of her entrance.

Only two other figures were in the room. Both were guards and were standing just a few feet away from the doors engrossed in a heated conversation when they glanced over to see who had entered. Both of their jaws dropped, but before either could signal their laird, Ellenor gestured for them to leave her alone with Cole. Immediately, they retreated outside, leaving her with a very tense and very angry husband. Just as Brighid was able to deduce Donald's mood from simple stances and slight movements, Ellenor was able to do the same.

Quietly, she glided over to where Cole was standing and slowly crept her arms around his middle. Instantly, the muscles in his arms and back went rigid, but just as quickly relaxed as she laid her cheek upon his lower shoulder and squeezed.

He stroked her forearm, which was still clutching his center, and asked, "What was that for?"

Ellenor kissed his back through his leine and then swiveled around to face him. "Is there anything you love that doesn't give you a headache?"

"I'm not sure whether or not I should be warmed or worried by your inclusion of yourself on that list."

Her mouth curved mischievously. "Both. But you can relax for now. I think Dugan has you preoccupied enough that you won't be tempted to try and intimidate me into obedience."

"I've known for some time that has never worked."

"And yet you keep trying."

He let go a deep chuckle. It was the first lighthearted

sound she had heard from him since their departure from McTiernay Castle. "I just like to see how you will rebuff the attempt," Cole teased. "Each time it is something different, usually amusing, and almost always it is at *your* expense and not mine."

Ellenor's mouth dropped open at the revelation. She considered it for several seconds, wanting to refute his claim, but couldn't. Then, she raised an eyebrow and gave him a half smile. "Hmm. But it got me what I wanted."

"And that was?"

"You, you big hulking Scot. I got you."

"Ah, *babag,* that you did," he murmured and lowered his mouth intimately over hers, tracing the soft fullness of her lips with his tongue. Her arms stole around his neck and her mouth opened as he continued the kiss, but neither of them moved to deepen its intensity. If they did, both knew neither of them would be able nor inspired to end things before experiencing full release. Instead, they simply enjoyed being with each other.

When Cole ended the kiss, Ellenor took her time before opening her eyes. She laid her cheek on his chest and just let him hold her. She hoped the simple embrace was helping to improve his spirits, but when she pulled back, she could see by his expression that it had only been a temporary reprieve. His eyes were staring at the fire once again, his mind swirling with the status of the clan.

"Where's Dugan?" she asked, trying to make her voice sound only curious, not concerned.

Her question was met with silence, and Ellenor was struck with the concept that Cole might be one of those men who never included their wives on clan decisions or happenings considered outside their responsibility.

The thought horrified her. A life kept in the dark was far from an appetizing one.

"Have you heard from Dugan?" she prompted again. This time her tone, while still soft, had a velvet strong edge to it. She hoped it would induce an answer. It did.

"I misjudged him," Cole stated simply, but there was no mistaking the anger in his staid calmness. He moved out of her arms and offered her a nearby chair to sit in.

She refused. Cole was distancing himself from her when he should have been leaning upon her for support. *He's new to friendship, a wife, even love,* she told herself and forced her jaw to unclench. She thought about hugging him again but knew that, even if he let her, it would not change what he was thinking.

Licking her lips, she tried another approach. "If that is true, then that would make me a bad judge of your character as well." Cole's eyes snapped to hers as she knew they would. "But it's not true." Her voice was not loud, but it rang out crisp and clear. "Your ability to read a person is unmatched by anyone I have ever known. My father was such a man, and yet, I doubt he would have recognized the real me as you did the day we met. It scared me then, knowing you possessed the ability to see things as they really are, not just as one presents them to be. Now I take comfort in it and so should you. Don't doubt yourself now. If Dugan is not here, then there is a reason. Just as there is a reason no one was sent to greet us. Don't use doubt to decide your course, use facts."

"And if I don't have them?"

"Then find them, Highlander, and show your people how you intend to rule."

Cole reached out and pulled her roughly into his arms. "Elle . . ." he whispered, his voice raspy with the suppressed emotion he refused to release. "God, how I love you." And then unable to hold back the desire any longer, he crushed her to him and took her mouth with savage mastery, devouring its softness.

Ellenor had been unprepared for the demanding intensity. His tongue was possessive, sensuous, letting her know just what he intended to do. She instinctively moved her body against his, massaging his hardness that was pressing against her, throbbing and demanding release and satisfaction. It matched her powerful need as shock waves of desire flowed through her entire body.

Cole released her lips and began trailing kisses down her throat, pushing her bliaut off her shoulder, seeking other delights he knew it hid. If it hadn't been for the knock on the door followed by the sound of it opening, he would have found out. He immediately broke off the kiss and shoved her behind him to fix her dress.

Ellenor heard footsteps echoing in the room, but it hadn't registered they were no longer alone. Her body ruled her mind and it was still burning with desire, aching with need for another kiss. The sound of another man's voice startled her into awareness.

"Laird, we know what has happened or at least some of it."

Ellenor stepped back into view and recognized Liam, one of the men who had elected to settle their wives before moving to the training fields.

"Explain," Cole demanded.

Liam glanced at Ellenor and then did as instructed. "We first went to the fields as you ordered. There was blood, but not enough to indicate a death and it looked several days old. We then followed a trail that led into a gulley. That was where I met Jaime. He was riding here. Fast."

Cole's eyes flew to the door and back to Liam. "Where is he?"

"Once he saw me, he stopped and ordered me to return immediately and bring you and my lady as quickly as possible."

Cole stilled as he assimilated the request. Ellenor felt his body harden and she knew why. Another man, besides him, had dared to dictate her presence. "Someone is hurt, and Jaime knows Hagatha taught me how to handle a needle. It must be serious, otherwise Jaime would have brought the man here rather than request that *we* ride out to him."

Cole's body remained rigid, but she knew he had heard her. "Go and get what you need. And tell the stable master to make ready all my men's horses for immediate riding."

There was a dangerous softness in his voice. Ellenor nodded and moved to exit the room. Just as she was closing the door shut behind her, she heard Liam say that war had broken out amongst the clan. She waited for a second, half expecting Cole to come out and change his mind about her riding into unknown hazards, but he didn't. She turned and raced across the lawn to the stables from which Brighid was just emerging.

Her brown eyes grew round and large. "What happened?"

"I cannot say, but someone is hurt, and if I were to guess, the person injured is Dugan. At least I hope he is."

Brighid frowned with confusion. "Did you say you *hope* Dugan was injured?"

Ellenor nodded and continued her march to the stables. "Otherwise, he is a dead man."

Just a little over three hours later, Ellenor knelt by a seriously injured Dugan, wondering what punishments the church would bestow on her if she wounded him further by punching him in the mouth. The man had no inkling of just how much he needed to stop talking.

The ride out had not been an easy one. They had passed the designated training fields shortly after they left Fàire Creachann and didn't arrive to where the men had gathered until almost two hours later. The ground was rocky and uneven, but it was the tension radiating from Cole that put everyone—including her—at unease.

Ellenor had thought that once they had found the men and heard what had happened, the hostility brewing in Cole would lessen, but now after hearing the explanations—or the lack of them—the result was just the opposite and she simply wished Dugan would be quiet.

"It was an accident. He would never have done it. Couldn't have. We're like brothers," Dugan mumbled. He was sweating profusely and it was a cold day. The man was in intense pain, but if Cole could see it—or cared—Ellenor couldn't tell.

"Are you saying Leith did this?" The question came from Cole.

Dugan swallowed and tried again. "I thought distance would help. It did. Ask Jaime. I just went too far. Never thought he would come here. Thought it would give him time."

Before he could finish, Ellenor shoved Dugan back down for what had to be the tenth time. The man was panicked and he should be, but right now, she needed him to lie still. "If you move again, I'll see to it that you're gagged."

Dugan's eyes momentarily focused on her face and lucidity came back into the blue, pain-filled pools. He stared back at her and murmured, "I'll lie still."

"Finally," Ellenor muttered and began to inspect his wound. It was deep and fever was sure to set in before morning. She ordered for one of the soldiers to heat their dagger in a fire and then searched her bag for a needle. She grabbed the beverage pouch from Dugan's hand and sniffed it, verifying it was ale. She poured some over the sharp object to clean the dirt off and then waved for the blade to be brought to her.

Realizing his hand was now empty, Dugan's mouth began to contort. Then he glanced at the gash in his lower left side. His face went green and Ellenor couldn't blame him. The puncture was deep and ugly.

"I'm ready to die. Made peace with the idea long time ago," he muttered, his words blurring together. "Just don't want to die with the laird thinking I'm a coward. You'll tell him, angel, won't you? Tell him, I'm no coward."

"I'll tell him," Ellenor promised just as she finished threading the needle. In an effort to divert his attention, she asked "How did this happen?" just as she pressed the hot metal against the wound.

Dugan managed to get out the word "spear" before his breath caught in his throat. His mouth pulled tight and a fine white line surrounded his lips. A second later, he was unconscious and Ellenor sighed in relief. It was much faster and easier to stitch a man who was not trying to attack the perpetrator of excruciating pain. Now able to take her time and ensure the stitches were even and small like Hagatha showed her, she sat back and concentrated on her task, listening to Jaime try to fill in the holes of Dugan's story.

"We lost one," Jaime said simply. His voice, however, made it clear how deeply he felt the absence.

"Who?" Cole demanded quietly.

"Ferris," Jaime answered. "He was assigned to watch for your arrival and return each night with an update. When he didn't arrive by sundown yesterday, Dugan and I knew something was wrong. I sent men to look, but they still haven't found him."

The only indication Cole had heard Jaime was the rigidity of his frame. Ferris had been a boy on the verge of becoming a man. His family had been wracked with loss and therefore had not been excited when their youngest son decided to join Cole and support him as a soldier. Maybe Cole should have said no, but Ferris was incredibly eager and loyal and would have jumped to do any task, including ones he should never have been assigned. Any loss was bad, but Ferris . . . he was one that would be mourned for some time.

Jaime felt the full weight of Cole's silence and felt partially to blame. "I should have expected it. When I agreed to Dugan's plan, I wasn't . . . I wasn't thinking, laird. I should have realized . . . I should have . . ." Jaime stopped himself and took a deep breath to gather his thoughts before speaking again. "Leith's cooperation goes beyond nonexistent. At night, he was sneaking into camp and building ill will amongst the ranks under my command. Dugan suggested we ride out here until your return. We weren't hiding exactly, but neither of us thought Leith driven enough to come this far just to cause mischief. Dugan hoped that if his men were kept away from Leith's bad influences, it would provide the time needed to regain their allegiance not to him, but to me . . . to you."

Cole's eyes shifted from Jaime down to the unconscious form and back again. He said nothing but waited for Jaime to continue.

"It seemed to be working or at least things appeared to be improving . . . that is, until last night. Many of the men felt protective of Ferris and believe Dugan is directly responsible for whatever happened to him."

"He's not the only one." Cole's statement was simple

and direct and held no inflection, which made it even more piercing.

Jaime gulped. "Aye, laird. Aye," he whispered. "Dugan didn't say much but he was mad, and in the middle of the night, he left with instructions to wait for his return. An hour after sunrise, he rode into camp barely alive with a hole through his left side. It was amazing he could stay on top of his horse. A few men and I followed his blood trail to where it happened, but Leith had disappeared into the hills. It would take days to find him and so I came back to find out what happened and . . . well, you heard Dugan. I have been able to make no more of his mutterings than you."

"Was he attacked by Leith?"

"Aye. It was Leith and he left enough clues he wanted us to know it."

"Or me," Cole sighed. He looked at the sky and raked his fingers through his loose hair. "Do you believe Dugan has been acting against me or my wishes?"

"Nay, but nor can I prove that he is a loyal supporter either."

"Then we will have to wait."

"For him to wake?" Jaime asked.

Cole looked at Dugan once more. "Or die," he answered simply.

Ellenor watched Cole's expression go void. It went blank as if all emotion had been drained from him. He was distancing himself right in front of her eyes. She wondered how far he would retreat and when he would return.

Ellenor listened and wished there were something she could say or do, but there was nothing. Cole's blue gaze shifted and caught her staring at him with questions she wasn't asking. He didn't answer them, but instead posed one in return. "Are you finished?"

Ellenor swallowed and renewed her attention on Dugan's wound. "I will be as soon as I get this poultice on. He needs to be back at Fàire Creachann, out of the cold and where he can be tended better." She glanced at the afternoon sun. It took two hours of hard riding to get where they were and it would be several more to return, especially with Dugan needing to be carried. Traveling at night was dangerous, but it couldn't be helped. "We'll have to stop often so that I can check the stitches and his bleeding."

Cole's deep blue eyes narrowed and then he shook his head. "You'll be returning with me. If Dugan arrives alive, you can tend him then." He then pivoted and barked out some clipped instructions.

Ellenor considered arguing, but Jaime stared at her and gave an almost imperceptible shake to his head. "Nay, my lady. The laird is right. The man who did that is still out there and it is more important to get you back to safety. I wasn't thinking when I asked you to come out here. I only knew if you hadn't come . . ."

"Dugan would be dead," Ellenor finished for him.

"Aye."

She swallowed and then knelt down to finish wrapping the poultice so that it would stay on the wound. She made the bindings a little tighter than preferable, but she hoped it would provide additional support to keep the gash from reopening. By the time she was done, Cole was back by her side, helping her to stand. Wordlessly, she allowed him to guide her to her horse and help her mount. Minutes later, they were gone and Dugan's fate was in the hands of the Lord.

The ride back was uneventful, but silent. No one felt the need to speak. In Ellenor's case, she didn't know what to say. They arrived and handed their weary dismounts to a sleepy stable master, who had just retired for the evening. Cole walked her to the odd-shaped tower she had guessed was the keep. He told her to go to the third floor and that he would return shortly. She nodded and watched him head across the grassy yard to the Lower Hall.

She was tempted to find Brighid and bring her up to speed. Her friend no doubt was pacing the floors, wondering what had happened and was probably fearing the worse. Unfortunately, Ellenor had no idea where she was. That was probably a blessing for Ellenor was not in the right frame of mind for company or being hammered with questions. Mostly because so many of them had no answers.

She longed for a place to organize her thoughts and consider what had been said, and even more important, what had *not* been said. For years that place had been a small lake where she enjoyed swimming in the nude. The water rushing over her skin had a calming effect that she thought unparalleled until the first night she had slept in Cole's arms. Here, at Fàire Creachann, water surrounded her, but it was inaccessible and far from calm. The crashing waves pounded the cliffs, but the sound had a hypnotic quality and Ellenor found herself drawn to its music.

Opting to delay going inside, she moved across the yard to the open area along the wall. The thick clouds from this morning had thinned, allowing pockets of moonlight to shine through on the castle and the sea. Ellenor stared at the glittering view. Memories of her father came forward, telling her to make a wish. Tonight, she wished for many things, but most of all, she yearned to know her husband a little better.

He loved her and she him, but that singular emotion

was far from insightful. Years from now, she would know what to expect and could prepare herself for his reaction. She would know if he would want to talk about his plans and, if so, when. She would know if he wanted feedback or if he would rather be left alone. A trust beyond their emotional bond would have been planted and cultivated, something only time could do. Meanwhile, she could only be herself and find out the hard way what was too little and too much. Regardless, she fully intended on being by Cole's side, supporting him in whatever way she could. The question was, would Cole accept it?

Ellenor did not intend to interfere with his responsibilities as laird, but sitting meekly by the side was not something she could endure for long . . . if at all. And nothing in their short relationship gave her any insight as to how Cole planned to integrate her with his life.

Oh, how she wished she knew her husband better.

Ellenor stared at the endless sea. A strong wind coming off the An Cuan Sgìth caused her to shiver. The clouds had started to thicken again, and the masses blocked the moon, turning the area nearly pitch black. Only the sound remained. The scene was a metaphor for the events that had been unfolding for weeks.

The attack had been almost inevitable. Even who was injured could have been predicted. Dugan's intentions had been on trying to help. That was obvious, even to the most unintelligent. His decision to move the men, however, was debatable. Then there was Leith, Dugan's best friend. Was he still? To know, Dugan needed to survive, and if he did live, he needed to prove just whom he was loyal to . . . his friend or his laird. Ellenor considered the puzzle for a while, but in the end was no closer to an opinion. Loyalty to friends ran deep with these Highlanders. Cole's promise to Robert proved that. However, honor was just as important, if not more, and Dugan had pledged his to Cole.

A bright light flickered across the yard and Ellenor glanced over her shoulder to see the hall's door open and several men step out. Cole was among them. The door swung shut again. Cole turned and began walking toward the keep but the rest headed toward the make-shift living quarters established near the well and old kitchen. Ellenor grimaced. Donald was among those shadows and that meant Brighid's temporary home was far from ideal.

Ellenor swung her gaze around to the keep. A light glimmered from two windows situated close to each other high along the tower wall. A fire was lit somewhere inside that room. Her and Cole's room, a place she had yet to see.

Cole must have seen her and adjusted his stride accordingly. When he reached her side, he pulled her into his arms and held her for several seconds, as if just having her close made things better. "Come, let's retire. On the way, I'll tell you what I can."

All the tension and worry of whether he would shut her out vanished with that one comment. Ellenor felt as if a large boulder that had been pressing down upon her was suddenly lifted. The need for explanations went with it. Just knowing he was willing to share was what she needed and he had given that to her.

Ellenor leaned into his side and allowed him to steer her toward the keep. "Tell me about Leith." It was the one subject she knew the littlest about and was the most dangerous.

Cole didn't answer, but Ellenor could feel his chest rise and fall quickly as if he were chuckling. "Leave it to my wife to ask about the one man everyone else avoided."

"Then what were you talking about?"

"Dugan."

Ellenor frowned. "What can you do or decide until you speak with him?"

"That wasn't the point."

Understanding suddenly overcame her. "Oh," she whispered. They had discussed Dugan to avoid discussing Leith. Ellenor could appreciate why. The men, no doubt Donald in particular, were grappling with the concept of someone treating their laird in such a way. A concept Ellenor had no problems facing. There were bad men in this world, and they did not always belong to a distant warring country. Sometimes they slept next to you. Pretending otherwise was a quick way to getting hurt . . . or worse. She had learned that the hard way.

"Tell me about Leith," she prompted again. And listened as Cole told her all he knew.

Chapter 15

"Roll over on your side," Ellenor instructed for the second time.

"Ahh, what would I do without you, love?" Dugan inquired dreamily as he did her bidding.

Ellenor raised an eyebrow but decided to let the endearment go. It wasn't the first time Dugan had tried flirting with her, but those other times he had been delirious with fever. "Well, at least you no longer think I am an angel sent down to guide your way to heaven," Ellenor replied.

"But I do," he countered. "The most beautiful Scottish angel in the land."

"I'm not Scottish," Ellenor informed him, leaning over to examine his wound. Her hair fell and he reached up to tuck it behind her ear. She jumped back out of reach.

Dugan was stunned. Her reaction had not been one of chastity, and recoils such as the one she just exhibited were not caused from mere discomfort. Every instinct in him screamed out that she needed protecting. Never did he want to see that look of panic in her eyes again—especially related to him.

"I promise not to hurt you."

Ellenor gave her head a little shake and forced ease into her expression and stance. She returned to his side and gave him a little push, indicating for him to roll back over. "Of course not. You just startled me."

"Well, just in case it was something more, know that I am the commander of this clan and can protect you. I will make sure you are well treated."

Ellenor's hands froze in shock. The man had no idea who she was. "I'm glad to hear it, because as Lady McTiernay and the chieftain's wife, I expect no less."

The blood drained out of Dugan's face. He reached over for the pitcher Brighid had left out for him and took several swigs. "You're . . . you're . . . the laird's wife? The one he went down to marry?"

"I am. Now, hold still."

The stitches had held during his transport to the castle, but the skin around them had grown red, puffy, and had begun to ooze stuff she knew wasn't part of the healing process. Fever had set in soon afterward. She had felt helpless, knowing only to keep cool compresses on him and keep replacing the poultice on his wound. She fed him some of the weed Hagatha said fought delirium, and after two long days, the fever was gone. The pain, however, wasn't.

Brighid had placed a couple of crocks of mead near him, and judging by the empty ones on the table and the nearly empty one in his hand, Dugan was grateful for the anesthetic help. He took another swallow as she finished. "Will I live?"

Ellenor smiled and said, "I need to replace your dressing, but yes, I think you will live. However, you will have to remain quiet for a couple of weeks and I expect by then you'll be howling about your living death." She walked over to where she had placed the herbs and began to make a paste.

Dugan swallowed the rest of the crock's contents and grunted. He tossed it on the floor and waved a finger in her direction. "I shouldn't say this so I won't. But you are pretty. I mean *really* pretty. And nice, too. Pretty and nice."

Ellenor glanced back and rolled her eyes. "And you, Commander, are drunk."

"Aye, very. Gotta be. The only thing to keep the pain away. Not to mention I got stabbed by my best friend."

"You try to induce sympathy where there is none."

Dugan tried to prop himself up on his elbows and groaned with agony.

Ellenor used her chin to point to the crocks full of mead. "Might want to watch the stuff."

"And you know what else you are? Honest. An honest angel sent here to help me."

"I'm not anyone's angel."

"You're the laird's."

Ellenor shook her head. Dugan would probably never believe Cole's nickname for her, *babag*. Filthy woman was about as far from angel as one could get.

She walked back over, sat down next to Dugan, and removed the old dressing. She grimaced as she cleaned the wound. She was hurting him, but he didn't say a word. He just held his breath. Finally she was done.

"Did I hurt you too much?"

Dugan shook his head. "Not comfortable, but that's not what's ailing me the most."

The man was green and Ellenor bit her bottom lip to keep from chuckling. "I'm guessing that you are not a drinker."

"Avoid the stuff usually. Seen what it does. Makes men say and do stuff that they shouldn't." He paused as Ellenor placed a new poultice against his side. "God, you are beautiful."

"And I'm nice and honest."

"And married to a man who doesn't like people."

Ellenor put Dugan's hand against the cloth to hold it in place as she began to bind his side. "Cole likes people."

Dugan shrugged. "Well, maybe, but people don't like him."

"I do."

"And *that* doesn't make sense. He's not likable! I'm likable. I mean, don't you like me?"

Any other time, Ellenor would have torn into Dugan, but she knew it was mostly the mead talking. "I must admit that I do."

"And you're surprised by that. I can tell. You like me, but you don't trust me."

Ellenor tied off the binding and stood up. "Trust has to be earned and we just met."

He watched as she went to the basin and cleaned her hands of his blood. "Your husband . . . everyone trusts him," Dugan slurred. "He commands respects and gets it. I try to do the same and even my own men ignore my orders."

Ellenor turned around, leaned against the table, and dried off her hands. "You're talking about Leith now."

"He was my friend. My best friend and he betrayed me."

"Can I ask you a question? How can you lead a friend? I've never met anyone who could."

Dugan tilted his brow with a look of uncertainty. "What do you mean?"

"Only that commands are issued from superiors, and friends are equal. Friends make decisions through agreement, so when you stepped into a leadership role, you cannot be surprised when those closest to you rebelled."

"So are you saying none of the men can be my friends? That sounds miserable. Not to mention lonely."

Ellenor stood up and went to look out the window.

Dugan was in the only other tower with a floor and a ceiling, and while his room wasn't nearly as large as those of the keep, it did have a lovely view. "You're right. It is lonely. Maybe that's why not just anyone can be a good leader."

"What about the laird?"

Ellenor turned around. "What about Cole?"

"Donald . . . Jaime. They are his friends."

A frown overcame her features. "I would say that they were the closest things he had to friends for a long while, but in the truest sense of the word? No. I don't think they ever will be. After being together for years, there is enormous respect and trust between them, but there is also a distance, one that will never be bridged. Cole gathers information. He listens, and then he makes his decisions alone. He always has."

"Don't know if I could do that. Have no friends."

"Cole has something better. Me."

Dugan took another swig of mead. "That makes twice he's beaten me. He's laird . . . and he has you."

"I'm not a prize."

"I doubt being laird is either."

Two pairs of eyes followed Ellenor. One watched in silence as she descended the staircase, enjoying how her hips swayed as she moved. The other stared from afar when she exited. One pair knew her movements intimately; the other had never seen her before.

One gaze was heated, thinking about the night, and her skin, and how he would tenderly caress it to make her come alive with desire only for him. The other gaze was very cool and firm. He thought about her as well. Pleasure came in different forms and it was rare to find a woman who agreed with his sadistic tastes. Even rarer was to find a woman who intrigued him. And this one did.

She was smiling just a little, as if she had a secret. Her expression was unguarded and tender, and both men yearned to know just what had made her laugh, if only to herself. Her head was arched slightly, revealing the delicate curve of her neck. She walked over and spoke to one of the servants, and each man imagined it was himself she was speaking to, hearing her voice, warm and sensual, whispering a willingness to indulge in his fantasies.

Loins tightened and hearts began to pound. Both men wanted her and they wanted her to want them. And for each, the strength of the sudden driving need was bothersome. For neither could have what they wanted . . . to be alone, with her, if only for a few minutes.

Both men began to make plans.

Only one man had the right.

Cole waited until Ellenor had left the tower to emerge from the shadows of the staircase. He couldn't remember the last time he had hidden from anything, but today he was glad he had followed his instincts.

Brighid had stopped by the hall to find her husband and found him instead. Cole had told her where Donald was and she had informed him that Dugan was finally awake. She had failed to mention, however, that Ellenor was tending him.

His hand was on the door and was about to give it a shove when Dugan's garbled attempts at seduction hit him like a broadsword to the head. Cole had managed to find just enough control to pull his hand back and sink onto the narrow sitting bench below the corridor window. He took a deep breath and reminded himself that pummeling an ignorant, drunken man may make him feel better, but it would not help him discern the truth. That was when he realized he didn't have to. All he had to do was listen.

And he did, and while he still didn't know why or how Dugan was injured, Cole had verified one thing and learned another. Dugan was a fool, but a loyal one.

Cole stepped into the room and stared at the semi-prone figure nursing a drink straight from the pitcher. Dugan's blue-gray eyes found and met Cole's piercing stare. He waved the pitcher haphazardly and said, "Come in. Hit me now and put me out of my misery, laird."

The man was incredibly drunk. It was amazing he could even speak. "Don't tempt me."

"Do you know who I was just talking to?"

"An angel."

Dugan's brows turned into deep furrows of confusion. "Damn you. Is there *nothing* you can't do? Now you're into reading a man's mind. Well, read away. I've nothing to hide except my shame and I can't even hide that anymore."

At the completion of the slurred speech, Cole realized the man had not been lying when he had said he never drank. Most men had learned at an early age how to hold their tongues, regardless of the amount they imbibed. Dugan was acting like a fifteen-year-old caught inside the buttery.

"Do you know what you have, laird?" And before Cole could respond, Dugan answered his own question. "An exceptional woman. And I mean exceptional. A golden angel and she belongs to you. So that makes you a winner three times now. And if you're the winner, then I guess I'm the loser. I've lost my best friend . . ." Dugan paused for another swallow, and before it was all down, he added, "And becoming laird—but that one . . . that one doesn't bother me so much now. Did at first, but now not so bad, and then this morning I learn that my angel is your wife. What is it with you Mc-Tiernays? I'm told your brother married himself a bonnie lass. Dunno myself. Never seen her, but I have seen your woman, and Lord knows you don't deserve a woman like that."

Cole walked over and plucked the pitcher out of Dugan's grasp. All men have secrets and even fools were entitled to keep a few. At the rate Dugan was rambling, the man would have nothing left to call his own. "I think in your case, pain is a better alternative to this stuff."

Dugan watched as Cole placed the crock on a table out of reach. He squeezed his eyes shut. "Damn stuff. Makes a man honest."

Cole shrugged in agreement and sat down in the single worn chair someone must have brought up from the hall. "Aye, that it does."

Dugan reopened his eyes and focused them on Cole relaxing in the chair. His legs were stretched out in front of him, his ankles crossed and fingers entwined. Even sitting silently, the man had an air of command and Dugan knew Cole was waiting for answers. Dugan took a deep breath and exhaled, trying to focus thoughts that refused to stay put. "The men—Leith's followers—I would hear them. Jaime didn't hear them. They made sure to keep silent when he was around, but not me. They didn't care if I knew about their discontent. They thought I wouldn't do anything about it, but I did.

"I wanted to bring the men together. Have them work and train together. I saw how the ones already under Jaime's leadership took pride in being part of a great army. These men . . . they used to be my men . . . but I could never give them the pride they had found these past few weeks. I wanted to give Leith . . . the others . . . the same thing."

Cole took advantage of the break. "Let me guess. It worked."

Dugan shook his head. "No. Leith was furious."

Cole pulled his legs in and leaned forward with his elbows on his knees. "I wasn't there, but I can assure you it worked. Otherwise, Leith would still be there today, building malcontent."

Dugan's face contorted as he considered just what Cole was trying to tell him. "So . . . it wasn't a bad idea?"

Cole cocked his head and shrugged his chin. "Well, not that one."

Dugan grimaced. "Aye. Leith was so angry. Accused me of attacking his credibility with the men and he withdrew them from the training sessions. I guess he thought I would just let him, but I told him that it was his choice, but he had to leave McTiernay land and never come back. He exploded and I could see it in his eyes. I knew then that he would attack if given a chance. I needed to give him time to calm down and leave."

"So you ordered Jaime to leave the fields to protect the men? They could have—"

"No!" Dugan growled and tried to sit up. He immediately winced in pain and collapsed back against the bedding that had been propping him up. "I did it to protect Leith. Your army against a couple of dozen men? They would have had no chance! And no matter what he had done, I had known Leith most of my life and I didn't want to be responsible for his death."

Cole didn't know whether to be impressed or disgusted by the man's misplaced loyalty. "So you ordered the men to be moved. Then what happened?"

Dugan's jaw clenched as he tried to distance himself emotionally from what had occurred. "I ordered a couple of sentries to watch for your return," Dugan began, sounding less and less inebriated. The man was fighting intense emotions; ones even large amounts of alcohol could not lessen. "One of them was supposed to return each night to update Jaime and me on their status and receive new orders. The night before you returned, one sentry never arrived. I thought . . . I thought Leith was just holding Ferris, forcing my hand, knowing I would come to him. But I was wrong."

"Is Ferris dead?"

Dugan squeezed his eyes shut and nodded, remembering the mangled body lying on the ground. "By the time I found them and I saw Ferris, beaten . . . I just . . . reacted. I raised my sword like a fool and Leith must have known I was going to kill him and took advantage of my anger." Dugan paused and then looked Cole straight in the eye. "He told me that it's over."

"Not yet," Cole promised and held Dugan's gaze for several seconds until he was sure the man knew his full meaning.

"Are you going after him then?"

Cole stood up and gave a simple shake to his head. "Won't have to. You're still alive and I'm still laird. He'll be back and I don't want there to be any confusion as to what will happen when he comes."

Dugan let go the breath he had been holding and nodded once. "Leith chose his path and it's one I will not save him from."

"We have one more matter to discuss."

Dugan tensed. He had been expecting this moment all day and it had been half the reason behind his drinking. Cole had every right to end his life, and while it was clear the laird was going to let him live, that act of mercy didn't equate to being a part of this clan, let alone retaining his responsibilities as a commander.

Cole pointed to his injury. "That's going to take a while to heal and I don't want Jaime or Donald arguing with you about whether or not you're ready to return, so I'm putting Jaime in charge of the all the men—permanently. Donald will continue as my second, in charge of the elite guard."

Dugan took a deep breath. "I understand," he said, exhaling.

"I'm going to be honest with you, Dugan. I think you are a talented soldier, but as a commander—"

"I'm terrible," Dugan interjected.

Cole arched his brows. "No . . . just foolish and that will change with time." He sighed. The man was defeated and no soldier would ever follow him until Dugan could once again respect himself. It only confirmed what Cole had decided. "I don't desire your battling skills, I require you for something else. The needs of this clan are numerous, and they are only growing as more and more of the nomadic families are finding their way to Fàire Creachann. Sometimes, it's days before I can meet with them and that's too long in some cases. I want you to assess their needs and oversee their work. Inform me of any major decisions to be made, and we'll meet each morning to discuss plans for the day and overall progression."

Dugan stared at Cole, his eyes filled with disbelief without blinking. "After what happened to . . ." he asked, unable to say the young soldier's name aloud.

"Ferris's death will be something you will have to live with, and so will I, but you didn't kill him. Remember that, especially at night."

Dugan nodded in understanding. The nightmares of Ferris's body, bloody and unmoving, were haunting and vivid, and Dugan doubted he would have another untroubled night of sleep again. "When I was riding back,

I thought I was going to die." He paused and licked his lips. "And I hoped I would. What you are offering will give me the chance to redeem myself."

"In whose eyes?" Cole prompted, curious to know just whom he needed to impress.

"My own," Dugan whispered.

Ellenor's scowl could be seen all the way across the courtyard as she exited the still incomplete kitchen. Extraordinary advancements had been happening over the past several weeks owing to Henri's guidance and Dugan's recruiting capabilities. The stables had been solidified, a smithy had been erected, and the Lower Hall was near complete. Ceilings had been either installed or reinforced on the lower floors of all the towers, creating storerooms. Even construction of the buttery had begun. No focus had been on the kitchens, the bake house, or any other room to take care of the basic needs of the castle. And Ellenor was getting furious that her requests were being disregarded or, as Henri put it, "delayed."

"Kitchens still a mess?"

Ellenor jumped, startled by the interruption of the internal monologue she was rehearsing for the next time she saw Cole or Dugan. "Even more so, and with no hope of changing in the near future. Henri won't even placate me by lying about when he will start," Ellenor spit.

Brighid let go a low whistle and fell in step beside her friend. "Guess I came at a bad time."

All of the sudden Ellenor stopped. "What are you doing here?" Three weeks earlier, Donald had ordered a cottage to be erected for them on the mainland. Ellenor wanted to argue but couldn't. There was very little space that was livable and the place he and Brighid had been staying in would eventually be used by castle servants. It was definitely not a home for the commander of the elite guard. So Brighid had left with both of them, promising to see each other at least every other day. Life, however, had had different plans. "I thought you were busy setting up home? Cole said that it was taking more time than Donald had anticipated."

"Oh, the roof and walls were up as promised," Brighid began sarcastically. "Chairs, tables, beds . . . those pesky little comforts have only just started to arrive."

"You've been sleeping on the ground?" Ellenor gasped.

"No. Donald has. I've been sleeping on top of him, and while that was nice for a day or two, I must admit that it's nice to have a bed. But there are still many who do not. The men and women are working as fast and hard as they can, but more families are arriving every day. I don't think anyone realized just how large this clan is going to be. I've been helping . . . which is why I haven't been around."

"No apologies necessary. I've been so busy training staff here . . . You know I think less than a dozen people have ever even been near a castle this size, let alone worked in one. So what finally drove you across the pass? Needed a break?"

"Two things. I came to find out about candles. We, and many others, are nearly out."

"If you have them, guard them well. We are nearly out everywhere, and neither Cole nor Dugan seems to care. I am no closer to finding a place for candlemaking than I am for weaving, spinning, or even washing our clothes. I actually have to have one of the maids bring Cole's and my laundry to the village so her mother—God bless her—can do it."

Ellenor almost mentioned her need for more soap but caught herself just in time. Last time she brought the subject up, she thought Brighid would never stop laughing at the idea of soap as a necessity, but Brighid was wrong. It *was* a necessity and Ellenor was almost out.

"I completely understand," Ellenor continued, "that it may be next summer before these people have a permanent area to do their duties, but every other day I have to find a new place for them to work! Henri keeps usurping any space I find and I would have his head if Cole didn't need it so much."

Brighid elbowed her friend. "Wasn't it you who said that if Cole could have a smithy, you could have a decent baker," she chided, hoping the light banter might cool the heated look in her friend's hazel eyes. It didn't work. "So, just talk with him."

"It's not Cole I am battling. It's Dugan! The man is on a mission, not only to prove himself to Cole, but to himself. He's afraid of being viewed as an invalid . . ."

Brighid started chuckling. "Dugan? Why, he's got every single woman in the village swooning over him."

"Ridiculous as it sounds, it scares him that it has been over a month and he still cannot swing a sword. He fears becoming weak and is determined to find another way of being worthy and capable in Cole's eyes. He spends all his time establishing order in the village . . ."

Brighid bobbed her head enthusiastically. "On that front, he is making excellent progress. The mood amongst the clansmen has changed quite dramatically in the past few weeks. The few squabbles that came up, Dugan handled quickly and fairly . . ."

"Fairly!" Ellenor hooted, uncaring who overheard. "The man doesn't understand the word. Every day he sends a few more men here to help support Henri in exchange for building a cottage, a bed, a table . . ."

"That sounds reasonable. You need the help and—"

Ellenor shot Brighid a sideways glance full of warning. "Not *women*. Men. Castle building is his focus, leaving my needs as Lady of Fàire Creachann unmet. He and Henri oversee the construction and Cole refuses to interfere. He thinks Dugan needs a chance to rebuild his self-esteem and will not counter any of his orders unless it jeopardizes the clan."

"You could try arguing with the laird. Always worked for Laurel."

"I started, but then Cole flattered me and said that my ability to outthink a man like Dugan was one of the reasons he loved me." Ellenor took a deep breath and sighed. "Now how could I argue after that?"

Brighid shrugged her shoulders. "I don't know, but I guess I just assumed all McTiernays fought."

Ellenor frowned at the generalization. "Cole and I have yet to seriously differ." She saw Brighid's brows rise in disbelief. "Oh, we've bickered, but to *really* disagree? No. At least not like Laurel and Conor. I think they quarreled every night after his return. Both of them seem to accept it as a way of life."

"It is a way of life!" Brighid cackled. "For them, but it's not that way for everyone. The laird does not erupt like his two eldest brothers."

"That's what I am afraid of. Cole internalizes his emotions."

"And you're just the opposite. Lord, the day you two *do* really fight, I hope Donald and I are off visiting family." She paused and gestured at all the workers, wood, and stones around them. "So, if you don't want to argue with Cole, what about Dugan? Have you tried him?"

"You mean the one and only time I've been able to find him?" Ellenor half asked, half grumbled. "He spends all of his time on the mainland and I've been so busy here that our paths only intersected once and he was quite difficult then. He claimed my requests, while important, were those of comfort, and safety came first. Well, today, mainland or not, I fully intend to meet with him and make him realize that it *is* the health of our people that's at risk. For the past week, I have been ill from the previous night's meal and it is no wonder with the state of the kitchens. The cooks are doing the best that they can but—"

Brighid grabbed Ellenor's arm, halting her march across the yard. "Good Lord, that's it."

"What's it?"

"Since the moment I saw you, I knew something was different. Why didn't you tell me you were with child? Are you and Cole trying to keep it a secret?"

The shock of Brighid's revelation hit Ellenor full force. She grabbed her throat and whispered, "You're wrong. I can't have a baby. Cole didn't want to start a family for a couple of years . . ."

Brighid snorted and crossed her arms. "Then he should have kept his hands off of you."

Ellenor vehemently shook her head. "No, I, too, didn't want to have a baby. Not so soon. There is so much to do."

Brighid rolled her eyes beneath closed lids, wondering how two such smart people could pretend that the rules of life and death did not apply to them. "Then I guess you should have kept your hands off, too."

"Don't say anything, Brighid. Not to Donald. Anyone. I need to think."

"Thinking won't change anything."

"I just need time to find a way to persuade Cole this is a good thing—a wonderful thing. But first, I'll need to convince myself."

"Well, don't wait too long. I suspect the laird enjoys

his nights, and if he's anything like Donald . . . he'll know soon enough."

Ellenor's jaw dropped. "You mean?"

Brighid grinned. "Aye. That was the second thing I came to tell you. It'll come during winter, of all times. But take heart, dear friend. Donald, my wonderful sweet and oh so emotionally rigid husband, actually hollered aloud he was so thrilled."

"He *has* been smiling a lot lately."

"Aye. So much so that the laird finally asked what's the matter with him. Donald said the laird actually looked jealous."

"I don't know whether to believe you or hug you for lying to me."

"I'll swear to every word."

Ellenor clasped Brighid's hand in hers. "Well, then this is cause for celebration. Duties can wait for a day. Besides I have yet to see your new home. If you don't mind, I think I will come to visit this afternoon."

Brighid nodded enthusiastically. "Please do. I am so scared and so excited and have been dying to share my news with you. And now we can commiserate with each other as we grow enormous." She embraced Ellenor. "This afternoon then?"

Ellenor gave her a final squeeze and let go. "I've got to take care of a few things and meet with Dugan, but then I'll be over directly."

Brighid grinned and waved good-bye. Ellenor returned the gesture, hoping her friend's excitement about becoming a mother was infectious.

Dark brown eyes watched Ellenor leave the stables and disappear into the keep. *A baby.* He had been stunned by the news, and by the sound of her voice, so had she.

Lady McTiernay was far from ecstatic about the idea of becoming a mother.

"You! Mind your business and stop staring at milady."

Leith fought the urge to strangle the stable master and returned his attention to the hay he was shoveling. A horse's stall had provided the perfect place to hide in plain sight. He had somewhere to sleep at night and he could always duck just out of sight—but not out of earshot—when needed. Most of the castle help did not recognize him, and it had been easy to avoid the few who could.

He had been biding his time and had even risked making friends with her ladyship. The woman was surprisingly intelligent, and a couple of times he found himself caught in the spell she wove around every man. He had seen Dugan's reaction the day she had spoken to him about getting more help. The fool had made the mistake of falling in love with her, and Leith refused to fall in the same trap. Women were trouble, but he had to admit Ellenor was different.

And what he just saw proved that.

By the tears forming in her eyes, being pregnant was the last thing she wanted to be. Maybe the image of love she gave off was not the truth. Perhaps Cole was not whom she wanted. Had she finally recognized her husband was a coward and infected all those who were underneath him with his own weakness?

Cole had destroyed his best friend, his hero, and in return, Leith vowed the false laird would lose his life. But maybe Cole didn't need to die . . . maybe the best way of hurting him was to let him live.

A delicious idea stole over Leith. The opportunity he had been waiting for had just arrived. With the exception of Dugan, all the commanders were at the training fields prepping for battle. They were waiting for him to return . . . something that would never happen, as he had never left. And Ellenor was leaving the protective surroundings of Fàire Creachann. Once on the mainland, her disappearance would go unmarked for hours.

Eventually, though, someone would notice and the great Cole McTiernay would seek him out. And Leith fully intended to let the man find him. He would give Cole a choice. He could watch his beautiful wife die or he could watch her choose to be with another man.

Either way, Cole McTiernay was destroyed.

Chapter 16

Dugan heard a sharp shrill female voice call his name and ignored it. Kenneth, however, had the opposite inclination. The older man had served with him for years, and when Dugan had merged his men with Cole, Kenneth had not been physically able to build the skills or develop the stamina Cole expected of his soldiers. And unlike the others in his situation who had elected to support Leith, Kenneth had remained loyal to Dugan. That loyalty had spread to include his new laird after seeing firsthand how Cole discovered and then utilized men's strengths.

"A lady asked to speak to you, sir."

"I believe I said *demanded*, not asked," corrected the female.

Dugan waved his hand for Kenneth to move aside and let the woman enter. He took a deep breath, trying to calm his already quickening pulse. Having been forewarned of Ellenor's vocal displeasure and promises of going mainland, he had been expecting this visit for several hours. He had also been dreading it.

The last time Ellenor had approached him with a request, he had almost done the unthinkable and told her of his feelings. Instead, he had fought his instinct to do whatever she requested and immediately left for the mainland, where he could fulfill his responsibilities without seeing her every day. In the past three weeks, he had thought he had conquered his attraction, but this morning when he learned of Ellenor's impending arrival, every emotion, every desire came rushing back to the surface. And he knew that staying with Laird McTiernay and seeing her ladyship—even infrequently—was not a burden he could withstand for long. But he had made a promise. He would see this clan was established and that Fàire Creachann was prepared to support the families who were depending upon Cole for protection. Then he would leave, and with him, he would take several hard-learned lessons and his pride.

The door opened. "Dugan, I don't care how busy you are, you can make time for me."

Dugan let go the breath he had been holding. Neither the voice nor the petite female frame standing in front of him belonged to Ellenor. Dark brown eyes fumed down at him. Dugan immediately jumped to his feet. "Brighid, I had not been told—"

"I am uninterested in why I was forced to wait so long for an audience," Brighid huffed, cutting him off. "I just want to know exactly what it is you said to Ellenor to upset her and why you find it necessary to make things so extraordinarily hard on her, especially in her condition."

Dugan opened his mouth and closed it twice before answering. "I did not know things were hard on her and am not sure what you mean by her condition. Is she unwell?"

Brighid bit her bottom lip, realizing her mistake. "No, she's just . . . um, tired, and you and Henri make things constantly more difficult by seizing any space she has to do the chores necessary to maintain a castle of this size."

"I had not realized—"

"Then what do you think Ellenor meant when she told you about the kitchens?" Brighid demanded.

Dugan's face was now full of confusion. "Lady Ellenor did not talk to me about the kitchens or anything else mainly because she has not been here to see me today."

Now it was Brighid's turn to look confused. "But she should have been here hours ago. She was supposed to see you and then come for a visit, but she never arrived. I had assumed Ellenor was so angry by your refusal that she didn't want to talk until she was in a better mood."

"I, too, had heard her ladyship was coming mainland, but she never arrived. Perhaps something interfered with her plans back at the keep."

Brighid frowned at him in concern. "I cannot imagine that to be true. She was quite insistent . . ."

Dugan massaged the back of his neck. Cole and Donald had left that morning for the training fields, and they were not due back until dinnertime, which was at least another couple of hours. That made it his responsibility to verify Lady McTiernay's well-being. "I'm sure she is busy with the keep, but I'll go and speak with her and ensure she is well and address any of those hardships you just spoke of."

"I'm going with you," Brighid stated matter-of-factly.

Dugan shrugged and opened the door. "Fine with me. Kenneth, you might as well come along, too, in case Lady McTiernay needs some help that cannot be addressed quickly."

Once all three had mounted a horse, they headed out of the village and crossed the narrow strip of land to enter Fàire Creachann. A quarter of an hour later, they were at the castle stables, handing their reins to the stable master. Dugan was about to follow Kenneth and Brighid, who were both waiting in the courtyard, when he turned and asked the stable master if he had seen Lady Ellenor lately.

"No, sir. Not for some time. This morning she retrieved her mount and headed towards the mainland, but has not yet returned."

"Was she alone?"

"I think maybe my new man accompanied her. I know he is quite taken with milady."

Dugan cocked his head, trying to remember whom he assigned to work the stables. There had been so many people he had sent over to support the castle, but he couldn't remember one of them being a stable boy. A steward would know and that was the one position he had yet to find anyone qualified to fill. "Can you describe the boy?"

The stable master chuckled. "Boy? That was no boy you sent me. He was a man. Built like you, he was. Looked like he should be fighting, not mucking out stalls, but he did as I asked. The only time I had to get on him was about her ladyship. As I said before, he's quite taken with her."

Dugan's heart suddenly stopped. "This man . . . was he near bald and a scar along his right cheek?"

"Aye, that's him."

Dugan grabbed the reins of his horse and ordered the stable master to prepare another. He jumped back on his mount and exited the stables calling for Kenneth. The man came running, along with Brighid. "Kenneth, ride out to the training fields as fast as you can. Leith's been here and he has Lady Ellenor. Tell the laird I am riding out to Glen Terrand. That's where

Leith will be waiting. Brighid, go find Liam. I think he
is at his cottage and tell him to round the elite guard."

"What are you going to do?"

Dugan stared at the gatehouse and said, "I'm going
to do what I should have done last time." He gave a
swift kick into the brown mare's sides and disappeared
through the gatehouse.

"Elle!"

There was no reply and Cole was starting to become
concerned. At first, he thought she was angry about his
late arrival. He had not been home for dinner for the
past five nights and Ellenor had made it clear, there
had better not be a sixth.

He had specifically left the training fields early to
ensure a timely arrival, but halfway between the fields
and Fàire Creachann, he encountered a young, panic-
stricken boy running to the village. His father had become trapped underneath a cart while harvesting his
crops and sent him for help.

Cole had hoped Ellenor would give him a chance to
explain, but when he arrived to an empty bedroom, he
knew he would first have to find her. He had already visited the two places she tended to go when she "needed
to think" and was about to head back to the solar when
he spied lights flickering from the Lower Hall. Was she
down there?

Cole made his way down the grassy slope, and when
he approached the entrance to the Lower Hall, he
heard several voices inside. All were deep. None were
female.

He opened the doors. The heads of his two commanders and his entire elite guard snapped up.

"Laird!" gushed Jaime, relief flooding into his expression. "You're all right!"

Cole entered the room and examined the looks of concern on all of his men's faces. "Of course I'm all right. Why wouldn't I be? Since when do my commanders and guard convene when I am a few hours late from helping out an injured farmer? Did my wife call for you?"

Cole was unsure why his question caused every man's face to suddenly turn ashen. Then he heard someone mutter, "He doesn't know."

"Know what?" Cole asked. His voice was low, calm, and full of authority.

Donald rounded the table and then paused, unsure of how close he wanted to be to the laird when he heard the news. "We believe Leith has Lady Ellenor. And until a few moments ago, we believed he had you as well."

Pain, intense and white-hot, flashed in Cole's eyes and then was gone. In its place was nothing. He walked over to where they were gathered. "Tell me your plan."

Jaime swallowed and Donald froze. The jolt of realizing how much their laird had changed hit them full force. Ellenor had breathed life into him, and in an instant, it had been ripped away. It was as if time had rewound four months, before he had met Ellenor, when he was still hollow, devoid of emotion and pain.

"If Dugan is right, her ladyship is being held at Glen Terrand," Jaime finally said. "The area is barren, with rock cliff walls to the north and only a few scattered trees. There is nothing to hide our approach."

"There'll be nothing hiding him either," Donald added.

Cole stood silently for a moment and then asked, "How long ago?"

"We suspect just before the noon meal, but we cannot be certain. The stable master saw her around that time leaving with someone who matches Leith's description."

"And Dugan?"

"About four hours ago. He left directly and sent Kenneth to the fields. We searched for you, but it was getting dark and so we convened here to decide the next steps."

Cole felt the weight of all eyes upon him. They expected him to have a grand plan, a sure strategy to safely find and rescue Ellenor. But he had nothing. His mind couldn't focus on anything. Only one thought kept circling, that he couldn't lose Ellenor.

Cole held each man's gaze, keeping his expression detached. He didn't want any of them knowing the terror inside him. "Where are the men?"

"Liam is gathering them in preparation for battle."

"Only the guard is coming," Cole ordered. "Jaime, you and the rest will remain here. Place some men inside Fàire Creachann, protect the village, and have the rest waiting at the pass. Slaughter all who arrive."

"You think it's a trap then," Donald murmured.

"I think it's an opportunity and one Leith will not ignore."

Donald nodded and ordered the men to get their mounts and prepare for an immediate departure. The confidence that had been missing minutes before had returned. The men, even his commanders, believed he understood Leith's plan and had one to counter it. They were only half right. Leith wanted, even expected, to die. He just intended to inflict a great amount of pain before doing so. Cole was reliving his greatest nightmare. Once again, he was the target and someone else would pay the price.

One of the men brought Steud to his side. Cole took the reins, trying to cut himself off emotionally as he had done with Robert. He yanked the leather straps and pulled his mount around the building to a dark shadow out of eyesight. His fingers wrapped around the pommel and instead of pulling himself up into the saddle, he sank against the large animal and buried his face in the rough mane.

Tears scalded his eyes, flooding them. The feeling of loss and hopelessness was not something he could suppress, hide, or ignore as he had with Robert. This time it was too great. He imagined Ellenor frightened and waiting for him to save her, looking expectantly into the darkness, wondering when he would arrive. He could not lose her. He would not lose her.

Rage swelled in his chest, choking every other emotion out. Wiping his eyes, Cole took a deep breath and mounted. He had not lost Ellenor yet and he had at least two hours of riding to devise a plan that ensured he never did. Nothing else mattered. Not his life, not being laird, nothing.

Cole rounded the building and was about to urge his mount into a lope across the yard when Brighid stepped into view.

"Laird!"

Cole stopped. "Brighid, what are you doing here? Trouble is coming. Go to the keep and wait for—"

"You're going after Ellenor, aren't you?"

Brighid was wringing her hands with worry. "I'll bring her home," Cole vowed.

"There is something you should know. Ellenor just found out this morning she is with child. You need to be careful. She's fragile and . . . just be careful."

Cole fought a new wave of emotion hitting him and immediately looked away. The hatred boiling in him

had done the impossible. It had grown to even greater
levels, and it would not lessen until he held Leith's neck
in his hands.

"I'll save them both," he choked and then left at a full
gallop. His men fell in behind.

Ellenor awoke confused. Her head pounded and
sharp pains shot through her arms and legs whenever
she tried to move them. It was dark, but light from a fire
beamed across the area so that she could see just enough
to be scared. Her arms were tied to the one tree in the
vicinity. No large rocks were in sight, just flat land that
ran right into the slope of an enormous mountain,
stretching beyond the campfire's ability to illuminate.
Instinctively, she squirmed and pulled her wrists, but the
binds were tight. Waves of nausea started to build and it
jolted Ellenor into awareness.

She and her baby were in danger.

All the fear and doubt she had felt earlier about
being pregnant vanished. This child was a piece of
Cole and the thought of it being taken from her para-
lyzed her with fear. Ellenor forced herself to sit still and
breathe.

On their wedding night, Cole had vowed to always
come for her and he would not break his promise now.
He would find her. It was her job to be alive when he did.

A shadowy figure caught her attention. She pretended to be unconscious and slumped in relief when
he walked on by. The figure joined his comrades. There
were seven total and all were huddled around a campfire located about hundred feet down the small, grassy
knoll. Their voices were hushed and she could make
out only one or two words, nothing to indicate where
she was or why she had been captured.

Someone cackled and Ellenor thought she recognized the sound. She leaned forward to concentrate when cool, firm fingers clasped her mouth. She instinctively jumped and gave a shrill that was muffled. Warm breath glided across her cheek and her spine went rigid. Hot tears began to form.

"My lady, it's me, Dugan."

Her heart thumped erratically. She didn't know whether he was there to help or if he was one of her assailants. She was afraid to guess. Then the pressure of the knots binding her wrists eased. "I am going to loosen your restraints, but it is important that you pretend you are still bound. You are being watched closely. It took me some time to make my way to you. The men have been watching the pass carefully but have taken a break to eat. Right now they are paying more attention to their food than to you."

Ellenor heard the fear in Dugan's voice and felt her pulse quicken in response. "Then why must I pretend to remain bound."

"Because someone would notice if you suddenly were able to get up and walk away. You wouldn't get ten yards and then they wouldn't chance you getting free again."

Ellenor whispered, "Where's Cole?"

"When I found out you were taken, I sent word for him to come here, but he doesn't know the terrain and my men are all over the area. His chances of making it through are slim."

Ellenor closed her eyes, her heart hoping Dugan was wrong. "You said these were your men."

One of the figures stood up and stretched, staring in their direction. Dugan sank back behind the tree before answering. "Most of them think they are doing this for me. Leith has told them their honor as Highlanders demands they do these things in retribution."

"Then go and speak to them. Tell them this is not what you want."

"I've tried, but they will not be convinced no matter what I say. They have already made up their minds."

Ellenor recognized the deep sense of loss in Dugan's voice. "You are speaking of Leith. It was he who did this."

"Aye, he and a handful of others," Dugan answered softly and began to work on her bindings again. "He . . . he intends to hurt me, doesn't he?" she asked, her voice low and raspy as she took in the full truth of her situation.

Dugan squeezed his eyes shut. The fear in her voice was a torment unlike any blade or spear had ever felt. He wanted to lie and ease her anxiety, but if he did, she might not listen and he had only one slim chance to save her life. "He plans to kill you."

"But why? Leith doesn't even know me."

Dugan scoffed. "You really don't know how you affect people, men in particular."

"You are not making any sense."

Dugan took a deep breath. "You don't know how much your husband changed after meeting you. The McTiernays are famed throughout the Highlands for many things, but your husband was known—and justifiably so—for his hardness."

The final knot was loosened and she was free. He held her wrists together. "Clasp your hands to appear still bound." After Ellenor did as he instructed, Dugan whispered, "Now, swing your legs to me. Move slowly so you don't catch their eye. That's right. Curl them, as if you are trying to get into a more comfortable position. I'll hold your hands so they don't break." Her bound ankles were finally within his reach and he began working on the knots underneath her skirts.

Ellenor swallowed. The more she was free, the more

she realized just how trapped she was. Only Dugan's voice was keeping her calm. "You were saying."

"Hmm? Oh . . . yeah. Your husband was the one McTiernay no one expected to marry."

"Why is that?"

"Come now, you have seen him scowl. Women are afraid of him. Hell, men are afraid of . . . don't move, one guard is looking at you. Don't say anything."

Ellenor bit the inside of her bottom lip as Dugan pinched her skin as he continued to work the difficult knots. Between her struggles and Dugan's aid, the rope had chafed her skin raw. She leaned back and closed her eyes, hoping Dugan would talk to her again. Finally, he did. "So, when Cole McTiernay—the hardhearted warrior whose deep hatred of the English is known to every Highland man, woman, and child—comes back with an English bride, only two things can explain it. Forced marriage or love. And it doesn't take long in your company to know which one it was. There, you're free."

Ellenor immediately moved to reextend her legs when Dugan caught her ankles. "You need to sit where your ankles are covered, milady, until it is time."

"You mean when Cole arrives?" she whispered, hoping he would say yes.

"This has never been Cole's battle," came Dugan's short reply. There was a hard brittleness she had never heard in his voice before. It startled her. "This has always been between Leith and me. He feels I betrayed him and seeks to destroy anything that I embrace. You, Cole, and next will be the clan. Now, when I leave you, I am going to reenter on the other side of the campsite. I'll meet Leith and pretend that I am joining him."

"What if he doesn't believe you?"

Dugan gave a small shake of his head. "Doesn't

matter. Either way he'll gather his men closer, either to welcome me or for vengeance. When he does, you need to run. There is a field behind you. Keep running until you see the rocks next to the cliffs. There is one big one, it's the only one taller than you. Are you listening?" Feeling her nod, Dugan continued, "There is a cave behind that boulder. Go to it and run deep inside. Do *not* try to run out of the pass. You will get caught and they will try to kill you immediately if that happens."

Ellenor swallowed. "When do I run?"

"When you hear me holler. That will be your cue. Get up and run as fast as you can. Can you do it?"

Ellenor's voice caught in her throat. Flashes of the night her father was murdered flickered through her mind. Of being held and fighting for her life. She had known fear then and conquered it to save her life. She could do so again. She *would* do so again.

"*Can you do it?*" Dugan asked more harshly.

Still unable to speak, Ellenor nodded.

"Good. The moon has not risen and the night should obscure their sight of you, but not completely. Run, Lady Ellenor, and God speed be with you."

It seemed as if hours had passed before Ellenor saw Dugan's shadow emerge on the other side of the campfire. His cantor was easy and slow, as if he was in no hurry. She watched him embrace each man as life-long friends and realized that was what they were. The man was caught in a horrible position few ever had to face. He had had to choose between honor and friendship. The price he had to pay for the choice was those he considered family. She wished for Dugan's sake this could have ended any other way.

It was still hard to hear, but with only Dugan and Leith talking, she could make out more of their conversation.

"I'm surprised you're here. I expected Cole."

"Your issue is with me. Not Cole and certainly not his wife," Dugan said, using his chin to point in Ellenor's direction.

Ellenor's heart sank. It was obvious Leith did not believe Dugan was there to join his cause.

"Aye, my issue is with you, but maybe if McTiernay were gone, you would remember your old loyalties. And his wife . . . consider that a bonus. She's not interested in you and never will be. I've watched how you pine after her. You even ran away to the mainland in an effort to remain loyal to your precious laird, but with him gone, she will be all yours."

"No, Leith."

The conversation was filled with tension, but the men had gathered closer, just as Dugan predicted. All eyes were on the two of them.

Leith shrugged. "Thought you might feel that way and have decided to claim her myself."

A shiver of horror ran up Ellenor's spine as Leith's words sank into understanding. She had almost missed her cue to run when Dugan belted out a loud "Never!" Her legs were stiff and unresponsive after hours of being bound. The blood surged through them as she forced herself to stand and then run. It felt as if she was moving in slow motion; her muscles refused to cooperate. Sharp pains shot through her legs with each step as blood surged through her semideadened limbs.

Past the edge of the light of the campfire, darkness enveloped her. She stumbled but kept moving until the rocks Dugan had told her about were in sight. The one large boulder stood out from the others and she began running toward it. That's when she heard the crunching footsteps of someone chasing her. Afraid to look back, she urged her legs to move faster.

It wasn't enough.

Something snagged her right arm, halting her run for freedom. Ellenor cringed as the large callused hand squeezed and hauled her up against his chest. The man wasn't tall, but he was broad and strong and his beard stank of sewage and rotten meat.

"Leith was right." The man sneered and Ellenor felt the sharp blade of a *sgian dubh* against her neck. "Aye, he thought it might be best if someone stayed behind to make sure nothing unexpected passed by and I think he would definitely consider you unexpected."

He half dragged, half carried her back to the campsite. As soon as they came in view, Leith broke off his conversation with Dugan and moved to leer at her. Ellenor strained against the bruising grip on her arm and the metal point pressing into her neck dug deeper. She felt her own blood trickle down her throat and between her breasts and ceased struggling.

"Aye, you better stop, Lady McTiernay." Leith saw her eyes pop open wide with astonishment. "You recognize me then." He bent down and placed his cheek against hers to whisper in her ear. She tried to jerk her head back, but he grabbed her chin and held it in place. "I had hoped for something more between you and I, but if Dugan is here, your husband cannot be far behind. I'll leave the choice to you. Choose me and live or choose your husband."

Ellenor curled her upper lip into a snarl. "And die?"

A sick laugh erupted from Leith's throat. "Not just die, *milady*. I intend to roll your lifeless body towards him."

"I'm tired. Lying down sounds good so I choose my husband," Ellenor spit. An instant later her cheek felt as if it were on fire.

Leith's reaction had been so fast, she had not been prepared for the sting associated with being slapped. She desperately wanted to show him no fear, no pain, but when he saw the tears trembling in her eyes, a look of immense satisfaction filled his expression.

"Your lady, Dugan, has finally lost some of her pride," Leith crooned and stepped closer to his ex-commander.

Ellenor glanced at Dugan, who was standing unarmed and motionless, just watching the scene unfold. His expression was so devoid of emotion, it was as if Leith had removed everything decent in him, leaving him vacant and incapable of saving himself, let alone her.

Then she saw Leith nod to the man holding her.

Ellenor could feel the blade begin to move. He was about to slice her throat, and in a moment, she would be dead. Cole would never forgive himself for breaking his promise to her.

She closed her eyes and suddenly heard a soft swish above her head. The hand holding her tight went slack and the *sgian* fell from his fingers. Ellenor tilted her head up and saw a long arrow protruding from her captor's skull just as the broad body fell on top of her, pinning her to the ground.

Agonizing pain struck her lower stomach as his body collided with hers on the hard earth. Her insides had been split into two and blood was pooling between her legs. Ellenor knew she was losing her baby and cried out for help.

Her screams blended with others saturating the night air. Metal was clashing in the distance and Ellenor craned her head to see if Cole had come, but it was not Cole fighting Leith. It was Dugan. The crazed look in his eye had disappeared and one of calm determination had taken over. Two bodies lay motionless and the others had disappeared. Only Leith remained and he would not be a victor today.

The pain in her stomach was growing. In desperation, she began to thrash in an effort to get the man off her. Without warning, the massive weight was suddenly gone and she was being swooped into arms, holding her incredibly tight.

She was about to renew her struggles when she felt the pressure of warm lips against her forehead that could belong to only one man. Ellenor threw her arms around him. "You kept your promise, Highlander. I knew you would," she murmured, her voice raspy with pain.

Metal clanked and Cole snapped his head in the direction of the sound. His face contorted. "Leith is mine," he said and moved to hand her over to Donald.

Ellenor grabbed his leine. "No, I need you, and this fight is *not* yours. It's Dugan's."

Cole narrowed his eyes. The blue had disappeared, leaving black holes with only pure hatred shining back. "It's mine. You cannot steal a laird's wife and plan to kill her without consequences." And before Ellenor could argue further, Cole was gone.

Donald placed her on top of Cole's horse and vanished into the darkness. The battle continued and she slumped against the neck of the horse for balance, trying to remain conscious.

She couldn't tell whether it was minutes or hours later when warm, gentle hands picked her up. But she knew it was too late for her and her baby. She heard Cole cry out. He must have felt the blood. It was everywhere.

A cool wind was on her cheek and she could hear Cole whisper in the distance, "Don't you leave me. Promise me you won't leave me, Ellenor."

Her green eyes couldn't focus on his face, but she

heard him. He had called her Ellenor. It was the first time Cole had ever called her by her name. She tried to promise but his horse began to move. Then new waves of pain struck.

The world went black.

Epilogue

Ellenor watched as the chubby little boy hesitantly let go of the table leg and took a step. He took another and then another. Pride erupted on his face and he began to clap his hands vigorously at his accomplishment. The dark curls surrounding his face began to bounce just before he fell. A loud "thunk" bounced off the walls as his head hit the carpeted floor. Instead of crying, he crawled back to the table leg and began the sequence again.

"He has to have an incredible headache," Ellenor leaned over and whispered to Brighid.

"Aye, you would think. The first time he fell, I rushed to his side in a panic but he was fine. Never cries, that one. I don't know whether to be proud or worried."

Donald walked over, swept the child up, and tossed him in the air. "Proud! He's strong, just like me. Aren't you, son?"

Squeals of delight erupted from the baby, getting attention from two other dark brown, curly-headed boys, who had been playing in the corner. Both marched over and began to tug on Donald's plaid, indicating that it was their turn. One by one, he tossed them in the air until he finally relented and got down on the ground to let them crawl all over him.

Ellenor laughed as she watched the huge Highlander wrestle with the three boys, feigning defeat. "Are you sure, Donald, you don't want to leave for Laird Schellden's with the other soldiers? The games are supposed to be quite large this year. If you hurry, you can still catch the men heading down to prove their prowess."

"I dare any of them to take on my three sons and come out the victor."

"I wonder," Brighid began, pointing at the four giggling figures, "if he would still be here if we had three daughters."

"Aye, I would be," Donald assured her as he pretended to succumb to the three-year-old's hold on his arm. The second oldest, who was two, grabbed his calf and held on for dear life as Donald began to swing his leg around in circles. The baby enjoyed falling onto his chest and hearing the loud "oaf" sound Donald made.

Brighid sighed with obvious happiness. "At one time I never thought I would even have a family, and now in just over four years, I have three boys."

Ellenor gave her friend a mocking wink and said, "If you don't want more, I suggest you keep your hands to yourself."

Before Brighid could respond, Donald piped in, unaware of the inside joke between the two women. "Nope. Now, we need to have three girls."

Brighid, who was drinking some water, began to choke. "Three?!"

"I believe the man said *three*." Ellenor laughed.

Brighid gave her friend a frosty glare. "Don't encourage him!" she ordered and then turned her attention back to her husband. "Can you imagine three more? I'm already going crazy and the only reason I haven't lost my mind is because of Ellenor. Three more and she really *will* order us to live back on the mainland."

Ellenor shook her head. "Never. I would miss you too much. Besides I need you here. More than you know."

Brighid's mouth twisted humorlessly. She leaned closer to whisper, "So when are you going to let Cole know? You wear that same glow you did four years ago, but I have yet to see that silly smile on the laird's face Donald always wears when he knows I'm expecting."

Apprehensively, Ellenor moistened her dry lips. "You're right, the smile's not there and it shouldn't be there. Cole and I agreed to have a small family, and after little Elle was born, he made me promise not to get pregnant again."

Brighid let go a soft hoot. "Well, it's not like you can create a baby on your own. He was there, wasn't he?"

Ellenor's dark golden eyebrows slanted into a frown. "Of course he was. He just . . . I . . . oh, how do I tell him? If I recall last time, *you* saved me the trouble."

Brighid threw her hands in the air. "No, dear friend. This time you are on your own. My only advice is don't wait. Blurt it out. Look, here's your chance."

The door to the Great Hall opened and Cole entered carrying a beautiful little girl with dark brown shoulder-length hair. They were singing, both to a different tempo and both out of key. Halfway across the room, the girl squirmed out of her daddy's grasp and began to run to the open arms of her mother.

"Mommy!"

"Elle, baby girl, I've missed you!" Ellenor said, swinging the three-year-old onto her lap.

A pink lip protruded from the cherub face and her brows puckered in frustration. "I'm not a baby anymore. I'm a big girl."

"Not to me. You'll always be my baby girl," Ellenor whispered, hugging the child close.

Little Elle pointed her finger toward Cole. "But Daddy says I am *his* baby. I don't want to be a baby. I want to be a big girl."

"And you are a big girl, sweetie," Ellenor reassured her.

Elle squirmed off the lap and toddled over to where the three boys were examining the scars along their daddy's arms. "My mommy has the best scratch," she announced. The boys ignored her. It wasn't the first time little Elle had talked about the deep scar along her mother's back. It fascinated her, as did the story of how it happened. Every night she would beg Cole to relay how he had saved her mother from the evil men.

Ellenor would listen and remember. She had thought she was losing Elle, and almost had, but not from internal hemorrhaging as she had thought that night. She had fallen onto the same knife that had almost sliced her throat. It had punctured her lower back. The healer said it was a miracle she had lived. But she had. And so had little Elle.

"There lies the fiercest of my guard," Cole said with a sigh as he watched Donald wrestle once more with his sons. "Who would have thought?"

"Speak for yourself, laird," Donald hollered as his boys began to wrestle with him anew.

"I was smart. I had a daughter and no more," Cole countered.

Ellenor swallowed. For the first couple of years when Brighid seemed to always be pregnant and producing nothing but sons, she had wondered if Cole wished he had the same—sons, and many of them. But she only had to see the pride in Cole's eyes when he looked at his daughter to know he truly was happy.

"What took you so long? The children have been

waiting anxiously for your return. You promised them a ride to the village," Donald reminded.

"Dugan," Cole exhaled.

Ellenor produced a tight-lipped smile. "What did Dugan need now? I thought he and Henri had a clear vision of how the curtain wall was to be erected." Once Fàire Creachann had been deemed complete by the master mason, Cole had decided that he and Dugan needed to focus on protecting the mainland village.

"They both agree that a wall is to be built, aye. But it seems there are many opinions as to how tall it should be and where it should be built. Some cottages will have to move, causing questions as to who should be so unlucky."

Ellenor closed her eyes and said, "But you already decided who would have to move."

"I didn't about the crops," Cole sighed. After four years of being laird, he had learned to deal with the constant pull of clansmen, but he doubted he would ever become accustomed to it. "I never decided just how many villagers could have crops inside the wall and who."

"And the verdict?"

"Ten families and this time I'm letting *Dugan* decide who they are."

Ellenor nodded with satisfaction. "Good. Hopefully that will keep him out of trouble for a while. When he's not busy, *I* am the one the ladies run to for help."

"Aye, they do. They want her to help *catch* him," Brighid added, remembering the last time Dugan had spent a significant amount of time in the village. Every day at least one—but as many as three and four— besotted girls would seek out Ellenor in hopes to learn how to win the man's affections. It always ended in wailing and an inordinate amount of tears.

Ellenor shook her head in resignation. "He shouldn't

encourage the women. He's far too smitten with most and refuses to commit to a single one."

Cole leaned over and gave her a light kiss on the cheek. "At least he's not smitten with you anymore."

Ellenor grimaced and shot Cole an exasperated look. "Oh he never really was. Mild infatuation was the most he ever felt for me, and after spending so much time with soldiers, it was no wonder he liked the first girl he saw."

"Well, he seems to have gotten over it." Donald chuckled. "The man breaks more hearts than anyone else I know. Claims he's cursed with good looks."

"I just hope to be around the day he spies a woman who doesn't fall so easily under his spell," Brighid said.

"Want him to experience a broken heart, eh?"

"No," Ellenor replied, elbowing her husband. "Brighid and I want him to be deliriously happy. Just like the two of you."

Cole arched a single brow and gave a slight "hrmph."

"The correct answer is 'He should be so lucky,'" Ellenor explained with a twinkle in her eye.

Cole picked up his little girl, swinging her around. She cackled and he grinned. "He'll never be as lucky as I. What else could a man want? I already have the perfect wife." He paused and bounced his daughter above his head. Her laughter filled the room. "And the perfect family."

Ellenor swallowed and glanced at Brighid, who widened her eyes and tilted her head, indicating she thought now was the time. "What if it weren't three . . . but four?" Ellenor blurted out.

Cole froze for a second and slowly lowered Elle to the floor. "More, Daddy! More!"

Brighid grabbed the little girl's hand and shushed her startled husband as she hurried everyone out of the room.

Still in shock, Cole was barely aware of the whines being ushered outside.

Ellenor began to wring her hands. "I know that we agreed to not have any more, but . . ." Suddenly she was in the air being twirled about.

"Are you sure?"

His bright blue eyes were sparkling, and she couldn't help laughing. "I'm sure."

"A baby?" Cole half asked, half exclaimed.

Ellenor's pounding heart began to beat differently. He seemed thrilled, but she needed to make sure. "Are you really happy? I mean—"

Cole cut her off, brushing his lips across hers before playfully nipping at her lower lip. Then, unable to resist the temptation, he caught and held her close for a deeper kiss. After several very satisfying minutes, he reassured her. "Very, love. But are you? Do you want another? After the last time . . ."

"I didn't think I did," Ellenor began, "but when I realized I was with child, I knew I wanted another baby very much. I was afraid you wouldn't . . ."

Cole placed a finger across her lips. "I love you and cannot think of a better gift you have ever given me than Elle. To know I will be doubly blessed brings me more happiness than any man has a right to."

Tears of happiness blinded Ellenor eyes. "That a promise?"

"Aye, a Highlander's promise."

More by Bestselling Author
Hannah Howell